# CHARCOAL AND SMOKE

## THE ELEMENTAL ARTIST

# JAMI FAIRLEIGH

Charcoal And Smoke
Copyright © 2023 by Fairleigh, Jami
All rights reserved.

Published by Kitsune Publishing
23515 NE Novelty Hill Rd, STE B221-309
Redmond, WA 98058
www.kitsunepublishing.co

The Library of Congress has catalogued the hardcover edition as follows:

Fairleigh, Jami, author
Charcoal and Smoke / Jami Fairleigh - First edition
ISBN 978-1-955428-15-6 (hardcover)
ISBN 978-1-955428-13-2 (paperback)
ISBN 978-1-955428-14-9 (lrg. print paperback)
ISBN 978-1-955428-12-5 (ebook)
ISBN 978-1-955428-16-3 (audiobook)

# CONTENT WARNING

Charcoal and Smoke is an adult fantasy novel which contains violence and gore. A full list of warnings is available at: https://jamifairleigh.com/cw-charcoal-and-smoke/

Or by scanning this QR code:

*For my siblings*

I am always doing that which I cannot do, in order that
I may learn how to do it.

**— PABLO PICASSO**

# CHAPTER ONE

The midmorning sun promised a warm day, and already the glare made my head pound as Ben and I followed my daughter into the shady barn. The scents of hay and horse and leather wrapped around me like a familiar blanket. Nearby, dust motes swirled in the single ray of sunshine streaming through a grimy window near the pitched roof.

Akiko strolled into the gloom and squealed. "Lady!" The mare's neck curved in a graceful arch as she reached for the child. Akiko's silky, black hair swung as she turned, her round face wreathed in smiles. "I missed you... and you, Sir Donkey!"

The little animal poked his head over the stall door and brayed like a rusty hinge. Charcoal barked once and glared at him with narrowed eyes, but the donkey didn't back away. His lips wiggled in an undignified grin as Akiko scratched behind his long ears.

Josephine's raspy singing stopped. She popped up from behind the stall wall and smiled. "Good, you're here. I need a word with everyone."

*This is my chance.* "Me too." My shoulders relaxed, and I

pulled in a deep breath. All week I'd waited for the right opportunity to express my concerns about traveling to Vegas Depot. Our decision to journey west on Olen's suggestion had been spontaneous... and irrational. Could we travel over thirty-six hundred kilometers on a hunch? We had no actual proof, nothing to go on except Olen's impression that a shape on my *Home* painting depicted the Strat tower in Vegas Depot. Plus, it wouldn't be the first time a scholar's opinion had led us astray; the reason we'd traveled to Toronto Depot was because another scholar had misidentified the tower.

With winter coming, I wanted to head south and regroup. Staying in one location would also make it easier for my cousin Talbot to find us. Any way I looked at it, it made sense to find somewhere to stay. But first, I needed to convince the others to change the plans we'd made.

Akiko disappeared into the deep shade near the back of the structure. "Hey look!"

Even squinting, I couldn't make out what she'd discovered. I ambled over and found her tugging her saddle from beneath a mountain of dusty leather. Her tongue stuck out the side of her mouth as she pulled on her tack.

Above us, Genevie's head popped over the edge of the loft. "Watch out below!"

"Hey," Ben protested in his deep, gravelly voice as his large, ornate saddle dropped onto the pile with a *thud*. "Don't throw our things into the dirt. My saddle is special to me."

"If you want a say in how the tasks get done, arrive earlier next time. Earl and I have been working our tails off to get us ready to leave on time."

Earl appeared at the top of the ladder, waved, and turned to descend. My cheeks burned, and I glued my eyes on Ben to keep from assessing Earl's *tail*.

"What tasks?" Ben folded his arms and frowned at Genevie. "All I see is a pile of mishandled tack."

Genevie made a rude, snorting noise. "Not only did we trim and shoe nine equines, but we also shifted a metric ton of straw to get to the tack *and* dragged everyone's stuff over the edge."

I should have gotten here earlier, too. If I convinced the others to postpone the trip, the effort Earl and Genevie had already made would be for naught. I cleared my throat to speak, but Genevie's silver flask caught the lone sunbeam. The reflection dazzled my left eye, making it tear.

When I wiped it dry, Akiko giggled. "Yeah, boo hoo. At least *you* didn't have to clean our bedrooms and bathrooms at the inn." She heaved a dramatic sigh and flopped backward onto the pile of leather, causing Ben's saddle to slide down the far side.

"Not you too," he said with exaggerated dismay. He bent down, grabbed the saddle, and hauled it onto his hip. "Let's tack up."

"Sorry, can't." Genevie stepped onto the creaking ladder. "I'm still waiting for the applause we've earned."

My window to call off the trip was closing, so I stalled, too. "Before we saddle, Josephine wanted a word."

"Sure did." She stepped into the aisleway, clapping two curry brushes together. They released a cloud of dust, enveloping her, and setting her coughing so hard she couldn't speak. While we waited for her to catch her breath, the wagon we'd hired groaned into the yard.

My heart sank, and the pressure in my head increased. If Olen was here, I'd lost my chance to say anything about our trip.

# CHAPTER TWO

Josephine caught her breath and straightened. "Good grief. Well, if our things have arrived, we should talk later." Josephine held her hand out to Akiko. "Come on. Let's say goodbye."

"Do I have to?" Akiko bit her lip. "I did it last night, and it was really hard."

Her sad expression sent a pang through me, but before I could reply, Genevie led her mares past us. "Then this one will be a breeze."

I followed the others and reached the door in time to watch Beck and Olen leap off the wagon. Away from the water, Gunther looked unsettled and out of place, like an old, rumpled blue heron. I ducked to pat Charcoal, using the movement to hide my smile.

But my throat thickened as Mama and Gunther climbed down. There was no reasonable way we could all stay together, but I'd miss Mama's warmth and her steady strength, not to mention her wisdom... and her cooking. And while I wasn't sure where I stood with Gunther, his gruff advice and uncanny ability to say the right thing and be in the right place had saved me several times.

Genevie sauntered past me to the side of the wagon and shielded her eyes. "Any problems?"

"None," said Beck, handing her a heavy sack. "Your horses all good?"

"Four feet, each and every one." Genevie crossed her muscled arms. "Earl helped me trim and shoe everyone except brownishgreyishyellowishblack."

"Sir Donkey is easier. Or Me-Lad-O." Akiko giggled. "Gunther taught me it." The way she smiled at Gunther was like a dagger to my heart.

*Akiko wants to stay.*

Gunther's beard rippled. He winked at her while handing Genevie a brown jug. "Good?"

Genevie shook the jug and grinned. "Very good. I have just the place for it." She studied the pile of crates and supplies around Ben. "You going to fit those supplies in *your* panniers, Hensly? My bags are full."

"They'll fit." Despite his certainty, Ben already sounded weary. "Come and watch me make magic."

Perhaps I could speak to the others after we reached the outskirts of the depot. There was no point in stalling any further. "I'll give you a hand."

Ben nodded. "Help me sort out the tack first."

Little puffs of dust rose from our footsteps as I padded after him into the barn. When we reached the pile, I glanced at Josephine. "Is there an efficient way to handle this?"

"This is typical Genevie. Act first, think later." Josephine shrugged. "Find your stuff, I guess."

I nodded and pulled a packsaddle from beneath a jumble of leathers.

"Nope, that's mine," called Genevie from the other side of the pile.

"It's beautiful." I examined the detail and rubbed my thumb over the stamped pattern of hammer and tongs. "Why did I leave my leathers so plain?"

"It's pretty until it's time to clean it." Genevie grinned. "The soap gets into every dent and divot. Massive pain."

"Better to be a plain Jane than a massive pain," sang Akiko as she tugged her bridle from the pile.

"Do you want help saddling Lady?"

The cheerful smile slid from her face. She bit her lip, glancing over at Mama and Gunther. "I wish we didn't have to leave."

Her plaintive expression tore at me and renewed my determination to say something to the others. "I know, Mouse. Come. I'll help you with Lady."

Akiko shook her head and squared her shoulders. "I'm not a little kid anymore."

Oxide and Magnesium nuzzled me and crunched the apple slices I'd brought while I watched Akiko saddle her mare. My geldings both appeared healthy and happy, but guilt twinged through me. *I should have visited them earlier.* After Akiko finished, I saddled Oxide, then heaved the packsaddle onto Magnesium. I'd barely secured it before both their heads popped up in curiosity.

Earl led a magnificent horse down the aisle. Muscles rippled beneath his black coat, which shone in the barn's dusty shade. His mane flowed along a thick, curving neck, and the forelock between his ears brushed the tip of his nose. He had enormous feet, well feathered, a short back, a powerful rump, and a full tail. He arched his neck to sniff noses with Oxide.

I leaned over the stall wall for a better look. "Who is this handsome fellow?"

The horse sniffed the back of my hand and bumped it for the apple slice I'd palmed.

Earl flashed me her lopsided grin. "Bruno, meet Matthew."

"Where did you find him?"

"His former owner runs the restaurant on the waterfront." She stroked the horse's glossy neck. "They've settled here permanently and traded Bruno for a year's worth of charcuterie."

"Charcuterie?"

"Mm. Dried and cured meats. I made salamis, pate, bresaola, and cecina at Mama's."

The memory of transporting bloody, wrapped packages to Mama's flashed across my mind's canvas. "You traded *frozen beef* for Bruno?"

"Yes." Earl laughed, her white teeth flashing in the dim light. "I knew I'd need a horse—I rode Akiko's mare to the depot, remember?"

Earl made her plans weeks ago. But between when she'd negotiated for Bruno and now... Bowman had died. "You're sure you want to come with us? It's not too late to change your mind."

Earl raised her eyebrow. "Are you uninviting me?"

I reddened and spluttered. "*No.* I want you—I mean, we want you to join us."

Flustered, I stopped. If I wasn't careful, I could become hopelessly besotted with Earl. It wasn't just her looks, though they didn't hurt. But her kindness toward Akiko, the sharp intelligence shining through her Emerald eyes, and the skillful way she cut through problems as easily as she cleaved meat were irresistible. There was also her compassion, forgiveness, and the grace she'd shown me time and again.

Earl's laugh rumbled, low and musical. "Good. I can't wait to see a buffalo."

*Buffalo.* It was another gut punch. Earl looked forward to the trip I'd been dreading. After all the work she'd completed to prepare for our trip, admitting my doubts could hurt her feelings. My gut twisted, but I pasted a smile on my face. "Think we will?"

"If I get the chance, I'm making us a buffalo salami." She winked and led Bruno from the barn.

I watched Earl go. I had nothing to offer her; no home, no permanent community, and no idea how to even romance a woman like Earl. Or any woman, for that matter. No, Earl and I should remain friends. *Platonic friends.*

Despite my certainty, I couldn't stop myself from picturing long days on the road with her. Or cozy nights by the fire. Or...

"Need a hand?" Ben asked.

I jumped, flashing him a guilty smile. "Sorry, are you waiting for me?"

"I'm finished, but you..." He leaned over Magnesium's stall door and gestured at the tack still sitting on the ground.

"Oh." I hesitated. "The panniers are heavier than I remember."

Ben chuckled. "Perhaps you've gotten soft, my depot friend." He picked up the nearest pannier and groaned. "Apparently, so have I." Together, we heaved it into place and buckled the leather straps. When we finished, we were panting, but Magnesium merely cocked his hip and sighed.

*Now or never.*

I glanced around to confirm none of the others were within earshot and took a deep breath. "Ben—"

"There you are," said Mama. "I have something for you." She held two, familiar brown bottles toward me.

I uncapped the first, the sharp pine scent making my eyes water. "From Freda?"

Mama nodded at Ben as he left the stall. "Bryer brought

them back."

Gunther clumped over to us while I wrapped the bottles in the soft towel Mama handed me. "Did Bryer find his lost boat?"

"Not yet, so he's hanging onto yours." Gunther snorted. "She's a fine boat, though 'tis needing a proper color."

"Why?"

"Well, 'twould be nigh impossible to find if he lands in the drink again."

"Right." I flashed Gunther a rueful grin, remembering the gray-brown color I'd used to camouflage the sailboat. "And a proper mariner stays out of the water."

"Aye, lad. Keep your keels wet and heels dry."

"I need to get this old bass back to the sea before he desiccates." Mama patted Gunther's cheek. "Keep your leg clean and dry, and use Freda's solution nightly."

"Promise." My throat thickened. Akiko was right; goodbyes were torturous.

*Time to go.*

With effort, I swallowed and led my horses outside. Ben was already on Zeus, his mule. Hera, his pack mule, waited, a patient expression on her long face. Akiko perched sideways on Lady, her silver mare, while Josephine fiddled with her stirrup from Fox's back. Bruno's dark coat flashed in the sun, contrasting with Earl's pale skin. Bertha, Genevie's buckskin mare, pinned her ears in annoyance at Gertie, Genevie's gray-spotted pack horse who rubbed her forehead on Bertha's rump.

"Are you sure you don't want to stay and party here, Genevie?" called Olen. "Jon and Cedrick are distraught by your leaving."

"The party is coming with me, thanks to Gunther." Genevie shook her flask. "Besides, there are plenty of other frogs in the pond. Take care of each other."

Beck grinned. "Likewise, sister."

My left calf protested as I mounted, but I kept my face impassive. Beneath me, the saddle was hard and foreign. I shifted to find a more comfortable position. Assuming every route we'd chosen was clear, it would still take months to travel the thirty-six hundred kilometers. We couldn't afford any further delays if we were going to go.

Even if my leg wasn't fully healed. Even when my heart wasn't ready to leave these people behind.

Should I call the entire trip off? We *could* stay in or near the depot. We had friends here, and in time, perhaps we could build the type of community Akiko needed. Somewhere safe where I could train her in art in secret.

But if we stayed, what would happen to my parents? Assuming my parents were in Vegas Depot... and assuming Carter knew who and where they were.

I sighed. There was no helping it. We needed to go, and we needed to go now before I lost my nerve.

The lump in my throat grew as Mama, Gunther, Beck, and Olen clustered together. I swallowed several times to clear it. "How can I ever thank you?"

"Find your family and send us word," said Mama.

I nodded. "Promise."

"I'll send more than a word," said Akiko. "I can do them all now."

Josephine cleared her throat. "*I'll* decide how much you know."

"I'm going to have school while we travel?" Akiko's eyes widened, dismay twisting her face.

Ben chuckled. "With me too. You're my primary kitchen helper."

"Oh boy," said Akiko, looking glum.

I leaned closer to her and lowered my voice. "I have lessons for you, too."

"Well, okay." She brightened, gave me an exaggerated wink, and handed me a piece of strawberry taffy.

I popped the candy into my mouth, letting the strawberry flavor chase away my bittersweet thoughts. Waving one last farewell, we pulled onto the road with Ben in the lead and me bringing up the rear. Donkey fell in step with Oxide, his head bobbing as he trotted beside us.

Ben led us through streets of crumbled buildings and rusted towers, the *clip-clop* of the horses' hooves on the cracked pavement echoing off the ruined structures. As we rode, my eyes slid to the upper-level windows, looking for ichthys signs. We'd heard nothing from Talbot since Carter's group fled the depot, but I trusted him to get word to us when he could.

We traveled beyond the frayed edges of Toronto Depot, and I turned my face to the sun, trying to picture the dusty plains and sculpted rocks of the desert southwest as Olen had described them. I'd grown up in the northeast, a child of cedar and snow, and couldn't fathom the landscape Olen's descriptions evoked. Despite our best efforts to prepare, we traveled into the unknown. Our destination was nearly a continent away, and the man who had threatened to harm my parents was somewhere ahead of us. With luck, our journey would be uneventful, but if not... I glanced back to where I secreted my sword into its usual spot in the spine of Magnesium's packsaddle.

As the others descended a hill, I twisted in my saddle for one last look at the spire above the jagged skyline. The tower had proved a false beacon, but I didn't regret the time we'd spent here. I allowed myself a lingering moment before turning to focus my eyes on the horizon. What was done was done, and what was to come would come.

My heart heavy, I bade farewell to those we'd lost and followed my friends toward our future.

# CHAPTER THREE

My resolve to stick to our plan eroded over the next week. Vegas Depot was months away, and with each kilometer, I was less sure we were traveling in the right direction. We could still head south and look for a community to overwinter with. There, we could wait for Talbot to send word while we evaluated our options.

Though being honest, it was hard to picture winter when surrounded by August's heat. The afternoon sun beat through the patchey tree canopy, as heavy as a weighted quilt. The damp heat, combined with Oxide's rhythmic swaying, lulled me into a semi-conscious, drowsy state. It took an effort to rouse myself and respond to Genevie when she said something. "Pardon?"

"Who are you daydreaming about?" While she wasn't yet slurring her words, she'd clearly been drinking for a while.

I reddened and she laughed.

"Boy, you've got it bad."

Even with my ever-present anxiety about whether we traveled in the right direction, the long, tedious days in the saddle left me plenty of time to think about Earl. And despite my decision to keep our friendship platonic, I'd traced the curve at the base of her back with my eyes and wondered about the texture of her flame-colored hair many times. In truth, I'd thought a lot about what it would feel like to kiss her.

My flush deepened, and to hide it from Genevie's probing gaze, I twisted to check on Magnesium. "Is his left pannier riding high?"

"So, you heard me," she said. "I asked if you wanted me to wait while you fixed it."

"Wait?" I glanced up and sighed. Ben and the others were out of sight. "Sorry. Lost in my thoughts."

I halted Oxide under the deep shade of a leafy oak and groaned as I dismounted. Even though we'd been traveling for a week, my hips hadn't adjusted to the long days in the saddle. On the bright side, riding a horse was less strenuous than pedaling a flier, giving my calf much-needed time to heal. The pain plaguing me for months was nearly gone; rare twinges were the only reminder.

While testing my leg, I studied Genevie. If she shared my reservations about the trip, she'd make an excellent ally in convincing the others to abandon our quest. "How far do you think we've traveled so far?"

"Too far for this heat." Genevie shrugged and wiped her forehead with the back of her arm. "Check Gertie's cinch while you're back there?"

I nodded and rubbed Magnesium's forehead. In response, the horse gave me an affectionate shove with his long nose. When Charcoal huffed his displeasure, I chuckled. "Don't you have something better to do?"

The dog swung his head southwest, then looked back my way. He sighed and sank to his belly, tongue lolling as he panted. But his ears pricked when a stick snapped under Donkey's hoof.

"Leave it," I said.

Charcoal ignored me and rose, staring east. Genevie stood in her stirrups and craned her neck.

"See anything?"

She shook her head. "Rabbit?"

Charcoal whined and trotted eastward to investigate.

When I heaved the pannier up, Magnesium swished his tail with displeasure. The pannier sagged as soon as I released it, and I shared a sigh with my horse.

"Do it right, Artist. The others will stop and wait for us… eventually. Probably." She snorted and took a long pull from her flask. "Why are you so slow today, anyway?"

If I wanted to recruit her, this was a great opening. But delivering bad news was the *worst*. I shrugged. "No reason." I pulled a heavy sack from the pannier and looked inside. "What are these? Rocks?"

"Akiko's souvenirs. She's been collecting one from each camp. And lunch break. And from every creek we've crossed." Genevie folded her arms. "Are you avoiding Earl?"

I ignored the question and dropped the sack of rocks on the ground. The next sack was heavy too, so I peered inside it. "Why am I carrying your farrier's tools?"

She twisted in her saddle. "Are you? What is Gertie carrying?"

I moved over to the heavy-boned, dun-colored mare. "Ah. You've got my art supplies."

Genevie swung from her saddle and dropped to the ground. "Perfect. We can use the mix-up as an excuse for not staying with the group. Plus, I can refill my flask, *and* you have time to tell me what's going on with you and Earl."

Charcoal reappeared at the top of the rise and barked.

Sweat trickled down my back as I tied Oxide's rein to a low branch. "Leave it, Charcoal. We've wasted enough time today."

Despite my words, Genevie's eyes brightened with interest. She tossed Bertha's rein to me and followed Charcoal over the hill. I muttered while I worked, willing them to return. By the time I'd sorted out the horses, they still weren't back. I stopped to listen and whistled.

Nothing.

I stomped up the hill, then descended into a thicket of bladdernut. This time when I whistled, Charcoal appeared. "Time to go. Get Genevie."

Instead of retrieving her, he barked.

There is no reasoning with a herding dog. Only arguments. Disagreements I rarely win. "Fine, show me." Thorny stems of black raspberry scraped at my face as I pushed through the brush. Charcoal led me down a faint game trail into a clearing.

Genevie nodded at me. Arms crossed, she gestured toward a log, a deep frown creasing her face.

Next to the log crouched a young coyote with its front paw trapped between two rusty metal bands. The bands were attached to a thick chain that snaked under the log. The coyote's snarled turned into a yowl, the high-pitched sound raising the hairs along my arms. I stopped when the coyote snarled and lunged at me.

My dog darted forward toward the coyote, but I called him back. "Charcoal! Down, stay." He obeyed, whining as I circled the trapped animal. She had the lankiness of an adolescent, but her lips pulled back, and her eyes narrowed with the mistrust of an older animal when I stepped closer.

I crouched and moved forward slowly, twigs crackling under my knee. "Easy, girl. Just here to help."

She sank toward the ground, her growl turning to a low-pitched whine. I scooted closer, weighing our options. If I did nothing, she'd likely die a slow, painful death. But she was young and frightened, and I wasn't sure I could make myself put her down. I patted the knife sheath on my hip. It was empty.

*Blast.*

"Gen, you have any tools on you?"

"No. But I could get some."

"Please do." When Genevie hesitated, I said, "I'm not sure I can help, but if you bring back a knife, we can end her suffering."

The coyote resumed her snarling when Genevie turned, and I waited until the animal calmed before moving closer.

*Can I release her?*

It was a dangerous option, especially since she clearly didn't want me to touch her, but when she whined again, she looked more like a frightened pup than a dangerous carnivore. Intent on my task, I ignored Genevie's return.

"Look who I found."

Akiko peered around Genevie, her eyes enormous. "How are you going to help it?"

"I'm not sure I can, Mouse."

Akiko squeaked when Genevie handed me a sheathed knife. "You can't hurt her!"

"Mouse—"

"Look, she's friendly."

Charcoal had belly crawled to the coyote and lay his head on his paws, nearly nose to nose with the trapped animal. When she relaxed her snarl, he swiped at her muzzle with his tongue. He turned his bright eyes to me, his pleading expression one I knew all too well.

Two against one. My shoulders sagged. "Keep quiet and I'll see what I can do."

Genevie swore. "What the blast are you doing?"

I held up my hand and crept closer to the frightened animal without taking my eyes off the coyote. "Calming her."

Genevie stepped closer, and the coyote rose on three legs, snarling.

"Easy, easy." I kept my voice low and melodious. "Gen, step back, will you?"

"It's a coil spring trap," she said. "To release the jaws, you'd need to press down on the levers evenly."

"Okay," I said.

She groaned. "It wasn't advice. There's no way the coyote will let you get close enough."

"She knows he's trying to help." The certainty in Akiko's tone made my heart warm as I moved closer.

"Use art," said Genevie. "Can you erase the trap?"

"It would take too long, and artists don't erase. Hush, and let me concentrate."

"You'll do anything to keep from discussing Earl." Genevie made a snorting noise. "Even risk your safety."

My neck flushed. For once, I hadn't been thinking about Earl.

*Until now.*

I swallowed, trying to calm my pulse. "To leave this poor animal now would be unforgivable. Besides, I'm nearly there."

I moved closer again, and although the coyote's growl deepened, she didn't move.

"Then talk to me about Earl," Genevie said. "I thought you had a thing for her."

"Had?" I asked, moving the back of my hand toward the coyote. It took effort to shove Earl off my mind's canvas, but I needed my entire focus.

The coyote tensed when my hand brushed her, but she didn't move. Charcoal whined and crawled closer.

"Mouse, can you keep Charcoal back?" I kept my tone soft, brushing the coyote's shoulder a second time.

"After you tell us what's going on between you and Earl." Genevie chuckled. "People like me need to know."

My heart thumped as I reached over and under the animal and grasped the two levers opposite the trap's jaws.

Her growl deepened.

"Or have you lost interest in Earl?"

My head whipped toward Genevie. "Lost interest?"

At my sudden movement, the coyote reared back, hit my chest, and snapped at my face. I jerked away, but not fast enough. Her teeth clamped onto my right hand. I howled, bowling backward.

"Matthew!" shouted Genevie, springing toward us.

My backward momentum pulled the coyote over backward, and she flipped upside down on top of me, her legs flailing, her teeth still clamped on my hand. Charcoal's frantic barking and Akiko's squeals ratcheted up the chaos.

I snaked my left arm around the coyote. "Get the trap open!"

The animal writhed on top of me, her growls and shrieks rising in tone and pitch, her fur musty and unpleasant against my face.

Genevie grunted, and a moment later, the coyote shivered. She twisted, released my hand, and bolted from my grasp, disappearing into the brush. Charcoal streaked after her. Akiko ran after them both before I could stop her.

Genevie released the trap with a jarring *snap*. "So, you *do* still have a thing for Earl?"

My chest heaved as I fought to catch my breath, my injured hand tucked tight against my chest. I glared at her. "Of course I do."

Genevie tossed a twig at my face and snorted when it

bounced off my forehead. "So why haven't you done anything about it?"

"Because it's better if we stay friends." My hand throbbed as I flexed it. Blood oozed from a dozen, needle-sharp punctures—beading Alizarin Carmine which darkened to Cadmium Purple when I smeared it across my filthy trousers. "She's still grieving Bowman. And I need to focus on Akiko." And because if she didn't feel the same way, there'd be no going back. "The timing is all wrong."

"Sounds flimsy." Genevie eyed my hand but tossed another twig toward me, anyway. "Do better."

"Can we patch me up first?" I waved my bloody hand at her.

She rose from the ground and offered her hand. "Sure. Assuming we're the ones carrying the first aid supplies today."

The path Genevie chose back was worse than the first, and we cursed as we forced our way through the brush. Several times, we stopped for fortifying swigs from her flask. By the time we reached the horses, we were both covered with scratches, sweat, and blood.

Unlike us, Charcoal appeared unfazed, lounging against the oak's trunk, a huge smile on his face. Next to him, Akiko beamed at me as she tugged on the dog's ears. "Everyone turned around to find us!"

Nearby, Earl leaned against a tree, looking cool and clean in its shade. I couldn't read her expression, but it didn't change when Genevie staggered past, weaving toward her mares.

Ben's face creased into a smile. He raised his eyebrow. "What the blast were you three doing?"

Josephine looked unamused as she marched toward me with her hands on her hips. "We won't get *anywhere* if we have to backtrack each time you two do not keep up."

To head off her scolding, I waved my blood-smeared hand. "We stopped to help Charcoal's new friend."

"She's right there." Akiko pointed at the brush. She held up an ordinary, gray rock. "I'm not going to name her so it will hurt less when she leaves. But I found a souvenir to remember the moment."

Josephine's face softened as she glanced from me to Akiko. "Of course you did." She sighed. "I'll get the disinfectant, but someone better explain what happened."

Genevie chuckled and drained her flask. "Have I ever told you guys about the time Matthew snuggled a coyote?"

# CHAPTER FOUR

For two weeks we picked our way through the vast forests of Red Maple, Bur Oak, and the Phthalo Green canopies of what Josephine identified as a Kentucky Coffee Tree.

When we broke out of the woods, I stopped Oxide to stare at the vast sea of waving grasses. The sun was still several centimeters above the horizon; the sky streaked with bands of Indian Yellow and Helios Red, which combined into a brilliant Rose Madder where they met the clouds.

This vast, empty landscape meant we'd reached the second stage of our trip. I'd grown up with crashing waves against a rocky shoreline on one side of the abbey and deep forest on the other, so this empty horizon unnerved me. When Olen had described the prairie, it had sounded romantic, but now all I could picture were long days in the saddle wading through prairie grasses under an unforgiving sun.

"Beautiful," Earl said. The setting sun bathed her in a golden light, turning her hair fire-bright. "Somehow I remember more sunrises than sunsets."

"Stunning." The timing for us wasn't right, but I still treasured these moments with Earl, hoarding each memory like goblins hoarded wealth in Genevie's favorite stories.

Earl looked away and drew in an audible breath.

Was she preparing to say something important? My heart pounded, and my palms wetted as my anticipation rose.

"Come on," she said. "Let's catch up to the others."

What did she want to say? As we rode, I nudged Oxide toward her, so our calves nearly brushed.

Earl smiled. "Matthew—"

My stomach's rumble interrupted her, protesting with an endless groaning whine.

Earl laughed and her posture relaxed. "It's clear what *you're* thinking about."

I winced. Once again, I'd missed the moment. "Pardon my gut. You were saying?" I pulled my hair up to let my neck cool off until Oxide took advantage of my inattention to stop and snatch a mouthful of grass.

"The heat over these open fields is brutal." Earl rolled her shoulders. "Do you think we're near our stop?"

Whatever I expected—*or hoped*—she would say, it wasn't that. Hoping to hide my disappointment, I kept my tone bright. "I wish I hadn't opened the map during our lunch break. Once Akiko saw 'dragon', it was over." My beard itched; I needed a bath. With luck, our visit with the dragon would be short and we'd reach the next community before dark. "Genevie teaming up with her didn't help."

"Kaskaskia Dragon." Earl drew out each syllable, like the phrase was magical. "What does it mean?"

"Who knows?" I grinned, remembering Akiko's squeals of excitement. "But it was on our way. After Detroit Depot, I couldn't tell her no."

Earl's mouth tightened. "I can't believe Carter's thugs ransacked *another* warehouse."

The depot had been in an uproar when we'd arrived. Carter's group had taken hand tools and all the art supplies from the warehouse. They had ransacked the seed library, too. "I keep wondering if we should have detoured to Chicago Depot."

"They might have hit it next, since..." Earl paused when Bruno shook his head. His bit jingled a merry tune, reminding me of the tinkle of Year's End bells. She patted the gigantic horse. "Since we have seen no signs of them since leaving the depot."

A mosquito whined near my ear, and I slapped my neck to warn it off. "Josephine said so too."

Earl flashed her lopsided grin. "Yet you continue to second guess our choices?"

"I don't, *really*, I—" Catching her expression, I chuckled. "Okay, I deserve that."

Earl's gaze slid sideways toward me. "Can I ask another question?"

I nodded and silently commanded my stomach to stay quiet. "Anything."

She toyed with Bruno's mane before asking, "Were you and Josephine—"

Her horse jumped sideways as Charcoal flushed a rabbit. It darted away in a gray-brown blur of panic. Charcoal gave an excited yip, but before he could give chase, the coyote pounced. The rabbit squealed once. It hung limp after the coyote gave it a tremendous shake.

I scowled at the coyote. She stared back, uncowed, before melting into the tall grass with her prize. I whistled to prevent Charcoal from following her and frowned at him. "If I didn't know you better, I'd think you were going feral, too."

He smiled, clearly unconcerned by the tone of my voice.

"He's no match for her feminine wiles," said Earl. "I can't believe she's still following us."

I flexed my hand. The punctures had nearly healed. "Me neither. I didn't think we'd see her again after the depot, but she's trailed after us like smoke. Your question?"

Earl blinked twice and blurted, "Were you and Josephine ever a couple?"

My voice cracked. "*Josephine?*"

Earl waited, her gaze even, saying nothing.

My face heated. I shook my head. "No. Why?"

"The two of you... you're close." Earl chewed on her lip. "I didn't think men and women could be friends."

"You and Bowmen were friends." As soon as the words were out, I longed to tear them from the air. It had been three weeks since his death, and guilt swamped me each time I thought of our escape from Welland Island.

"We were different." Earl sighed and faced the sunset, her expression wistful. "Besides, Bowman liked men."

"I'm sorry." Though I'd apologized many times, the words sprang forward. I shoved back another flare of guilt. "I miss him too."

"It's still unreal." Her eyes sharpened. "But quit changing the subject. You and Josephine?"

"Me and Josephine." I watched Charcoal bound through the tall grass. "When we first met, there might have been a spark, but it didn't catch. She met Ben soon after."

"She's important to you."

"Like a sister," I agreed. "What about it?"

Earl shrugged. "In my experience, men and women can't be friends."

I straightened. "That's absurd. Genevie is my friend. You're my friend."

Earl's lips drooped. But before I could clarify my meaning,

Akiko screeched from somewhere ahead of us. My head whipped around in time to see her race Lady up a hill. Genevie streaked after them; her mares stretched flat as they galloped after my daughter.

I tightened my grip on Magnesium's lead and kicked Oxide forward. The humid air billowed with the scent of crushed grass, and my eyes teared as we hurtled after them, Charcoal sprinting beside us. Cresting the hill, Oxide halted in a series of short bounces and nearly unseated me. My heart thrashed like a trapped bird. I dropped to the ground and sprinted toward Genevie. "What's wrong? Where's Akiko?"

A smile split Genevie's face. She pointed.

Akiko's eyes glowed as she waded through the waving grasses toward us. "We're here, and there's a *dragon*." She pulled on me, her hands fire-hot against mine. "Come on, let's free it!"

My breath caught. A thin, spiked, silver neck rose nearly five meters above the tall grasses and shrubs. Under Akiko's direction, we pulled and trampled the grasses and vines back from the beast until we could easily walk around it.

The creature was approximately ten meters long and stood on its hind feet, supported by its tail. It had two, comically short grasping arms halfway up its neck, balanced by a pair of ludi-crously small bat wings.

When we'd finished, Genevie slung her arm around my shoulders. "I waited my whole life to see a dragon, and now I've seen three."

"Three?" I asked, while Akiko raced beneath the sculpture.

"Beck's queen, the dragon you put on the front of the *Marybelle*, and this." She cocked her head, her flask near her lips. "Why didn't I think of cobbling together a giant, metal sculpture?"

"A lack of imagination?" I smirked when she shoved my shoulder. "We're friends, aren't we?"

"After that comment?" Genevie's eyes narrowed. "Why?"

"Well, I—"

"Who have you been talking to?"

"No, I meant—"

"What have you heard?"

Chuckling, I gave up. "Never mind."

"Pushover." She set her palm against the dragon's side and patted it. "Spill, Artist."

"Earl doesn't think men and women can be friends."

Genevie raised her eyebrows. "It's probably true when you look like her." She sighed. "I looked like a potato until I hit puberty, and afterward, I was a potato with tits. But the boys didn't find me intimidating, and the girls didn't see me as competition. I was free to make friends, pursue love interests, and develop my sparkling personality without judgment."

I stared at her. "A potato?"

"With tits," she agreed.

She offered me her flask. The sour smell of bourbon wafted toward me. I shook my head, and she took another long drink. Before our fishing trip on the *Marybelle*, I'd rarely seen Genevie drink more than a glass of ale. But since departing the depot, the occasional nips had turned into a daily descent into inebriation. My throat tightened at the now-familiar burble of liquid as she guzzled from her flask.

When I cleared my throat, she waved it toward me. I took it and feigned taking a swig. Even so, the bourbon burned my lips and tongue where it touched me. "And Earl wasn't free?"

Genevie looked thoughtful as she gazed up at the shining sculpture. "I suspect she had it harder. With her looks, men and women would have been more invested in how she appeared than interested in who she was."

"But that's transactional." I shook my head. "Besides, what about Ben and Josephine? They were friends first."

Genevie shrugged and reached for her flask. "Are you saying Ben wasn't interested in Josephine from the start? Because if you are, you're either lying to yourself or a fool."

Genevie was right. Ben had expressed interest—romantic interest—in Josephine from the moment they'd met. "So, there's no hope? Men and non-potato women can't be friends?"

When Genevie shrugged, I swallowed hard. If Genevie was right, I could either tell Earl how I felt about her or say nothing and continue to enjoy her friendship. And if I admitted my feelings to Earl, and she felt differently? I'd have poisoned my chance at a friendship and the opportunity to spend more time with her. It wasn't worth the risk. Besides, I needed to focus on Akiko and on reaching my parents.

Charcoal and Akiko shadow-boxed beneath the dragon's belly, Charcoal hopping on his hind legs. The coyote watched their antics from the edge of the beaten-down grass.

"In my experience, friendship with *anyone* is hard to maintain when one party retreats into their head and abandons the conversation." Genevie's eyes danced when I reddened. "Besides, if you truly want to know what Earl thinks, why don't you talk to *her* about it? Here's your chance."

The coyote melted into the deepening dusk as Ben, Josephine, and Earl rode toward us.

Ben halted his mule and leaned forward, shaking his head. "There really is a dragon."

"Told you!" Akiko skipped out from under the beast's belly. "What's for dinner?"

Ben's eyes crinkled. "It depends on what the group decides."

"We have choices?" Akiko asked.

Josephine folded forward and draped her arms around

Fox's neck. The chestnut horse bobbed his head, wiggling his lips as Josephine scratched his chest. "We shouldn't be far from the community of Vandalia. Should we make camp here or continue?"

"Stay here!" said Akiko, twirling.

"Why?" asked Ben.

Akiko's eyes bulged, and she stopped spinning. "Because there's a *dragon*."

"Duh," said Genevie, nodding.

Silently, we watched fireflies flicker and wink as they floated over the tall grasses.

Ben cleared his throat. "What does everyone else want to do?"

What I wanted to say was I wanted a night under a roof, away from the heat, humidity, and whining insects.

But Earl hugged herself and said, "It's romantic here."

Akiko squealed in agreement, and my desire to continue to the town shriveled. I shrugged, so Ben twisted to look at Josephine.

"I'm good either way," she said.

Ben sighed and scratched at the stubble along his jaw. "Then it's my decision. I—"

Magnesium interrupted by groaning and folding his legs. Without waiting to be unsaddled, he settled on the ground with a contented sigh. His eyes bright, he leaned against a pannier and snatched a mouthful of grass.

"Too late! Magnesium decided for us." Akiko chortled and twirled again. "Tonight, we sleep under a dragon!"

# CHAPTER FIVE

Akiko's face reddened, and she raised her chin. "No. You can go, but I'm staying here."

It was her first public meltdown on this trip. Her tantrum mortified me. Worse, it thwarted our plans for an early morning departure. She'd been so happy after our reunion in Toronto Depot. I'd hoped this bad behavior was behind us.

"Akiko, I will not ask a fourth time," I said, keeping my voice measured and reasonable.

The others gathered around the horses; their attention rapt on meaningless tasks. I flushed harder and lowered my voice. "You're making everyone uncomfortable."

Anger flashed across Akiko's face. "If you want the bedrolls stowed, *you* stow them."

My lips compressed and nostrils flared as I sucked in another breath. "Okay, but here's the thing. Stowing the bedrolls is *your* job." A vise clamped around my eyes as I gestured toward the others. "Everyone has a job. Ben and Earl cook. Josephine and Genevie take care of the horses. I set up and tear down camp. You stow the bedrolls and gather firewood."

She said nothing, but her chin jutted, and she crossed her arms.

I counted how many shades of green I could identify in my peripheral vision before continuing. "Akiko, this seems to be about more than bedrolls." When her mouth softened, I continued, "Can you tell me why you want to stay?"

Charcoal leaned against her leg and looked up, his tongue lolling.

When Akiko hesitated, I sat cross-legged on the trampled grass. "Talk to me, Mouse."

She frowned and buried her face in Charcoal's fur. "I want to stay because I want to live in a community with a dragon on its green."

"But..." I looked around. "Akiko, there's no community here."

Her eyes glinted with unshed tears. "But there could be. I could put one here. Build it right around this dragon and stop traveling."

My heart squeezed at the plaintive expression on her face, but a chill raced down my spine. I could pull the parental card and insist she behave, but what if she rebelled and drew attention to the secret we'd been carrying? If I forced her on her horse, my actions would do little to soothe her worries. Worse, it could bring on more meltdowns.

That I agreed with her made it worse. But this was neither the right time nor place to settle. Plus, I still didn't know how to explain my reluctance to continue to Vegas Depot to the others. They had traveled so far, and lost so much, to help me find my family. But if I couldn't share Akiko's secret, how could they understand why my goals had changed?

It took little effort to soften my tone or expression. "Traveling can be tedious, huh?"

She nodded without looking at me. "And there's no one to talk to."

My eyebrows shot up in mock surprise, and I crossed my arms. "No one? If memory serves, the only time you're not chattering is when you're asleep. And sometimes you even talk then."

When surprise crossed her face, I knew I'd reached her. She wavered as though wanting to hang onto her original complaint, but gave in and grinned. "No way."

"Way. Between your mumbling and Ben's farting, I get no sleep at all."

Akiko cackled. "Ben farts?"

"All. The. Time." I poked my finger in her side until she squirmed. "Why do you think I ask you to put Josephine's bedroll between Ben and the fire?"

"Oh." Akiko scrambled to her feet. "Okay, I'll keep it in mind when we stop tonight. Our secret."

"Our secret," I agreed, making a dramatic farting noise as I stood. "Mouse, when we stop traveling, I promise we will have a dragon on our green."

"Cross your heart?"

"I swear it."

Akiko scrambled to her feet and carried the bedrolls to the horses. When she handed Ben his bedding, she cackled, flashing me an exaggerated wink. Ben shot me a puzzled look, and it took every gram of my composure to shrug as though I didn't know why.

Despite our late start, we reached the community of Vandalia in less than an hour. If we stayed focused, we'd need little time to gather supplies and could make up the time we'd lost this morning. Turning down the main street, Akiko and I rode side by side, singing the ribald song I'd taught her at top volume.

Akiko's eyes danced as she sang, "The steamboat went to—"

I matched her enthusiasm and vigor as I cut in, "*Hell*-o, operator, give me number nine. And if you disconnect me, I'll cut off your—"

"*Behind* the yellow curtain, there lay a piece of glass. Miss Suzy sat upon it and cut her little—"

"*Ask* me no more—" I stopped singing to stare at a gray pony tied to the hitching rail.

Akiko bounced on top of Lady, her voice shrill with frustration. "Matthew, *no*. You say—"

I stopped Oxide in the middle of the street. "Doesn't that look like My Darling?"

Josephine's head whipped to the left. "What?"

Before Akiko could respond, the pony dropped to the ground and rolled in the dirt, raising a cloud of dust. "It *is* My Darling!" The hairs on my arms rose.

*Sally.*

"Pickled flaming fisheyes!" a voice screeched from the nearest building. "You better not crush my saddle, you bag of pigeon brains!"

"Shut your mouth, Sally Park. There are ladies present!" bellowed Genevie.

A swinging door shrieked open, and Sally stood in the doorway. "Where?" she countered in a hard voice dripping with scorn. "I see dung heads, dirty socks, and a party of pig gravy!"

Josephine openly wept as she flew toward the older

woman. They clung together, trembling. Genevie vaulted from her mare and raced toward them, wrapping her arms around both women. Akiko squirmed into the knot of sobbing women and disappeared in the middle. Even Ben's smile was wide enough to split his head, and he too jumped down from his mule, leaving me and Earl to corral the unsupervised animals milling in the middle of the street.

"Guess they know her," said Earl, her grin rueful.

"Guess so," I said, as I gestured toward the herd. "Help me hitch them?"

By the time we'd tied the last horse, our friends had disappeared. "Shall we?" I asked, keeping my voice light and offering my elbow. Earl said nothing but linked her arm through mine.

Inside the dim room, Sally waited near the threshold with her hands on her hips. She peered through the spectacles perched on the tip of her nose and snorted. "Blazing inferno, were you *always* this handsome?"

On the street, she'd appeared unchanged, but the distance had hidden the depth of the lines at the corners of her eyes and mouth. They had deepened, suggesting she'd been living in a perpetual state of worry.

My voice cracked. "Son of a sea cook, have I missed *you*."

Sally folded me into her arms, and I fought back the sting in my eyes. She trembled against me, her arms around me like steel bands. Memories crashed over me, and I closed my eyes, patting the bony area between her shoulder blades.

When her shaking slowed, she sighed, gave me one last squeeze, and faced Earl. "Burned gravy, you are a looker. Who are you, and what are your plans for this turd suit?"

I choked back a laugh. "Earl, meet Sally Park, administrator. Sally, this is Earl Kildare, butcher."

Sally's eyebrow rose. "A butcher, eh?"

Earl's lips curved. "Heya, Sally. I've heard... *colorful* things about you."

Sally turned to me and poked her finger into my chest.

"Ow, Sally! What?"

"Why are you here, and" –she stopped, her voice cracking– "what took you so *long*?"

I wrapped my arms around her and held her as she wept.

When her tears slowed, she pulled back and gave me a watery smile. "Don't you dare tell *anyone* I have feelings left."

"No one would believe me, anyway." I offered an arm to each woman. "Come, let's talk."

We rejoined the group at the large table Ben had arranged. Sally's eyebrows shot up when Ben brushed Josephine's temple with his lips. "I see I've missed something."

"Yeah, me," said Genevie, thumping her chest.

Akiko giggled and slapped her chest, too. "Me more?"

"Without a doubt. How have you grown *so* much?" Sally shook her head and feigned amazement. "Did Matthew learn how to cook?"

"Hardly," Earl said. She blushed when all heads snapped toward her. "Too soon?"

Everyone laughed, and she relaxed. My cheeks burned from smiling so much, and the wink Earl flashed me didn't help.

Over pints of lager and moon-shaped meat pies filled with chunks of beef and potato, we filled Sally in on our travels and what had transpired in Toronto Depot.

Sally's eyes darkened at Ben's mention of Talbot. He'd have ground to make up when he and Sally met. If they met. I pushed away the twisting ache of uncertainty.

Sally patted my hand. "This Reverend Carter sounds like a spit-covered fudge puppy. I'm sorry you haven't found your birth parents. What's next?"

"Fudge puppy. Good one." Akiko chortled. "We're going to Vegas Depot. You'll come too?"

Sally took a deep breath, but when she released it, she nodded. "If you'll have me." She turned toward me. "I left you before—"

"But you're back *now*." I gripped her hand. "Do come. Without you, the power goes to Ben's head. He gets insufferable."

"We suffer, Sally." Akiko pinched her nose shut.

"Well," said Sally, her eyes wet. "Should I organize rooms for you? They're probably getting tight because of tonight's minstrel show. I may have more luck if I can offer art in trade."

Everyone else exclaimed with excitement, but my gut clenched. A minstrel show? After what we'd been through with the revivalists, uneasiness arose in me when people mentioned minstrels. But even if I said no, there was little chance I'd talk the others into skipping the show. And, like Akiko, I wanted Sally to come with us, so I buried my misgivings and smiled. "Anything for you, Sally."

Her throat convulsed several times before she drew in a shaky breath. "Tonight, we'll share one of Tony's deep-dish wonders and attend a minstrel show. Tomorrow, we'll head across the great empty... together."

# CHAPTER SIX

I didn't stop to set up our camp until I was sure we were out of sight of Vandalia.

Akiko sighed, her mouth twisting as I hoisted the tarpaulin over the rope. "It's not fair."

"Fair?" I wiped the sweat off my forehead with the back of my arm. "What's with the face?"

Her scowl deepened. She crossed her arms and sighed again. "Since you're the one doing the improvement for hospitality, why are *we* camping in the dirt? The others got rooms."

"There were only two empty rooms."

"Wrong." Her lip poked out. "Three rooms."

I tightened my knot and hid my smile. For a week, I'd been looking for a few private hours to continue Akiko's art lessons but hadn't found an opportunity until now. "Well, I wasn't willing to kick Sally out of her room."

"Because she's old, or because you're scared?"

"Both?" I grinned, securing the rope.

"Fine. What about Genevie and Earl?"

"They desperately wanted baths. Please set up our bedrolls."

"You need a bath more than they do." Akiko sighed and pulled our bedding from Donkey's packsaddle. "But giving Ben and Josephine a room was smart."

"Smart?" I squatted to rub Charcoal's belly.

"Keeps Ben's farts from burning us up," she muttered.

"Right." I snorted, picturing Ben's face when Akiko finally shared the joke with him. "We'll be in town tonight for dinner and the minstrel show, so we're only sleeping here. And since it's just the two of us, we can study."

Akiko brightened. "Art lesson?"

I made an exaggerated show of scanning in every direction before nodding. "Yes. Plus, I'll show you how to make charcoal." I pulled out the bundle of sticks I'd collected while traveling through the woods, each roughly the diameter of my thumb. "I have several types of oak, willow, and maple... and a favor to ask."

"Okay. This is *way* better than staying in town." Akiko kneeled next to me and picked up the sticks. "What's the favor?"

I sat back on my heels, ignoring the cartwheels inside my stomach. "I want to learn how to create. Will you teach me?" If I could create like she could, I could establish a home for us nearly anywhere. We wouldn't even need a nearby community or depot for supplies.

"Me teach *you*?" She looked doubtful. "But I'm a kid."

"So? A good artist is always learning, and you know something I don't." I nudged her shoulder. "In trade for your lesson, I'll teach you about value and essence. You need to understand both to draw with charcoal. Deal?"

The smile she gave me made my heart swell. "Deal. Let's

start with an egg," she said, pointing at the cast iron pan where I'd nestled four eggs to boil for breakfast.

"Perfect." I glanced around our meager campsite. "Why don't you set up the lesson while I get a fire burning?"

Once my fire caught, I rejoined Akiko. She folded a towel on top of one of the upturned empty panniers. "For the egg."

"Noted." I settled next to her on the grass and pulled out my sketchpad and pencil, enjoying the peaceful moment. The scents of crushed clover, nodding onion, and wild oats mingled with the wood smoke in the humid air. In the distance, a rusted metal silo from *Before* loomed over the sea of grass. Charcoal sprawled on his back, his legs splayed and his belly soaking in the sun's heat. The coyote lay near him, her eyes watchful.

When I finished sharpening my pencil, Akiko straightened, her expression serious. "First, draw an egg."

When I opened my mouth to make a joke, her frown— nearly identical to Josephine's expression of annoyance— convinced me otherwise. I bent to my task and illustrated a speckled egg.

"Ooh, fancy," said Akiko, when I showed her my sketch-book. "Next, pick up your egg with your brain fingers. Focus on its shape and how smooth it is. When you can hold it and feel the weight, draw it on the towel."

Brain fingers? A part of me wanted to argue, to tell Akiko why it wouldn't work, but I pushed away my inner cynic, drew in a deep breath, and nodded. I stared at my drawing, exam-ining each speckle, the texture of the shell, the faint shine. The world retreated as I focused. Even the ever-present drone of insects softened like I'd slipped underwater. As the illustrated egg blurred, the egg in my mind sharpened and crystallized. I let it roll across my mind's canvas, noticing minute details, like the weighty pause prior to each revolution.

When I set my pencil tip near the paper, the sensation was

almost as though I drew directly on the egg's shell. Waves of energy pulsed through my arms as I worked, unlike the usual tingle I felt when I altered the physical world. Faster and faster, I sketched until an egg sat nestled upon the towel on my page.

"Matthew!"

Akiko's voice broke through my trance-like state. My chest heaved as I gasped for air, drenched in sweat.

Charcoal stared at me, his body radiating tension.

"What happened?" Akiko's voice was barely a whisper. I lifted my sketchbook to show her my drawing. But she ignored it, pointing at the pannier.

A speckled egg sat upon the towel.

*I did it.*

A wild joy bubbled up, and I sprang toward the egg. It mirrored exactly the egg I'd drawn, and its weight and smooth shell were perfect. Eager to crack it open, I raised my hand.

"Wait, stop!" Akiko held out the cast iron pan. "I think you moved the egg."

My shoulders sagged, and I clutched a fistful of my wet shirt. "Are you sure?"

"We had four eggs, didn't we?"

I nodded, staring at the egg in my hand, my heart heavy.

"Three eggs are in the pan."

I sighed. "I'll try again."

"Give me back your egg first."

My chest tight, I handed it over and returned to my place. This time I drew a plain egg with no color deviations. After holding it with my mind and letting it solidify, I drew the three-dimensional shape. The pulsing shocks were no less vibrant, so when I raised my eyes to the pannier, the sight of an egg was more of a reassurance than a surprise. "Mouse, how many eggs do you have?"

Akiko sighed. "Three."

Disappointment curled through me. Saying nothing, I returned the egg to her. Given the effort it took to transport the egg, why didn't I have more to show for it? When Akiko created, the process appeared effortless. I had created *nothing*, yet the effort left my muscles weak and rubbery, like I'd sprinted for hours through deep sand. If I'd been at the abbey, I would have tried again and again until I mastered the skill. But I was no longer a lad, and I'd promised to teach her about value, so I set aside my frustration.

"The fire is ready for us to make charcoal." I poked at the fire with our shovel, moving the red-orange coals to the side. "Let's bury the sticks."

Akiko dug a shallow trench in the hot ash and dropped in our branches. Once we'd covered them, I pushed the glowing embers over the sticks and rebuilt the fire. Sweat poured down my face. The day was too hot to sit near a fire, but if we squandered this opportunity, we might not have another for months. "Is there any water left?"

"Yup."

Akiko waited until I was mid-swallow to ask, "What are your intentions with Earl?"

I snorted, the water burning as it sprayed out my nostrils. Wincing, I wiped my face on my sleeve. "What?"

Akiko shrugged. "Sally asked Ben about your intentions with Earl. Are you planning something?"

"No plans." My face flushed. "Not yet."

She bent over her sketchbook. "If you change your mind, let me know."

"Would it bother you if I changed my mind?"

She said nothing.

My heart thumped as I waited for her response. Why had I asked?

The silence lengthened, and tiny bubbles appeared around the edges of the pot.

"I like Earl." Akiko's words were slow and measured, as if she'd mulled the question with deliberation. "So, if you do, I'll help you get a great plan."

*This kid.*

"Thank you." I bowed, marshaled my emotions, and cleared my throat. "Want to start your lesson while we wait for our eggs to boil?"

Akiko nodded, her expression brightening.

"We'll start with essence. A charcoal drawing is immediate. Visceral." I waggled my favorite charcoal pencil near her face until she giggled and relaxed. "The medium doesn't allow for much nuance, so the composition must be intentional. Good, so far?" I stopped and waited for her to nod. She did, but the furrow on her brow warned me she didn't understand.

"Okay. Unlike a landscape where you are not required to set a focal point, a charcoal sketch *must* have a subject. It's what we call the essence... it's the point of the drawing. Once you've captured your subject, only add details to highlight the essence, and nothing else. With charcoal, less is more."

Akiko's frown deepened, so I held my fingers to frame Charcoal lying in the grass. "Let's say Charcoal is our subject. If you sketched with graphite, you might draw the entire vignette; him, the ground, the sky, clouds. But when using charcoal, we add flowers and grasses solely to highlight or anchor the essence."

Akiko giggled, and I looked up from my finger frame. "What?"

"You're using charcoal to highlight Charcoal in a charcoal."

It *was* absurd, but I feigned offense. I even held my expression until Akiko crossed her eyes and stuck her tongue out. The tension I'd been carrying for weeks dropped away as I chuckled. "If you please, Miss Sugiyama?"

"Professor." The sarcasm she layered into her reply was a perfect mimic of Josephine, and I barked a laugh. "Value is the range from black to white. If zero is white and ten is black, what value would you give your trousers?"

Akiko plucked at the fabric. "Seven?"

"High marks for you, young miss. Head of the class. Questions?"

"Why does value matter?"

"Ah." I opened my sketchbook and ignored the flare of disappointment at my egg sketches. Flipping to a new page, I drew a thin rectangle at the top and portioned it into roughly five squares. "This end is the white, and this end is the black."

Akiko crowded close to watch me fill in the black square with my deepest charcoal.

"Value matters because we use neither white nor black to draw." I filled in the middle squares, creating a gradient. "When we draw with charcoal, we won't allow our shadows more than a value of six or seven. Can you guess what value we assign our lightest strokes?"

Akiko traced the rectangle at the top of the page with her pointer finger. "Three or four?"

"Exactly." With sweeping strokes, I drew an outline of Charcoal's face on the page. I kept the pressure light to rough in his markings and features. Once his face was set, I worked on deepening the patches around each eye, leaving a speckled white area around his muzzle, between his eyes, and up over his forehead. "Although the black color around his eyes and along the edges of his ears is deep, I'm going to use a value of six to shade it. Can you tell me why?"

Akiko bent over the drawing, studying it while I worked. The waves of concentration emanating from her were nearly tangible, but it wasn't until I started shading the area under his ears using a value of eight that she made the connection. "You're using a deeper value to show shine!"

Her happy, excited expression was my reward for putting her needs before my own. I grinned. "Exactly."

"Keep going." She watched, her face rapt, as I worked on Charcoal's portrait. When I set down my charcoal, she sighed. "You're a better teacher than me."

"You're a better student." I kissed her forehead, tasting salt. "And I have more practice at teaching."

"But less practice at creating." She folded her arms and frowned, her expression thoughtful. "You should try again. We need to get your value from a zero to a five."

"I'd settle for a three," I muttered, picking up my sketchbook. After flipping to a new page, I lifted the canteen, but it was empty. I waggled it, narrowing my eyes. "Can you create a cup of water?"

"Don't know." Her brow furrowed. "Let's see." She scribbled for a few minutes and a cup appeared on the pannier. She sprang up and trotted over, but her shoulders sagged. "A cup, yes, but no water."

# CHAPTER SEVEN

It was late afternoon by the time I was ready to work on the improvement. A sizable crowd had amassed on Vandalia's community green, so we stood at the edge, looking for the others.

Sally waved us over. "The news about your art got out, and they've been arriving all day. At this point, I'm not sure which show they've come to see. Matthew and Akiko Sugiyama," she said, by way of introduction, "this is Trudie Barnes, Vandalia's administrator."

"Well met." I had my easel and satchel of art supplies under my right arm, so rather than juggling or dropping everything, I extended my left hand.

Barnes took it, but her grip was loose and hesitant, adding to the awkwardness of the moment. "Uh, right," she said, staring at my shoulder. She straightened and turned toward the green, but the way she wiped her right hand on her trousers brought Akiko's opinion of my cleanliness to mind.

I squirmed, flushing. Done was done, and if my improvement was suitably impressive, perhaps the crowd would over-look my grimy, disheveled state.

Earl had yet to see me improve more than a chicken coop, but although I'd been excited to show off my skills, my earlier efforts to create an egg had worn me out. This lackluster meeting with the disengaged administrator hadn't helped, either. Still, if I wanted to show Earl what I was truly capable of, I needed the administrator to ask for something grand.

I summoned all my energy and flashed Barnes a smile I hoped dazzled. "What improvement can I make for you, Administrator?"

Barnes wiped both of her palms along her legs before answering. "We've been meaning to build a larger shelter on the green. Our carpenter was supposed to tear down the gazebo by now." She pointed. "But she had a baby, and her apprentice isn't up to a large project on her own."

I nodded, scanning the green. The area was extensive enough to house a substantial building if they didn't mind losing some of the open space. "Should I put the shelter where the gazebo is?"

Barnes didn't answer me and looked at Sally.

Sally patted her shoulder. "Why don't I organize Matthew for you? There must be a million details for you to attend to today."

Barnes gave Sally a grateful smile and hurried off without another word.

"Did I do something wrong?" I asked, following Sally toward the gazebo. "She didn't like me much."

"Don't you worry about it." Sally climbed the gazebo's steps and turned to assess the crowd. "We need to move these people back."

I dropped the satchel and opened the easel with a *snap*. "Why wasn't Barnes pleased to meet me?"

"Leave it alone." Sally glowered, her eyes glinting with a warning. She turned toward Akiko. "Child, can you tell those people to back up? Let's clear everyone from the man in the blue-striped shirt to the lady with the baby on the red blanket."

Akiko nodded and scampered toward the crowd.

"It's not unusual for administrators to fawn over me when they meet me," I muttered.

"Listen here, young man. She had a sex dream about you during her nap and hadn't composed herself before you showed up. Okay? Can we focus now?"

My face flamed as I clipped the paper to the easel. "What should the shelter look like?"

Sally threw up her hands. "You be the artist, and I'll be the administrator. Bye now."

Akiko bounded up to me. "I told them. Where is Sally going?"

"Akiko, fetch Ben." My ego and self-importance shriveled, sending my confidence plummeting.

She narrowed her eyes. "Why?"

This wasn't the time. "Because I asked."

A hurt expression crossed her face, and she scurried away before I could apologize. My spirits even lower, I sketched a half-dozen shelter ideas.

The rumble in Ben's voice startled me from my work. "Akiko said you're cross."

"I'm not—" I closed my eyes and drew a deep breath before starting again. "They've asked for a shelter but provided no direction about the style. Do you like any of these?"

Ben folded his arms and looked over my proposals. "They're nice."

I made a face. I wasn't going for *nice*. Nice wouldn't impress Earl. "Nice?"

"This one is elegant." He pointed at a structure with finials. "And this drawing is impressive."

"But?"

Ben rubbed his jaw and squinted across the green. "Tell me what the administrator said."

"Their carpenter was supposed to tear down the gazebo and build a larger shelter, but she had a baby." Ben waited, but I shrugged. "Nothing more." I pointed to the sketch of the Norse-inspired lodge house. "Should I do something like this, but add skylights?" Ben's expression told me *all* my designs were wrong. "Fine." I took a deep breath and fought the urge to throw my things on the ground. "If they commissioned *you* to engineer a shelter, what would you build?"

As though he'd been waiting for my invitation, Ben took my pencil. "Something like this." He drew a simple peaked roof supported by vertical poles.

It was nothing but a roof on stilts. "That's it? No skylights? No adornments?"

"Yes. They need shade in the summer, so no skylights." Ben studied his sketch. "If you want to deliver more, add a sheet-metal roof like the gazebo, and some kind of hardscape under the shelter."

"No walls, no adornments, no skylights." I shook my head. This wouldn't impress anyone, but I was honor-bound to paint the improvement they asked for.

"What's wrong?" Ben handed the pencil back to me, his mouth drooping in a parody of mine.

Despite myself and my poor mood, I chuckled. "This will take but a few minutes."

Ben grinned back. "Good. They'll appreciate having time to decorate it for tonight's show."

By the time Akiko returned, I'd already finished sketching the gazebo. I opened my mouth to apologize, but she snatched my discarded sheets and examined them. "What are we doing?"

I pointed to Ben's sketch.

She pouted as she studied it. "That's all?"

*Exactly.*

While this improvement wouldn't impress either of us, my duty and training kicked in. I was an *artist*, and these people had come to watch artwork. "Ready?"

My single-word question rippled through the air and an unnatural hush fell over the green as every set of eyes focused on me. Even the birds stopped chirping as if they too held their breaths. The energy of the crowd's focus raised the hairs along my arms as I approached my easel.

Since there was no point trying to drag out the simple improvement, I didn't bother to close my eyes or salute the sun or any of the other nonsense I'd incorporated into my demonstrations. Instead, I focused on transforming the gazebo into the best version of the simple shelter Ben had suggested. My fingers tingled as I used the gazebo's front left support as my anchor point and enlarged the building, extending it to a rectangular shape roughly twelve meters wide and twenty meters long.

The wood shifted and splintered as I worked, each *crack* drawing excited cries from the people on the green. Once the basic structure was done, I used the copper sheeting from the gazebo's edges to roll out sheets of copper roofing. I raised seams in the roof from the ridge cap to the edges. To offset the garish shade of the fresh copper, I sketched an aged patina over it.

The stone at the base of the gazebo's steps provided a starting point, and I covered the ground beneath the shelter with interlocking limestone pavers. Finished, I stared at the unassuming building, unimpressed and underwhelmed. The crowd cheered and clapped, but I paid them no attention.

Akiko sidled up next to me and poked my side with her elbow. "Know what it needs?"

I waggled my eyebrows at her. "An egg?"

"A weathervane?" Ben asked at the same time.

Akiko's eyes widened. "Yes! It's even better than my idea."

Ben beamed. "In what shape?"

"Duh." Akiko rolled her eyes and stared at me, as though confident I would read her thoughts.

The building's roof was long and plain: no cockerel or swimming fish would do.

"Duh," I repeated. Setting my pencil on the page, I drew a two-dimensional version of the Kaskaskia dragon, complete with his absurd wings and tiny front arms. That did it. The crowd's applause kicked up several notches, the thunderous noise waking several babes. The little ones wailed as I added one last detail, changing the dragon's arms, so he held an egg.

Akiko rewarded me for this last detail with a huge smile, sending my heart soaring. But it swelled to bursting when she pointed to where Earl clapped and cheered along with the others in the crowd.

# CHAPTER EIGHT

Although the evening air hung damp and heavy around Vandalia, we refused to let the oppressive heat conquer our spirits. We made our way to the new shelter on the green, following the excited crowd. Akiko skipped between Ben and me, hanging from our hands to jump over Charcoal every chance she got.

The community's excitement was infectious, and although I outwardly sported the same bemused expression as Ben, the child within me yearned to leap and caper like Akiko. Even after the day's trials and everything we'd learned about the revivalists' minstrel shows, I was still high on the exhilaration and praise my artwork had yielded. Now, I was wild to lose myself in the pleasure of an evening of stories and songs. Plus, tomorrow we'd start the next grueling phase of our journey.

We *deserved* one night of fun.

Earl, Josephine, and Genevie paused at the edge of the shelter, waiting for seats.

Ben slowed too and dropped Akiko's hand to rub his stomach. "Dinner was marvelous."

"So good," said Akiko, rubbing her own stomach. "I could eat it every day."

The keeper had called the meat pie he set before us a 'meatza'. It had a thick, chewy crust and chunks of spiced lamb sausage and onion tumbled in a savory tomato-garlic sauce, redolent with basil and oregano. The keeper had topped the pie with handfuls of shredded cheese. They melted into long, glistening strings like strands of spider silk as he served us wedges of the meaty pie.

Grinning, I rubbed my stomach, too. "Tony might be my favorite keeper, ever."

Ben locked eyes with me over Akiko's head. "Wasn't Earl a keeper when you met her?"

Akiko snickered. "I'm telling!"

"Sure, fine." I picked her up and slung her over my shoulder. "It's not like you and I need to remain friends." I strode down the aisle and deposited the giggling girl into Genevie's lap. "Here. She's *your* problem tonight."

Akiko's cackles made me chuckle as I sat on the bench behind my friends. Ben slid in next to me but bent forward to tap Josephine on the shoulder. After he murmured something to her, she leaned over to speak with Earl. Earl flashed a smile at Ben and traded places with him. My heart fluttered like a wild bird as I scooted over to make more room for her. She slid onto the bench next to me, flashing her lopsided grin.

Akiko popped up over Genevie's shoulder. "Hey Earl, guess what Matthew—"

When I dragged my finger across my throat, Akiko giggled and slithered back into Genevie's lap.

"Keeping secrets, Artist?" Earl arched her brow.

My mouth went dry as I scrambled for a pithy response... and found nothing. "No."

Ben's back shook with laughter, but I curbed the urge to

shove him when Sally stopped at our bench. "Room for one more?"

Earl nodded and slid closer to me, our thighs brushing. Ripples of delight snaked through me, and my leg jerked in response to the contact.

Sally leaned forward across Earl. "Beautiful work, Matthew. The administrator was beyond impressed and asked me to convey her gratitude."

The administrator wasn't the woman I'd hoped to impress. I gave Sally a small smile.

Earl tilted her head back to gaze up. "It's so pretty, hung with these lanterns." Earl gestured at the rafters. "You created a marvel."

Heat bloomed in my chest. This time, my smile was genuine. The end of her long braid brushed my arm, sending shivers racing through me. My groin tightened as she shifted closer, smelling of sun and wild bergamot. I longed to wrap my arms around her. Instead, I took a deep breath, inhaling her scent. "What did you do today?"

The crowd hushed as a man stood and faced us.

Earl leaned closer, her breath warm and soft in my ear. "Gathered herbs on the prairie with Ben."

Her proximity left me senseless. I swallowed, but Earl didn't notice; her focus locked on the man standing before us.

"Welcome, friends. My name is Jessie Copeland, and it's my pleasure to entertain you tonight. I'll start with a song." Nodding at Administrator Barnes, Copeland closed his eyes and brought a long, cylindrical instrument to his mouth.

"What is that?" Earl whispered.

Her hair tickled my nose as I whispered, "Oboe."

She brushed her fingers along mine, sending a jolt through my body so strong my heart lurched in a strange double beat.

Copeland blew a long wavering note but stopped when the crowd clapped.

I didn't care—*couldn't care*—about his performance anymore. My attention was on Earl, my eyes glued to the tiny patch of skin where her finger brushed mine. Each minute movement of her finger, pale and smooth compared with mine, sent chills through me. Was it on purpose? Was she aware of the effect she had on me?

A hush spread over the audience, the anticipatory energy reminding me of my earlier artwork. To distract myself from Earl, I glanced forward, curious to see how Copeland handled himself. His eyes gleamed. When the crowd's attention ripened into stillness, he brought the instrument to his lips again. Three notes in, the hairs on the back of my neck stood.

*The Lady of Shalott.*

My gaze bore into the minstrel, my attention fracturing between the present and the memories cascading across my mind's canvas.

The last time I'd heard a minstrel perform had been in Mama's inn on Hanlan's Island when Talbot had sung the poem to me and Olen. Even after Copeland finished the song and moved on to tell an unrelated story, my scalp prickled as if each hair vibrated with memory. Although I was vaguely aware of the crowd laughing and sighing at Copeland's performance, I couldn't focus, couldn't push Talbot's face from my mind's canvas. Talbot was also a minstrel, and minstrels were rare. So, was the song a coincidence... or a message?

Earl's hand on my arm brought me back to the present, and I flinched. My friends stood around me with quizzical expressions as the crowd filtered from the shelter.

*I missed the entire show.*

"Sorry, I—" I stopped, my gaze sharpening on the minstrel packing his things. "I'll be right back."

Copeland had stepped from the shelter when I caught up with him. He turned, a pleasant look on his face when I cleared my throat, but my mind went blank.

*Should I ask?*

If I didn't and the song had been a message from Talbot, I would miss it. But if I said the wrong thing, it could expose me... if this man was part of Carter's operation.

After a beat, the minstrel nodded. "Thanks for coming. I hope you enjoyed yourself."

A roaring filled my ears.

*Now or never, Artist.*

Before he could turn away, I blurted, "I've heard one of your songs before."

Copeland nodded, his smile benign. "We minstrels swap stories on occasion."

"No, I mean..." I swallowed and took a deep breath. I had to get this right. "Pardon me. I recognized the tune from the *Lady of Shalott.*" As I spoke, I traced an arc in the dirt with my toe. My pulse jumped and my mouth went dry, but Copeland's expression didn't change. "I enjoyed it."

"It's an old poem," he said. Although his tone conveyed polite disinterest, he squared his shoulders, and his chin came up.

Was I right? Had Talbot sent a message through Copeland?

"Tennyson, if I remember correctly." I traced the same arc with my toe. "From *Before?*"

Copeland stepped closer. "I believe you're correct." My heart pounded while he appraised me. "I believe Lord Alfred Isaiah Tennyson wrote it in a week, circa 1412." As he spoke, he completed the ichthys with his right foot.

*I was right.*

My vision narrowed, and I struggled to catch my breath.

But instead of delivering Talbot's message, he said, "Good evening, Artist."

My mind went blank as he ambled into the night and disappeared into the dark. Long after he'd vanished from sight, I stared, hoping he'd return, my thoughts a roaring jumble.

But Copeland didn't reappear. Eventually, the prickling on the back of my neck reminded me I was under observation. Feigning nonchalance, I turned, scuffing the marks in the dirt as I faced my friends. They waited for me under the shelter, and when I opened my mouth, Josephine shook her head, her gesture reminding me we were not alone; volunteers from Vandalia bustled around us, blowing out lanterns and stacking benches.

"Call it a night?" asked Genevie, her voice uncharacteristically flat.

Akiko sprawled across a bench, asleep. I hoisted her onto my hip, and she snuggled against me, draping her thin arms around my neck. I brushed her hair away from my cheek. "Sure. See you tomorrow." It would be better to tell them about the minstrel and my suspicions after we were out of earshot of the strangers.

My friends paired off, heading toward their beds. From the gathering shadows, I watched them go. The minstrel had told me nothing, but what if he *had* a message to deliver, but I'd flubbed the exchange? Without Akiko's sleepy weight, hot and solid, grounding me against the waves of anxiety and doubt crashing over me, I may have run bellowing into the dark.

# CHAPTER NINE

I'd planned to tell the others about the minstrel's message first thing, but the steady stream of people leaving Vandalia left us little privacy as we rode westward. While I waited, I turned the minstrel's words over and over, trying to make sense of them. If it was a message, I couldn't figure it out. I stared dully at the horizon until I caught my name on the wind. My head snapped up. We were finally alone. "Last night—"

Akiko's song turned into a shriek of glee as a small rodent popped up from the ground and stood on its hind legs. Several more rose from holes and whistled in alarm as we passed. Charcoal and the coyote pounced, but the lightning-quick rodents appeared and disappeared faster than either canine could react, sending us into gales of laughter.

I caught my breath long enough to mimic the rodents' whistle. Several popped up to pipe alarms, then disappeared again. "What are they? A community of weasels?"

"A coterie of prairie dogs," said Josephine.

Genevie leaned forward to squint past Ben and me. "What?"

Josephine flapped her hand at the rodents. "A family of prairie dogs is called a coterie."

"Dogs?" asked Akiko as she loped Lady in a circle around us. In response, Ben's mule Zeus pinned his long ears and shook his head, glaring at the mare.

"They're a type of ground squirrel," Josephine called. "Please slow Lady. It's dangerous to run a horse over ground littered with so many holes."

Akiko's mare stopped abruptly, her tail swishing with displeasure. "Sorry!" Akiko called over her shoulder. She pointed at yet another coterie of whistling rodents. "Maybe we'll see a coterie of rabbits if we keep our eyes peeled!"

"Warren," muttered Josephine.

I turned my face toward Ben to hide my smile. Ben grinned and held up three fingers, silently counting down.

Before he reached one, Josephine muttered, "Sorry," and urged Fox into a quickened, single-foot cadence to catch up with the girl. "Akiko, a family group of rabbits is called a warren!"

Genevie chuckled and slowed, moving Bertha toward us. As they pulled alongside, the mare pinned her ears at Oxide, giving him a nasty glare. He snorted and moved toward Ben's mule. I corrected my horse but sympathized with his reaction.

*Girls are trouble.*

The five of us rode abreast through the muggy heat without speaking. The wind sighed through the grasses, setting it sway-ing. Monarch butterflies glided and soared around us, erupting from patches of milkweed as we rode past them.

Genevie sighed. "On the off chance you haven't noticed, we're all waiting to hear what happened last night."

"Patiently," added Earl.

"Right." I waved a gnat away from my face. "There's not much to tell."

"What did he say?" asked Sally, leaning forward to peer around Ben.

"Nothing but nonsense," Ben answered.

Genevie snorted. "Obviously."

"What?" asked Sally, her tone querulous.

Ben sighed, but slowed and moved to Sally's right.

She glared first at me and then at him. "Are you implying I'm too old to hear Matthew properly?"

"My ears are larger than yours, Sally," said Ben, with a straight face.

"Barnacle butt nugget," she said, before turning toward me. "Well?"

"Last night, the minstrel started his show with the *Lady of Shalott*." I twisted to check on Magnesium and Donkey. "Talbot sang the same song before you all arrived in Toronto Depot."

"Talbot," Genevie said, clucking her tongue while shaking her head. "Talbot plays the oboe?"

"No, the guitar." My breath caught at the memory of Talbot's beautiful tenor. Would I ever hear it again? "The lyrics are from a poem written *Before*, by a chap called Tennyson."

Ben shrugged when no one responded. "Maybe Josephine knows something about him."

Genevie pulled her flask out. "What did the minstrel say when you spoke?"

"Nothing. Not really. The song was a coincidence." Akiko rode her mare in a graceful circle around Josephine and Fox. By the end of this trip, she'd be as good a horsewoman as Josephine. "Or maybe I did or said something to prevent him from delivering the message."

Sally squinted from under her wide-brimmed hat. "Then why are you so broody today?"

I froze, my mouth going dry. Earl was as still as a sculpture on Bruno. He stalked forward on stiff legs, his head elevated, ears pointed, and nostrils flared. They stared ahead at Akiko, who was on the ground creeping toward a monster.

The giant beast leaped away from her and thundered toward the southwestern horizon, leaving a cloud of dust in its wake. Fox plunged and bucked beneath Josephine. She struggled to settle the panicking horse and dropped Lady's rein. The mare bolted east.

"Charcoal, get Lady," I shouted, kicking Oxide. I galloped across the grasslands toward Akiko, with Josephine's warnings about prairie dog holes blaring across my mind's canvas. Somehow, my luck held, and we reached Akiko without a mishap. I slowed Oxide to a stop, but Magnesium ran past us, wrapping his lead around my waist. By the time I'd untangled myself, Ben had grabbed Fox's reins. Josephine's legs shook as she dismounted.

"Did you see it?" Akiko asked, when I reached her.

I gripped her shoulders and scanned her. "Are you okay? Are you hurt?"

Akiko beamed. "Did you see how close I got?"

"It was a buffalo," said Earl, her voice soft. She stared west. "Was it as big as it looked?"

"It was massive," said Josephine, "like a shaggy cow with horns."

As my fear receded, resentment bubbled in my gut. Why hadn't I insisted Akiko stay close? At muffled hoofbeats, I turned and waded through the horses to catch Lady. "Good boy, Charcoal."

One of Akiko's reins had broken, but otherwise, the mare looked fine. "Gen, can you check Lady? I'll look for a set of spare reins."

I dug through Magnesium's panniers but found nothing useful. "We need to pony Lady for now. I'll repair the leather when we stop for lunch."

Akiko waved but continued to chatter with the others about the buffalo.

Ben, Genevie, and I already had pack animals, leaving Earl, Sally, and Josephine with a free hand. Fox was flighty, but Josephine was the strongest rider in our party, so I gritted my teeth. "Are you up for ponying a horse? Either Lady or Magnesium."

"Yes." Josephine took a deep breath and patted Ben's chest, stepping back from him. She must have caught my expression because the smile slipped from her face. "I'm sorry—Akiko needed a comfort break, and the buffalo must have been lying in the grass. We didn't see it until Akiko flushed him out, and Fox" —she stopped to pat the chestnut gelding— "well, you saw."

I couldn't manage more than a curt nod. We would all have to be more cautious in the future. None of us knew what dangers lurked unseen in the grass sea.

Once everyone was back on their horses, we followed the buffalo's tracks. It had trampled a wide swath of grass when it fled, but on either side of the trail, the grass was tall enough to hide another napping beast. For once, I was glad Charcoal and the coyote ranged through the surrounding brush. I didn't trust our horsemanship—or the horses' nerves—if we flushed another gigantic animal.

The humidity continued to rise, and by midday, everyone was lethargic, our collective torpor broken only by someone occasionally snapping at someone else. My head pounded. With our tempers short, I kept my thoughts to myself.

Ben shaded his eyes to scan the horizon and straightened. Something about his posture intrigued me. I squeezed Oxide to brighten his step until we were abreast with Ben. "What did you see?"

"Trees. I thought we could take a break in the shade."

"Finally," groaned Akiko, from behind Josephine. "This was the most boring ride *ever*."

Josephine stiffened, and her lips compressed, but she said nothing. However, the look on her face told me she was still blaming herself for what might have happened.

*Might have... but didn't.*

It wasn't Josephine's fault; Akiko's encounter with the buffalo could have happened with any of us nearby. I caught Josephine's eye and mouthed, "Thank you." Her shoulders relaxed and a hint of a smile crossed her face as she rolled her eyes in Akiko's direction. To show her I understood, I shrugged with exaggerated helplessness. We smiled, the bands of pressure around my chest falling away.

The stand of trees Ben had noticed stood at the crest of a bluff, and the valley's floor opened up as we rode toward the edge.

Earl made a choked noise. "*Look.*"

Buffaloes scattered the length and breadth of the valley floor.

"Blistering toad warts, there must be hundreds of them," said Sally.

"They look peaceful from here," said Ben. He tied Zeus to a low branch and sighed, patting the mule. "I don't know how we'll get past them, but that's Josephine's problem."

She snorted and helped Akiko down. "We could let this monkey try to pet them again."

"*No*," I said, when Akiko turned her hopeful face toward me. "If we're sacrificing anyone, send Genevie."

"Gallant." Earl snickered as she loosened the cinch on Bruno's saddle. "Don't forget to ask Josephine about the poem."

Josephine looked at me. "Poem?"

I cringed. A part of me had hoped everyone else had forgotten about it, since I hadn't planned to bring it up again. Now, she'd get focused and intense, like a terrier hunting a rat. But since I had messed up the exchange with the minstrel, I had nothing to tell her.

Ben squeezed her shoulder. "I'm starting lunch."

Josephine patted his hand but kept her focus on me. "What poem?"

"From last night," I said, pulling out my art supplies. "I thought the minstrel might have had a message from Talbot for me, but he didn't."

Josephine pursed her lips hard enough to discolor the scars on her cheek. "Let me be the judge."

I sighed, frowning at Akiko's damaged bridle. Josephine wouldn't let this go. "I mentioned I'd heard the *Lady of Shalott* before, and he agreed it was a poem written *Before*."

"How dull," said Genevie. She lifted her hair and fanned her neck. "I miss the woods. It's too hot out here."

"What did the minstrel say *exactly*?" Josephine asked.

I shrugged. "I said the poem was by Tennyson, and he agreed."

"How? He said 'yes'?"

My fingers tingled as I repaired Akiko's bridle. "He said Lord Alfred Isaiah Tennyson, circa 1412, wrote the poem in a week. He also said goodnight and called me artist."

Josephine frowned, tugging on her lip. "1412?"

I nodded, shaking out my hands. "Mouse, put this back on Lady."

"What is it, Josephine?" asked Sally.

"I think we need to stop at the nearest depot." Josephine tilted her head. "It's possible you received a message after all."

Outwardly I stilled, but inside, my stomach flopped like a

fish out of water. Had I received a message, after all? "Are you sure?"

"I don't know what Talbot is trying to convey," Josephine said, "but if memory serves, Tennyson wrote the poem in the 1800s."

# CHAPTER TEN

A cloud of dust erupted as Genevie closed her book with a snap. "There's nothing here, Josephine."

We'd dug through the records in Louis Depot for two days, but all we'd found was mildew and mold. If we wanted to decode Talbot's message, we needed better information. Even one book about Tennyson could tell us if Josephine was right and the minstrel had delivered a message.

"I agree." Josephine's shoulders drooped. "How important to you is this?"

I studied the towering stacks of mildewing books. "If it is a message from Talbot, I need to figure it out."

"A big if." Ben sighed as Sally erupted into her third sneezing fit. "What are our options?"

Josephine tapped her fingers along her jaw. "We could continue to search the records here..."

"Or?" prompted Genevie.

"Or travel to Kansas Depot and search their records." Josephine winced as we groaned in unison. "The librarian told me the records in Kansas Depot are properly cataloged and in better shape."

This depot stop had been an utter waste of time. The records in Louis Depot were a mess, and they had no art supplies in the warehouse. To top it off, they'd asked for Josephine's help in cataloging supplies and Earl's butchery in exchange for hospitality, giving me no opportunity to showcase my art *or* spend time with Earl.

"We should do everyone a favor and remove Louis Depot from every map." My eyes itched, but I fought the urge to rub them. Genevie hadn't, and hers were red and swollen. "How much time will Kansas Depot add to our trip, Mouse?"

Akiko beamed as she spread a map on her table. She traced her fingers along routes, humming under her breath. "None. We're nearly there already, and we can go straight to Vegas Depot from there."

Ben rubbed his jaw, the stubble rasping beneath his fingertips as he studied the map over her shoulder. "The northern route crosses more mountain ranges, but otherwise, Akiko's right." He looked at Josephine. "Are you confident we'll find answers in Kansas Depot?"

Josephine shrugged. "We have a fair chance, assuming they saved a selection of literature."

"I move we escape this dungeon, collect Earl, and go get us some answers," said Genevie. "Can I get a second?"

I hesitated. What if I made the wrong choice? If we stayed here, we might still find answers, and we'd already completed our side of the bargain Sally had struck for hospitality. While Kansas Depot might have better records, we'd have to negotiate for hospitality again, causing a further delay.

Sally sneezed several times. "Earl should be finished by this afternoon," she said, dabbing at her nose with a handkerchief.

"Ben and I can use the time to gather supplies while we wait. It's up to you, Matthew."

Towering stacks of moldy books waited. We could spend days here and still come up empty. "Okay, let's try the next depot."

Ben grinned and snapped his book shut. "I hoped you'd agree. The supplies here haven't impressed me. Another depot will give me a chance to get us better outfitted."

Everyone else nodded, lifting my spirits. I'd made the right choice. If Talbot's message proved important, it might even provide information about my parents or Carter's movements.

Ben stood and rolled his shoulders. "What are you two going to do?"

Akiko and I looked at each other. I poked her side. "Find a patch of shade and look pretty?"

"Eggs-actly," she replied.

My pulse quickened. Akiko was right—I should use the opportunity to practice creating again. "Meet at the livery around two?"

A cloud of gray-green dust enveloped Josephine as she flipped open another book. "See you soon."

***

ONCE OUTSIDE, AKIKO GROANED. EVEN THOUGH I welcomed the fresh air, the heat and humidity overwhelmed me. Charcoal planted himself in a tiny patch of shade, panting.

"Why is it so hot?" Akiko drooped like a cut flower. "And where is everyone?"

"Inside?"

"Duh. This depot is boring. And empty."

I held my hand out. "Come on. My sketchbook is in my

saddlebags, so let's see if the hostler will let us lay in his water trough."

Even Akiko's giggle was subdued as we ambled toward the livery. If it was this hot all the way to Vegas Depot, the sun would scorch us crisp. Nothing but cinders by the time we arrived. But we couldn't wait for temperate weather. Assuming my parents were in the depot, each day of delay potentially put them in greater danger.

The cooler temperature inside the shady barn made Akiko sigh. "Can we work in here?"

"Good idea." As I surveyed the area, my gaze settled on a half-buried covered wagon. If we had a wagon, we'd have shelter whenever we needed it.

"Or half a good idea," I said as the hostler entered the livery. "Keeper, I'm interested in your wagon."

The hostler squinted at the wagon, then at me. "If I trade you my wagon, how will I finish moving my hay?"

Based on the dusty detritus stacked around the wagon, he hadn't used it in years, but I kept my expression neutral. "I could stack your hay at the back of the barn for you."

"I'm going to build new stalls along the back wall." The keeper smirked. "I planned to move the hay to the loft."

*With a wagon?*

I studied the wagon again. Was it worth the work? The shade would be welcome, and I could find another wagon, but it would take time. "I'll stack the hay in the loft and build stalls—"

"Done," he interrupted. "But if you're taking the wagon, you might as well clear out the rest of this junk and build the stalls along this wall, nearer the water."

"Right." I sighed.

It was too hot to paint, so I sketched the scene with my favorite charcoal pencil. When the hostler wasn't looking, I tried creating a new bale, but only pulled one from the stack, leaving a gap. Sweat poured down my back, but moving the bale was no harder than moving the egg had been. I studied the ladder. Could I move the hay into the loft with my art? The effort may be as strenuous as physically hauling each bale up the ladder, but would be quicker.

I climbed the ladder until I could see into the loft and set my sketchbook on the loft floor. Standing on the ladder, I drew the space, then descended.

Akiko met me at the base. "What are you doing?"

"An experiment." I sketched the first bale into the loft. The effort to move the hay with art left me panting. I drained my canteen and studied the stack. Could I move more than one at a time?

*Why not try?*

Four bales were as difficult as one, but no harder. I tried a block of eight bales and found the same. The effort was in moving the item, not the size, bulk, or weight of them. Cheered, I continued to move the hay in chunks, pausing occasionally to climb the ladder and reassess the remaining loft space.

Once I moved the hay, I cleared away the junk blocking the wagon, rolled the wagon outside, and improved the barn, creating an orderly set of box stalls along the wall, all with art.

Akiko didn't appear impressed as we climbed inside the covered wagon. "Why do we want a dusty old wagon, anyway?"

"I don't see a dusty old wagon."

She peered at me as if trying to understand a joke. "What do you see?"

I slapped the wooden wall with my palm and grinned at the hollow boom. "A mobile shade station. A classroom. Perhaps even enough privacy to practice art."

"Oh!" Akiko brightened. "I see it too!"

While we waited, I practiced creating a variety of small objects Akiko found in the barn, but again, all I did was transport existing items. The effort lessened with practice, but why it cost as much energy to move a bolt as a stack of lumber perplexed me.

Ben's face darkened when I shared my vision. "A wagon limits our route options."

"The route we've picked looks open," I said, glancing at Akiko for confirmation. "What could go wrong?"

His frown deepened. "What if the pavement is impassible or we crack a wheel?"

Josephine's face reddened. "A wagon would let us carry more supplies. What if we need to transport something heavy, like water?"

Ben shook his head, but Josephine marched across the barn to line up with us, standing shoulder to shoulder with me. Chin high, she crossed her arms as though taking a stand.

I turned toward Sally and Genevie. "How about you?"

"None of us know how to drive a wagon." Sally scowled and joined Ben. "I'm good at riding now, so you can't make this old lady learn to drive."

We turned toward Genevie. A smile flitted across her face as she evaluated us. "A wagon could be useful." Triumph flooded me until she stepped to Ben's side.

"What are you doing over there?" asked Akiko.

Genevie shrugged and gurgled from her flask. "If we have more cargo space, Ben will bring more stuff."

"Hey," Ben protested. "Whose side are you on?"

Her flask flashed a second time. "It's not about sides."

"We're four against three," said Akiko.

"Charcoal doesn't count," said Ben.

Akiko sighed. "Then how will we decide?"

"Let Earl choose," Genevie said. I narrowed my eyes, but

she ignored me and continued, "But let her pick without us arguing our sides."

"Why?" asked Akiko. "Matthew already did the work."

"We shouldn't make Earl choose between what she thinks and who she likes," Genevie answered, without taking her eyes off me.

*Who she likes.* Genevie's words sent a shiver of thrill through me.

"Why not?" Akiko asked again. "Josephine didn't choose Ben."

"Hey!" Ben protested again.

"Hey, what?" Earl sauntered into the livery, carrying two string-wrapped parcels. "What's going on?"

"We're trying to decide if we need a wagon like this one," said Akiko, giving each of us a meaningful look. "What do *you* think?"

A strange fluttering filled my chest as Earl tilted her head back to evaluate the wagon. Glancing at the hayloft and the newly built stalls, Earl set her parcels in the wagon. "It's a great idea."

Akiko cheered, Ben groaned, and I beamed at Earl.

Sally sighed. "Who will pull the wagon?"

"The mules," Josephine and I said together.

"Guess I better learn to drive." Ben eyed the parcels Earl had set down. "What did you bring?"

"Smoked mutton," said Earl. "I thought it would make a pleasant change. The dried chicken travels well, but I'm tired of it."

"Did they have sacks of dried beans in the market?" Ben asked.

"And so it begins," muttered Genevie. "We better hit the road before Ben's inner hoarder escapes."

# CHAPTER ELEVEN

The impressive warehouse in Kansas Depot gleamed in the late morning sun. Ben stopped the wagon in front of the main doors and craned his neck.

Genevie whistled. "You're sure this is it?"

Josephine nodded and shaded her eyes, tilting her head backward. "It's beautiful."

The building soared nearly thirty meters above the ground, its facade graced by three, enormous, arched windows stretching upward four stories from the ground. Two shorter buildings flanked the grand entrance. It *was* beautiful, but the meticulous gardens around the building raised my spirits more. The grass was uniformly green, and the hedges sported crisp edges. A community who kept ornamental gardens with this kind of care surely maintained precious records with as much consideration. My confidence soared. If the minstrel *had* delivered a message to decode, we would find our answers here.

"How long should we stay?" Sally asked me.

We needed time to work out Talbot's message, but there

was still a vast distance between us and Vegas Depot. "Is three days enough?"

When everyone nodded, Sally snapped into administrator mode. "Right, here's the plan. Josephine, tie Fox to the wagon and head in to begin your search. The rest of us will find livery."

Sally turned toward Ben. "You and Earl gather supplies while Genevie and I negotiate for rooms, supplies, and hospitality."

It was rare for Sally to assign Earl and me a task together since our duties rarely overlapped, but I couldn't help the crestfallen feeling each time she sent us in separate directions. Earl caught me staring at her and lifted a shoulder in a half-hearted shrug.

Was she disappointed, too?

Somehow, the possibility cheered me. Perhaps Ben would be quick, and Earl would join us in the library.

"What about us?" asked Akiko.

"I'd love your company," said Josephine. "There's bound to be maps inside, so maybe you can learn the terrain while I start a list of records to review."

Akiko brightened and leaned forward to dismount. "Okay, great."

"Stop!"

Akiko froze at my tone.

"After the shenanigans in Toronto Depot, I'm not letting you out of my sight." Akiko's lip poked out, but she sat back. "After you help me get the horses and Donkey settled, we'll find Josephine *together*."

"But I'm tired of the sun." When I didn't relent, Akiko sighed and picked up her reins. "Fine, let's go."

Unlike the isolated tower warehouse in Louis Depot, they laid the warehouse in Kansas Depot out like a small community, complete with lodging and livery. It took us less than an hour to get the horses settled, arrange for rooms, and rejoin Josephine.

"That was fast," she said when we joined her at a large wooden table.

Akiko clambered into a wooden chair and motioned me to push her in. Its feet squealed across the smooth concrete, the noise reverberating in the large chamber. Charcoal yipped until I pulled out a chair for him, too. He smiled as I pushed him in, then laid his chin on the table's top.

"Our rooms are in the warehouse," Akiko told Josephine as she unfolded the first map, "so we can stay inside for three days if we want to."

"Charcoal will need to go outside," I said, eyeing the stacks of books Josephine had amassed. "Are you researching or reading for pleasure?"

Josephine's face pinked. "Maybe both?" She pushed a smaller stack of books toward me. "Look, I was right."

I flipped the book open to the bookmarked page. "Lord Alfred Tennyson." I glanced at Josephine. "So?"

She tapped her pencil on a page of notes. "You told me the minstrel said Lord Alfred *Isaiah* Tennyson."

"Right." I stared at the picture of Tennyson, a stern-faced man with a massive beard and cold eyes. "Circa 1412. But this says he published the poem in 1833."

"Exactly," said Josephine, her eyes glowing.

"Eggs-actly," muttered Akiko, without looking up.

I flipped the page and scanned it. "The minstrel got his name wrong. It happens."

"His name... of course." Josephine's head snapped up. "Of *course*." She pushed her chair back hard enough to shake the table and topple her tower of books but didn't stop to look back when the books clattered onto the table and floor.

Akiko stared at me with her brow furrowed, but I had no explanation for her. "Diarrhea emergency?"

Akiko cackled and returned to her map, leaving me to pick up the books.

Josephine reappeared ten minutes later, flushed and breathless. "I found it. Look."

She lay an enormous book with gilt-edged pages onto the table and pointed.

I stood and leaned over the table. "What?"

"Isaiah 14:12."

I shrugged. "And?"

Josephine blinked, then shrugged. "This is the Bible."

*The Bible.*

The hairs on the back of my neck rose, but Josephine didn't notice my unease. "Isaiah is one book, and 14:12 refers to the chapter and verse."

Akiko didn't look up as she traced a route on the map with her finger. "What's it say?"

Josephine cleared her throat. "How you have fallen from Heaven, morning star, son of the dawn! You have been cast down to the earth, you who once laid low the nations!"

When she finished, I waited, but she said nothing else. I clasped my hands to keep from fidgeting. "Terrific. What does it mean?"

Josephine's excitement faded. "Good question."

"Maybe Talbot is stuck in a hole," said Akiko.

The cartoon image of Talbot with his foot caught in a prairie dog's burrow crossed my mind's canvas and struck me as absurdly funny. Akiko looked up when I chuckled, then eyed the other books Josephine had brought. "What are those?"

"Bibles."

Charcoal leaned against me. "There's more than one Bible?" I asked, scratching his head.

"Sort of." Josephine's eyes shone. "There's one Bible, but many translations. I thought a different version could give us more. Here's the passage from the King James translation. 'How art thou fallen from Heaven, O Lucifer, son of the morning! How art thou cut down to the ground, which didst weaken the nations!'"

"Still in a hole," said Akiko. "But they marked no holes on the map."

I stretched, staring out the window. "I've never heard of the Lucifer star."

"Star..." Josephine's brow furrowed, then cleared. "Oh, Morning Star. It was another name for Lucifer."

"Who?"

"Um, another name for Christianity's devil."

I shook my head. "He's the devil, a star, and a man?"

"Yes, and also an angel." Josephine squirmed at my bark of incredulous laughter. "You're right; it's a confusing story."

"I like stories," said Akiko. She propped her head on her hand and waited.

Josephine flicked her pencil, scribing in the air. "Okay, from my memory, Satan was an archangel—"

I tapped my fist against the table. "Who is Satan?"

"Same guy," said Josephine. "He has a bunch more names and titles, so keep up."

Akiko snickered. "Yeah, keep up."

Josephine smiled and continued, "Even though he was already the highest-status angel, Lucifer—*same guy*—had an argument with God. In response, God pushed him out of Heaven, and he fell to earth."

The story made no sense. "What did they argue about?"

"Probably about who should be in charge." Josephine snorted and rolled her eyes, making Akiko giggle. "Anyway, the passage refers to the point in the mythology when God cast the angel out of Heaven. He fell to the earth, was demonized, and became the devil."

Akiko gasped. "Look!"

Charcoal jumped onto the table to investigate.

I pointed at the floor. "Off!"

After he jumped down, I circled behind Akiko and craned my neck. "What?"

"Angel Falls." Akiko jabbed at the map. "And it's near an abbey!"

"Is she right?" Chills slid down my spine. "Could Talbot have meant Angel Falls?"

"Maybe, but when?" Josephine snapped her fingers. "A week. The minstrel said Tennyson wrote the poem in a week."

"It's been five days since I received the message." I studied the map. The falls were near a small community called Lansing. "So, in two days?"

"What if the message isn't from Talbot?" Josephine sat back, her expression troubled. Her eyes hardened. "And even if it is, should we trust him? It could be from Talbot and *still* be a trap."

Josephine's suspicions were understandable—her sole encounter with him had been after the battle in Wakefield, when Whistler had died. She only knew Talbot as the man who had tried to prevent me from traveling.

But I'd gotten to know my cousin during my time in Toronto Depot. I trusted him, and Talbot knew I'd recognize the tune of the *Lady of Shalott*. The message *had* to be from him. It was possible we'd guessed the wrong location, but even if Talbot didn't show up, I wanted to visit the abbey, anyway. And if Josephine was right, and it was a trap... well, I'd worry about that later.

"The message is from Talbot. I'm certain." I studied the map. "Plus, two days gives me a chance to visit the abbey first."

Akiko straightened, but I shook my head. After what had happened in Toronto Depot, I didn't want her anywhere near an abbey until I'd evaluated their allegiance. I rolled my neck and groaned as several vertebrates popped. "I'm too young to be this old. Let's find Earl and the others."

Akiko smirked and folded the map. "I'm too old to be this young, so I'm ready to 'splore, too."

"*Explore*," corrected Josephine as she opened another book. "Since I'm exactly the right age, I'm going to stay and poke around."

# CHAPTER TWELVE

Akiko chattered as I watched shadows shorten through sparkling windows. If I focused beyond the gardens, the air shimmered in the day's heat, but the temperature in the dining hall was pleasantly cool. My stomach growled again, rumbling through the empty room.

Akiko stopped her story to snicker and pat my belly. "You should have eaten breakfast."

"They'll serve lunch soon. I hope." Impatient to leave for Leavenworth Abbey, I'd skipped breakfast to complete the improvements requested by the librarians. My plan was to leave as soon as I'd eaten, even though the day's heat would be at its worst.

A door opened, making us turn. Earl stalked into the dining hall, the air around her crackling. She paused near the threshold, scanned the large room, squared her shoulders, and strode toward us.

"Did you see the red flash?" whispered Akiko.

"She's angry. Did we do something?"

When Earl dropped onto the bench, Akiko squirmed. "If we did it, blame Matthew."

Earl's smile was strained. "It's that obvious?"

"What happened?" I asked, pouring a glass of water for her.

She took the glass and rolled it along its edge. "The man I bargained with cheated me."

"What?" My pulse started thudding in my temple. "What happened?"

Her glass hit the table with a *clunk,* spilling water. "I agreed to show him how to make bresaola in exchange for enough meat to make some for us, too. But after I finished the lesson, he claimed I offered to teach my technique if he supplied the meat."

"But that's not fair!" Akiko turned toward me, her face expectant.

"Sometimes life isn't fair, Mouse." If I offered, would Earl ask me to track the man down with her? Although angry on her behalf, I forced myself to take a deep breath, relax my fists, and keep my voice mild. "What can I do?"

"I'm too mad to think straight." The hair that escaped her braids fluttered as she blew out her breath. "And I'd slap his stupid face if he was within arm's reach, anyway."

"Tell me what he looks like," I said, flipping open my sketchbook. I roughed in a face, changing the features as Earl described him. When I finished, a man with heavy jowls, a snub nose, and a crescent-shaped scar above his left eyebrow stared belligerently from the page.

"It's perfect." Earl's mouth tightened. "What are you going to do with it?"

"This won't do much to fix things for you," I said as I drew block letters on the page, "but perhaps he'll think twice about trying to cheat anyone else." I turned the page toward them.

"This man cheats," read Akiko. "Do not trust him to fulfill his bargains."

"The librarians can have a scholar make copies and distribute them around the depot." I tore the page from the sketchbook. "You may have a case with the administrators if you want to pursue restitution."

"We're not staying long enough to bother, so no." She toyed with her water glass again. "But all bets are off if I run into him again."

"Why don't you come with me?" I asked, surprising myself. "I'm taking a side trip to visit Leavenworth Abbey."

"Is it far?"

"Roughly fifty kilometers, assuming the map was accurate. Maybe six hours if I push Oxide?"

I expected the distance to be a deterrence, but Earl's brow smoothed. "Yes, I'd like that. Ever since we visited Niagara, I've been curious about the abbey system." She drummed her fingers on the table. "When are we leaving?"

"Leaving?" asked Genevie. She dropped onto the bench near Akiko. "Where are we going?"

"*They're* going to Leavenworth Abbey," Akiko said, her voice glum. "*We're* staying here."

A surprised expression crossed Earl's face, and her eyes flicked toward me.

*She thought we'd go as a group.*

Before Earl could back out, I wrapped my arm around Akiko. "There's an abbey northwest of the depot. I've finished my work here, so while you're all busy, Earl and I are visiting it. I want to see if they know anything about Carter's artists. We'll be back before it's time to leave the depot."

Akiko stiffened when I didn't mention Angel Falls, but thankfully remained silent.

"After the day I've had, I needed something to stop my

mind from spiraling." Earl straightened and grinned. "Thanks. I'm looking forward to it."

*Time alone with Earl.*

My stomach leaped and twisted, but I quelled my excitement. I could use this opportunity to deepen our friendship. Perhaps I'd even prove to Earl that men and women could be friends.

Akiko jabbered on about workable routes to Vegas Depot, while Genevie shot me pointed looks, but I ignored her. Genevie could think whatever she wanted. My focus needed to remain on Akiko—and maybe Talbot, too. Besides, my decision to keep our relationship platonic had released me from the pressure I'd put on myself to impress Earl, leaving me free to enjoy her company. It was better for everyone if Earl and I remained friends, anyway. This trip would give us a real chance to connect without pointed glances and prying questions. By the time we returned, maybe even Genevie would understand. "Gen, while I'm gone, do you mind if Akiko bunks with you?"

Genevie smiled and pointed at Akiko. "Sleepover!"

Akiko's eyes gleamed as she clapped. "Do you have another dragon story?"

"Bet we can find one while we're here. We'll ask Josephine when she comes to lunch."

"Goody!" Akiko turned to me. "Leave now."

I chuckled, but Earl stood, taking Akiko's directive seriously.

"Why not?" she asked, her voice soft. "I'm too wound up to eat, and it won't take long to get our horses ready."

My stomach protested, but I ignored the hunger pang. If we didn't go now, Earl could change her mind. I'd choose time alone with her over a full belly any day. Besides, if Akiko was to be believed, I could afford to skip another meal. "Sure. Gen, can you ask a librarian to have this distributed?"

Genevie studied the portrait. "I hope he deserves this. No one will bargain with him after this."

I shrugged. "Integrity is important."

"It's the most important quality one can have," said Earl, her eyes flashing. "Without integrity, there cannot be trust, and without trust, you have nothing."

"Here, here," said Genevie, banging her fist on the table. She smiled broadly at Earl. "When you return, I'd like to get to know you better."

Although Genevie's tone was friendly, her statement sounded like a challenge. I caught my breath, hoping Earl wouldn't use it as an excuse to shut down.

To my delight, Earl raised her chin. "I look forward to it."

THE ROUTE OUT OF THE DEPOT WAS TOO NARROW TO RIDE abreast, but when we broke onto the open prairie, I held Oxide back until he and Bruno were shoulder to shoulder. But even after we were side by side, Earl didn't speak.

I stared at the horizon, scanning the rolling land and hills, and suppressed a shiver. "Long ride ahead of us." I glanced sideways at Earl. She pressed her lips into a straight line, her gaze fixed on some distant point.

*So much for deepening our friendship.*

Charcoal ranged around us as we flowed down the old pavement, and the ever-present coyote trailed thirty meters behind us.

Perhaps I had to start the conversation. After glancing at Earl, I took a deep breath. "Please don't repeat this, but it's good to get away from everyone."

Earl raised her eyebrow. "You don't have to put on an act for my benefit."

"I love them, but sometimes I miss the days when I traveled alone." A sheepish grin slid onto my face. "There's a relief to being alone. No worries about hurting someone's feelings, no anxiety about letting anyone down."

My spirits lifted when Earl chuckled and nodded. "You're speaking my truth, Artist."

We rode past a building that stretched forever, its intact concrete block wall like a cliff. "Why do you suppose they needed such large buildings?"

She shook her head. "The people from *Before* confound me, and the more I travel, the more confused I get. Perhaps it's a better question for Josephine."

I wouldn't let her wiggle out of our conversation so easily. "You know, Josephine didn't like me much when we met." I watched a hawk circle above us in the heat-rippled air. "Come to think of it, Ben didn't either."

Earl looked interested. "You're close now."

"We've been through a lot together. You should know Genevie is exactly who she presents. There's no artifice to her. When she says she wants to know you better, she means it."

Earl bit her lip. "Growing up, I didn't have many female friends. Or male friends, for that matter."

"Sounds lonely," I said. "Although, I suppose my childhood wasn't much different."

"What was it like?"

My heart warmed at her question. If she was interested enough to ask about me, maybe this trip *would* be good for our friendship. Memories scrolled across my mind's canvas.

"By design, there's a distance between the boys and masters in an abbey. There were fifteen of us in my class, and we were an average size. While we got along, there was a thread of competition woven through everything we did, so I spent a lot of time by myself." I glanced down at my dog. "In a lot of ways, Charcoal was my best friend."

He glanced up briefly at the mention of his name, then focused on the horizon again. Next to him, the coyote ignored us.

"The people in Star Creek were kind, but because I was a fosterling, I changed households constantly and they shuttled me back and forth as families expanded or contracted. After my apprenticeship, I carved out a place for myself, and I'd already established a home for myself by the time Bowman moved to the community."

"Can I ask you something?"

"Tell you what." She studied me. "While we're out here, why don't we agree to say exactly what we mean?"

I grinned at her. "You want the unvarnished truth."

"Do I?"

"The last step when creating a painting is applying a varnish. It evens the brushwork, brightens colors, and puts a protective sheen over everything. Even mediocre paintings look better when varnished, so to take the measure of an artist's skill, you appraise their unvarnished works."

"Perfect. Ask me anything, but in exchange, I get to ask you a question too."

Despite the day's heat, a shiver tracked down my spine. What if she asked something I didn't want to answer? If I declined, would she shut down? I didn't want to lose this chance, but I wasn't ready for a tough conversation.

*Especially about Bowman.*

Earl raised her eyebrow at my hesitation, so I nodded and chose an easy topic. "How did you end up with the name of Earl?"

She sighed. "Can I take back what I said? Let's go back to being awkwardly polite."

I laughed. "Not a chance."

"Prepare yourself for a sad tale, and don't you dare show pity."

*Pity?* In a voice too eager, I said, "Promise."

Earl swallowed, then sighed. "No one named me."

"What?"

"Fosterling, remember?" She pressed her lips together. "They called me 'Girl', which led to 'Irl,' which led to Earl."

My dismay must have shown because she narrowed her eyes. "There's your pity face and your first broken promise. To make up for it, you owe me a pitiable secret about *you*."

Again, my face must have betrayed me because Earl laughed. "The memory you're trying to forget is my payment, Artist."

"Fair is fair, Butcher." Heat crawled up my neck as I cleared my throat. "This is something I've shared with no one, so if I hear a whisper from *anyone*, I'll know the source of my betrayal."

Earl nodded. "Proceed."

After glancing around to make sure no one was around, I curled my toes in my boots and leaned toward Earl to mutter, "Genevie gave me my first and only kiss."

# CHAPTER THIRTEEN

After traveling tens of kilometers across an empty prairie occupied by little more than an occasional iron lamppost, arriving at the massive abbey was jarring. The building stood alone, towering over the sea of grass and prairie flowers. It appeared vaguely crescent-shaped, with the front edifice set in the middle of the concave curve. The abbey was three stories high, but they fashioned the bottom story from white marble blocks, which created a handsome foundation and an eye-catching contrast between the vibrant greens of the rolling prairie and the red brick supporting the upper two stories.

The grand front entrance featured a peaked gable supported by four massive ionic columns. The primary entrance was glass—something I'd never seen at an abbey—and framed by a curved lintel made from the same white marble blocks. It was an expansive building meant to inspire and intimidate, both of which landed.

"I assumed the abbey would be near a cooperative community of some sort." Earl brought Bruno to a halt and bit her lip. "Are you sure they'll welcome my visit?"

Based on her looks alone, I knew the masters would welcome us, so I smiled to reassure her. "Yes. But if you're not comfortable, we'll go. We have several hours of daylight left. If needs must, we can return to the last filling station we passed."

Earl squared her shoulders and nodded.

The glass doors opened before we arrived, and four masters in black robes waited for us on the circular brick paving.

I halted Oxide before we reached the paving and dismounted, leading him on foot.

The men waited with pleasant expressions.

"Good evening, brothers. *Ego autem* Popham."

One man stepped forward, smiling. "Welcome, brother. I'm Cecil Grossett. This is Jamal Washington, Hassan Callcut, and Royce Lingard."

"Well met. I'm Matthew Sugiyama, and this is my friend Earl Kildare. We're traveling toward Vegas Depot but stopped to visit."

Grossett smiled. "We offer hospitality to you both for a price. Our headmaster will demand a visit from you, Brother Sugiyama. We request Ms. Kildare pose for two classes."

Although I'd expected these terms, a sensation of déjà vu swept over me. I turned toward Earl. "They want you to model for their students."

Pink spots appeared high on her cheekbones, but I turned to Grossett. "What medium?"

"My sculpture class," said Callcut.

"Upper-grade pastels," said Washington at the same time.

Grossett sighed. "This is why every master vies to greet travelers."

I chuckled and turned back toward Earl. "The sculpture class will be about ninety minutes, but the pastel class shouldn't be longer than three-quarters of an hour."

She leaned down and murmured in my ear. "Clothed?"

The warmth of her breath and the image of Earl posing nude were too much at once. My groin tightened and my mouth went dry as I floundered for words. Mute, I nodded.

"We have a bargain." Washington's teeth gleamed.

Brother Lingard held Bruno's reins while Earl dismounted. She rewarded him with a smile and a soft, "Thank you." He blushed, taking Oxide's reins from me too.

We followed the other three men through the glass front doors. The atrium was sunlit and cheerful, the polished, white limestone floors immaculate. Tall urns of curly willow, royal fern, and a type of sedge unfamiliar to me graced the entry.

Washington and Callcut excused themselves, leaving us to follow Grossett down a long hallway filled with offset doors. I glanced inside the open doors we passed. The interior rooms all had windows facing an internal courtyard, while the exterior rooms boasted vast views of the empty prairie.

Grossett stopped at a door on the far end of the hallway and knocked twice.

"Come," called a voice from inside.

"Headmaster Tanaka, I've brought Brother Sugiyama and Ms. Kildare."

*The name Tanaka sounds Japanese.*

Chills raced down my arms as I craned my neck to examine the headmaster. He was younger than I'd expected, fifteen years my senior at most. He was shorter than me and had a broad chest, close-cropped hair, and a single patch of hair under his bottom lip.

"Sugiyama? Let me think." He snapped his fingers. "Cedar mountain, am I right?" He rounded his desk, thrusting his hand out. "Tanaka roughly translates to the center of the rice paddy, which I guess works since I've spent my life in the middle of an enormous field." He released my hand and stepped around me to shake Earl's hand, too. "Come in, come in, both of you. Have a seat."

We obeyed, sliding into armchairs.

Tanaka perched on the edge of his desk and studied me, then Earl, then me again. "I'm sure they've already demanded Ms. Kildare sit for at least two classes, but your face is also nearly symmetrical. Will you pose for our students as well?"

I blinked, overwhelmed by Tanaka's energy. "Yes, Headmaster."

"Andrew, please. Away from the students, I'm Andrew Tanaka. Grossett, you're making me nervous. Take a seat, man." Tanaka strode around his desk but ignored his chair. He pulled a rolled document from a shelf and spread it across his desk. "Where did you study, Sugiyama?"

"Popham, and it's Matthew."

Andrew smiled and circled Popham. "Great, terrific. Popham has quite a reputation, but let me guess." He leaned against his desk and snapped his fingers. "Head boy?"

I chuckled. "It still shows?"

Andrew's teeth flashed. "A touch. You'll need a few more years to round down the edges. So, Head Boy Matthew, why have you come to Leavenworth Abbey?" He leaned forward. "If you've come for a staff position, it's yours."

Warmth bubbled in my chest, but I shook my head. "Thank you, but no. I have several questions..." I stopped and stole a glance at Grossett. Could I trust them? If I admitted what I knew and they worked with Carter, I'd put Earl and me in danger. But if I said nothing and Carter showed up, they'd be unwarned.

Andrew shook his head, as if expecting my question. "Grossett is my number two. He'll leave if you want to talk in private, but I'll tell him everything you've said later, anyway."

Grossett chuckled and settled deeper into his chair. "We have an hour before dinner."

Earl relaxed into her chair, seemingly unconcerned by me sharing our knowledge.

I liked both men immediately, and my intuition said I could trust them, so I took a deep breath. "We've recently traveled from Toronto Depot." My gaze flicked back and forth between the men, but neither reacted. "I had occasion to visit both Niagara and Erie Abbeys while we were there."

Andrew's gaze flicked to the map. From my position, I couldn't tell if the abbeys were on it. They waited, their eyes curious and faces open.

"Together, the abbeys had roughly sixty masters and a hundred students. However, over the course of our stay, we learned both abbeys worked for a man called Reverend Carter."

I stopped, but when neither man appeared to recognize the name, I drew in a breath. "I believe Reverend Carter is attempting to revive religion. Specifically, the Christian faith from *Before*."

Both men appeared startled, and Andrew ran both his palms over his head. "Cecil, have you heard anything about this?"

Grossett shook his head. "Not a thing." He turned to me, his brow knit. "Do you have any names?"

"Headmaster McCully was in charge of Niagara Abbey, but they abandoned Erie Abbey before I visited it."

Andrew's mouth tightened, and he shook his head. "It's not a name I'm familiar with. Where are the abbeys?"

"South of Toronto Depot."

He scanned the map, then shook his head.

"Both are now empty," added Earl. Her words, though softly spoken, had a galvanizing effect on both men.

"Both?" Andrew paced behind his desk. "Why?"

"They left the abbeys in Carter's service."

Grossett leaned forward, his left leg jittering. "Andrew, I should notify the other masters."

Andrew nodded. "I hate to say it, but I'd like to reinstate a watch." He looked at me, his eyes troubled. "Are they friendly?"

When I hesitated, his eyes hardened. "What else?"

"Carter and his people ransacked the warehouse in Toronto Depot before they left."

"Heading this way?" asked Grossett. When I nodded, he swore.

"We know they cleaned out the warehouse in Detroit Depot. Nothing else." I turned toward Andrew. "They took all the art supplies from both depots. The librarians in Kansas Depot told me Leavenworth Abbey has the remaining art supplies in this region."

Andrew sighed. "You've noticed how empty the area is?"

Earl tilted her head. "There's almost nothing from *Before* left around here."

"Blasted prairie fires," said Grossett. "Brick doesn't burn, and we have metal shutters to protect our doors and windows. We've survived, but few grasslands communities remain here long."

I shivered. Ever since Brookfield had burned, flames had plagued my nightmares, charred skulls grinning at me from a flickering inferno.

Andrew bounced on the balls of his feet. "Louis Depot, Kansas Depot, and Oklahoma Depot are it, and we're the last abbey left on the prairie. Long ago, a headmaster had all three depots scoured for art supplies. They stored the supplies they found in our subbasement." He snapped his fingers as though an idea had occurred to him. "If you need anything, give Grossett a list. We have plenty."

"Thank you. I need turpentine, and the depots we passed had none."

When Andrew and Cecil exchanged troubled glances at my request, the hairs on my neck rose. Their stockpile of art supplies meant Leavenworth Abbey was a rich resource... and a target.

# CHAPTER FOURTEEN

Earl laughed when I popped my head into the auberge. "You look quite dashing in your borrowed robes."

I lowered my eyes, smoothing the dark material. "It's both strange and familiar to wear them again." I glanced around the richly appointed room.

*Alone.*

During our travels, it had been near impossible to find time alone with Earl, let alone privacy. Now, assuming our unvarnished truth pact was still in place, I could ask her every question I'd wondered about since meeting her. A surge of nervous energy coursed through me, leaving me tongue-tied and awkward. Given our platonic status, it surprised me.

Charcoal jumped onto Earl's bed and stretched out. He grumbled twice before laying his head on her pillow. While I envied his ease around her, a muffled clang echoed through the courtyard.

*Sword practice.*

I looked up, but they had blacked out the windows facing the courtyard.

"I guess they don't want me to see what they're doing." Earl shrugged. "Do you trust them?"

"Yes." The simple answer broke through my nerves, giving me the confidence to cross the room and sink into a large, leather armchair. I beamed at her. This was what I'd hoped for—uninterrupted private time alone with Earl. The chance to sit and chat with her like I did with any friend. "I like Headmaster Tanaka."

"He's intense, but I like him too. How did your class go?"

I grimaced and flopped onto the armchair. "An hour is entirely too long to have students stare at you like you're a piece of fruit. I didn't enjoy being discussed like I wasn't present, either."

"Congratulations, you've experienced what it's like to be a woman."

I raised my arms in a victory pose. "What do I win?"

"Empathy."

I chuckled. "How was the sculpture class? What pose did you choose?" When Earl's lips curved, I sat forward. "Tell me."

"After they told me I could choose any pose, I asked to visit the kitchen."

"And?"

"Found a roast."

"You carved meat?" My belly shook with laughter, and I gasped for air.

"I'm a butcher." She shrugged and flashed me her lopsided grin. "When they discussed me, I pretended it was the meat they judged."

I chuckled, drying my eyes. "I should insist Grossett show me the sculptures. With luck, they'll cast at least one in bronze." I chuckled again, picturing a curl of meat forever preserved in burnished metal.

"What should I expect from the pastel class?"

"Right, I forgot you had another class today."

The urge to join the class subdued the pang of disappointment. I'd longed to paint Earl since we'd met. I rarely worked with pastels but could dust off my rusty skills, assuming it was okay with her. "Would you mind if I sit in?"

Earl hugged herself. "Would it be weird?"

"Not at all. You'll have a friend in the room." Even though I kept my tone light and cheerful, I wasn't sure either of us believed it.

"I'm nervous."

I raised my eyebrow. "Why?"

"You are artists… and I've seen what you're capable of."

"We never alter life models." I took her hands in mine. "Students practice portraiture to refine their critical eye and work toward capturing a moment."

She squeezed my fingers. "Thanks."

Charcoal raised his head, and Brother Washington knocked on the open door. "Ready?"

My breath caught when Earl entered the classroom. Instead of her usual overalls, she wore a long-sleeved, green dress. The material had a shine, like satin, and the skirt swirled around her as she walked, brushing her bare calves. Her hair flowed freely, nearly reaching her waist. As she followed Washington toward the platform, she carried a bouquet of wildflowers collected from the prairie. He tossed a pale-green rug over the wood before escorting her up and taking her bouquet from her.

Earl assumed a square, neutral posture with her arms hanging loosely at her sides and raised her chin. Around me, pencils scratched as the boys sketched her proportions. I didn't need to. I'd long ago memorized the ratios of her legs to torso, arms to legs, and shoulders to hips, so I used the time to watch her.

"Ready?" Washington asked, handing her the flowers. Earl took a deep breath, nodded, and stepped forward on her left leg, lifting the flowers toward the sky. The pose turned her into a triangle, the hypotenuse line unbroken from the flowers, down her arm, back, and through her right leg to where her toe touched the platform.

"This pose will last fifteen minutes. Go."

An effervescent sensation filled me. I chose a light-gray crayon to capture the angles of the pose. Once done, I switched to the green pastel and worked in swift strokes to capture the curves and folds in the material. As I worked, my belly relaxed, pulling air deep into my lungs. The anxiety I'd carried for so long unspooled, leaving lightness behind. It took little time to remember the pleasure of working with pastels, and I could nearly imagine the texture of Earl's cheek as I smoothed the pigment with the tip of my finger.

"Time," Washington called.

Pages flipped as Earl brought the flowers down toward her right ankle. The movement caught her hair over her left shoulder, where it draped like a fiery curtain. Because she hadn't moved her feet, the folds of material deepened, adding an illusion of movement.

I worked feverishly, but too soon, Washington called "Time," and Earl dropped the pose.

The boys set down their materials and clapped long after she'd stepped down from the platform.

She smiled at them as she walked toward me. "May I see?" she asked, gesturing at my easel.

When I stepped back, Earl caught her breath. "It looks like

I'm dancing." Her eyes glowed, nearly the same color as the dress. "It's beautiful."

"It's what I saw."

"Admirable," said a voice behind me. "Popham taught you well."

I spun and bowed. "Headmaster Tanaka."

He smiled at Earl. "Please excuse us, Ms. Kildare."

She nodded and followed Washington from the classroom without looking back.

"We rarely allow our life models to dine with us," Tanaka began. "I would have made an exception for Ms. Kildare, but unfortunately, I need to explain our situation to the lads and junior masters tonight. You're welcome to dine with us, but I'll have Ms. Kildare's meal sent to the auberge."

"I understand. I'll join her if you don't mind." This was perfect—an evening alone with Earl, away from probing stares.

"Not at all." He paused, waiting for the students to leave the classroom before gesturing at my pastel. "If you change your mind, join our staff as a senior master. My offer won't expire. I suspect we have much in common, and I'm genuinely sorry we won't have longer together."

Warmth coursed through me. If I posed it as a hypothetical, could I ask Tanaka about Akiko's gift? His words and actions seemed sincere, and nothing about him triggered my intuition.

*I didn't suspect Robin Pritchard or Headmaster McCully, either.*

*Say nothing.*

"I am too, Headmaster. Thank you for your hospitality. And the offer."

Boys and masters alike stopped Charcoal and me several times on our way to the auberge. By the time we reached it, Earl had changed back into her usual attire and had nearly finished braiding her hair.

"You look troubled again," she said to my reflection in the mirror. "What is it? Open and honest, remember?"

"Right." I pulled the robe over my head and tossed it over the chair, realizing too late that Charcoal was already there. The robe landed on him, and he swung his covered head back and forth. When he grumbled but did nothing to remove it, Earl giggled and crossed the room to pull it off him. He leaned against the chair's arm, smiling at her.

Earl rubbed his cheek before holding the robe out toward me. "Won't you need this for dinner?"

"No. Tanaka said you're dining here, so I'm joining you. I'm sorry for the poor hospitality."

Earl waved away my apology, and her smile appeared genuine. "It's fine. Actually, it's a relief. Everyone here stares."

"Stares?"

"All the time." She dropped the robe over the stool near the mirror. "It's unnerving. I've been judged by my appearance my entire life, but never as overtly as this."

"It's not personal," I said, sinking onto the corner of her bed. "You're just..."

She waited. When I said nothing, she lifted her eyebrow. "Yes?"

I traced her face with my eyes, roaming over its oval shape, high cheekbones, and wide mouth. When I paused too long on her mouth, Earl shifted.

"You're beautiful," I said. "Objectively, spectacularly, and devastatingly beautiful."

Earl crossed her arms and took a step backward. "You can stop now."

"I've made you uncomfortable."

She nodded, and I sighed. "After my experience as a model in the portraiture class, I can sympathize. From my perspective —from any artist's perspective—you are a fascinating subject.

The symmetry of your features, your unusual coloring, and the presence with which you hold yourself combine into something more than human. Any artist who doesn't stare at you is a man who has lost his sight."

I rubbed my hands together. "I catch myself staring too, and I've sketched you from memory many times. Long ago, the artists from *Before* often returned to their favorite models, immortalizing them. Over many compositions and scenes, they attempted to capture their essence, something more foundational than appearance. You've helped me understand why."

"So, it's a professional interest?" Earl's posture softened. "Purely?"

"Ah." I flopped backward on her bed. "Maybe not. We are men, after all." The bed shifted as Earl sat next to me. I bolted upright.

She stared at her hands, slid her eyes sideways, and tilted her head toward me. "So."

A dozen centimeters separated our shoulders. My mouth went dry. I gazed into her eyes, falling into them again. "So."

"You've had one kiss and one kiss only?"

My gaze locked on her lips. I nodded, my heart crashing around my chest.

"Unless you are a man who refuses to kiss—which I can't imagine—Genevie is your sole sexual experience. With women, at least."

Bands of pressure wound around me. I searched her eyes for derision or judgment but found only compassion. Heat flooded my face. "With anyone. Is it off-putting?"

"No." She leaned even closer. "But it explains a lot,"

My hands spasmed along my thighs and words deserted me. There was too little air in the room, and my breath hitched.

A knock on the door shattered the moment. We jumped apart like guilty children as a black-robed man pushed a wheeled cart into the room. He had shiny, dark hair swept neatly to the side, and a thin, angular face. He stopped, wide-eyed. "Hullo, beautiful people."

Earl and I glanced at each other, then back at him.

"Wow," he said. "I'd heard from the others, but... wow." He pushed the cart toward the table and pulled off the white cloth covering the top. "I'm Dante, and you have way too few words to say between you. Did I interrupt something?" He arched his brow, and the suggestive way he stared first at the bed and then at us broke my stasis.

I sprang to my feet and crossed the room in two large bounds. "Not at all."

Earl leaned forward, gripping the corner of the mattress. "Dante, you said?"

"Dante Ruiz." He set two plates on the table, flashing me a coquettish expression. "I brought quiche, and I'm joining you for dinner," he said, setting a third plate on the table.

My stomach dropped, but Earl smiled and pulled out a chair. "Lovely."

Dante set the quiche and a leafy green salad on the table before perching on the second chair.

Why was I so disappointed? Dante had interrupted a moment, but since Earl and I were just friends, it shouldn't matter. In truth, I should be grateful for the interruption. But I wasn't. I slid into the remaining chair and pasted a smile on my face. Under the table, Charcoal nosed my hands, preventing me from rubbing my wrist.

"Now," said Dante as he served a wedge of quiche to Earl. "I'm told you're traveling to Vegas Depot."

"We are," said Earl, passing me the salad bowl. "Have you been?"

"No, but I want to go, which is where you come in." Dante beamed as he slid the quiche onto my plate.

"Oh?" I picked off a piece of the crust and passed it to Charcoal.

Dante peered under the table. "Oh, hullo, little chap." He rifled through the crockery on the cart before his brow smoothed. "You don't mind eating from a saucer, do you?" He put a large piece of quiche on the small plate before catching my expression. "No?"

"It's fine. His name is Charcoal."

"Of *course* it is. Clever boy." Dante scratched under Charcoal's chin and set the food on the floor before resuming his pitch. "Now, I *yearn* to visit Vegas Depot, and happily, you're already going. I've packed my bags, so please don't say no."

My first instinct was to decline his plea, but Earl laughed. I picked up my fork but set it down again. Perhaps his request was a joke? "Why do you want to leave?"

Dante leaned forward, motioning us to do the same. Earl did, her eyes bright with interest.

"I've already dated everyone here." Dante's voice dropped an octave. "Everyone appropriate." He cut a tiny piece of quiche with his fork and stared at it, his voice returning to its normal pitch. "I'm lonely and on a quest for love. Since everyone knows love is the *most* important thing, you'll say yes... right?"

My gaze snapped to Earl, but I dragged it away.

Dante smiled brightly and waved his fork. "I'll miss the cooking here, but I mean, if I have a whole abbey full of interesting men to meet, I'll make do."

'No' hovered near the tip of my tongue, but Earl seemed charmed by his request. A pang snaked through me. If we agreed to take him, Earl wouldn't be the "new" person anymore. I'd planned to ease her loneliness with *my* friendship... but could she have too many friends? "We'll need to ask the rest of our group, but I believe in love, too. With Earl and me on your side, I doubt they'll say no."

Dante beamed, but it was Earl's delighted laugh and the way she lay her hand over mine that convinced me I'd made the right choice.

# CHAPTER FIFTEEN

We'd warned Dante the final decision would depend on the rest of our group but found him waiting for us in the atrium after breakfast. I pressed my lips together, scrambling for a polite way to tell him he'd have to wait. "We need to ask the rest of the group before we can take you."

Dante shrugged. "I've said my goodbyes and am ready to go, so let's trust in love to triumph." Unfazed by my expression, he leaned forward to kiss Earl's cheek. "You look pretty."

She laughed, and they chatted while I brooded.

When a boy led Oxide and Bruno to the front entrance, Dante drooped. "I don't have a horse!"

His look of distress was almost comical, but Earl soothed him, her hands fluttering as she proposed a solution. "You can ride Bruno, and I'll ride with Matthew."

I was prepared to argue—we *could* return to the abbey for Dante later. But the fantasy of spending the day with Earl's arms wrapped around me was too enticing. Besides, I needed to make my rendezvous with Talbot. I couldn't risk an argument, so I said nothing and nodded.

Dante clapped his hands and lifted two bags. "Where do these go?"

I sighed. Done is done. They chatted while I rearranged our tack, moving Oxide's saddlebags onto Bruno and lashing Dante's valises on top of them. "As long as we keep to a walk, I think this will work." I held Bruno's reins out toward Dante.

He beamed at Earl and approached the large animal. "You are a pretty brute, aren't you?" When he reached Bruno's shoulder, Dante clapped. "Now, how do we do this?"

My heart lurched into my throat. "You don't know how to ride?"

Dante's eyes danced as he shook his head. "But I'm *eager* to learn."

It took everything I had not to groan. "It's over twenty-one hundred kilometers from Kansas Depot to Vegas Depot."

"Plenty of time for me to practice, right?"

I sighed and pointed at his left leg. "Bend at the knee, and I'll hoist you up."

"Oh," said Dante as he settled onto Bruno. He crouched forward like he wanted to hug the horse's neck. "He's much taller than he looked. What do I do with these?" he asked, flapping Bruno's reins. Per his training, the horse stepped sideways. Dante dropped both reins and grabbed the saddle horn.

I turned toward Earl, widening my eyes, but she smiled. "Matthew can pony Bruno for you until you're more comfortable."

Dante's smile was grateful. "Yes, thank you."

After mounting Oxide and pulling Earl up behind me, I waited for her to settle. Dante handed me Bruno's reins with a shaking hand.

"I'm new to riding, too," said Earl, nestling her cheek into my back. "You'll be fine."

They chatted as we rode southwest, talking about nothing

and everything. Earl was both soft and solid against me, and since Oxide didn't seem to mind the extra weight, I relaxed into the feeling. For once, the humidity was low, and though the day was warm, the steady crosswind kept the temperature comfortable. Fortunate, because our progress was slow.

"Ouch," said Dante as he staggered, bow-legged, during our first break. "Girl, your horse done broke my pelvis."

She laughed as she rubbed the small of her back. "It gets better, I promise."

Near midafternoon, we rode toward a cluster of buildings. They were short, made from concrete blocks, and had steel-covered, pitched roofs. The community was the type I'd normally pass without stopping, but after the long hours of crossing empty prairie, Earl squeezed me. "It's nice to see something. Anything."

"If that's another filling station, I'm ready for a break," called Dante.

"Me too," murmured Earl, tightening her arm around my belly. "I'm hungry."

The station's keeper smiled broadly when we introduced ourselves and our professions. "Well met. I can offer a meal of sliced bread, soft cheese, and an assortment of my gourmet pickled vegetables."

Dante and Earl turned matching hopeful expressions toward me. I scratched at my beard. "What would you like?"

The keeper rubbed his palms together, his eyes gleaming. "My brother-in-law built me a wood-burning bread oven out back, but the opening is too small for my peel. Widen it, and I'm happy to feed and house you."

I wavered. The task was simple, but I was impatient to reach the rendezvous spot. Lansing, the community nearest the falls, shouldn't be far; could I convince Earl and Dante to continue on?

"I'll make the improvement," said Dante. "My sketchbook is at the top of my bags."

"Oh, good." Earl sank onto one of the padded chairs and patted it. "Can I offer you a seat?"

I bit my lip and shook my head. "I need to check something Akiko noticed on the map. If you want a break, wait here and I'll return as quickly as I can."

Dante flapped his hand. "I'm happy to stay as long as you need. Overnight even."

The keeper beamed. "You're most welcome."

Earl sliced bread, spread it with cheese, and layered strips of pickled, red bell pepper across them. She closed it and handed it to me, flashing me a shy smile. "See you later."

Oxide looked wistfully at the meal I pulled him away from, but Bruno didn't seem concerned about being left behind. It took less than an hour to reach Lansing. The community bustled with people. I rode past several workshops displaying crafts and wares in their front windows, and past a market stall where a man unpacked a crate of tomatoes.

At the end of the road, I found a hitching rail and a trail leading into a stand of trees. The sign said 'Angel Falls, Pedestrian Trail'. There were no other horses tied nearby, but I dismounted and secured Oxide before hiking up the trail. Charcoal was at my side right away, happy I was on foot once more. It took us a quarter-hour to arrive at the falls.

"This is it?"

At most, Angel Falls was a meter and a half tall. A dull shelf of flat rock over which brown water sheeted into a shallow plunge pool. It was a pretty enough spot, and if my nerves hadn't been flipping, I might have enjoyed sketching the scene. I sat on a bench to wait, rubbing my thumbs over each other as I listened to the birdsong.

A few people strolled by, and a gaggle of children around

Akiko's age splashed in the shallows at the base of the plunge until a harried-looking man called them away.

Near dusk, footsteps approached. I looked up but didn't recognize the man. He lit standing lanterns along the trail. The flames gutted and danced as a breeze filtered through the trees.

Charcoal leaned against my leg and sighed. I stood and stretched, twisting left and right. Should I stay? Charcoal yawned, making me yawn, too.

"Let's check on Oxide."

We walked to the trailhead, where Oxide dozed. He woke, blinking sleepy eyes, but shifted his weight from his right to left hip and closed his eyes when I rubbed his forehead. I sighed, scanning the road for anyone familiar. There were fewer people out now, and a single flat-bottom wagon was the last vehicle left on the street. Would Talbot come?

We wandered back up the lantern-lit trail in no particular hurry, so when he called my name, it caught me by surprise.

*Talbot.*

I swayed. "You're here."

He rose from the bench I'd vacated and stepped forward to hug me. His embrace was warm and familiar, and a shudder of relief ran through me, my knees nearly buckling.

When I pulled back, my worries dropped away like stones. "It's good to see you."

He smiled. "I wasn't sure you'd get my message."

"It wasn't the best plan." I narrowed my eyes. "What if I hadn't attended the minstrel's show?"

Talbot ran his hands through his hair. "This is the fourth meeting spot I've waited at. It isn't easy to get away from Carter, and I wasn't certain which direction you'd travel. I made the best guesses I could. Hullo, Charcoal."

I raised my chin. "You knew I'd head toward Vegas Depot?"

Talbot nodded. "After Olen mentioned he was from the southwest, I knew he'd recognize the tower in *Home*."

My hands balled. Why hadn't Talbot just told me himself?

"Your—" Talbot broke off, staring into the woods. "Are you alone?"

"Yes." I checked Charcoal, but he gazed in the opposite direction. "What were you saying?"

"Your parents aren't in Vegas Depot," said Talbot, his attention still focused on the woods. "Did you hear something?"

*Not in Vegas Depot?*

If true, we had traveled nearly three-quarters of the way to the depot for *nothing*. My gut twisted. "I hear nothing. They aren't—"

Talbot interrupted my question by raising his hand. Simultaneously, Charcoal's hackles rose. I turned, gasping at the stranger swinging flames toward me. Talbot shoved my shoulder hard, and I plunged into the brush, twisting in time to see the man strike Talbot across the face with the pitch-covered torch.

Talbot cried out, falling to his knees as Charcoal launched into an attack. Snarling, he leaped up to bite the man's arm. The man wheeled backward, kicked at the dog, and dropped his torch. Time slowed as he stepped backward over the edge of the falls and fell from sight.

I sprang to my feet and crossed the trail to look over the edge. The drop had been short, but the man had fallen backward and landed across two boulders. He stared at the darkening skies with unseeing eyes, his head twisted at an unnatural angle. My stomach lurched, and I backed away from the edge on shaking legs. I wobbled toward Talbot who was curled in a fetal position on the ground. "Are you okay?"

"Run," he cried. "Get away!"

I shook my head, but Talbot couldn't see my gesture.

He clawed at his face, ripping at the scorched skin around his eyes. Blisters rose from the raw flesh, and I blanched as I caught his wrists. "It's fine. He fell. Don't touch your face."

We needed help, but I was ten minutes from my horse, forty minutes from Earl, and roughly eight hours from Ben and the others.

*Now what?*

"It burns!"

"I'll get a cool cloth." I returned to the water above the falls, but I couldn't stop staring at the dead man. My knees threatened to buckle, so I turned my face upstream and tore a strip from my undertunic while trying to catch my breath. Crouching down, I wetted the cloth, fighting nausea and trying not to think about the dead man lying downstream.

I returned to Talbot's side. "Can you sit up?" He struggled into a seated position, groping for me until I caught his hands. "How did you get here?" I asked, dabbing at his injuries.

"Got a lift." He clutched my forearms, tears streaming down his blistered face. "Parcel delivery."

*He has no transportation.*

His hands tightened on mine. "Is it safe? Are we safe?"

I nodded, but he couldn't see me. "Yes, we're fine. He—he's dead."

"Dead?" Talbot shuddered, but his grip loosened.

"Who was he?"

Talbot didn't answer. He wagged his head, his right hand fluttering toward his face. The motion reminded me of Josephine, back when I'd first met her.

"Don't touch it." I glanced around the clearing, but there was nothing here. Nothing but the burbling water and a dead body. "I need to get you to a healer."

He clutched my hand. "I can't trust anyone. It's why I

couldn't give the minstrels a simple message for you. If Carter sent someone for us, he knows—"

"Okay, okay," I said to soothe him. "Earl and Dante are at a filling station. I need to retrieve them, but afterward, I'll get you to Josephine and the others in the Depot."

Talbot reached for me again. "Don't leave me—I can't see."

"I know, but I only have one horse." Frustration bubbled up, making me groan. "I have no choice. If I take you with me, I'll have four people to move." Two of whom couldn't ride, but that was a problem for later. "Listen, I'm going to hide you off the trail, in the brush. If you're quiet, no one will know you're here. I'll be back as soon as I can."

Talbot stilled, and his mouth drooped. "You'll return?"

"*Yes.*" My heart cracked as I pulled him to his feet. "Come on."

Talbot stumbled after me, crashing through the brush. When I judged we'd traveled far enough from the trail, I helped him sit at the base of a large oak. He shivered in the warm night air, wrapping his arms around him, so I unbuttoned my outer tunic and draped it over his shoulders. I turned to go, but he looked so small and defenseless huddled at the base of the tree I couldn't move.

"Matthew?" he asked, as if unsure if I was still there.

"I'm going now, but Charcoal will stay with you. I'll be back as soon as I can."

Charcoal gave me a pained look but didn't protest when Talbot clutched him close. I left before either could call me back, dread and anxiety roiling in my gut.

# CHAPTER SIXTEEN

It didn't take long to reach the filling station, and Oxide nickered happily when I left him with Bruno and a flake of hay. I hurried into the building, prioritizing the tasks we needed to tackle.

*Get Dante and Earl ready to go.*

*Saddle Bruno.*

*Ride to Lansing.*

*Retrieve Talbot and Charcoal.*

*Arrange transportation to Kansas Depot.*

*Find a healer.*

At least the first task on the list would take no time at all. The door into the filling station banged open, and Dante looked up from his sketchbook. I glanced around, but he was alone.

"Where's Earl?"

Dante shrugged. "She went to bed an hour ago."

I groaned and rubbed my face. We didn't have time for this. "It took me longer than I expected."

Dante stretched and smiled. "You caught *me* just in time.

I'm heading off to bed now if you..." He hooked his thumb toward the hallway and smiled suggestively. When my breath came out in a rattling hiss, he shrugged. "Worth a shot."

"I'm sorry. It wasn't a rejection of you. I mean, it was, it *is*, but I'm..." I stopped, collected myself, and tried again. "No one is going to bed. We need to leave."

"Now?" Dante blinked and held up a finger, wagging it back and forth. "Did I hear you say no to my invitation, no to bed, and also that we're leaving this cozy little nest?"

"Yes."

"Ah. Hoped I heard wrong." He sighed. "Well, I guess I'll ask my testicles to retreat into my torso again. Wake the fair maiden, and I'll meet you near my borrowed brute."

To be polite, I chuckled, but the smile slid from my face when I stepped into the corridor. It had five doors, all closed. It wasn't late, but no one would thank me for waking them.

I tapped on the first door but heard no response. Loud snores emanated from the next, so I crossed to the other side of the hallway. Bed springs squeaked when I knocked. The keeper, wearing a long dressing gown, jerked the door open. His mulish expression disappeared when he recognized me.

"Welcome back," he said. "Yours is the room at the end of the hall."

"I'm sorry, but we need to leave. Can I settle up with you?"

"Your friend has provided more than enough help. But if you're not staying the night, I'm in *your* debt." He wrung his hands and looked distraught. "I'd planned a breakfast for tomorrow, but the food isn't ready."

"It's no matter, and I need to find my friend. Dante said she went to bed?"

The keeper gestured toward the door across from him. "At least let me scramble eggs and fry bacon. Won't take a half hour."

My stomach rumbled, but I shook my head as I knocked on Earl's door. "Sorry, no. We need first aid supplies if you have any to spare."

Earl opened the door, her eyes clouded with sleep. "Did you say first aid?"

"Yes. We need to go." I looked over her head at the keeper. "There's been an accident, and an acquaintance of mine was burned."

The keeper shuffled his feet and sighed. "I have a good calendula salve. We see a lot of burns in these parts. I'll meet you in the barn."

Earl ducked back into her room but re-emerged moments later. Clad in her overalls, she handed me her boots and padded barefoot toward the common room as she braided her hair.

"Your shirt is on backward." I followed her down the hall. "And inside out."

She said nothing, but the side of her mouth quirked as she pulled on her left boot. "My eyes are up here."

I stammered an apology, but she tugged on her right boot and stepped into the night.

***

ON THE RIDE BACK TO LANSING, I RELAYED WHAT HAD happened. Earl squeezed me before sliding off Oxide. "You go get Talbot, and we'll figure out transport to the depot."

I nodded as a wave of fatigue enveloped me. On foot, I hurried up the street, pausing at the trailhead to the falls. No one was watching or lurking in the shadows. My neck ached from the tension.

*Hurry, Artist.*

I needed to get Talbot away from here before anyone discovered the dead man. Deep shadows flanked the lantern-lit trail, and my heart crashed to a stop at a pair of glowing eyes. I snatched a standing lantern with shaking hands and pointed it at the eyes. The now-familiar coyote blinked at me before melting back into the brush.

"Talbot?" I called, shoving the lantern's pike back into the ground. It sagged to one side, the guttering flame descending toward the brush.

No response.

I whistled and tried without success to straighten the torch.

The brush moved and Charcoal appeared. He scampered toward me, a relieved expression on his face. When he reached me, he leaned against my leg, pushing against my hand as I fondled his ears. "I'm back, chap. Where's Talbot?"

The dog sighed and swung his head toward the dark.

"Get Talbot."

He trotted into the brush, and I pulled the lantern from the ground to follow him. It took longer to reach Talbot than I expected because he'd moved from where I'd left him.

"Matthew?"

I wiped sweat from my forehead. "Ready to go?"

"Go where?"

"The depot." I reached down and clutched his waving hand, pulling him to his feet. "Come, Earl is organizing transport."

Talbot stayed rooted to the ground. "Is it safe?"

"I don't know." His hand tightened on mine. "But we can't stay here," I said. "Come on."

With the lantern in one hand, and Talbot clutching the other, I had no way to protect my face as I pushed my way through the brush toward the trail, branches scraping and clawing at me the entire way. Once we were back on the trail, I took a breath to collect myself, but the flickering lanterns illuminated Talbot's injury. Nauseous, I replanted the lantern and tugged on Talbot's arm. "This way."

Our progress down the root-covered trail was slow, and when we reached the street, my heart plummeted. Our horses were gone.

"Is everything okay?" asked Talbot.

*Now what?*

"Fine," I lied, scanning the street again. "A bit farther."

Before we reached mid-block, Dante hissed at us from a shadowed alley. "Over here!"

Talbot halted. "Who is that?"

"Dante."

"Dante who?"

I rewound my memory, searching for Dante's last name. "Rodriguez? Ramirez?" I tugged on Talbot's arm. "He's an artist I met at Leavenworth Abbey."

Talbot didn't move. "Why is he here?"

*Good question.*

"He wants to travel to Vegas Depot with us." Talbot stiffened and I sighed, but he allowed me to guide him into the alley. "I agreed before you told me my parents aren't there. I'll tell him later."

My gut twisted. We'd traveled nearly halfway already, and my parents weren't even in Vegas Depot. I hadn't given myself time to process Talbot's news, but saying it out loud left a deep, sorrowful ache behind.

Earl, clear-eyed and action-ready, hurried toward us and slipped under Talbot's other arm. "We have first aid supplies, and I've sorted a ride for Dante and Talbot. Let's get back and find a healer before we leave for Vegas Depot."

I guided Talbot toward the waiting wagon, where Dante sat next to the driver. "If my parents aren't in the depot, there's no reason to continue—"

Talbot's grip on my arm tightened. "Your parents aren't in the depot, but your sister is."

*My sister?*

Ice slid down my spine as he continued, his voice hoarse. "If Carter knows about me, Erena isn't safe either."

# CHAPTER SEVENTEEN

Talbot's words left me numb, and I rode to the depot in silence.

*Sister.*

The strange blankness in my mind refused to budge. Throughout the years I'd yearned for answers about my birth family, I'd only ever imagined my parents. Never had I considered siblings. The word 'sister' conjured only a montage of moments shared with Josephine.

Talbot was near frantic to warn Erena, but my concern was for him. At last count, Carter commanded more than a hundred people. If he suspected Talbot, there could be others coming for Talbot, too.

*We need to get away from here.*

The buildings were dimly lit and quiet by the time we reached the warehouse compound, but I didn't hesitate to wake our group.

Once she'd blinked the sleep from her eyes, the efficiency with which Sally organized a response astonished me. That

Dante and Talbot, neither of whom could ride, would accompany us to Vegas Depot, barely caused a blip.

"Put Talbot in my bed," she said. "Ben, find Librarian Keely and ask for a healer. Josephine and I will reorganize the supplies in the wagon to make room for Talbot."

My shoulders sagged; everything would be fine now. "What else should I do?"

She peered at me. "If you're up to it, I agreed to several minor improvements to cover the supplies Ben wanted."

"Sure." I had completed my improvements before I left. How much more had Ben grabbed? "We'll see what we can do."

Genevie dragged in so late the sky was already lightening.

Sally made a clucking noise. "You reek. Bathe first, then sleep. I'll wake you when it's time to go."

Genevie blinked and stumbled off in a cloud of sour whiskey and stale sweat, not bothering to ask why we were leaving or who Dante was.

Dante raised his eyebrow, but I shrugged, too weary to explain. While we sketched, Akiko hugged Charcoal and chattered about warehouse gossip. I couldn't make sense of her words, but Dante smiled at her energy. She watched him work with as much attention as she paid me, but asked no technical questions. As hungry as she was to learn about art, her caution made me proud.

By dawn, we were nearly ready to depart. Exhaustion made me woozy, but I couldn't relax. My nerves jumped at every sound, and my mind found assailants in every shadow. And each time I imagined my sister, my mind's canvas blanked.

"Breakfast time." Oblivious to my haste, Sally settled herself into a chair next to Talbot's bed. "If someone will bring me a cup of tea and a sticky bun, I'll watch him while you eat."

Ben nodded, herding us toward the dining hall. I followed the others, but he grabbed my arm. "Go bathe."

I looked down at my stained and ripped clothes. Talbot's safety was more important than my cleanliness, but the distaste on Sally's face when Genevie had staggered in flashed across my mind's canvas. "How bad am I?"

"Rank." His nose wrinkled. "I'll make you a plate."

If Carter's people had found the man at Angel Falls, they would head here next. "Do we even have time for breakfast?"

Ben studied me before speaking. "If we sneak away in the dark, people will notice. It's better to wait."

He was right. My shoulders sagged, but I nodded and headed to the showers.

CLEAN, WHOLE, AND DAMP, I ENTERED THE DINING HALL in time to watch everyone rise from the tables. Ben handed me two wrapped sandwiches before I could complain. My stomach rumbled as I tore open the first package. Charcoal nosed me, and despite my hands shaking with hunger, I shared it with him as I walked toward my horses.

I handed the second sandwich to Josephine to hold while I mounted Oxide. "Thanks. It's good to see you."

She smiled and handed me my sandwich. "Let's talk once we're back in the open."

Ben flicked his mules, and the wagon lurched forward. As the wagon rumbled past me, Dante leaned forward to wave, his hand fluttering. Sally and Akiko rode by next, followed by Josephine and Earl.

Genevie waited for them to pass by before waving me alongside. Our hoofbeats echoed off the rotten buildings as we followed the others down the cracked pavement.

Unlike earlier, she looked clear-eyed and sharp. "So... what the blast happened?"

I tore into my second sandwich and mumbled, "Don't even know where to start."

Genevie pressed her lips together and twitched Gertie's rope.

I stuffed the rest of the sandwich in my mouth, and Charcoal threw me a disgruntled look before trotting off to join the coyote. When I swallowed the last bite, I cleared my throat. "The trip to Leavenworth wasn't what I expected."

"No kidding. You left with one woman and returned with two extra men." Genevie eyed me. "If I'd known you were man shopping, I might have come with you. What was the abbey like?"

"Strange. The building sits by itself on the prairie, like a monument." I sighed. "It's as isolated as Niagara Abbey was."

"An island of men in a sea of grass. My loss."

"Are you looking for a new man?" It might explain her drinking.

"Not necessarily a man, but I miss having *someone* in my life. I'm not talking about sex—sex is always available." Her shoulders hunched as if seeking to escape a memory. "Speaking of sex..."

"*Nothing* happened." Ahead of us, Earl rode beside Josephine. "We're just friends." But what if Dante hadn't joined us for dinner in the abbey? Before he'd shown up, the blazing energy between us had been intense.

*Done was done.* I sighed.

Genevie held her flask out toward me. "How does it feel to have a sister?"

"It's bizarre." I waved off the flask; the sun was barely above the horizon. Was I already supposed to know what I felt about the news? I hadn't even had time to wrap my brain around the disappointment that my parents weren't in Vegas Depot. Trust Genevie to ferret out yet another subject I wasn't ready to talk about. *A sister.* Josephine wasn't close to her brothers, and as far as I knew, Ben, Earl, and Akiko were only children. "Do you have siblings?"

"Technically, no. My mother raised my cousins, though, so I grew up with them."

"Where are they now?"

"They died when I was fifteen." Genevie's mouth tightened. "They were in a depot bunkhouse, and someone closed the fireplace flue. No one woke up in time."

My stomach churned. "They burned?"

Genevie shook her head. "They died in their sleep from carbon monoxide poisoning."

"How many?"

She grimaced. "Thirteen."

"Horrific."

"I know. It's why my mother moved. The guilt... she settled farther south. I planned to join her after I finished my apprenticeship, but I met Whistler."

"Then Sally knew your cousins."

Genevie grinned. "She'll tell you they were a couple of hooligans." Her smile faded. "Their deaths hit her hard. Death is hard, full stop."

The dead man at the bottom of the waterfall flashed onto my mind's canvas, and my breakfast threatened to come back up. I checked the road behind us, and though no one had appeared to have followed us from the depot, I couldn't shake the hunted feeling as we rode across the prairie.

# CHAPTER EIGHTEEN

Everyone brightened when Ben stopped the wagon for lunch in the shade of a trio of honey locust trees. Their branches drooped in the heat, their foliage a showy Cadmium Gold.

Genevie pulled her flask from her pommel bag and took a long drink. She wiped her mouth and held it out to me, but the whiff of whiskey was enough to unsettle my stomach. "Thanks, but no."

Could I ask the group to postpone the break? We had traveled six hours from the depot, but I wanted to put as much distance between us and it as possible. Each kilometer increased our safety... and diminished the chance anyone could follow us. But everyone appeared exhausted. We had forgone sleep to ensure our early departure, so how could I ask them to travel without breaks? Sighing, I tied my horses, then checked on Talbot. He still hadn't woken.

"Has he said anything?" I asked Ben.

He shook his head. "Dante gave him something around ten. He's been quiet ever since."

Dante was on the other side of the clearing chatting with Josephine, Earl, and Sally. Catching my eye, he smiled, his hand fluttering like a butterfly.

I waved back. "How did you find Dante?"

Ben hesitated. "He's... friendly. What's with her?" he asked, pointing to where Akiko lay in the grass, frowning at our newest map. Charcoal lay beside her, his chin resting on the small of her back while he watched Donkey snuffle through the grass.

I shrugged at Ben, then ambled toward Akiko. "That's quite a frown."

She looked up, her eyes troubled. "I don't know where to go next."

I dropped to the grass beside Akiko and tickled her ear with a purple coneflower. "Next?"

She slapped the flower away. "There's a big river but no bridges. Look."

As tempting as it was to tease her frown away, Akiko never exaggerated these things. If the river was large enough, it could give pursuers time to catch up. Unease twisted and coiled through me. I craned my neck to look at the map. "There's a bridge here, but it's south."

"How far south?" asked Sally, approaching from the other side of the map.

"The first bridge..." Akiko slapped her palm on the map, making Donkey snort. "It doesn't matter because right after, there's another river, and another and another." She scowled. "It's all squiggles."

Ben joined us, glancing from me to Akiko. "What's wrong?"

"This is the land of squiggles," she muttered.

I studied the map, but she was right. Every route with an intact bridge ended, taking us farther into the shaded areas designating swamps or estuaries. I'd assumed the prairie lands would be wide open, making tracking us near impossible. But if there were few choices, could someone follow while remaining out of sight?

"Can we go north?" asked Ben.

"No, no, nope," said Dante. "Uh-uh." He shrugged, his shoulders nearly reaching his ears. "Talbot said that Carter fellow is setting up something *fierce* in the north."

If Carter had settled in the north, nothing could compel me to take Akiko anywhere near there. "So, we go west." Akiko frowned and tapped the large river west of us, but I shrugged. "We'll figure it out when we get there."

***

THE RIVER WAS WORSE THAN I'D EXPECTED. THE LONGER I stared at it, the wider it grew. From the edge of the bluff, the far shore was approximately three kilometers away, across the swath of sluggish, brown water.

"We need to find another place to cross." Josephine's mouth tightened. "I'll go north."

"Keep Gertie for me, and I'll go south," said Genevie. "Do us some good to blow the cobwebs out of our ears."

Chucking her flask into the river would be more helpful than a gallop, but I said nothing and leaned forward to take Gertie's lead. Genevie saluted me, spun Bertha south, and took off at a dead run.

Startled, Gertie followed. She jerked at the end of her lead, then cow-kicked Magnesium. He grunted and swung to the side, knocking into Oxide. I glared at them while turning Oxide to untangle the three of us. "Quit!"

Once the horses settled, I picketed them to the trees and checked on Talbot again. His cheek was hot and dry to my touch, but whatever Dante had given him had worked, and he slumbered on.

Ben gestured toward the storm clouds building north and east of us when I rejoined the others. "We need to cross the river before either of those storms hit."

Earl patted Bruno, who danced from side to side. She was even more pale than usual, but when she spoke, her voice was clear. "I—I can't swim."

Terrific. "Neither can Akiko, so we need a solid plan to cross it." Though I'd intended to reassure her, Earl paled more, making her freckles more pronounced.

"Here comes Josephine," called Akiko, pointing north.

We waited silently, and when they got closer, Josephine slowed Fox to a trot. The chestnut was drenched with sweat, his sides heaving as he jogged toward us, but Josephine was pink-cheeked and smiling. "We're in luck; I found a ferry. Is Genevie back yet?"

I shook my head. "Why don't you take the others to the ferry and get the loading process started? I'll wait for Genevie." For once, no one argued. I watched the others trudge out of sight. The minutes stretched interminably, giving me plenty of time to brood.

When Genevie finally appeared, she whistled a merry tune and was clearly in no hurry. By the time she reached me, I'd checked the tack on all three horses, untied them, and climbed onto Oxide. Bertha wasn't even sweaty. Worse, the bright spots on Genevie's cheeks told me she'd continued working on her flask during her 'gallop'. I must have scowled because Genevie frowned and snatched Gertie's lead from me. "Where did everyone go?"

I gritted my teeth. "Josephine found a ferry."

"Oh, good. There's nowhere to cross south of here."

She leaned forward to dismount, so I spun Oxide north. "Come on. They're waiting."

The skies east of us were now an ominous Amethyst, and the steady eastward wind nearly flattened the grasses. Relentless, it carried the scent of hot algae and minerals as we rode north. By the time we arrived, Ben had the mules and wagon loaded. Lady and My Darling were also on the ferry, tied to the back of the wagon. Earl waved and loaded Bruno.

Josephine cantered Fox toward us, her forehead creased. When she reached us, her voice was thin and rushed. "There's not enough room for everyone on the ferry, and the ferry-woman isn't sure she'll make it back before the storms hit."

I evaluated the flat boat. "How many can she carry?"

"Besides the wagon and the mules, she can take seven."

I counted the horses on my fingers and looked up. "Then we're fine. I'm sure we can squeeze Donkey on somewhere."

Josephine shook her head. "While we waited, an older couple showed up. They're in a dreadful hurry."

I groaned and glared at Genevie. "Then we have two and a half horses too many."

Josephine nodded, her brow wrinkling.

We could insist our party stay together and force the older couple to wait, but it didn't feel right. Especially when it was Genevie's fault we hadn't arrived together. If anyone should stay behind, it was her.

Genevie swayed in her saddle.

I rubbed my face and sighed. Done was done. "Okay, I'll wait here. You should both load now."

Genevie wavered and sloshed her flask. "Jo should go first."

Josephine shook her head. "With everything going on, you'll be more useful to Ben. Besides, if I stay with Matthew, Donkey can go with the rest of you."

"Are you sure?" I glanced at the sluggish water. "The next crossing might be rough if the rains hit hard enough."

Josephine appeared resigned but calm. "I can handle it. Why don't I hold your horses while you help Genevie load the rest?"

The other horses crowded forward when Genevie led her mares onto the ferry, both animals stomping their feet and swishing their tails. "Calm down, girls!" Genevie bellowed.

I squeezed Donkey past the angry mares and settled him between Lady and My Darling, nodding to Sally. I turned to go, but Akiko sprang toward me and clung to my waist. "Mouse, we need to get this ferry moving."

"I don't want to go without you." Tears leaked down her cheeks, and she tightened her grip on me.

"Charcoal, come!" The dog worked his way through the livestock and panted happily when he reached us. "Can you watch him for me? He's going to be upset his herd isn't staying together."

Akiko hesitated, but nodded, releasing me to crouch down and hug him.

I slipped backward off the boat and waved at the ferry captain. She nodded, and the steam wheel hissed as she guided the ferry forward.

When he realized I wasn't staying on the boat, Charcoal began barking, his volume increasing as the gap between us grew. But despite Charcoal's vocal distress, my anxiety lessened. Each meter the ferry traveled took Talbot farther out of reach from any pursuers.

The ferry was several hundred meters into the river when a commotion broke out on the deck, followed by a splash.

"Here comes Charcoal," murmured Josephine.

I sighed but stared at the sky, where a single flake fluttered from above. "Snow?" I caught it in my hand where it lay on my palm, feathery soft.

*Ash.*

My gut twisted, but I said nothing and waded into the muddy, brown water to haul Charcoal from the river.

When she spoke, Josephine's voice was barely a whisper. "Is that smoke?"

"Yes." I dumped Charcoal onto the bank. "The prairie is burning."

# CHAPTER NINETEEN

There was nothing to do but wait.

I fidgeted, my gaze revolving from the dark clouds north of us to the hill behind us, to the ferry slowly scrolling across the water.

By the time the ferry reached a quarter of the way across the river, Charcoal was beside himself. He paced, panting. He circled us incessantly, agitating the horses. The third time Magnesium kicked at him, I grabbed Charcoal by the ruff of his neck and pinned him to the ground. He cowered as I scolded him, but as soon as I released him, he was up and pacing again.

The coyote crept closer. She remained out of reach, but her willingness to come near us increased my sense of urgency. I studied the river again. "Is the current increasing?"

Josephine scanned the water and shook her head. "I don't think so." She sighed and stroked Fox's neck. "Have you ever swum a horse?"

"No." My stomach lurched as I imagined swimming in the brown water. I checked the ferry's progress and glared at Charcoal again. He laid down, panting, but as soon as I looked away, he was back on his feet, circling us. "Will it come to that?"

"No, I'm sure we're fine. The wind is blowing east toward Kansas Depot."

I swallowed and checked the ferry again. The return voyage would be faster, and we'd board in a flash. "Did Ben tell you Dante propositioned him?"

"Ben could do worse." Josephine chuckled, but it sounded strained. "Speaking of Ben, you could try one of his breathing exercises."

I took a deep breath and held it for a count of four before releasing it slowly. I repeated the process until my heart calmed, trying to ignore Charcoal's interminable circling. The bands of pressure encircling my chest eased, and I rolled my neck to relax my shoulders. "The Headmaster at Leavenworth was not at all what I expected."

"Oh?" Josephine turned toward me, her smile warm, as if thankful for the distraction. "Tell me."

Even as I pictured Tanaka, my gaze slid to the ferry and the northern horizon before I focused on Josephine. "First, he was ten or fifteen years older than I."

"Is that unusual?"

Was it? "I don't know. Leavenworth was the fourth abbey— the fourth *occupied* abbey—I've visited. Tanaka was quick to smile and crackled with energy. I'd never met another artist with a Japanese heritage either."

"Any chance you're related?"

"Who knows? Maybe." I leaned my elbows on Oxide's saddle and studied the river again. "Life is funny, isn't it?"

Josephine's expression turned thoughtful. "What did he say when you told him about McCully?"

"He said little, but he increased the guard and doubled the defensive drilling time for everyone." Remembering Tanaka's response made me wince. With everything happening in Toronto Depot, I'd forgotten about the self-defense lessons I'd promised Akiko. "It's what I assumed McCully would do when I warned him about Carter."

The ferry neared the halfway mark, the figures on deck barely distinguishable.

Josephine tugged on her lip while watching the ferry. "Then some abbeys are *not* spreading religion."

"You're right. I hadn't made the connection." I released a long breath, gazing west, north, and east. Other than the coyote moving closer, nothing had changed.

Charcoal licked the coyote's snout on his next circuit. She whined in response, and after he passed, her gaze fixed on me again.

I jerked my chin in her direction. "What do you think of her?"

"The coyote?" Josephine glanced over her shoulder. "She unnerved me at first, but she's become a part of the scenery." She thought for a moment. "You're like a Pied Piper."

I blinked. "A what?"

Josephine rested her cheek against Fox, her eyes locked on the ferry. "It was a legend from *Before*, about a rat catcher with a magic pipe. He wandered around the countryside, offering his services. If a town hired him, he'd play a tune to lead the rats away."

Fox snorted when Charcoal's circle tightened, but Josephine stroked the horse's neck to settle him. "However, one town refused to pay him after he had rid them of their rats. In retaliation, he played a tune, and the town's children followed him, never to be seen again."

I shuddered. "Thanks?"

"You're like the benevolent version. You've charmed Sir

Donkey, Akiko, and now the coyote." She chuckled. "Me too, I suppose."

I smiled back as a gust of wind lifted the hair from my neck.

Even before Josephine's smile dropped her smile, her face paled, highlighting the scars wheeling across her face.

My voice was little more than a whisper. "The wind."

In unison, we turned and stared at the hillside behind us. The smoke's scent had strengthened, and when I checked the ferry's progress, the span between us appeared hazy.

I tried to swallow, but my mouth was too dry. It went drier still when Charcoal's whine deepened into a growl. My heart hammered as I stared at the hill behind us.

*Nothing.*

I scanned the eastern skyline from north to south. "See anything?"

"No, but the ferry is nearly to the far shore." Fox danced sideways, and she murmured, "Easy boy."

When I turned toward the ferry, the wind gusted westward, blowing my hair across my face. I froze, gooseflesh rising along my arms. The wind gusted again, bringing smoke, thick and bitter.

"Matthew," said Josephine, her voice low.

We waited, our gazes locked on each other.

A wisp of smoke blew past us, and Josephine took a deep breath. "We're going to have to swim."

I blinked, allowing my gaze to flick from her to the hillside behind her.

*Fire.*

Icy sweat trickled down my spine.

"Let's go," she said. Somehow, she held her composure as she mounted Fox and walked him into the water.

Flames raced down the slope behind us, sending Charcoal into a barking frenzy.

Josephine twisted in her saddle to face me. "Listen, I know Oxide isn't fond of water. When he can't feel the ground, he's going to panic, but stay with him. Keep his head pointed at the far shore. His body will fully submerge, and you'll float off him."

I tried to breathe while checking my cinch, but my lungs wouldn't cooperate, and my hands shook.

"Once Oxide is swimming, release Magnesium. He'll follow."

Josephine had Fox in belly-deep water by the time I sprang onto Oxide. I kicked him toward the water, glancing over my shoulder. The lead rope jerked Magnesium. He staggered sideways, his eyes rolling at the flames behind us. The panniers shifted as he staggered, further unbalancing him.

*They're too heavy. He won't make it.*

I vaulted from Oxide and sprinted to Magnesium, my fingers fumbling with the pannier's buckles.

The coyote screeched, her ears flat against her head as flames rushed toward us. The sound sent ice down my spine. Charcoal darted toward her and pulled her toward the water, but she dug her feet into the soft mud and screamed again.

The first pannier hit the ground with a *thud*, startling Oxide. He fought me as I pulled him toward Magnesium's other side.

The brush near Magnesium's tail caught.

I dropped Oxide's reins and caught the buckles on the remaining pannier as Magnesium swung his haunches toward me. When they released, I slapped Magnesium's rump, screaming, "Go!"

Magnesium leaped forward but reversed course, backing toward the shore when the water reached his chest. Oxide plunged beside me, his eyes rolling in panic, but I grabbed his rein and used it to whip Magnesium until the horse launched forward. He submerged under the brown water before his head popped back up. He followed Fox and Josephine without a backward glance.

The smoke and heat seared my throat as I tried to get my foot into Oxide's offside stirrup. Unused to mounting from the wrong side, my foot got stuck. Oxide spun, knocking me over, and I hit the ground. Several blades of grass near my eyes shimmered before lighting. I scrambled to my feet, grabbed Oxide's reins, and dragged him toward the water. He whinnied, splashing into the shallows as the coyote screeched.

Oxide lunged forward but fell to his front knees, chest deep. He froze, and I used the opportunity to snatch the coyote with my left arm and jump onto the horse. She writhed and clawed at my arm, and Oxide bugled his alarm and he lunged into the deeper water. I nearly went over backward, but I grabbed a handful of his mane in time.

Oxide's bucking motion smoothed. As Josephine had predicted, my body floated to the river's surface. The shock of cold water left me gasping, and the current pulled at me as I aligned my body with Oxide's. Despite my maneuvers, the coyote went limp, but her growl rumbled too near my face as Oxide dragged us west.

The roar of the flames merged with Oxide's snorts, and his pace quickened. He surged forward as if determined to catch up with Magnesium and swept past Charcoal, whose nose was barely above water. Panic flared in Charcoal's eyes as Oxide's wake swamped him. With my left arm occupied with the coyote, and my right hand entangled in Oxide's mane, I had no way of helping my dog.

If I let go to grab him, Oxide would pull away, and I couldn't swim with two canines under my arm. If I switched my hands, I could lose the coyote, and I didn't know how well she could swim. But if I did nothing, Charcoal wouldn't make it.

My heart wrenched as Charcoal's nose slid under the water again. "Charcoal, come!"

His eyes brightened at the sound of my voice, and he struggled harder, his nose rising above the water.

"Good boy—good chap. Come!"

He sped up more, his eyes locked on me.

"Come on!" Images of picking him from his whelping box sprang onto my mind's canvas. He'd been round and soft, his floppy ears two perfect black triangles. The memory of his puppy breath and the sensation of his needle-sharp baby teeth stung my eyes. He swam closer, nearly within reach. "Good boy! Just a little more. Come on Charcoal, come!"

If I did this, I had one shot. The far shore was an eternity away, and without help, Charcoal wouldn't make it.

I nodded my head in time to Oxide's rhythmic snorting as the dog swam closer.

*One shot.*

Charcoal faltered before speeding up again, and I shouted encouragement. He'd nearly reached my shoulder when I shifted my body, floating nearer to him as I counted Oxide's snorts.

*Three... two... one.*

On the off-beat of Oxide's forward movement, I released my grip on his mane. Kicking as fast and hard as I could, I scooped my right arm around Charcoal and reached forward to bury my fingers in the floating tangle of Oxide's mane. I grunted as my grip locked into the horse's hair, and quit kicking. Charcoal rested his head on my biceps, his body pushed forward by my chest. I treasured the warmth of him; even with the exertion, the chilly water sucked feeling away from my body.

The extra drag slowed Oxide, but he continued swimming, and the far shore drew closer. I relaxed onto my right side, and Charcoal licked my face as I pulled the coyote in closer to him, using him as a buffer between me and her.

Magnesium snorted behind us, the sound never in sync with Oxide's breaths. My mind drifted while I floated along, so when Oxide's pace changed, the sensation jarred me senseless. Oxide bounded forward, trying to rip my right arm from my shoulder. I released Charcoal and the coyote, hoping neither would be kicked by the horse's flailing legs. Oxide continued to lunge forward through the shallow water in a hopping-plunge, his hind hoof striking my limp legs. I shouted as pain reeled down my leg and my feet dragged over the river's muddy bottom.

Oxide climbed from the river, yanking me toward the bank. My body sagged as I lost buoyancy. With my right hand locked in his mane and my back against his shoulder, I couldn't turn or get my feet beneath me. Because I couldn't let go, I hopped along with him, shouting his name until he finally stopped. He trembled as I scrambled in the thigh-deep water, trying to stand. I continued to shout his name until Ben wrapped his arms around me. He lifted me long enough to allow me to untangle my fingers, and when he released me, my legs buckled. I dropped to my knees, spluttering as my head submerged beneath the murky water.

Ben hauled me from the water again. My chest heaving, I spat out river water, heavy with minerals and rust. South of us, Genevie chased Magnesium. He galloped through the knee-deep water, his tail high with panic.

"Charcoal?" I gasped.

"There," said Ben, pointing.

On the shore, Charcoal lay on his side panting, with Akiko

crouched over him. Halfway up the bank, the coyote shook, spraying water from her coat in a silver arc.

Catching my breath, I patted Oxide's rump. His hind legs shook, but he bobbed his head, licking and chewing. I leaned against him and turned east. The sight of the charred hillside roiled my stomach. Shrubs burned like candles along the water's edge, releasing oily black smoke into the air. The memory of a fire-blackened skull popped onto my mind's canvas, and I vomited into the river, my sick adding to the fire's stench.

# CHAPTER TWENTY

Sally waited with me on the shore while the others chased after my loose horse. Her eyes were bright, but she said nothing and patted my cheek while we waited for them. I cradled my strained hand to my chest. Akiko squirmed between us, taking my other hand. She squeezed it, her hand fire-hot in mine.

Genevie joined us last, having run the farthest. She was more clear-eyed than earlier, as if the afternoon's events had sobered her.

"Are we all here?" asked Sally, peering around at us.

"Except for Talbot," muttered Akiko.

My desire to get Talbot away from the depot reignited the moment I glanced at the wagon. For all I knew, they were after him because of me, which also put Akiko in danger. "Does he know we're okay?"

Ben shook his head. "He slept through the whole thing."

"How?" Josephine tilted her head back to look up at Ben. "Hasn't he been out for hours?"

Ben focused on Dante, and a sly smile slid across the artist's face. "He was in tremendous pain, and I have hashish."

"You have hash?" Genevie's eyes brightened. "I have pain."

Dante giggled. "Come see me later."

"Enough." Sally clapped her hands twice, lowering them after we refocused on her.

"What's hash?" whispered Akiko.

Bending forward, I whispered, "Don't know." I gave her temple a quick peck, and she snuggled closer to me, pulling my left arm across her collarbones. Her warmth seeped through my wet clothes.

"... or set up here along the river," said Ben.

I'd missed the first part, but didn't have the energy to ask him to repeat it.

Earl folded her arms. "How likely is another fire?"

Ben scanned the sky north of us. "The fire on the other side has burned itself out, but if we get another thunderstorm, it's possible this side will light up too."

"So," said Dante, his hands fluttering while he spoke, "we can camp here, or continue west, or travel north, or wander south?" He waited, his palms facing the sky, but no one said anything. "I mean, it sounds like the only option off the table is crossing back over the river."

Akiko's snort was nearly a snicker, earning her a glare from Sally.

"Come on, people!" Dante threw his arms up. When no one responded, he puffed his cheeks. "Let's decide."

"Oxide has a gash on his left hind leg," said Genevie. "Fox and Magnesium are fine, but both are exhausted."

"As am I," said Josephine.

My heart sank. Camping near the river would offer some protection if another fire broke out, but we'd also be visible from the other side. I'd rather chance leaving the riverbank and traveling west.

Sally looked at me, and I shrugged. Although it was unlikely anyone followed us through the fire, I still wanted to put more distance between us and Kansas Depot. "I don't want to look at *that* all night." I jerked my chin at the charred hillside across the river and Akiko tightened her grip on my left forearm. "Let's keep riding."

"You have no horse to ride," said Genevie.

"What about Magnesium?" asked Akiko.

My gaze slid to where Genevie had tied my packhorse. He was still wearing his packsaddle's rigging... but nothing else. Dismay flooded through me, and I groaned.

Sally paled. "What is it?"

"We've lost our art supplies."

"*What?*" Dante's shriek rang in my ears.

I winced. "I had to drop the panniers to give Magnesium a chance. Each pannier was nearly forty kilograms *without* the weight of the water."

Ben's frown deepened. "What else were you carrying?"

My mind went blank. "I don't know. Someone packed for me."

Genevie sighed and ticked her fingers. "Art supplies, clothes, the maps, and Dante's brown bag."

"My *valise?*" Dante shook his hands, his face creased with alarm.

Sally made a note on her clipboard. "What was in it?"

Dante's melodramatic posture was so comical it took every gram of my control not to laugh. He stood with one hand on his left hip and the other on his chest, his face a mask of outraged indignation. "Only *all* of my winter clothes, my favorite riding boots, and my spare brush."

"But you don't ride," said Akiko. Her mouth twitched like she, too, suppressed her giggles.

Dante glanced down at her. "Little girl, you don't have to *sit* on a horse to wear a magnificent pair of boots. If I'd known travel was like *this*, I might not have left home."

*Home.*

My mouth went dry, and it was my turn to panic. "What about my painting?"

Genevie's eyes brightened. "It's safe in the wagon, along with your sword and Dante's short swords."

Dante went silent and dropped his arms. "Well, it's something."

When he raised both arms, sweeping them back and forth in double arcs, Akiko copied him, a delighted expression on her face. "It's like a 'W'!" She spun away from me and twirled toward the wagon.

My gaze flicked to Genevie, but she shook her head. "They're wrapped and secured up in the ceiling struts. She can't reach them."

I took a deep breath but nodded. If my coat was in the panniers, my sketchbook was gone. The small sketchbook I carried for tiny improvements was in my trouser pocket, but it was wet, and I'd lost my pencil. My stomach twisted—the loss of art supplies was a blow. If we needed hospitality or supplies, it would be hard to find hosts willing to support a group as large as ours, with only butchering or smithing to trade. Ben's engineering and Josephine's scholarly arts were valuable, but their professions required time or materials beyond what was workable while traveling.

Tanaka had mentioned the former headmaster at Leavenworth Abbey had scoured the prairie for art supplies, but maybe they had overlooked some. Besides, even if the next depot held no supplies, traveling to it would move us farther from Kansas Depot. "Since we've lost our art supplies, I suggest we detour to the nearest depot."

Josephine's brow wrinkled. "I'm not sure I remember which was the nearest."

I scanned the hillside for Akiko. "Hey, Mouse!"

She grinned when I beckoned and popped into the circle between Earl and Genevie. Her grin widened as she mimicked them, folding her arms across her chest.

My mouth quirked, and I failed to keep the smile from my voice. "Do you remember which depot was closest to here?"

Her brow wrinkled, and she shifted her feet to copy Genevie's stance. "There were two, but I think Oklahoma Depot was closer."

Genevie smirked as she noticed Akiko's posture. She shifted her weight and raised her left leg. Without changing her expression, Akiko copied her again.

"Oklahoma Depot was on the southern route, wasn't it?" asked Ben.

Still standing on one leg, Genevie raised her left arm. Akiko copied her again.

Josephine's lips twitched. "Yes. Does it matter?"

Ben shook his head. "I remember thinking the northern route was more mountainous, and the southern was more arid."

"Perfect." I raised my left arm and leg to copy Genevie and Akiko. "After this swim, I'm good with dry for a while."

Akiko's chest shook as Josephine and Dante raised their left legs and arms to join us.

"Earl?" asked Sally.

Earl scanned our faces before shrugging. "I can't swim, so dry works for me." She raised neither her arm nor leg but flashed me her lopsided grin and took a step backward away from the circle.

Ben released an extravagant sigh and raised his arm and leg, leaving only Sally standing in the circle on two feet. In unison, we stared at her. Akiko's face turned bright red, and she clamped her lips to suppress her giggles.

"Nun on a bun, we're heading south," said Sally, raising her left leg and arm.

One-legged, we stood in the circle grinning at each other until something thumped inside the wagon and Talbot shouted, "Where the blast is everyone?"

---

By the time we stopped for the night, I was exhausted. We turned in after a hasty meal, but each time I closed my eyes, my thoughts spun and whirled. As the others drifted off, I shifted again, trying to find a comfortable position. Everything ached. Wide-eyed, I stared at the canvas tarpaulin above me, barely visible in the dark, longing for sleep. For any escape from the relentless scrolling of the day's events across my mind's canvas. From recalling every stupid choice and decision I'd made. Fresh waves of pain continuously rolled through my shoulders, sending spasms down my arms and my fingers twitching. The pain berated me for my foolishness.

*Akiko needs a home.*

With no home and no family, she couldn't afford to lose me, too. It was my responsibility to find a home for her, a safe place for her to grow into her dazzling talent. My need to find a safe place for her renewed the familiar heartache and yearning to find my parents. But not for answers to the questions plaguing me my life over—not unless those answers could also provide me guidance on how to protect my daughter. While everyone here loved her, none of them had a home either. Worse, none of them knew how to nurture an artist. But if I found my birth family, Akiko would have someone to care for her if something happened to me.

Charcoal shifted his chin, his breath like a warm question against my hand, and I gave in, sat up, and slid the dog from my chest. He sighed and pushed himself into a sitting position, ready as ever to accompany me. Maybe a walk would settle my mind and bring on sleep.

As quietly as I could, I rose and stepped out from under the shelter. The wind sighed across the grasses, and even though we'd traveled hours after leaving the river, a faint scent of char lingered in the air.

Charcoal trailed behind me as I wandered up a hill, pausing at the sound of ripping grass. "Hullo, Sir Donkey." No matter who tied him to the picket string at night, we found him loose each morning.

The little animal's head popped up, his long ears swiveling in the moonlight. I rubbed the donkey's ears, and Charcoal huffed before trotting toward a stand of shrubs near the crest of the hill.

In the dark, someone murmured Charcoal's name. Cresting the hill, I found Earl sitting on a rocky outcropping. She shone in the moonlight, and my heart fluttered. In the steadiest voice I could manage, I said, "Butcher."

She leaned backward, resting her weight on her hands. "Artist."

I settled into the grass near her rock and lay back to look at the stars. "Couldn't sleep?"

"We still doing the unvarnished truth thing?"

I rolled over onto my side and propped my head up, thankful for the dark, thankful she couldn't see the guilt twisting my face. "Absolutely."

"To see you on the riverbank with the wall of fire racing toward you" –Earl's voice cracked– "terrified me."

"Me too." I rolled back and traced a constellation with my finger. "Remember when I told you about Brookfield burning?"

"Mm."

"Ever since, my nightmares have involved Akiko disappearing or flames." My arm thudded on the grass. "Or both."

When Earl said nothing, I traced her profile against the starry sky with my finger. The movement reminded me of the pastel class... and our lost art supplies. I balled my fists and pressed them into the ground as hard as I could. "What are you afraid of, Earl?"

"Besides watching you dance in the flames?"

I snorted.

"To disappear without a ripple." Earl tilted her face up toward the sky, but her eyes were closed. "Perhaps it's why I never learned to swim."

The donkey shuffled, restless, and I sat up, scanning the moonlit grass behind us. Less than five meters away, the coyote froze and sank to her belly. "Hullo. If I hadn't lost my art supplies, I'd sketch you to find your name."

When Earl twisted, the coyote flattened and slunk into the shadows. "Dante calls her Neblina."

"Neb Leena?"

"Neblina. He said it meant mist or smoke or something, in Spanish."

"I like it." I mouthed the unfamiliar word as the skittish animal crawled toward me. Her wide eyes reminded me of Charcoal's earlier panic.

*Something's wrong.*

The hairs on my arms rose, and I sat up, twisting.

Earl tensed. "What is it?"

I rose and scanned the horizon in every direction, my nerves jumping. "Have you heard thunder?"

"No." Earl slipped off her rock and scanned the northern sky. "What is it? Another fire?"

"I'm not sure," I said, glancing at Neblina.

I'd barely finished the statement before the wind gusted, bringing the scent of rain and decay. The donkey's head whipped up, and he brayed before scrambling down the hill toward the wagon and horses.

"There!" Earl pointed south.

Lightning flashed, and the smell of rain grew stronger. A long rumble rolled across the grass, and Neblina pressed herself against my leg.

Alarm snaked through me. *Not again.* "Come on!"

We raced down the hill, and I skidded to a stop at the shelter. "Wake up!"

"What is it?" Ben asked, fumbling with the flint. I shielded my eyes from the flare of sparks.

"There's a storm, south." Earl wheezed as she fought to catch her breath, her face so pale she gleamed in the dim light.

Dante bolted up and gasped as another round of lightning flashed. "Twister!"

"A what?" asked Genevie, buckling her belt.

"It's a twister!" Dante's face was now nearly as pale as Earl's. We gaped at him until he spun twice. "A funnel! We need to get underground *now*."

"Where?" demanded Sally, her voice shrill and tight.

Josephine pulled her hair back and tried to secure it, but the gusting winds tore it from her fingers. "Are you talking about a tornado?"

Dante screeched, "Yes!"

Josephine's eyes widened, and she turned toward Ben. "It's a rotational storm with the power to suck things up."

Akiko tugged on Josephine's sleeve with enormous eyes. "What kinds of things?"

"Dirt, water, even *cows!*" Dante spun, shrieking, "Move!"

"Where?" Sally bellowed again.

Josephine whipped around to face me. "Can't you draw something?"

Her fear sent my heart crashing. "With what? We lost *all* our art supplies."

Akiko tugged on my tunic. "What about charcoal?"

I turned, looking for my dog.

"It's in the wagon," said Akiko, "in one of Genevie's empty buckets."

*Our homemade charcoal.*

"Get it, please," I said, my voice barely a whisper. Even with charcoal, I needed *something* to improve, but we were on open grasslands.

The winds strengthened, and the horses whinnied, pulling at their pickets. Why had I insisted we move farther into the empty prairie? At least at the river, we could have sheltered along its narrow banks. We'd have been safer at the toe of the slope than out here on the wide-open plains.

"Okay, so how do we get underground?" Ben spread his hands wide. "What are we talking about? A cave?"

Earl's voice was tight as she crowded closer to me. "Can you draw a cave large enough to hold all the horses?"

Earl pressing against me brought Neblina to mind, and my imagination briefly painted pointed ears onto Earl's head. When I shook my head to reset my focus, her face fell, and she stepped away from me. I wanted to protest the misunderstanding, but this wasn't the time. The lightning strikes were closer now, the thunderclaps increasing in frequency. Each boom sent my thoughts spinning while freezing my muscles in place. A horse whinnied in panic. It was too much; the attack on Talbot, the prairie fire, fording the river. How much more could we endure?

Genevie shoved my shoulder. "What about the overpass?"

"There's a small creek in the gully, but it shouldn't be more than ankle deep." Josephine twisted toward me, her expression hopeful. "Can you work with it?"

I squinted through the dark, trying to picture the overpass. "Is it wide enough to shelter everyone?"

"If not, you'll use *art*." Dante's breath came in gasps as he wrung his hands.

*Art.*

Dante's words cleared my head and freed my feet. I was already moving past the picket line toward the overpass when Ben pushed his way through the milling horses toward his mules. He shouted, "Hurry—we haven't much time!"

# CHAPTER TWENTY-ONE

Akiko darted from the wagon with the charcoal. I took the bucket from her, and we sprinted toward the overpass. I slipped and staggered down the incline, the bucket banging against my thigh like a discordant bell. My feet splashed in the shallow water, but I ignored the cold and raced up the gully. Behind me, a large splash followed Dante's yelp. I slowed and turned, but Akiko was already helping him up.

The overpass supported two widths of pavement, each nearly four meters wide. Together they spanned a ten-meter gully, supported on either side by large concrete blocks. Man-made slopes led up from each side of the gully, meeting the pavement near the apex on each side. In the dark, the structure looked intact, but the uneven sliver of light in the center showed the paved surface was weak and sagging.

Genevie splashed into the gully, leading two horses in each hand. She voiced the question rattling in my mind. "Is it big enough?"

It wasn't, but it was the best option we had. "We'll make it work."

Akiko darted forward and took Lady and Magnesium from Genevie, pulling them farther under the edge. Donkey crowded in behind them, his ears flicking and twisting as he brayed.

"Move up," Sally ordered from behind them.

Genevie pushed her mares to the side but handed their leads to Sally. "Here. I'm going to go help Ben."

"We need light!" I called to Genevie.

Dante stepped out from under the overpass, shivering in the moonlight. "Light for what? We have nothing to draw on."

Josephine hurried toward us, carrying a lantern. It swung as she moved, casting grotesque shadows on the concrete supports.

Akiko clutched at my arm. "You drew on the tower."

"You're a genius." I beckoned to Josephine. "Can you hold the lamp while we work?"

She nodded, her face white. Behind her, Fox danced from side to side, his neck and chest covered with sweat. When Josephine raised the lamp, he swung sideways and knocked Akiko over. She fell face down into the shallow water. I bellowed and crashed into the horse's hip with my shoulder, knocking him away from Akiko. I snatched her from the water, and she clung to me, sobbing. When I attempted to set her down, she fought me, entwining her arms around my neck and her fingers through my hair.

*We're running out of time.*

Instead of consoling her, I dropped to my knees. When her feet touched the ground, she stumbled backward.

I reached out to grip her shoulders and steady her, then didn't let go until she focused her dark eyes on me. "If the storm comes this way, the horses will panic. I need you to climb up and sit under the overpass, out of the way."

She shook her head and flung her arms around my neck,

but I peeled them off me. "Listen! Keep Charcoal safe for me. We don't want him trampled, right?" I pointed at where he circled the nervous horses, snapping at their heels. "Please?"

Her chest shuddered with sobs, but she trotted up the incline and tucked herself onto the ledge at the top.

I snapped my fingers at my dog. "Charcoal, watch Akiko!"

He looked where I pointed and galloped up the incline to guard the girl. Donkey followed them, climbing as far as he could up the slope.

With Akiko and Charcoal out of immediate danger, I evaluated the scene. Ben had maneuvered the wagon into the gully, but with our horses milling in the center of the overpass, his mules couldn't move forward.

Josephine thrust the lantern toward me while assessing the melee. "Here. I'm needed elsewhere."

I fumbled with the lantern and nearly dropped it when my finger sizzled against the hot glass. My yelp startled Fox, who whinnied, setting the other horses off. Genevie's mare swung sideways and crashed into Bruno. He reared, his eyes rolling, nearly pulling Earl off her feet.

My heart beat so hard it was hard to focus my eyes, so I closed them. Ben and the others could handle the horses. My efforts were best used here. "We need to extend the overhang on both sides."

"How?" Dante's eyes were glassy, his pupils so dilated his iris looked black in the lantern's strangled light. "What are we doing?"

The words stuck in my dry mouth. "Drawing."

"We can't!" Dante stepped closer, panting, his breath fetid with panic.

It took everything I had not to swing the lantern at his head. Arguing would get us nowhere. Without the storm, I would have circled the structure to find the best vantage, but it would reach us in minutes. Our best shot was to work on each side independently.

"Dante, can you extend the far side while I work on this one?"

"Extend what? The *overpass*?" His head whipped toward the front side of the structure before swinging back. "Are you crazy?"

Instinct told me to slap sense into him, but Headmaster Sinclair's voice popped into my head. "Inspire, instruct, and when all else fails, attend to it yourself."

"Okay, how about something smaller?" I pointed at the narrow gap above us, between the lanes of travel. "Can you close the gap?"

Dante nodded, so I took a handful of charcoal and handed him the bucket. "I'm going to work near the edge, so why don't you draw on this post?" I left before he could protest, climbing part way up the incline to skirt the milling horses.

"Bring their noses into the center," Josephine shouted as I passed.

The wind picked up as I neared the northern side of the overpass, the sound eerie. Within seconds, hail crashed down in a thunderous roar. The pellets bounced and skittered, and the lantern's hot glass shattered. On reflex, I dropped it, wincing as the flame hissed out.

The wagon shuddered, the wood creaking as Ben's mules strained to pull it farther under the shelter. From within the wagon, Talbot's slurred shouts frazzled my nerves even more. Genevie staggered toward me carrying a second lantern, and I tried not to judge her unsteady gait. To focus myself, I took a deep breath before sketching the scene on the concrete support wall. At regular intervals, I trotted into the open gully to get a better perspective of the structure I sketched. Rain lashed me in uneven gusts, and the tempo of the lightning strikes increased. Each flash illuminated the sky—Burnt Umber with Diaoxazine Purple undertones.

Between my anxiety and the electricity in the air, I couldn't tell if the sensation in my hands was from art or nerves, but the dark beneath the overpass deepened as I widened the pavement covering us. A rumbling roar reverberated across the prairie, turning my muscles to smoke.

The deepened darkness meant we were safer, but it didn't make it easier to maneuver through the crowded space. To avoid the crush in the center, I scrambled and clawed my way up the other incline and staggered south.

The gap between the lanes was nearly closed, and when Dante shouted for more light, several additional lanterns flared. I shielded my eyes and turned my head, scanning the top of the slope. Akiko was still where I'd sent her. Charcoal covered her lap and Neblina huddled nearby, nearly within her arm's reach. Akiko waved, and I waved back before skidding down the hill toward the southern opening.

This side offered a vast view of the prairie. Lightning strobes intermittently turned the sky an opaque Olive Green, illuminating the funnel's dark shape.

"Hurry, Matthew," muttered Sally.

My first stroke was too violent and crumbled the piece of charcoal I'd been using. I dug into my pocket for another piece of charcoal as the grasses pulsed and danced like waves before a winter storm on the Atlantic. I sketched with short, rapid strokes to set the scene, then hurried toward the opening for an outside view of the structure. Sally grabbed a handful of my tunic.

"Sally, let go!"

Her eyes flicked from me to the funnel shape, but she wouldn't, or couldn't, release the fabric. Desperation clawed at me, and I twisted, tearing the tunic off over my head. I raced into the storm and scanned the scene, trying to memorize the slopes, the lines, the shadows. When I sprinted back to my drawing, Sally was still standing where I'd left her, my tunic in her hands. The second time I passed her, she crumpled, clutching the garment to her chest. I bellowed for Genevie's help but raced past Sally, back to my drawing.

The din of the storm increased. I sketched feverishly while my mind labeled the sounds. There came whistling, like a kettle about to blow, joining the rumbling crash of a spring tide rolling into sea caves. Debris whipped around me as I worked, as though the storm fought my art. Something struck me, and pain seared above my right eyebrow. Blood and sweat dripped down my face, stinging my eyes.

When I'd drawn the scene, I closed my eyes and set my intention. To start this last bit of artwork, I blocked everything out—the panicking horses, the fiery blood running down my face, the roar of the storm, my fear. Everything receded until nothing remained—nothing but the manifestation of my vision. My hand moved to alter my sketch even before my eyes refocused on my illustration. I worked in a state of calm, transforming the simple overpass into a tunnel.

The overhang above me stretched toward the prairie, the light underneath fading. The winds diminished, settling the horses.

*We did it.*

I slumped, my chest heaving as I struggled to catch my breath. With hands on my hips, I spat copper and salt from my mouth. Once my breathing had evened out, I climbed the slope and joined Sally and Akiko. As I approached them, Sally held my tunic out toward me. I took it from her and wiped my face, then shrugged it on. "Everyone okay?"

They nodded, and Akiko pushed Charcoal off her to crawl

into my lap. She wound her arms around my neck and lay her cheek against my neck.

Outside, the lightning flashes continued, illuminating the swirl of debris near the opening. Inside, the lanterns guttered and danced, but the horses remained calm, their noses turned into the center of a circle where Ben, Genevie, and Josephine stood back-to-back.

On the wagon's front seat, Dante clutched Earl against him. He nodded when I waved, but his gaze tracked upward as the pitch of the storm changed. "This improvement was wicked smart, brother."

The pressure of the surrounding air increased, causing Akiko to tense. I stroked the back of her head, but my eyes remained glued to the pavement above us, ready to bolt if cracks appeared. The lantern guttered and threw strange shadows across the faces of the people I loved. "We're safe," I murmured. "We did it."

# CHAPTER TWENTY-TWO

The aftermath of the storm astonished even Dante, the only one of us with any experience of the spiraling land funnels. It cut a swath through the prairie twenty-meters wide, a track of barren dirt stretching as far as we could see. The storm had left little of our campsite, and despite Ben's constant reminders and admonishments, only he, Sally, and Akiko had stored their saddles in the back of the wagon. The loss was calamitous. Even if we hadn't already agreed to replenish our supplies in Oklahoma Depot, the storm had forced our hands.

"We have four riding horses without saddles," said Genevie. She raised one hand, ticking off our names. "Fox, Oxide, Bruno, and Bertha."

"My saddle might fit Bertha," said Ben, "but we're roughly two days from Oklahoma Depot."

"You better stretch it to three days." Josephine sighed and leaned against Fox. "If I'm riding bareback, we're not traveling eighty kilometers each day."

"I'm no good bareback, but if I can have the saddle, I can at least take the pack string," said Genevie, an apologetic expression on her face.

I shook my head. "We may as well let them wander free. They can graze while they walk. It's not like they're carrying anything, anyhow."

We followed the barren dirt track south, with the sun beating down upon us. An occasional tree, wretched and grasping at the sun-bleached sky, renewed the churning in my gut, reminding me of what we'd narrowly escaped.

Without a saddle, I struggled to ride Oxide. I slithered and slipped across his back, wincing when my tail bone jarred against his spine. My thighs burned from trying to clamp onto his swinging shoulders, and more than once, my testicles got pinched between his spine and my upper thigh when I slid to one side. Earl trailed behind me on Bruno, but when I attempted to twist toward her, I nearly unseated myself and spent the next several minutes trying to pull myself back to the center.

Unlike us, Josephine floated around on Fox, and even raced Akiko and Sally. Their peals of laughter made my grim experience even more irritating.

The wagon lurched to a halt, its wheel sinking into the loamy dirt.

*Not again.*

I slid from Oxide, groaning, and tottered forward to help push it out. Before I reached it, a flash hit my mind's canvas. I had had no intuitions about *Home* since leaving Toronto Depot, and I brightened, trotting toward the wagon, eager to see where this shape fit.

*I have no art supplies.*

The disappointment crawling through me must have been visible in my expression.

"I know," said Dante. "What a pain. This is what, the fourth time today?" His face scrunched as we put our shoulders against the backboard and shoved the wagon. With our help, Ben's mules pulled it from the rut, and Dante scowled at his hand. "Dirty."

If we'd been on a hard-packed surface, I might have asked to travel on the wagon too. But adding my weight would increase the likelihood of getting the wagon stuck and slow us further. "Leg up?" I asked him.

The afternoon shadows had grown long. Akiko raced toward me, her hand covering her mouth.

"What is it?" I asked as she swung Lady alongside Oxide.

She lowered her hand and made a gagging motion. "We found a channel of death."

I blinked. "A what?"

"A channel of death."

Sally trotted toward us.

"A channel of death?" I asked when she joined us.

Sally clucked her tongue. "The storm left a rotting crap sack behind."

"Dead fish, frogs, and prairie dogs," said Akiko. She pretended to gag again. "But it's not the worst part."

I wrinkled my nose as I pictured the scene. "What's worse than a swath of storm-killed animals?"

Akiko made a disgusted noise. "The coyote ate some of it, and Charcoal rolled on a squished fish."

"Animals," Sally said, her nose wrinkling.

"He's sleeping with you tonight," Akiko and I said in unison. I scrambled for another retort, but Akiko cackled and kicked Lady into a lope to catch up to the wagon.

Sally glanced behind us. "They've been conversing all day."

I steadied myself with my left hand on Oxide's neck to look back at Earl and Genevie. "About what?"

Sally's smile stretched wider as I squirmed, rubbing the back of my neck with my hand. Akiko's squeals drew my eyes forward, where she raced toward the horizon with Josephine beside her.

"Come on," said Sally, kicking My Darling into a jog.

Oxide obliged, and I bounced on top of him like a sack of potatoes until he caught up with My Darling.

Ben smiled at us. "They're scouting for a campsite."

*Finally.*

I squinted and shaded my eyes. "Is that a depot?"

"Looks like it." Ben clucked to his mules. "Or at least the remnants of one. I thought it would be better to camp near something we could shelter in—if needed."

Josephine and Akiko returned a quarter-hour later, their smiles wide and eyes bright.

"It's a long-abandoned depot," said Josephine.

"No one home," Akiko reported. "We-cheeta."

"Wichita," Josephine corrected.

Ben and I exchanged glances. Would an abandoned depot be safe? We may find shelter but wouldn't see danger coming until it was upon us.

"I'm ready for a break," said Dante, rubbing the small of his back. "This wagon isn't the luxurious ride I'd envisioned."

It took effort to swallow my retort and not complain about the pain in my tailbone, testicles, or even my rubbery legs. But I also wanted to stop for the day. "It's an opportunity for shelter and shade. I'm in."

Ben's nod was slow, but he hastened his mules. We made no progress toward the distant buildings over the next hour. If Josephine and Akiko hadn't already ventured nearer, it would have been easy to dismiss the jagged skyline as a mirage or shared hallucination. But I locked my attention on the horizon and hung on grimly. Eventually, the distant structures sharpened.

The dirt track gave way to cracked, buckled pavement. Despite Ben's care, the wagon jolted and bounced along the route. We passed slowly through a kilometer of crumbling concrete foundations before we neared what must have been the core of the depot.

Oxide and I sighed in unison as we passed beneath the shade of a towering building. The air was thick with rust and something like kerosene, and if anyone lived here, the clatter of our hoofbeats crashing off the stone and concrete structures would have heralded our arrival.

No one came.

We weaved our way toward the center of the depot. Many structures had fallen, choking the roads with rusted debris. Few standing buildings remained, and none of them appeared whole.

When Ben pulled the wagon to a stop before a four-story building, Akiko squealed and vaulted from Lady. "A castle!"

"Not so fast!" I slid from Oxide and staggered toward her. "Where do you think you're going?"

"Just 'sploring." Akiko scuffed her toe on the pavement, kicking at a dandelion. The weed's fluff exploded and floated toward me.

"The buildings aren't safe, Mouse." I craned my neck to look up. The rounded corner of the building led to a peaked turret. I shivered, reminded of the room they had trapped me in on Welland Island.

"Definitely not," said Dante, strolling around the corner. When he beckoned, I handed Oxide and Lady's reins to Josephine and followed them.

The limestone blocks on the north side of the building had

fallen, leaving the structure open to the air, like a child's dollhouse. We backed up, craning our necks.

"I wish we could go up there," said Akiko, sighing. "I miss air views."

A tower extended upward from the middle of the building, some fifty-odd meters up. What looked like a wooden rowboat hung from one point, near a round hole in the wall's face.

I shivered, remembering Beck's boat while wondering about the power of a storm capable of hurling a heavy boat over fifty meters into the air.

***

WE FOUND THE OKLAHOMA DEPOT WAREHOUSE IN AN odd, domed building. Its roof sported interlocking, triangle-shaped panels, in an eye-popping gold.

"Heya, Travelers. Well met." The librarians beamed at us.

"Thank you. I'm Sally Park, and we're here for saddles, dried foodstuffs, and art supplies."

The head librarian's expression turned dour. "Ah."

Sally sighed and turned toward us. "Why don't you scavenge while Ben, Genevie, and I negotiate for hospitality?"

Why they bothered was a mystery to me, considering the doubt on the librarians' faces, but the rest of us wandered south, drawn by several towers hulking above the cracked pavement and prairie grasses. The first listed to one side, like a rotted tooth, but south of it stood three towers untouched by time, ranging between seven and nine stories tall.

Josephine tried the first door, but it stuck. "Can you force this one?" She stepped aside and gestured at it.

Earl and Akiko flashed me expectant smiles, so I rammed my shoulder into the door until it gave a tortured groan and opened. The air inside was dead and still, thick with dust and mildew, but cooler than outside. I rubbed my bruised shoulder and followed them down the first hall, peering into the empty rooms we passed. Perhaps they had already picked the depot clean of anything useful.

"We're supposed to find something usable here?" Dante scrunched his nose. "This place is as useless as Wichita Depot."

Earl sighed and crossed her arms. "Why don't we split up and search separately?"

I squinted at the sunlight glinting off the intact glass. If we couldn't barter, Akiko could create saddles, but to do so without exposing her secret required privacy.

*Privacy and a blasted good explanation.*

Josephine shrugged, but Dante nodded. "I'll take the tallest tower if you tell me what we're looking for."

Josephine tugged on her lip. "Housewares or leather furniture? Anything we can fashion into a saddle, I suppose." She held her hand out to Akiko. "Want to come with me?"

Akiko nodded and skipped toward her, but I cleared my throat. "Actually, since there are three towers and three of you, I thought Akiko and I could explore the brick buildings across the street."

Akiko skipped back toward me, but when we stepped back into the heat, she wilted and turned sullen. Her shoes made a harsh rasp as she dragged them across the fractured pavement, and I made a point of ignoring her sighs. The hot wind flicked my hair into my eyes, but other than Akiko's sighs and the scraping of Charcoal and Neblina's nails, the depot was silent as we crossed the roadway.

Akiko halted when I didn't stop at the first dwelling. "Aren't we searching here?"

I shaded my eyes and gestured at the buildings the others were searching. "I want privacy, so we don't have to lie to anyone."

Charcoal panted and moved into a patch of shade created by the dwelling's porch. Neblina trailed after him, her ears pricked and eyes watchful.

Akiko's eyes widened. "You're going to try creating again?"

"If we can find a suitable surface to draw on." I pulled a piece of our homemade charcoal from my pocket and wiggled it. "If it doesn't work, I have another idea, but I'll need your help."

We walked for more than a half hour while I searched for signs of children. At last, we found a dwelling with a rusted swing set in its side yard.

"Why here?" asked Akiko.

I shoved open the door. Sunlight poured through gaps in the back wall, but the structure seemed safe enough. "If I can't manifest a saddle, you're going to create toy horses wearing saddles."

The building creaked as we skirted a hole in the floor. A broad plank table stood near a large, broken window. I pulled out a chair for Akiko.

"Stay here while I look for something to draw on."

She nodded and climbed into the chair. A weary expression crossed her face. "It's almost as hot in here as outside."

I handed her my canteen. "Here."

I climbed up to the second floor, the stairs shaking and groaning with each step. The ceiling on the upper level had more holes than roof, and the wooden floors beneath each hole were dark with rot. The first bedroom was bare. In the second, several crows fled, their caws trailing after them when I opened the door. In the third room, I found books and the toys I'd been hoping for. None of the mildewed creatures were horses, but I pulled several off the pile, sneezing at the dust I raised by touching them.

Out of curiosity, I turned to the bookcase. The spine of the first book crackled when I opened it, but the illustrations inside were undamaged and compelling. I studied the style before grabbing as many as I could carry.

Downstairs, Akiko was at the table where I'd left her, drawing on a large sheet.

My brows knit. "Where did you find that?"

She pointed to a bare spot on the wall. "It hung loose, so I pulled it off." She fingered the material. "It's like paper-cloth. What are those?" Her nose wrinkled when I set down the moldy, pillow-like toys.

Charcoal sniffed them but backed away, sneezing.

"Toys," I said as I pulled another strip of paper from the wall. "For scale."

"Scale?"

I nodded and lay my sheet on the table. "If I can't manifest a saddle, I need you to create saddles to fit stuffed toys like these."

Akiko's brow furrowed. "Why? I could create real saddles."

"Because it would be much harder to explain how we 'happened' to find exactly the four saddles we needed." I stacked the pile of children's books I'd brought down. "Look through these for a saddle to copy." She opened her mouth to argue, but I continued before she could. "The saddles you create must look like toys. We'll take them back so Dante and I can improve them into real, usable tack."

Akiko released her breath like a hiss. "Wicked smart plan."

# CHAPTER TWENTY-THREE

The terrain west of Oklahoma Depot was drier and more ragged. Within a week, the lush prairie grasses gave way to shorter, scrubby grasses growing in red and blue-tinted bunches. Spiky, spreading shrubs boasting vibrant yellow, orange, and red tubular flowers grew between the grasses alongside familiar purple coneflowers. Lemon beebalm perfumed the hot winds with a citrusy scent.

The days blended into each other, giving me plenty of time to brood about Carter, Talbot, Erena, and a home for Akiko. Given the heat and increasingly short supply of water, we couldn't hurry our pace, but the landscape neither inspired me nor invited us to linger.

Determined to maintain the status quo with Earl, I spent the long days away from her and tried to content myself with watching the western mountains grow ever larger. If Earl noticed my polite distance, she neither did nor said anything about it. Instead, she spent her traveling hours chatting with Dante, Josephine, and Ben.

Genevie spent her days alone, her eyes clouded from drink.

No one else seemed to mind, so I said nothing either. But I took to riding sweep so I could monitor her.

Oxide snatched mouthfuls of Yellow Indiangrass as we walked, and Akiko laughed at the spray of gold and purple flowers hanging from his mouth.

Josephine brandished the field guide she'd found in Oklahoma Depot. "Please identify these."

Akiko pretended to groan at the lesson but poured over the guide and identified each plant we encountered as we trudged westward under the September sun.

The plants weren't the only thing changing. While still muggy, the air was no longer an oppressive, wet blanket wrapped around us. Even better, the temperature cooled as soon as the sun set, meaning I could finally catch up on lost sleep.

In the evenings, swarms of starlings swooped and twisted in a mesmerizing dance. Their wings beat a rasping sigh, reminding me of waves lapping across a sandy beach. They painted pictures across the dusky sky, like charcoal dust on paper.

"Another murmuration," said Josephine as she reclined against Ben. "The birds are so attuned to each other they rarely collide."

"How?" asked Akiko.

When Josephine shrugged, Akiko looked at me.

"Perhaps they can sense and use the energy of the flock." My voice trailed off when Earl shifted her attention from the birds to me. Though I took care each night to put the fire between us, her gaze still had the power to stir me. I swallowed. "Or maybe one clever bird orchestrates the entire routine."

As Earl's lips curved, Dante clapped his hands. "In my next life, I wish to be a starling. I will swoop and fly and never be lonely again." Without warning, he jumped to his feet and ran around the group with his arms outstretched. Akiko leaped up to join him, and together, they twirled and giggled as Charcoal tried to marshal them back into the group.

When the birds landed en masse in a whispered hush, Talbot crossed his arms. "I wish I could see them." For weeks he'd ridden in the dark, the bandages covering his eyes. Even with his eyelids closed, he found the sun's light painful, so he traveled inside the swaying wagon by himself.

A pang jolted through me. "The sun's down now. Let's change your bandage."

Talbot's chin lifted like he was smelling the air. "If there's enough water, I could use a wash."

Sally grimaced. Water had become increasingly hard to find, and we'd taken to using our stores for drinking and cooking, letting the animals slurp their fill from fetid ponds and pools whenever we found one.

I ignored Ben's head shake and clasped Talbot's shoulder. "Sure. I'll help you." I escorted Talbot to the far side of the wagon to undress and circled back to fill a pail.

Sally gripped my forearm after I'd stoppered the cask. "We shouldn't be wasting water."

I chewed on my lip and nodded. "Right, but he's enduring a nightmare, and he got burned trying to protect me. I'll give up my share for tomorrow—I saved most of my water today."

Sally sighed but released my arm.

I held the bucket for Talbot as he unwound the linen bandage from his head. After dunking the grimy rag into the water, he swiped it across his skin. He started with his face and moved to his limbs before finishing with his armpits and groin. Talbot sighed as he worked, and when he finished, he took the bucket from me and dumped the last quarter of it over his head.

"I'm human again," he said, his skin puckering in the cooling air. "You can't know how much I needed it."

My back was sticky with sweat and the pale-yellow pollen floating behind the wagon coated my grimy face, but I said nothing and opened the jar of salve. I hesitated before smearing it on his eyelids. "Your skin is still raw. Are we doing more harm than good?"

"The healer in Oklahoma Depot said it was to be expected." Talbot shivered under my touch. "I have faith."

He waited while I wound a fresh bandage around his eyes before groping for his clothing. His skin had already dried, but he wrinkled his nose as he pulled his tunic back over his head. "I hate to ask, but I need this washed."

The washtub I'd improved for Mama flashed onto my mind's canvas. We'd brought nothing like it, nor did we have a kettle large enough to change. Or lye or water to wash with. I put a smile in my voice for his benefit. "I'll do it the next time I wash mine." My stomach rumbled. "Come on. I smell food."

Ben ladled beans simmered with salted pork belly into bowls and passed them around. The dish was savory with hints of sage and rosemary, and the two heaping bowlfuls I devoured left me heavy and lethargic.

After Josephine and Sally finished washing the dishes, Talbot clapped his hands. "I believe it was Genevie's turn to choose a subject."

Akiko squealed and squeezed between Ben and Josephine. I hid my smile and glanced around our campsite for where Akiko had laid my bedroll.

"Me again, already?" Genevie groaned as she flopped onto her bedroll, propping her shoulders against her saddle. Her brows knit, and the silver flask flashed in the firelight. She opened her mouth but belched.

The sound caused Sir Donkey's head to snap up. When he brayed his displeasure, Genevie flushed, and she patted her chest. "Sorry. Beans."

"Beans it is," said Talbot.

Genevie sat up. "No, I meant—"

"You said beans!" Akiko chortled and stared at Talbot with an expectant smile. "Well? Do you know a story about beans?"

When I spotted my bedroll, I sat grinning at Dante. He'd wrapped his arms around his knees and sported a delighted smile as he waited for Talbot to begin.

Each night we tried to stump Talbot, searching for any subject he didn't have a song or story about. So far, no one had found the bottom of his deep reservoir of tales. Dante had bet me no one would best Talbot before we reached Vegas Depot, and he was probably right.

"Why, yes." Talbot tapped his jaw and raised his finger. "Once, an old woman set about to make her dinner. She brought a pot of beans and several handfuls of straw to her hearth."

Talbot paused and leaned forward, lowering his voice. "She thrust the pot onto the embers and set the straw to ignite. But her eyes were old, and her hearing was poor, so she didn't see what happened next."

Talbot leaned back as Earl settled next to me. In our many weeks of travel, we never ended the day side by side. My pulse leaped; with her beside me, I wouldn't fall asleep.

Akiko wriggled up onto her knees, nearly bouncing with impatience. "What happened?"

Talbot swung his head as if checking no one else was within earshot. "A bean fell out of the pot and landed on the straw, which she hadn't yet burned. At nearly the same moment, the fire popped, and an ember landed right next to the bean." When Akiko gasped, Talbot lowered his voice, and everyone leaned in.

"To be friendly, they had a quick chat and soon learned they had each fled their doom. Since none wanted the old woman to correct her mistake, they conspired to take a trip together."

Akiko jumped up, cackling. "The bean and straw and ember take a trip?"

"Just so," said Talbot. "Shall I continue?"

Ben pulled Akiko back down and folded his arms around her. "Please." Akiko gave a happy sigh and wriggled backward between Ben and Josephine.

"The bean and the straw and the ember trundled down the path until they came to a narrow stream. As he was the tallest, the straw offered to lie across the stream and let the others pass. They agreed it was a good idea, but the ember started across the straw first. He made it halfway before getting scared by the water rushing below the straw. He froze—"

"I know what that's like," said Akiko, jumping up. "I got stuck crossing over a river, too."

"We remember," said Sally. "Sit down, child."

Akiko skipped to Sally and settled next to her. "Go on, Uncle Talbot."

It was the first time she'd called him uncle. It gave me chills, but worked a greater effect on Talbot. His throat convulsed as he swallowed several times before continuing. When he did, his voice was scratchy. "The delay was too much for the straw, and it scorched brown before snapping in two. At once, the straw and the ember fell into the stream and disappeared."

His lips curved at Akiko's gasp. "The bean, being a silly bean, found the situation hilarious and laughed and laughed until its sides burst. It lay like a broken piece of mush until a wise tailor with a kind heart heard its plaintive cries. The tailor sewed the bean up, which is why most beans today have a seam down one side."

Genevie sat up. "Do they?"

Dante laughed and clapped his hands. "A song please!"

"No, a riddle," Josephine called.

"I bet he has one that does both," Earl murmured near my ear. Her voice and warm breath sent shivers sliding down my spine. She lay back on her bedroll, and I longed to join her.

Talbot sighed. "If someone will bring my guitar, I'll do both at once."

Akiko scrambled into the wagon. When she shimmied back down, she had the guitar we'd found in Oklahoma Depot clutched in her hand. Breathless, she placed it on Talbot's lap before returning to her spot next to Sally.

Earl sat up while Talbot strummed the guitar to tune it. "Told you." Her warm breath tickled my ear, sending shudders through me.

Talbot launched into a mournful tune about cherries and chicken bones, but I could concentrate on nothing but Earl—her closeness, her scent. I lay back and slowed my breathing by counting the stars. Earl lay back too, her shoulder brushing mine. Our breaths synced, and despite my misgivings, a drowsy torpor fell over me, the sounds of the others drifting away.

"Nut king slapper, watch out!"

Sally's voice jolted me awake, and I opened my eyes in time to see Bruno rear, his platter-sized hooves waving in the air above us. Without thinking, I twisted left, grabbed Earl's shoulder, and pulled her right. She rolled on top of my chest and lay on me, stunned, as Bruno plunged up and down, the *thud* of his hooves pierced by his screams of rage.

Josephine raced over to pull the horse away from us, and I wrapped my arms around Earl as she trembled, her heart knocking so hard it could leave bruises on my chest, too.

"You okay?" Ben stooped next to Earl and straightened, holding a battered and mangled snake. Akiko gasped and described the scene to Talbot.

His voice was tight. "Matthew?"

"We're fine." My voice cracked, and I cleared my throat after Earl rolled off me. "Fine."

Ben frowned as he examined the carcass. "This looks ominous." He pinched the tail and shook it, the sound like dried rice pouring into a pot.

Josephine examined it before flipping through the field guide Akiko had left on her bedroll. "Here. I think it's a rattlesnake." She scanned the page. She looked up, her face troubled. "It says rattlesnakes are vipers with hollow fangs capable of injecting venom. If bitten, the remedy is anti-venom. The guide says to tourniquet the limb to prevent the poison from spreading."

Akiko's eyes were enormous in her pale face. "Why do they rattle?"

"To warn animals to stay away from them." Josephine pursed her lips and looked at us.

"Did you hear a rattle?" I asked Earl. She shook her head.

"Here's more." Josephine scanned the page. "Rattlesnakes can't regulate their body temperatures and seek heat sources to stay warm."

Everyone sprang to their feet.

Genevie's eyes flashed as she shook out her bedroll. Her voice bordered on belligerent. "Better be room in the wagon, Talbot, because you're getting a roommate. I may be the toughest one here, but I'm not sleeping on the ground again —*ever*."

# CHAPTER TWENTY-FOUR

The unrelenting heat intensified as we continued west. To combat the weather, we'd taken to rising near dawn to take advantage of the cooler morning hours. It also afforded the horses, mules, and Donkey more time to graze, which became increasingly important as the vegetation thinned, too.

The last community we'd encountered had been three dwellings squatting in the middle of nothing. We'd stopped, hoping to find a healer for Talbot. A lady there bathed his wounds and gave me a homemade ointment to apply, but it didn't help much.

We pressed on, though we stopped to speak with the few people we encountered. Each time, I asked about a healer. Two of the travelers mumbled something about a boneyard, but upon finding we had no water to share, moved on.

After our experience with the rattlesnake, I improved the wagon so three bunks folded down from each side. The weather was so dry we didn't worry about shelter. The configuration left the top bunk on each side uncovered, but they also boasted unobstructed views of the starry sky.

Genevie moved into the wagon to sleep beside Talbot. Akiko and Charcoal fit snuggly on the padded driver's bench, leaving Ben, Dante, Sally, Josephine, Earl, and me on the fold-down bunks. At first, we balanced the wagon by putting Ben, Josephine, and Sally on the same side, but privacy soon became more of a concern than weight distribution—the diminishing vegetation made making one's toilet even harder.

I'd taken to waking first, slipping from my bunk, and finishing my daily movement before either Ben or Dante woke. This morning, like many others, my eyes shot open with the first trill of birdsong. The predawn sky had a misty, opalescent quality as I trudged away from the wagon, a short-handled spade in one hand and a handful of corn husks in the other. Neblina ranged ahead of me, as silent as smoke, as the pebbled, sandy soil crunched and squeaked beneath my boots.

The landscape lent little cover. Short, stubby, brown grasses grew in clumps around low-growing, greasy shrubs, which shed a scent like heavy, rain-laden clouds. The trees, such as they were, were sparse. They made me uneasy with their grasping, gnarled hands, long-bladed leaves, and shaggy bark. The roots of the older trees reminded me of dusty feet. Like someone had entombed a dozen people standing back-to-back in scaly wood. Had cursed them to stand under the open sky for an eternity.

By the time I'd put sufficient distance between the wagon and myself, the mountains appeared to be on fire; the sky painted in violent Cadmium Red. I stopped to watch, awestruck, as slashes of Carmine and Helios Red painted the underside of the clouds.

No one near the wagon appeared to be stirring yet, so I backed a few steps and loosened the laces on my trousers. My bowels shivered and rumbled with anticipation. The sunrise's performance continued, the colors shifting toward oranges and golds as I shimmied my trousers down. They were stiff with dried sweat and road dust and made an unpleasant rasp as I lowered them. I leaned forward, resting my belly on my thighs before rocking my weight backward into a squat. I didn't even have time to sigh before fangs sank into my flesh.

I sprang forward, bellowing, and half-hobbled, half-hopped toward the wagon, gathering my trousers as I went.

Ben reached me first, his face pale under his deep tan. "What's happened?"

"Snake bite!" I turned my uncovered posterior toward him, then spun away when Josephine, Earl, and Sally rounded the wagon. "Get back!"

My shout caused Josephine to throw her arms wide, preventing the other women from moving forward. Akiko jumped off the front of the wagon and started toward us, but Dante grabbed her arm and hauled her backward, too.

Genevie stuck her head out, her hair wild. "Why all the noise?"

Ben's grip on my arm tightened. "Are you sure?"

"Yes!" Why wasn't he *doing* anything?

Ben bent to stare at my wound. "Did you hear a rattle?"

My vision swam as shudders racked me. "No, but I'm blasted sure a pair of fangs sunk into me."

While Ben examined me, Josephine appeared with her guidebook. She flipped pages and scanned the text, her brow furrowing.

"Well?" My vision narrowed as I struggled to catch my breath.

"It says to prevent strenuous physical activity and get the victim to medical help." She looked up. "We need to find you anti-venom."

"Where?" My voice was nearly a shriek as I spun, flinging one arm wide at the open, empty terrain. Someone giggled as I unwittingly flashed my injured nudity at the others, and my face burned as I snatched my trousers. "The last community was two days back, and we don't even know if they *had* anti-venom."

Nearer the wagon, Talbot swayed. "You're sure it was a snake?"

"I see the marks." Sally's eyes clouded with what I assumed was concern, but she gripped my elbow. "We'll find someone who can help, but since you can't ride, come on."

Fear burned away the last of my dignity and shame, so I let her pull me toward the wagon. The wind was cool against my exposed skin as I clambered into it and flopped belly-first onto Genevie's bedroll.

"What now?" asked Talbot. "Head toward Vegas Depot?"

I blinked furiously and nodded, trying to swallow the lump of panic threatening to block my throat. Talbot prodded my shoulder, unable to see me nodding.

"Yes. I think so."

The wagon creaked forward. Even laying on my stomach, the ride was far from easy—many of the jolts hard enough to crack my chin against the wooden decking through Genevie's bedroll. My stomach churned and nausea roiled. Even when the sun turned the wagon into an oven, I couldn't stop shivering. To distract me, Talbot launched into a poem about a raven. The words flowed rhythmically, his sonorous voice sending me into a drowsy trance.

The cessation of the wagon's movement was nearly as jarring as the snakebite. I lifted my head and gasped. With my limited view, I couldn't identify the strange object from *Before*. My gaze roved over the glinting metal, the frayed edges dripping with wires.

Talbot's chin lifted. "What? What is it?"

I lifted my torso onto my arms and turned to look over my shoulder, gaping at the alien structure. "I think it's an aircraft."

A man with shaggy, matted hair popped into view. He wore several strands of pebbles on a wire which clacked as he moved. "Heya, Travelers."

"Hullo?"

"I'm Hiram Spiegel, and your friends sent me to assess your affliction." He clambered into the wagon and squeezed between me and the wagon's wall, shoving me down when I tried to rise. "There's a good lad."

Hiram's necklaces clunked against my back as he bent over me to pull the towel back. "How long ago was the event?"

My dry throat tightened further as he probed my flesh. "Sunrise."

He sat back. "Thought so."

"Will he make it?" asked Talbot.

"Afraid so." Hiram stepped over me and squatted next to Talbot. "Might as well look at you while I'm here. Your pretty lass is sawing up my old goat, so I may as well earn my keep."

A fiery sensation churned in my heart. I propped myself onto my elbow, hope making my voice thin. "I'm going to be okay?"

"Mm," said Hiram, unwinding Talbot's bandage. "Next time, don't sit on a cactus."

Talbot's chuckle turned into a hiss as Hiram pulled the bandage from his skin. Red and white streaks mottled his raw flesh.

Hiram's touch looked gentle as he prodded the swollen skin around Talbot's eyes. "This still hurt?"

Talbot grunted.

"Good. Since you still have feeling, the burn isn't full thickness and may yet heal." Hiram patted my shoulder. "Pull your trousers up, lad, and get me a fresh bandage."

Heat flushed my neck and burned my face as I fumbled with my trouser laces. "Here," I said, pulling a clean bandage from the sack.

Hiram wound it around Talbot's head, tying a neat knot to secure it. "I wish I could help more, but we have none to spare."

"What does he need?"

Hiram patted Talbot's shoulder before climbing down. "Water."

I blinked and nearly fell from the wagon in my hurry to follow him. My injured posterior protested, but I ignored it. "Water?"

"Your brother is dehydrated. Burns remove a lot of water from the system, and he hasn't been drinking enough."

My stomach clenched. Sally had been right—I should have insisted Talbot drink the water, not waste it on a bath. "Thank you, Hiram. I appreciate—" I stopped, my jaw dropping open as I spun a slow circle.

Ben had stopped the wagon at the edge of what appeared to be a forest of aircraft. They lay in neat rows, one after the other. Some were whole, but others had been ravaged by time, scavengers, or both.

"What is this place?"

"Welcome to the Nelson Boneyard. Come and look around." He squeezed Talbot's elbow. "You can come too, son. My poor Betsy goat should be loins and hams by now."

Talbot took my arm, and we followed Hiram toward the laughter and smell of food.

When we arrived, Ben's greeting was too loud and uncharacteristically jovial. "Hail the wagon, boys! Did Hiram fix your butt?"

"I'm fine," I said, startled by Ben's glassy eyes and dopey grin. "What have you gotten yourself into?"

"They call it spike." Genevie snorted. She was also flushed, but she'd had weeks to become accustomed to an inebriated state. "I call it 'Ben's-not-driving' juice. You cleared and good to go? Did we load up on anti-venom?"

"Something like that." I avoided her eyes until she chuckled. I sighed. "Does everyone know?"

"You bet. Sally rode ahead to look for help. She told us if it *had* been snakebite, you would have died hours ago."

Josephine struggled to wrestle Ben into his seat, the picture improving my mood markedly. I smiled, glancing around. "Where's everyone else?"

"Earl is butchering Hiram's goat, Sally is chatting up their foxy administrator, and Dante is" —she waggled her eyebrows– "busy."

"Oh?"

She leaned closer, leering. "He makes... 'friends', fast."

I smirked and helped Talbot onto a bench in the shade of an aircraft's wing. "Dante is a friendly fellow."

Charcoal streaked past us with what looked like a bloody leg in his mouth, Neblina hot behind him. Akiko trotted after them and caught sight of me. She waved with both hands, each red with gore.

"What have you gotten into?"

"Earl was learning me how to butcher."

I caught her wrists and shook her arms. "Why haven't you washed?"

"Miss Nelly told me to take a sand bath."

"A what?" I stared at Hiram.

He nodded, his ornamental pebbles clattering. "A sand bath. We hoard our water for important things."

"Like spike!" Ben giggled.

I tapped the sandy soil with my foot. "So, she rubs her hands on the ground?"

Akiko crouched, her palms hovering over the dirt, but

Hiram shook his head. "If your hands are dry, I'll show you where the sand drum is."

"Okay!"

I followed them past two aircraft with blue and white checkered curtains in the windows. "Do people live in these?"

"About thirty of us do." Hiram directed Akiko to a round steel drum. "Here we are. Take a handful, step away from the drum, and rub your hands together briskly." He turned toward me. "They keep out snakes and muffle the wind. When it gets chilly in the winter, we pile dried brush and tumbleweeds underneath to burn. They take the bite off the cold and don't damage the metal."

Akiko held her palms up for inspection.

Hiram nodded, but I flipped them over. "Sand or water, you still have to wash the backs of your hands."

"How?" She flopped the backs of her hands together until Hiram mimed washing one hand with the other.

I smiled at him as we waited for her to finish. "How far to Vegas Depot?"

"You'll make it by sundown, but I don't envy your journey."

I stiffened. "Is it dangerous?"

"No, but there's not enough room in the wagon for three of you to lie down, and neither the big man nor your brother can ride." Hiram shrugged. "While it wasn't a snake bite, you put a couple of good-sized holes in your hide. I'm betting you won't appreciate another five hours in the saddle."

# CHAPTER TWENTY-FIVE

The first hour in the saddle was as bad as Hiram predicted. Oxide's normally smooth gait tossed me around like popcorn kernels in a hot pan. No matter which way I leaned, I couldn't stop the saddle from contacting the sores on my backside. At our first break, I hopped off, intending to walk, but walking was no better. The others said nothing about my yelps and squeaks, leaving me with the pretense of dignity. I'd never liked them more.

We arrived at the outskirts of the depot after sunset. Despite being weary and thirsty, we'd *made* it. Our smiles flashed in the gathering gloom.

Akiko stopped Lady next to a sign on the ground. "Welcome to Fabulous Las Vegas, Nevada." Her brow furrowed. "What does it mean?"

"Las Vegas means 'The Meadows' in Spanish." Dante wrapped his arms around himself. "Sometimes Nevada means 'snow-covered,' and sometimes it means 'snow-capped,' but I hope I'm translating wrong. I came to the desert to get away from snow!"

Genevie snorted. "Not much grass here now."

"Or snow," said Akiko, peering into the dusk.

The outskirts of the depot were quiet and dark. The wind whistled through the crumbling buildings, carrying the fetid scents of sewage and rust.

"Come on," said Sally. She clucked to My Darling as Genevie tapped Zeus. The mule flicked his tail but leaned forward into his harness.

I waited for Josephine and Akiko to pass so I could ride beside Earl. We'd arrived, and it was time to refresh our friendship. I wiped my damp palms on my trousers. "I can't believe we're finally here. What are you looking forward to?"

Earl's grin split her face. "An enormous hat and fresh fruit. What about you?"

"Privacy, a snake-free bed, and a bath," I said.

This was a lie. What I wanted, needed—*craved*—was a glass of water larger than my head. Thirst, thick and bitter, clawed at my throat, but all day I'd fought to ignore it, trying not to swallow. Before leaving the Boneyard, I'd donated my remaining water to her for her knives. The water had been precious—and Talbot needed more—but her distress at Hiram's suggestion to clean her bloody knives and bone saw with sand was unendurable.

But as a result, I'd spent the rest of the day miserable, parched by the sun and the dusty road, until all I could think about was water. No matter. I'd drink my fill once Sally got us settled.

The administrator arrived to negotiate with Sally before we caught up to her. Ben's snores rumbled from the wagon. "How will we get him out?" I asked Josephine.

"The silly oaf will sleep it off in there." She shook her head. "Serves him right."

Sally shook hands with the administrator and walked

toward us with energetic steps. "Family meeting! Come, gather around."

"This isn't quite what I'd pictured, but hey, hurray, we're here!" Dante climbed off the wagon, groaning and rubbing the small of his back. "So, Miss Sally, what's the news, and where we gonna snooze?"

The sight of Akiko chortling at Dante's rhyme lifted my spirits, so I joined in. "Come on, Park, it's getting dark!"

Sally peered through her spectacles and clucked her tongue. "I have dwelling assignments, but they're not ideal. I say we go with it and revisit the issue later if we can." She waited for us to nod before continuing. "Now, they only use ground-floor units, so we're housed in different complexes."

The surrounding buildings ranged from one hundred to nearly two hundred meters, but all the upper-floor windows were dark. "Are the buildings unstable?"

Sally shook her head. "It's a water issue. Josephine, Ben, and Genevie are in the Wyndham complex. It's the farthest away, but nearest to the livery."

She handed a scrap of paper to Josephine. I craned my neck to see what was on it and Josephine flashed the crude map toward me.

Sally frowned at her notes. "Matthew, you, Akiko, Talbot, and Dante will stay at the Tropic." She peered at us. "The administrator said it's the nicest assignment, so no complaints. Earl and I are across the street in the Copperfield complex."

I couldn't help glancing at Earl to see if she was as disappointed at the split as me.

Genevie thumped her foot against the side of the wagon. "What about me?"

Sally whirled, her hands on her hips. "You're staying in the Wyndham. Do listen." Missing the colorful gesture Genevie made behind her back, Sally continued, "Since the Copperfield is midway, let's meet for breakfast at nine to work out assignments and labor hours. Now, before we head to bed, I have something to say."

We flashed each other guilty expressions. Had we already done or said something wrong?

"This trip wasn't easy, and went more wrong than right, but we've made it... and nearly in one piece." She swallowed several times before continuing. "I'm proud of us, of what we've accomplished together, and am grateful you invited me to rejoin you."

My heart filled with gratitude for each member of the group. Together, we'd worked through many obstacles and setbacks, endured heat and long days in the saddle, and traveled an astonishing distance. The trip wouldn't have been possible without our four-legged friends either, so I leaned forward and wrapped my arms around Oxide's neck. He bobbed his head and snorted, but his ears wiggled when my fingers scratched his favorite spot.

After Sally's moving words, I was reluctant to dampen the group's mood, but I asked my question, anyway. "What about Erena?" My sister's name was strange on my tongue, and as expected, the smiles slid from everyone's faces.

Unable to see their expressions, Talbot nodded. "Yes. We need to find her right away."

"I know." Sally pressed her lips together. "But we're exhausted, and the administrator promised to make introductions for us tomorrow."

"Is it safe to search for Erena openly?" As tired as I was, the delay was a gift.

"Probably not," she said, and the corners of Talbot's mouth drooped. "Let's keep it between us for now, at least until we learn more about the depot and the people here."

"A good night's sleep will help." Josephine's expression was sympathetic, and she tossed a wry glance at the wagon. "And I promise to keep Ben away from spike until we find her. Here, I'll take your horses to the livery so you can get Talbot settled in."

I flashed her a grateful smile and helped Akiko down. While gathering our reins to hand the horses to Josephine, I caught Earl's lingering look. Perhaps she was disappointed after all. I held her gaze until she pinked and turned Bruno to follow Sally. She glanced over her shoulder to see if I was still watching, sending my heart soaring. I jumped when Josephine cleared her throat, but the leering grin she flashed me was so out of character I barked a laugh.

After handing her our horses, I led Talbot into a garish, ornate building, the lobby's lanterns throwing grotesque shadows across the gilded walls.

A red-faced porter sporting a stringy mustache showed us to our assigned dwellings. One had a sitting area, a kitchenette, and two bedrooms. The other two rooms were singles. Dante took the room across the hallway, leaving the single next to ours for Talbot.

A door on the shared wall had strange locks and no doorknob. "Can we combine these rooms?"

The porter sighed but unlatched the interior door between the suite and Talbot's room.

I led Talbot to his bed, then strode toward the kitchenette. My hand shook as I turned the tap, but no water poured from the faucet.

"Your water allotment includes a half hour at nine and again at six." The porter shrugged. "Welcome to Vegas Depot."

"Have some of mine." Talbot sloshed the water inside his canteen.

My throat tightened, but I pushed the canteen toward him. "You drink it. I'll beg some from Mouse." From the other room,

Akiko shook her canteen to show it was empty, but I lifted my finger to my lips, warning her to remain silent. "You need it more, cousin."

Unlike me, Akiko wasn't ready to sleep and kept up a constant stream of chatter after Talbot retired. Eventually, she tired of my grunts and single-word responses and turned her attention to Charcoal. When she poked him, he groaned and batted her finger away, but swiped at her cheek with his tongue.

Too tired and thirsty to rise from my chair, I leaned my head against the wall. Tomorrow, I'd drink my fill, then figure out how to find a woman I hadn't met, in a depot I didn't know, without using her name *or* openly looking for her.

Akiko and Charcoal jumped onto my bed, waking me. Thirsty and disoriented, I closed my eyes and pretended to sleep, but her cheerful chatter was infectious.

"Fine. Get Talbot up."

"He's up and ready!"

We stopped in the hallway to collect Dante before heading across the street to meet the others in the Copperfield. We were in good spirits as we made our way to the dining hall, but the mood at the table was sour when we arrived. Ben's face was bleak and tight, as if he'd been sculpted from granite. Something was off between him and Josephine, and her movements telegraphed aggravation. In full administrator mode, Sally's greeting was perfunctory. Worse, Earl didn't react to our arrival. She appeared preoccupied and even more withdrawn than usual, showing no hint of the flirtatious energy we'd shared last night.

"I'm starved, and you're late, so we started without you.

Pass the syrup?" Genevie was at least cheerful, but the bourbon wafting across the table from her made me wonder if she'd been to bed at all.

When Ben didn't move, Josephine reached across him, grabbed the syrup, and set it down with a *thud*.

He rubbed his palms over his face. "Sorry, Jo."

"So you said." She pushed her empty glass toward me as a porter delivered a pitcher of water to our table. I filled the empty glasses, my throat tight with thirst.

Sally reviewed her notes. "I've spoken with Francis Lee, an administrator, and have assignments for Josephine, Ben, and Genevie."

I nodded, passing glasses to Talbot and Akiko.

Sally sipped her water. "Ben, their resident engineer needs help to complete a special project. You're to meet her at the archway after midmorning bells."

The water left in the pitcher barely filled my glass halfway. I downed it in a single swallow. "One more?"

Our server frowned and gestured at the table. "You've had your allotment."

"Then I'm sorry to ask. We arrived late last night, and we're still parched from our travels."

He leaned closer, his breath reeking of onions. "We don't like guzzlers around these parts." He snatched the pitcher from me and padded away, disappearing into the kitchens.

I sank back down and stared at Talbot's half-finished glass. Across the table, Ben sipped his water but pushed his untouched plate away.

Genevie stabbed one of Ben's sausages and waved it as she asked, "What about me?"

Sally frowned as she flipped a page. "The hostler wants your help to trim and shoe livestock." She looked up. "You have what you need?"

"Unfortunately." Genevie's expression turned glum. Catching my raised eyebrow, she pantomimed fanning herself. "Nothing like standing over molten steel on a scorching day."

Sally scribbled something and addressed Josephine. "Francis said the librarians here are all new." Sally sighed. "If I read her hints right, the three of them barely have the smarts of a marsh tit, so you're to help organize the warehouse."

She turned to address Dante and me. "You both have today off. I let the administrator know we've brought two artists, but neither of you can make any improvements until you've replenished your art supplies."

"We have our homemade charcoal," I said, glancing around the table.

Sally sighed. "Do you, or do you not, want to search for Erena?"

I pressed my lips together and nodded.

"Good. Now, Francis mentioned the depot runs a daily market at Sayzar's. It's" —the pages rustled as she flipped through the stack— "about three kilometers north. You can accompany Ben." She sat back and drained her water glass.

Earl cleared her throat. "I'd like to see the market too if I don't have an assignment this morning."

"Good idea. See if you can find your cohorts there." Sally tapped her notes. "If we don't find butchering work, I'm afraid they'll assign you with labor hours."

Before we could stand, Akiko plucked an empty bowl from the center of the table. "Charcoal is thirsty, so if you're not finishing your water, pour it here." She held the collected water for him, and my throat tightened as he slurped it happily. But even Charcoal didn't get to drink his fill—Akiko pushed him away and took the bowl back when he'd drunk half. He followed her, whining and hopping on his hind legs.

Mystified, Dante, Earl, and I followed her, threading down

hallways toward the exit. Outside, the sunlight dazzled, the day's heat already breathtaking.

Akiko glanced around, and her brow furrowed. "Can you whistle?"

I tried, but my mouth was too dry.

Akiko frowned like I'd purposefully failed, so I bit my tongue to make it water. My second attempt succeeded, but my whistle was weak, and the note wavered. Even so, Neblina appeared as if by magic. She hesitated in the shadows at the edge of the plaza, so Akiko shoved the bowl toward me. "Here. She won't let me get close enough yet."

I walked the bowl toward the skittish animal. Charcoal trotted next to me, bumping my leg with hopeful eyes. When I bent to set it down, he rushed forward, but I pushed my foot against his chest. "Sorry, chap. You've had your allotment."

He sat and whined but didn't rush the bowl again. Neblina waited until I backed up several steps. She relaxed and drank with dainty laps until a greasy sausage landed on the pavement near her with a *splat*. Startled, she jumped backward, then darted forward to snatch it. After she melted into the shrubbery, I let Charcoal lick the empty bowl.

"Let's get Ben." Akiko struggled to pull the door open. She stopped and panted. "It's too hot. Why do people live here?"

"I love the heat." Dante winked, opening the door for her. "But I'm still thawing from *years* of winter on the prairie."

# CHAPTER TWENTY-SIX

While we waited for Ben outside the Copperfield, the temperature rose several degrees.

"It must be thirty-five out here. In October." Dante raised his arms and spun. "Glorious."

He and Earl continued joking about something, but I was too distracted, thirsty, and hot to join in their fun. How could I find Erena? While I agreed we should keep our search discreet, how would I learn anything about her without asking questions?

"Can we go? It's too hot." Akiko scowled at us from a tiny patch of shade next to the building.

"Maybe we should. Ben looked rough, and Akiko's right—it's too hot to stand around." I flapped the collar of my tunic. "Besides, we need allies, and the market might be a good place to forge relationships."

"And supplies," agreed Dante. He scrutinized the crude map Sally had given Akiko. "Sure, let's go."

Sayzar's Market occupied an imposing, multi-story concrete structure. The exterior was styled with predominantly

Doric columns, though the main entryway included Corinthian details and Romanesque arches.

"Odd," said Dante, narrowing his eyes as he studied the building.

Catching Akiko's curious expression, I tried to explain. "We study many of the old masters at the abbeys, so we're familiar with Greek and Roman architecture."

"Which is this?" asked Earl.

"Both," said Dante. "How delightfully tacky. I love it here!"

Shops primarily occupied the first three floors. When we asked about the day market, a deeply tanned, smiling woman directed us to a staircase and told us to climb to the fourth floor. Our footsteps clanged on the metal staircase as we climbed, the discordant sound unsettling.

On the fourth floor, the bustle of commerce and the layout of the stalls reminded me of Toronto Depot's market. A searing wind fluttered through the open sides of the structure, but the deep shade created a welcome coolness and respite from the morning's heat.

"Maybe we should split up," said Dante, staring at a handsome man setting crates of eggs on a table. "We might cover more ground if we don't travel in a cluster."

I smirked. "Good hunting."

"Hunting?" Akiko looked around. "Here?"

"For art supplies," I said to cover my gaffe. "And useful contacts."

Charcoal trailed Akiko as she led the way down the first aisle, her head swiveling. Even with my greater height, I struggled to take in everything; the market was crowded with people and wares. Earl sauntered beside me. Several times, our fingers brushed as we strolled. Each contact quickened my breath, but the longer touches sent thrilling shivers through me.

On the sixth floor, Earl stopped to chat at a stall displaying a variety of dried meats. Akiko used Earl's distraction as an excuse to cross the aisle to admire a display of carved whistles. I followed, but nothing in the carver's stall caught my interest. The adjoining stall offered woven blankets in a variety of intricate, geometric patterns.

Across the aisle, a tall man with broad shoulders and a sharply defined jaw joined Earl and the stall's keeper. Earl's posture changed, and the way she moved looked almost coquettish.

Something ugly flared inside me.

Earl laughed at something the man said, touching his arm. My fists bunched. She shook her head and gestured toward us, and I jumped.

I didn't want them to know I'd been watching, so pretending to browse, I reached for the nearest blanket.

When my fingertips brushed the weaving, the memory of yesterday's desert sunrise, before I'd squatted on the cactus, flooded back. It was like I was there, watching the sky change, feeling the morning chill, listening to the bird calls. I snatched my hand back and stared at the weaving. The pattern wove interlocking diamonds of Azo Yellow, Cadmium Orange, and Pyrrole Red. A jagged black line crossed the midpoint, like the mountain range.

"You like it?"

I looked up and nodded at the vendor, a plump woman with a pleasant face and frizzy, blonde hair. "Yours?"

She shook her head. "I'm minding the stall. Look around. I'll be back in a moment if anything catches your eye."

I nodded and moved farther into the booth. Nothing like this had happened to me before. Had it been a fluke? My fingers twitched as I turned slowly, trying to decide what to touch next. My gaze snagged on a blanket hanging over a bar at the stall. After checking to make sure Earl and Akiko were distracted, I approached the blanket. My breathing shallowed. The design reminded me of waves during a slack tide, and the color palette set my insides buzzing.

"What are you looking at?" Akiko squeezed into the stall next to me.

"The palette reminds me of *Home*. A murky gray with cool green undertones."

"Winsor Violet mixed with Undersea Green." Akiko beamed. She'd memorized all the pigments I carried on our journey to Toronto Depot. "Weird."

I touched the blanket and smelled the sea. Screeching gulls and the patter of rain on water replaced the market's sounds, and my knees buckled as a wave of homesickness swamped me.

"Matthew?"

The desert heat, sounds, and smells returned like a wallop. I staggered backward, my senses reeling. Akiko bit her lips, her eyes clouded with worry.

"I'm fine, Mouse." Drawing in a deep breath through my mouth, the air tasted of creosote, mineral sands, and jasmine, not salt. I pointed at a vivid, Jade Green blanket woven with interspersed Potters Pink and Wisteria polka dots. "Touch this?"

She pinched the corner and gasped. "It's a meadow!" She reached forward to grab the next blanket, but I spotted frizzy, blonde hair bobbing toward us. I pulled Akiko's hand away and smiled at the stall's keeper.

"Did a little shopping myself." She set down a honey-scented candle. "Make any decisions?"

"Not... yet." Akiko squirmed, but I gave her a warning squeeze. "We'll come back. Are these here every day?"

The keeper smiled. "Nearly, so visit anytime."

# CHAPTER TWENTY-SEVEN

Earl raised her eyebrow when we rejoined her. "Blankets?"

"Just browsing." I gestured to Akiko, who was already wandering up the aisle. "You look pleased."

"Do I?" Earl laughed as we followed Akiko. "I may have made a friend."

Though a scathing reply hovered near the tip of my tongue, Earl's sunny smile softened me. This wasn't the time for snark or sarcasm, so I adopted a teasing tone. "You mean men and women *can* be friends?"

She smiled and took my arm. "Perhaps."

We continued down the aisle, browsing. Near the center of the space, a shaft of brilliant sunlight delivered the scents of frying oil and salt. Akiko and Charcoal scampered up the ramp, paused at the top, and raced back down toward us.

"Hungry?" Akiko flashed me a beseeching smile. "I am."

We strolled up the ramp which led to the top floor of the market. The sun dazzled my eyes, and I shaded them as I took in the throngs of people wandering around the vendor stalls.

"Let's find out how payment works first; I brought no charcoal with me."

Charcoal looked at me and lifted his nose. It quivered, shaking the line of drool hanging from his muzzle.

Near the end of the first row, a man scribbled notes on a clipboard. We approached him, passing several stalls redolent with warm sugar.

"Heya, I'm Matthew Sugiyama."

The man nodded without looking up, his tiny braids swaying with the movement. "Staying where?"

"The Tropic."

His gaze snapped up. "Welcome, Artist."

I blinked. No one else in the depot had expressed excitement at meeting me. "Am I on your list?"

He shook his head and the beads on the ends of his braids clattered. Behind him, Akiko shook her hair, mimicking his movement.

"We reserve the Tropic for minstrels and artists, so I had a fifty-fifty chance of getting it right." He made a note on his clipboard and handed me a wooden button stamped with '333'. "Show this to any vendor, and they'll mark it down. The administrators will sort it out later." He turned to Earl. "Do you need a chit, too?"

I shook my head, but Earl stepped forward. "Yes, I'm Earl Kildare, staying in the Copperfield." He made another note and dug into his satchel. "Eleven."

Her lips curved as she flashed it at me. "My favorite number."

Akiko tugged at my hand. "We okay to eat now?"

He nodded and waved us toward the stalls. "Enjoy!"

Earl stopped at a stall with grilled chicken skewered on sticks. My stomach growled, but Akiko tugged on me. "Look!"

We watched a vendor lower a wire mesh basket into a vat of

bubbling oil. The oil hissed and burbled, emitting a spicy scent unfamiliar to me, and reigniting my thirst.

"Who's next?" the vendor called.

A woman wearing a broad straw hat stepped forward, flashed her chit, and murmured something. The vendor nodded, drained the basket, and dumped the contents into a gleaming metal bowl. I stared as the vendor sprinkled the bowl with flakes of salt and tossed the bowl. She put the fried food into a woven basket and pushed it across the counter. "Next?"

I leaned forward. "Are those *grasshoppers?*"

The vendor nodded and brushed her sweaty bangs away from her face with the back of her meaty forearm. "One or two?"

I grimaced, but Akiko piped up, "One!"

The vendor grinned at the girl. "Spicy or regular?"

Akiko's face scrunched. She chewed her lip and squinted at me.

The vendor flashed me a knowing smile. "First time, eh? I recommend regular."

The idea of eating regular *or* spicy fried insects turned my stomach, but Earl looked as intrigued as Akiko. I swallowed. "Regular, thanks."

The vendor put a huge scoop into a basket. "Eat them quick; they're best hot." Akiko took them and scurried toward the tables at the end of the aisle.

I showed the vendor my chit and her eyes widened. "Very good, sir. If you need anything else, you come right back here, got it?"

She held my gaze longer than I was used to, so I glanced around before leaning forward. "Does anyone vend... water?"

She smiled and tapped the side of her nose. "Visit my friend Ruben. He makes the street tacos at the end of the next aisle. But" —she leaned forward and licked her lips— "make sure you ask to *pick your cut.*"

"Pick my cut."

She nodded and straightened. "Welcome to Vegas Depot. Next?"

Akiko and Charcoal had eaten nearly half the grasshoppers by the time we caught up. Her eyes glowed as she shoved the greasy basket toward me. "Here!"

I took an insect and grimaced at it, but Earl nibbled on one without hesitation. "They're good."

My nostrils flared, but to refuse now was impossible. I closed my eyes and popped the insect into my mouth. It was crunchy, and the heat and salt coating my tongue made my stomach cry for another. "It's like a fried, shell-on shrimp!"

"Tasty," said Akiko, giving another grasshopper to Charcoal. He smacked his lips and sneezed, then begged for another.

I reached for one too, but Akiko slapped my hand. "Manners!"

"May I have another fried bug, *please?*"

She beamed and handed me the rest of the basket. "What's next?"

I hooked my thumb toward the end of the aisle. "Street tacos."

"Okay." She skipped ahead of us.

Earl took another grasshopper when I offered, nibbling the legs off one by one as we strolled after Akiko. "What are street tacos?"

"No clue. The grasshopper woman recommended them."

When we reached the stall, I approached the rotund, pale man. His hair was nearly Cadmium Orange, and he cocked his finger at Earl. "Fellow gingers are always welcome! What can I get you?"

Something in his amiable manner put me at ease. "Street taco?" I said, flashing my chit. "You're Ruben?"

"Sure am. How many and what kind of taco would you like?"

Earl and Akiko shrugged in unison. Not wanting to admit our ignorance, I answered his question with another. "What would you recommend?"

"Today, my carnitas are perfection, but the lengua has been walking away faster than I can cook it."

"We'd like three carnitas, please." After a heartbeat, I added, "But I'd like to choose the cut, if I may."

Ruben's smile broadened as he pulled back the cloth covering his doorway. "Come on in."

We crowded into the tiny kitchen space behind him. The air was hotter inside, but fragrant with oil and an herb I didn't recognize. Ruben said nothing as he dragged a crate forward and opened the lid. Inside were aluminum canteens. He handed the first two to Earl and Akiko. My hands shook as I took the third. Somehow the water was still cold, and though it had a faint sulfurous odor, I sucked it down greedily.

"Again?"

I nodded and nearly drank the second as fast.

Ruben sat on a second crate and opened one for himself after handing me a third canteen. He drank deeply and smacked his mouth, reminding me of Charcoal.

Akiko looked at Ruben but pointed at Charcoal. "May I?"

He nodded until she kneeled to share her canteen with the dog. "None of that now. You'll spill too much." He groaned, climbed to his feet, and rummaged through the crockery piled on the counter, handing her a rust-colored, earthen bowl. "Use this."

When we'd finished our water, Ruben set the empty canteens upside down in the crate. "Our secret, mind. These depot folk get fair twisted about guzzlers. So, carnitas, you said?"

Emboldened, I grinned. "Sure, but we don't know what they are. Or what street tacos are."

"Ah." Ruben's face pinked. "You're new to the southwest."

"We are, but we're enjoying its flavors so far." Water-drunk, I shook my basket of fried grasshoppers. "Besides, you said they're perfection, so how can we go wrong?"

"My man!" Ruben beamed. "It gives me a reason to turn your chit in, too. Never know when an administrator is watching. Head outside, and I'll assemble your tacos."

Even with the illicit water swelling my belly, the carnitas sent my senses swooning. Ruben pulled pork he'd simmered in fat from a bubbling vat and grilled it with slivers of onion and a green vegetable he said was cactus. He put the pork on flattened corn crepes and topped it with wafer-thin slices of sweet-hot radish and sprigs of an herb I didn't recognize.

The pork was hot and savory, the edges crispy. The crunch of the radish, the sweet corn wrapping, and the fresh herb—a cross between mint and parsley—combined into one of the most satisfying bites I'd ever experienced. The flavors and textures burst forward, and I moaned, stuffing the rest of the taco into my mouth. When I'd finished chewing, I wiped my mouth and licked the side of my hand. "Ruben, your taco might be the best thing I've ever put in my mouth."

Ruben's belly shook as he laughed. "My man! Another?"

When I nodded, he set to work. I sensed Ruben was a man who knew how to get things, but could I trust him enough to ask about my sister? Illicit water was one thing, and besides, we paid for it. But until we got to know Ruben better, it was safer to opt for discretion. Happily, getting to know him better would also provide a terrific excuse to return for another crack at his marvelous food.

# CHAPTER TWENTY-EIGHT

We browsed the vendors in the market for another hour. It was the perfect way to spend time with Earl; we had a shared goal and no pressure to make small talk.

But our meal made Akiko drowsy, then cranky. "Can we go back yet?"

I wasn't ready to return to the Tropic and wanted Earl to stay too. "Let's find Dante and see if he will take you back."

We searched three floors of market stalls but didn't find him. Akiko dragged her feet, glowering.

"Akiko, I need to meet the chattier vendors."

Earl brushed my forearm. "Why don't I take her back?"

I hesitated. I didn't want her to go, but it might prevent a meltdown. "Are you sure?"

She smiled. "Walk us out."

When we passed the stall with the woven blankets, I stopped. "What do you think of these?"

"Pretty." Earl fingered the same blanket I'd touched first, but her expression didn't change. "You'll be back for dinner?"

"Absolutely. What time did Sally say dinner was?"

Earl shrugged. "After evening bells."

Even though her words and tone were benign, there was something flirtatious in her expression. Akiko didn't notice, but a thrill shot through me. Did Earl have something more in mind than dinner? I watched her shepherd Charcoal and Akiko toward the exit, but neither of them looked back.

Over the next several hours, I strolled the market, making mental notes of things we might need, and people who may be useful to know. I took special care with the chattier vendors, figuring they could be my best shot at finding Erena. As I worked through the stalls, my thoughts repeatedly returned to Earl and the hint of promise in her eyes.

One stall I visited featured exquisite wooden carvings sculpted with such astonishing detail they could have been artist-made. The vendor was a morose, older woman, disinclined to chat, so I swallowed my curiosity, flashed my chit, and pocketed a beautiful little buffalo as a gift for Earl.

When bells tolled, I jumped, nearly knocking over a heavy, earthen serving bowl. "Evening bells?"

"Oh yeah." The potter's eyes sparkled, and she pointed. "Quitting time."

Around us, the energy of the market transformed. The noise increased as the vendors packed their wares, shouting and laughing with each other.

Despite my large lunch, my stomach rumbled. I fingered the buffalo carving in my pocket and my heart skipped a happy beat. "Thanks for everything. The exit is...?"

She pointed and winked. "See you tomorrow."

I jogged toward the staircase. It rang with footsteps as I joined the throng, clambering down it. Reaching the bottom, I followed the crowd onto the road, but nothing looked familiar. The heat hadn't lessened, and I dripped with sweat as I turned down routes, looking for anything familiar.

The buildings crowded closer as I trotted down unfamiliar lanes, trying to find a vista open enough to get my bearings. My stomach rumbled again and again. If I didn't find my way soon, I'd miss dinner. Perhaps I could sweet-talk a porter into bringing me a plate of leftovers.

When the bells tolled next, I spun, trying to pinpoint the tower's location. We'd passed it on the way to the market, so if I could find it, it shouldn't be difficult to make my way to the Copperfield afterward. My instincts told me to take the next left, so I did, expecting to find the ornate arch and tower. Instead, I stopped short, my breath rattling in my chest.

Ahead of me was what could only be the Strat. Like the tower in Toronto Depot, the Strat was taller than the surrounding buildings and was also a slender, white spire with a bulb near the top. But while it dominated the depot's skyline, it was barely half as tall as the spire in Toronto Depot.

I exhaled, my breath a hiss. If this was the Strat, I'd traveled north, not south—entirely in the wrong direction. Not only would I miss dinner, but I also had a fair distance to walk, which meant less time to spend with Earl.

Frustrated, I spun, then froze. Three men stood behind me. They were each a head taller than the next, creating a sloping gradient. Shoulder to shoulder, they blocked my path. I would have found them comical had they not fidgeted and flashed each other furtive glances.

They were following me. Alarms blared in my head, and I waited for two thundering heartbeats before sprinting east.

"Talbot!" one of them shouted.

Twilight descended as I raced down a narrow alleyway. Near the end, I paused, listening to their pounding footsteps and shouts. They tried to flank me by running down parallel passages. I turned and sprinted north. Their calls echoed off abandoned buildings, but I used every evasive maneuver I could think of, slipping into narrow gaps between buildings and hiding in the shadows as they ran past. Despite my roundabout route, I worked my way south and burst from the dense cluster of buildings near the livery. I darted into the shadowy barn. My chest heaved. Sweat poured down my face as I listened for my pursuers.

Nothing.

While I waited, the familiar scent of horses and hay wrapped around me, slowing my pounding heart. Oxide nickered from his stall, and I patted him before taking a deep breath and trotting south toward the Copperfield.

I stumbled into the Copperfield's dining hall, expecting it to be empty, but my friends lounged around the same table we'd breakfasted at. I opened my mouth to blurt what had happened, but their relaxed, cheerful expressions stopped me. Gone were the pinched squints from too much sun and the worry about too little water in the alien landscape.

I pulled out my chair. "Where's Ben?"

"He skipped dinner and went to bed." Genevie raised her eyebrows. "We weren't sure you'd make it." For once, she was clear and sharp like the Genevie of old.

I flopped into my chair and gulped the water Earl poured for me. Should I say something? Ben wasn't here, and what could any of them do tonight? Perhaps it would be better to wait until morning, and not upset everyone needlessly. "Sorry, I got sidetracked at the market," I said, wiping my mouth. "And got turned around on the way here."

Akiko leaned her head against my upper arm. "Dinner wasn't as good as lunch. Salad and these corn cake things. They were okay, but we ate them all."

"Did you learn anything useful in the market?" Talbot asked.

"Nothing concrete, but I met people who may be useful

later." I sighed and picked at the bowl of wilted greens Sally passed me. "What about everyone else?"

"Dante made a friend," said Akiko. "That's why we couldn't find him in the market."

"So did Genevie," Dante said in his teasing tone.

My eyebrows lifted. "Do tell."

Genevie grinned. "They came into the smithy to ask about a trade."

I waggled a cucumber stick at her. "Name?"

"River," Akiko answered. "*And* they're part of the Avalon Society."

"Not again." I groaned. "They're everywhere."

"Akiko said their complex is across the street." Although Talbot's voice remained neutral, the tightness around his mouth reminded me how much he disliked the organization.

"The Avalon Society is here, in the depot?" I straightened, frowning.

Sally clucked her tongue. "The monstrosity, west of the Tropic. You didn't see it?"

I shook my head. "Our rooms are on the east side, and we came straight here this morning." I turned toward Earl. "Thanks for watching Akiko this afternoon."

"Watching?" Akiko narrowed her eyes.

I poked her ribs until she giggled. "You don't have the best track record of staying found in depots."

"We had fun." Earl grinned at the girl. "Remember the couple I chatted with in the market?"

The sharp-jawed man flashed onto my mind's canvas, but I dismissed him. "The dried meat lady?"

Akiko cackled. "Dried meat lady!"

"They've invited me out to their ranch where they raise game and other exotics." Earl's gaze was steady. "They're considering bringing a butcher on site to process the meat rather than transport live animals into the depot."

Was Earl considering *staying* in Vegas Depot? A pang tore through me. I'd traveled here to find and warn my sister, but I had no intention of staying after we found her. "How far is the ranch?"

"Twelve kilometers west of the depot." Earl filled my glass again. "Sally, can you work it out with the administrators?"

Sally raised her chin. "No problem." She shifted her gaze to Josephine. "Any luck in the warehouse?"

Josephine shook her head. "Not yet. The place is a mess." Her words conveyed disappointment, but her eyes sparkled.

"A lot to sort and organize?" I grinned at her as I picked through the salad.

"Yes. I did find new pack saddles for Gertie and Magnesium though." A smile lit her twisted face. "I'll search for art supplies for you and Dante next."

"Take your time." Dante stretched, catlike. "I'm fully prepared to enjoy some time off."

Genevie snorted. "Because the last two months have been so grueling?"

Dante tossed his head. "It takes a lot of effort to look like this." He framed his face with his palms and batted his eyelashes at Akiko.

"Sure does!" She giggled and copied him.

Beneath the table, Charcoal nosed my hands. I handed him a chunk of tomato, and though he took it, he chewed with little enthusiasm.

Pouncing on the lull in the conversation, Genevie stood, yawned, and stretched. "Boy, am I ready for bed."

"Braggart." Dante snickered.

Genevie leered at him. "Can I help it if I'm irresistible?" She glanced at Josephine. "River is coming over later..."

Josephine nodded, pushing back from the table. "The room is yours. I'll bunk with Ben." She pinked when we smirked at her. "Oh bother, you're like a pack of nosy grannies."

"I resemble that remark," muttered Sally, stacking her papers and tapping them against the table. "We done here?"

My heart sank when Earl stood, too. Maybe I'd misread the situation. The group was ready to go, so I stood to escort Talbot back. Perhaps tomorrow would be better. "Breakfast?" I asked Earl.

My heart plummeted into my sweaty boots when she shook her head. "I'm heading west to the ranch first thing."

"We'll be here," said Sally. "Let's get an earlier start tomorrow. Say, seven?"

"Is the sun even *up* at seven?" Dante made a comical face.

Akiko smirked at his expression. "That's for us to know and you to find out."

The street was empty when we stepped outside. Wanting to see the Avalon Society's compound, I led Talbot west.

Akiko stamped her foot and pointed south. "We're staying *there*."

"I know, but I thought we'd walk around the long way."

She pouted until Dante sighed. "I'll walk you back, Short Stuff."

Akiko brightened and took his hand. "Goody. Later, gators."

"We're just walking around the corner. It will take an extra three minutes."

"See you," she sang, snapping her fingers for Charcoal.

"Fine." I cleared my throat as they crossed the street. "You don't mind the extra walk?"

Talbot's teeth gleamed in the dusky light. "After being cooped in a room all day, I welcome the chance to stretch my legs."

"Tomorrow will be better." Despite my assertion, guilt curdled the meager meal I'd consumed. Why hadn't I considered Talbot's needs even once today? "Can you tell me anything about Erena to help me find her?"

A hot, eastward wind lifted my hair as we trudged west.

I wasn't sure Talbot would answer until he cleared his throat. "I haven't seen her in twenty years. From my mother's letters, I know she settled in Vegas Depot, but not much else." He paused, shaking his head. When he continued, his voice was subdued. "As children, we were close. She was at my house so much it was like she was my sister."

I scanned the street before we turned the corner.

*Empty.*

"I'm not much use right now, but I can stay with Akiko while you search for Erena. I should have enough stories and songs to keep her entertained for a few days at least." Talbot sighed, and his grip tightened on my arm. "I'd reach out to my network for answers, but if Carter is after me, I'm not sure how to proceed. Did you see any ichthys notations today?"

We turned the corner, and I froze.

"Matthew? What is it?"

"A fairy tale farce." I stared at the building and its comical, pointed towers and battlements. Even at this hour, guards patrolled the roof, their posture relaxed as they passed each crenel.

"What is?"

"The Avalon Society's compound." My eyes narrowed as I read the sign out front. "*Excalibur.*"

# CHAPTER TWENTY-NINE

Genevie and Sally were alone at the breakfast table when we arrived. My face fell. I'd planned to tell everyone about last night's events over breakfast. "Small crew so far."

Genevie waved her mug. "Ben and Earl took off at sunrise, but they'll be back for dinner."

I sighed and pushed Akiko's chair to the table. My news would hold until then.

Sally peered at Genevie. "How do *you* know?"

"Zeus and Bruno needed shoes, so I met Tager this morning."

My head snapped up. "Who's Tager?"

"Earl's rancher." Genevie whistled. "If I hadn't already met River, Tager might have turned my head. He's quite a fellow."

A burning flutter ignited in my gut. Was Tager the sharp-jawed man from the market?

Genevie turned toward Sally. "If you can handle my absence today, River asked me on a day trip."

Sally consulted her schedule, frowning. "You're free today."

A teenager with close-cropped hair delivered a platter with bright-gold cakes and strips of bacon. He set down a small pitcher. "Anything else?"

I picked up the pitcher and sniffed it. "What's this?"

The boy's response sounded more like a question than an answer. "Syrup?"

I poured several drops onto my plate. It was the color of faded Nickel Titanate and thinner than honey. "It's not maple."

The boy's brows knit. "Sir?"

Genevie forked two of the golden cakes onto her plate. "What kind of syrup is it?"

The boy's expression cleared. "Agave. Anything else?"

"We're fine, thank you," said Sally, dismissing the boy before I could ask for a mug of tea.

I put a corn cake and two strips of bacon on Talbot's plate. "Syrup?" He shook his head and poked his plate until he found the food.

Akiko watched with her mouth hanging open until I elbowed her. When I held the platter for her, she put bacon and cakes on both of our plates. But when I passed the platter across the table to Genevie, Akiko set my plate on the floor for Charcoal.

Genevie snorted, handed me a plate, and passed the platter back. "Where's Dante?"

I shrugged. "We knocked, but we heard a muffled thud and a clear 'no' when we asked if he wanted to come."

"That's not *all* we heard." Akiko smirked and puffed up. "Want to know what else he said?"

Genevie grinned and leaned forward, but I cleared my throat. "It's neither polite nor appropriate to repeat what he said."

Akiko pouted until Genevie mouthed, "Tell me later."

I ignored their collusion. "Where's Josephine?"

"Warehouse," Sally and Genevie said in unison. Sally clucked her tongue, and Genevie rolled her eyes, but I couldn't tell why and waited for Genevie to swallow her mouthful. "She skipped breakfast and left in a huff."

"Are she and Ben fighting?"

Genevie raised her shoulders and widened her eyes. "It's neither polite nor appropriate to repeat what we heard."

Talbot chuckled, but the idea of Josephine and Ben out of sorts made me uneasy. They were perfect for each other... and had been since meeting in Rochester Depot last winter. But if *they* had troubles, what chance did Earl and I have? Especially now that Earl had met Tager.

Before I could sink into another broody funk, Sally snapped her fingers near my face. "Are you returning to the market today?"

I'd intended to spend time with Talbot, but the way Sally pursed her lips warned me to agree. "I suppose. I haven't checked out the shops on the lower levels, and I'd like to talk to a vendor."

Beside me, Akiko stilled. "The blanket lady?"

I nodded. "Can you keep Talbot company today?" Before Akiko could argue, I lowered my voice, "He was all by himself yesterday."

She pressed her lips together and leaned forward to glance at him. He appeared listless and pushed the food around his plate apathetically. If it was an act to convince Akiko to stay with him, it was a marvelous performance.

Not ready to concede defeat, Akiko eyed Genevie. "You and River..."

Genevie's eyes slid sideways, and a small, private smile lifted her lips, so I cleared my throat. "They already have plans. Besides, Talbot has stories he needs to try out."

Akiko brightened. "I can help with those."

"Good," said Sally. "Because the administrator has asked for a minstrel show tomorrow night."

"Well," said Talbot, "I welcome the chance to earn my keep." He looked pleased, his composure back.

The men last night had been after Talbot. A show wasn't safe, but he and Sally didn't know because I hadn't told them about the chase.

"More than *your* keep." Sally grinned, brightening. "The show will cover Dante, Matthew, and Akiko too."

My gut twisted, the bacon turning bitter in my mouth.

"Then you *really* need my help, Uncle Talbot." Akiko rose and piled all the remaining food onto her plate before taking Talbot's hand. "Come on. You can help me feed Neblina before we practice."

Foreboding filled me. Should I stay with them until we figured out what was going on?

When I stood to escort them back to our quarters, Sally tugged on my tunic.

"I need your help. I'm assigned labor hours at the market, but I haven't been there yet. Can you explain how the chits work on the way?"

While I scrambled for a polite way to decline, Genevie snorted. "Of course, he will. Matthew, the gallant, would never let a damsel sort out her own distress."

Sally chuckled in agreement, leaving me with no way to refuse.

"Right." Bands of pressure wrapped around me as Akiko led Talbot toward the door. "Let me get Talbot back first."

"I can do it," Akiko called. "Bye!"

Charcoal's head swung back and forth as the distance between us widened. "Go with them." He huffed and trotted after them, his ears pricked and alert.

"Come on." Sally plucked at my sleeve as Akiko pushed the door open. "I can't be late for my first shift."

I needed to focus on my search for Erena, but watching them go, I wanted to bail on Sally and stay. But how much trouble could they get into in the Tropic? Dante was across the hallway, and this place wasn't like Toronto Depot. They'd be fine.

"Ask Dante if you need anything," I called.

And though Akiko waved in agreement, I couldn't help but worry.

# CHAPTER THIRTY

We walked toward the market through deserted streets. The morning was already sweltering, hinting the day's temperature would beat yesterday's heat. Worried the men were still prowling the depot looking for Talbot, my gaze darted around. Beside me, Sally remained unusually quiet.

As my gaze roamed, I caught Sally worrying at her lip. "Is something wrong?"

"I have a peculiar feeling, like I've forgotten something, and it's driving me mad." She sighed. "Is it obvious?"

"Perhaps it's this place. The heat."

"Mm. What's going on with you and Earl?"

"Why? Did she say something?" I straightened.

Sally squinted. "Was she supposed to?"

I said nothing until we passed the bell tower and turned west. "I don't know what I'm doing with her."

"Shocking." The corners of her mouth quirked, taking the sting out of her statement.

My chuckle turned rueful. "I've admitted it to her, too."

"I never married, so I have no useful advice for you." Sally stopped and faced me, taking my hand. "But I was a young woman once."

I waited, searching her face.

"All people want the same thing—to be heard, seen, felt, and understood." She patted my hand. "Now, where's this market?"

When I pointed, she squared her shoulders. "Good. Tell me how chits work."

As we climbed the stairs, I explained the system as I understood it, showing her my chit.

A group of people conversing broke apart when we paused on the fourth-floor landing.

A woman wearing an extravagantly large, floppy hat approached us. "Sally Park?"

"Reporting for duty," said Sally. She turned to me. "Good luck today. If I hear anything, I'll let you know." She marched toward the others, her chin held high. The group enveloped her with welcoming chatter, so I headed back down to the ground level.

The keepers buzzed around their shops, but from the side-eye glances they gave me, I understood the market was not yet open for custom.

*Perhaps it's a sign.*

I could postpone the search and return to the Tropic. I could warn Talbot and watch over him and Akiko until Ben and the others returned tonight. But even if he knew about the men, I couldn't imagine a scenario where Talbot would leave the depot without warning Erena. The longer it took to find my sister, the longer we were stuck in the depot. Plus, the shops would soon open, and it would be easier to talk to the shopkeepers before they got busy.

I wandered down the street until I found a bench in a thin strip of shade. Within a quarter-hour, the day market's vendors began arriving, and the narrow route was choked with wagons and carts filled with wares. A group of people gathered near the main stairwell. At some signal I couldn't see, they began the work of porting the vendor's goods up the stairs toward the day market. Given the sloping ramp which connected each floor, hand-carrying each item up the stairs struck me as inefficient. But by the time the midmorning bells rang, every parcel had been carried up, and the wagons had rumbled away.

The shopkeepers were also ready for customers and called greetings to the people passing their doors. As before, I methodically worked my way through the three levels of shops, lingering with the chattier craftsmen. With each interaction, I looked for opportunities to mention Erena's name, but when I did, no one recognized it. Despite the lack of results, I continued, in part, to distract myself from Talbot and the impending minstrel show. Plus, if I exhausted every avenue of inquiry, maybe I could talk him into temporarily leaving the depot.

By midday, my stomach growled, so I climbed to the top level to visit the food vendors. The open air shimmered under the midday sun. Thick crowds browsed the vendors' stalls, so I skirted around the back edge to reach Ruben's stall.

I grinned at the big man. "Hullo, Ruben."

"My man! Today, my asada is perfection. Care to try it?"

I pretended to consider his offer. "Can I choose my cut?"

He beamed. "Come on in."

Once inside, Ruben mopped his brow and kicked the insulated box toward me. I stooped and pulled out two canteens, handing him one. I drank deeply, then peered into the canteen. "Where do you find extra water?"

"I have a good feeling about you, Artist." Ruben groaned and lowered himself onto the other crate. "Ask me again when we're better acquainted."

"Fair enough." I sipped and glanced around the small area. "What else do you have?"

He shrugged, but his eyes gleamed. "Bits and pieces, here and there."

I leaned against the wooden butcher block, my gaze roving over the crates and lidded containers. "I grew up in an abbey."

Ruben nodded, conveying polite interest.

"Each class had a boy who could" –I drank again– "procure things."

Ruben's smile broadened, but he said nothing.

"Whenever one of these resourceful lads graduated, within days, a new name would emerge. I *always* made it a point to befriend the boy."

Ruben finished his canteen and smacked his lips. He twisted the cap back on and reached his hand out.

After I hauled him to his feet, I clapped him on the back. "So, what is asada?"

"Vinegar-marinated meat. You'll love it."

While I waited for Ruben to prepare my tacos, we chatted about the market, and he gave me advice on which vendors to avoid. Again, I brought up Erena's name casually, but Ruben didn't react.

The asada was every bit as good as Ruben promised, but it turned to dust in my mouth when another vendor stopped by to discuss the minstrel show with Ruben. The knowledgeable way they discussed the logistics of serving the expected crowds confirmed my worst fears. With the depot buzzing with excitement about Talbot's show, there was no way the men who chased me hadn't heard about it. I weighed my options. I could postpone my search and return to the Tropic to warn him, but if everyone knew about the show, they also knew where to find Talbot since the depot housed artists and minstrels in the Tropic.

Yet... if everyone in the depot knew about the show, wouldn't the news also reach my sister? Maybe she'd already heard and reunited with Talbot.

Hope crackled through me. I waved farewell to Ruben and hit the stairwell. My feet were a blur as I descended to the fourth floor, intending to tell Sally I planned to go. She wasn't where I'd left her, but while searching for her, I found the blanket stall tucked into a corner near the northern stairwell. This time, a stony-faced, older man attended the stall. He had sharp cheekbones and sunken eyes, as though he'd been ill a long time. His eyes were sharp and a deep, vivid Cobalt Blue, but conveyed distrust.

"Are you the weaver?"

"No." His eyes flashed, and he crossed his arms. "You here for a blanket?"

"Not today."

He grunted and turned away.

I hesitated before asking, "Why is the stall in a different location today?"

The man rounded on me like I'd insulted his mother. "I haven't the time or the inclination to chat, so unless you're here for a blanket, *leave.*"

His hostility left me gaping. My stomach filled with lead, and I fought to steady my voice. "There's no need to be rude."

"You think me rude?" He glared, crossed his arms, and raised his voice. "I'm stuck in the corner because the idiot woman in charge of this floor had neither the discernment nor the foresight to hold our usual space."

The vendor in the next stall popped out, her voice sharp and strident. "Market rules, Marcus. It's first come first serve, so next time, don't roll in at the last minute and expect special favors."

Marcus recoiled like a snake. "Touch nothing!" Without another word, he stalked off.

When I looked at the woman, she shrugged. "Avalon Society," she said, as if it was all the explanation I needed.

* * *

My thoughts churned as I headed toward the Tropic. Other than another memorable lunch, the day had been a waste. The unpleasant exchange with Marcus aside, I'd found no art supplies, and learned nothing about Erena.

Why hadn't I listened to my intuition and stayed with Talbot?

But done was done, and now, hot, footsore, and thirsty, all I wanted was to get out of the sun and rest.

Based on the porter's map, the quickest route from Sayzar's to the Tropic was the same broad road separating the Tropic from the Excalibur. I had plenty of time to scowl at the crenelated castle compound on my way back to the Tropic. The scolding from Marcus had done little to improve my mood. Or my impression of the Avalon Society.

The interior of the Tropic was cooler than outside, and I sighed with relief. But when I reached our rooms, neither Talbot nor Akiko was there. Anxiety coiled in my gut as I scanned the room for clues to where they'd gone. It was too late for lunch, so I crossed the hallway, hoping Dante would know something.

I knocked, and to my relief, Akiko opened the door. "Hi! Come in. We're doing art."

My knees wobbled and my mouth went dry, but when I stepped into the room, Dante appeared as relaxed and cheerful as usual.

*Akiko hadn't shared our secret.*

To hide my relief, I bent to pet Charcoal. Talbot wasn't in the room, but the bathroom door was closed and occupied, based on the noises inside it. I took a deep breath to calm my racing heart. "What are you improving?"

"My wardrobe. The water wardens here won't give me an extra ration for laundry, so I'm altering my clothes. At the least, I'll be presentable at tomorrow's performance." Dante held up a large piece of paper and blew away the charcoal dust before studying me with pursed lips. "Need me to do yours too?"

I glanced down at my grimy clothes and grimaced. I needed to freshen up, but I didn't want to clean my clothes before I'd washed my body.

The bathroom door popped open. A man dressed in a Prussian Blue jumpsuit waved a pipe wrench. "I've opened the valves, so you'll have running water at nine and six." When Dante opened his mouth, the man shook the wrench. "Don't even ask—I can't turn on the water out of band. Besides, you're lucky your allotment comes at six. Unlike some, you'll have plenty of time to wash up before the show."

After he'd gone, I checked the bathroom to make sure Talbot wasn't in there before turning to the others. "Speaking of the show, where's Talbot?"

"In our rooms." My heart squeezed as Akiko's brow furrowed. "Isn't he?"

# CHAPTER THIRTY-ONE

My gut twisted. Not wanting to alarm Akiko, I shrugged and feigned interest in Dante's work. He sketched his clothing smooth, the stains fading into nothing. Akiko sighed happily and peppered him with questions, but my thoughts raced. Where could Talbot have gone? Perhaps he'd taken a wrong turn and had gotten lost in the compound.

"I'm taking Charcoal out for a quick walk, but you guys stay here, out of the heat."

Akiko barely acknowledged my statement, but Dante beamed. "Thanks—I don't want to stop while I'm on a roll."

I retraced my steps across the hallway, but Talbot hadn't returned. Charcoal sighed as though he'd believed my lie. He jumped onto the bed and flopped over, grumbling. His eyes tracked me as I paced the room, gnawing on my thumbnail.

"What now?" I asked.

Charcoal's ears twitched.

Nothing in our rooms suggested where Talbot had gone, so I entered his room through the adjoining door. He'd made his bed, and nestled his guitar in a fuzzy blanket on the single armchair near the window. In the bathroom, he had laid his brush and toothbrush neatly on the counter. His tidiness was a feat for someone who couldn't see.

My chest tightened, imagining the care he'd taken with his things. Perhaps he'd left a clue with his belongings. I bit my lip and glanced around his room, then shrugged and opened the first drawer. Like us, Talbot traveled light, but going through his few belongings without his permission made me uneasy. When I finished searching his dresser, I checked both nightstands.

Nothing.

If he'd hidden something under his mattress, there was no way I could pretend I'd found it by accident. But what if something happened to him and I later learned I could have prevented it? I slid my hands between the mattress and the frame but found nothing. After pulling the furniture away from the walls, I sat on his bed, stumped.

Maybe there wasn't anything to find.

My shoulders sagged until I noticed his dresser had a decorative front edge, leaving no gap between the bottom drawer and the floor. I kneeled and pulled the bottom drawer out. In the cavity between the bottom of the drawer and the floor were four linen-wrapped parcels.

A noise from the hallway caught my breath. I sprang to my feet and bounded to the door, but whoever had made the noise was already gone. To be safe, I bolted both doors before returning to Talbot's things.

The first parcel was a thick stack of envelopes. They were bound with twine, so I set them aside. The second parcel contained a diary. He had written his last entry over a month ago, before his injury. His penmanship was smooth and sure—elegant, like him. A lump grew in my throat as I traced his flowing script with my finger. But recognizing my name, I slapped the book shut.

*Not now.*

The third parcel contained a well-thumbed book with the thinnest pages I'd ever seen. He had slipped sheets of paper between the pages—snippets of poetry, song lyrics, and story ideas. I next examined the densely printed text, the hairs on the back of my neck standing.

*A Bible?*

Nearly every page I flipped to showed underlined text or margin notes. Some were scholarly, but he'd written others like questions, as if conversing with someone over the meaning of the passages. Heaviness filled my core. There was so much about Talbot I didn't know. I'd spent our journey too distracted to do much more than helping him through his toilet or with his meals. If we got him back, I'd do better.

I clenched my jaw. "*When* we get him back."

Setting the Bible down, I unwrapped the last parcel. My throat tightened and my breath caught in a gasping sob. Talbot had framed the pencil sketch I'd made of Gabriel, the dead minstrel Josephine and I had found on the side of the road. At the time, I hadn't known who he was, but after we'd buried him, we'd found my name in the letters Talbot had sent him. It had been the first piece of tangible proof someone knew about my family.

*Family.*

We'd come to Vegas Depot to find my sister but had lost my cousin. I stared at Talbot's parcels. These things were precious to him, so either he planned to return...

"Or he didn't leave voluntarily." My words lingered in the room like an unpleasant odor. My hands trembled as I re-wrapped his things, putting each back as I'd found it.

Talbot didn't have a horse, so there was little point in

checking the livery. Genevie had gone out with River, and Sally was at the market, so neither of them would have any information. Ben and Earl had left early this morning, leaving only Josephine. It was midafternoon, but knowing her, she'd still be digging through musty stacks of papers in the warehouse.

I knocked and opened Dante's door without waiting for a response. He was still sitting at his desk, but Akiko had fallen asleep and lay curled into a ball on his bed. I kept my voice low. "Taking Charcoal for a longer walk. Be back later."

Dante waggled his fingers and flashed a cheerful smile.

The lobby was empty, and no porter appeared when I rang the desk bell. Charcoal whined near the exterior door, so I opened it for him.

The heat outside was like a blast from an oven. Charcoal lifted his leg on a yellowed shrub while I glanced around.

The street was deserted, and I'd seen no warehouse signs, but Sally said it wasn't far. When Charcoal finished, we walked to the corner. The market was north, but ahead of me was the Excalibur. As before, guards strolled the upper perimeter, so if they'd been on shift when Talbot left, it was possible they'd seen something. But if they had, would they tell me?

Every time I'd asked one of their communities for aid, their help came with strings. And while I hadn't ruled out joining one of their communities someday, many of my interactions with them had been unpleasant. Still, Talbot was out there somewhere wandering through this heat, and it wasn't safe for him in the depot.

I sighed, squared my shoulders, and crossed the broad road. A portcullis blocked the main gate, so I called through it. "Hullo?"

A middle-aged woman popped her head around the corner. She stopped a meter from the gate and folded her arms. "Yes?"

"Heya... Lady," I said, unsure how to address her. "I'm Matthew Sugiyama."

Her expression didn't change.

"Matthew Sugiyama, Artist."

"Yes?"

I blinked. This was the first time I'd had to introduce myself to a member of the Avalon Society. "I'm staying at the Tropic, and my cousin wandered from our rooms sometime today. He's unmistakable—he looks like me, but he's wearing bandages around his head, covering his eyes."

Her expression remained unchanged. "And?"

"Have you seen him?"

She shrugged.

I licked my lips. "Sorry, perhaps I've handled this poorly. May I speak to your administrator?"

Her brow wrinkled, but she nodded and left. She returned accompanied by Marcus, the man who had shouted at me in the market.

He stopped when he saw me, eyes narrowed. "What?"

"I'm Matthew Sugiyama, Artist..." My voice trailed off when the woman rolled her eyes. "I'm looking for my cousin."

"He's not here."

"No, I—"

"Anything else?" Marcus interrupted.

I barely managed to swallow my words and keep my opinion of him to myself. "Where is the warehouse?"

"Head south and take the first right." Marcus turned, his back stiff.

"Have I offended you, Marcus? It *is* Marcus, isn't it?"

He stiffened. "We are the Avalon Society, and we have helped you *enough*."

They left without another word, leaving me gaping.

It took Charcoal and me nearly twenty minutes to walk to the warehouse under the scorching sun. Once there, a friendly librarian gave us each a brief drink before escorting us to where Josephine worked. As I'd expected, she'd made a nest of sorts and sat on the floor surrounded by stacks of files, loose papers, and books.

She smiled when I approached. "Whatever are you two doing here? Did you find Erena?"

I shook my head and reached down to help her up. "No, and now Talbot's gone too."

"What?"

I flinched at her tone. "I take it he hasn't been here?"

Josephine stretched, her spine popping. "Ooh, I guess I haven't been moving enough." When she straightened, her gaze was clear and steady. "I haven't seen him. Where do you think he's gone?"

I slouched against the wall. "Best case, he needed to stretch his legs, but got turned around and wandered away."

Josephine tugged on her lip and nodded. "But after what had happened at Angel Falls..." Though her voice trailed off, we both knew what she'd left unvoiced. She squared her shoulders. "Stay positive. Perhaps we can organize a search party. One librarian here acts as a sort of ambassador with many other groups and has an extensive network of associates. Let's ask him for advice."

When I didn't move, Josephine searched my face. "There's more, isn't there?"

"Yes."

"There always is." She sighed. "Tell me."

My ego protested, but if I didn't tell Josephine now, explaining myself later would be impossible. "Last night, men chased me." She paled, but I held up my hand to prevent her from speaking. "They mistook me for Talbot, but I lost them in the dark. It's why I was late for dinner."

"Matthew," Josephine groaned.

"I know. *I know.* If Ben had been there, I would have said something, but you all looked relaxed and happy. And I didn't have answers or anything..."

She swallowed. Nodded. "You know what this means, right?"

I nodded, my gut churning as she reached for my hand. "Talbot didn't wander off."

"What now?" She squeezed my hand.

"Everyone should be back tonight for dinner," I said, squeezing back, "so it's time for a family meeting."

# CHAPTER THIRTY-TWO

After leaving Josephine, I searched the areas south and east of the Tropic for Talbot. Finding nothing, I returned to walk her back to the Copperfield. Intermittent gusts carried a scorching heat and sapped my nervous energy. Still, I wasn't looking forward to confessing what had happened. While trudging northward, I relayed my run-in with Marcus.

Josephine's jaw tightened, and her voice took on a hard edge when we passed the Excalibur. "His rudeness doesn't surprise me." She glared at their compound until we turned the corner. "I'm glad their attempts to recruit you never worked."

I managed a noncommittal nod and pulled the door open for her and Charcoal. Now wasn't the time to admit I hadn't yet decided where Akiko and I would settle. Marcus had been unpleasant and disagreeable, but many of the Avalon Society members I'd interacted with had been warm and kind.

The butterflies fluttering in my gut sank into a leaden mass as I followed Josephine into the dining room. Unless Talbot had reappeared while I was out, I was about to ruin everyone's evening. Confessing what had happened was as appealing as throwing myself on a funeral pyre, and for at least three heartbeats, I seriously considered turning and sprinting away.

As if she'd heard my thoughts, Josephine slowed and slipped behind me. She put her hand, warm and steady, on my mid-back. When I hesitated, she gave me a gentle push. But even with her encouragement, my forward progress faltered. As reluctant as I was to tell everyone what had happened, the sight of Earl laughing glued my feet to the floor.

She'd thrown her head back, her red-orange hair hanging behind her in a smooth curtain, like a waterfall made of fire. Her torso mirrored the smooth line of her throat, and her arm raised with the grace of a dancer. Time slowed as I attempted to capture the scene on my mind's canvas—Earl in her posture of surprised delight, Dante's face alight with mirth, Akiko beaming at them, her mouth wide open.

Genevie had noticed us, so I locked my gaze on her questioning expression. Now more than ever, I couldn't afford the distraction Earl presented.

The pressure of Josephine's hand increased. "Ready?"

My breath caught, but I nodded and stepped forward. When Ben saw us, he paused his conversation, his smile warm and loving. I grinned back until Josephine, the more likely recipient of Ben's admiration, brushed past me. To hide my reddening face, I kissed the top of Sally's head, grimacing at the two empty chairs next to her. Mine... and Talbot's.

I swallowed, gripped the back of Talbot's empty chair, and cleared my throat. "Before I lose my nerve, I need to tell you something."

Everyone froze, their smiles slipping from their faces.

"After leaving the market last night, three men chased me." I held my hand up to prevent Genevie's question. "I don't know who they were, but they didn't look friendly. When they shouted Talbot's name, I ran. They chased me for a while, but I lost them." Eyes burned into me, and I stared at the table. "I should have said something last night, but... well, I'm telling you now."

Ben set his fork on his plate with a *clink*. His voice deepened when he processed bad news, and now it was full of gravel. "Matthew—"

"It gets worse," I interrupted. "Today, when I got back from the market, Talbot wasn't in his room."

Dante's fork paused halfway to his mouth. "What?"

"I looked for him and even went to the Excalibur to see if Talbot had wandered by, but either they hadn't seen him, or they didn't care to help me."

The silence following my admissions was tangible, like a great judgmental beast. It circled me, its breath hot against my neck.

Sally was the first to breach the quiet. "He can't be gone. He's scheduled to *perform* tomorrow night."

"It may be how they knew where to find him, Sally." Josephine clamped her lips together, as if to keep from saying more.

"You're sure they've taken him?" Genevie's tone implied more of a statement than a question, and I nodded.

Akiko burst into tears. "It's my fault, isn't it?"

I folded her into my arms. "No, it's not."

"But I was supposed to watch him," she wailed. "If I'd stayed with him, he'd be fine!"

When I kissed the crown of her head, her hair smelled like charcoal and the floral pomade oil Dante used to smooth his hair. If Akiko *had* been with Talbot, would they have taken her too? Chills ran up my arms. "It's not your fault, I promise. But we need to look for him, so can I ask a favor?"

Akiko nodded as though I had asked her, even though my

gaze was fixed on Earl. Earl nodded, and I mouthed 'thank you' before continuing.

"Can you stay with Earl while I look for him? I don't want you in our rooms, just in case."

Akiko's fierce hug squeezed my heart. When she released me, everyone but Dante and Sally stood, leaving their uneaten meals. A surge of gratitude flooded through me.

From her growing stack of pages, Sally pulled out a crude map, and we clustered around her. The map depicted the rough shape of the depot, and once we'd pinpointed our location, I showed them the area I'd searched.

"I'll go south," said Josephine. "While I'm there, I can ask the librarians for contacts."

"The idea of striding into the sunset appeals, so I'll go west. Besides, it gives me an excuse to see River again," said Genevie. She looked at me. "What about you?"

The evening bells had rung, so the market would be disassembling. With luck, Ruben might still be waiting for porters to clear the rooftop stalls. "North."

"Leaving me east," said Ben. "What exactly are we looking for?"

Josephine tugged her lip. "I doubt they carried him. With luck, someone saw a bandaged man escorted away from the Tropic."

"Or a few men carrying a rolled rug, or pushing a large cart, or—" Genevie stopped when she caught me glaring. She followed my gaze and blanched at Akiko's terrified expression. "Or riding an enormous pig. Anything really."

Ben drained his water glass and wiped his mouth on his sleeve. "Let's go."

"Check in with me before you go to bed," said Sally. "No matter the hour."

I nodded and whistled for Charcoal, but Earl caught my eye.

"Are you okay?" Her hand was cool against my forearm.

"You mean other than letting everyone down yet again?" I grimaced at the bitterness in my voice.

Earl brushed my cheek with her hand. "There's time for that later."

"You're right." I caught her hand, and before I could stop myself, blurted, "Will you have dinner with me tomorrow night? Just the two of us? I know my timing is terrible, but something always gets in the way."

Earl's cheeks pinked, and she gazed down at our entwined hands. "You only had to ask. Besides, once you find Talbot, we'll want to celebrate."

My heart hammered, and in another act of daring, I brought her hand to my lips and brushed it before releasing her and fleeing from the Copperfield.

My heart sang as Charcoal and I trotted toward Sayzar's, but when we arrived, few vendors remained. None of them knew when Ruben had departed or where he lived, so I descended the metal stairs, walked back to the broad route, and turned north toward the tower. "Come on, Charcoal."

When the man had attacked us in Angel Falls, I'd assumed he'd been swinging for me. Talbot throwing himself in front of me had reinforced it, but what if Talbot had been the target all along? If Carter's people had found out Talbot was a spy, perhaps they'd taken him to... to what? Punish him? Return him to Carter?

The hot wind gusted as we walked. It carried a fiddle's song, the music luring us as we wound through the empty buildings. We followed it until a burst of raucous laughter spilled from an open doorway. We crossed the street, and the door swung open again. A couple emerged and held the door for us.

The room was too warm, too bright, and awash with people. The aroma of fried onions and peppers curled around me, and my stomach lurched. Charcoal tossed a hopeful look my way, but after scanning the patrons, I shook my head. "We're not staying, chap."

I flagged down a girl pushing a mop and bucket around the kitchen. "Pardon, Lady, but are you the keeper?"

She brushed the hair plastered to her forehead away with the back of her arm and pointed at a short, swarthy man. "Talk to Jack."

Jack rubbed his balding pate and listened to me describe Ruben but shook his head. "Sorry. This place keeps me busy, and I don't get to the market often."

Though hot, the dry, evening air was a relief after the steamy din of the pub. We continued north toward the glimmering tower. Reaching the base, I stopped to retie the flopping lace on my left boot. When I straightened, a mark on the building across the road caught my eye.

*Ichthys.*

In Toronto Depot, Talbot had told me the sign was used to help travelers find fellow believers. This symbol was on the twelfth floor and fifth window. If I remembered correctly, it meant I'd find the Christian safe house twelve blocks north, on the fifth door.

I hesitated and debated what to do next. If I was wrong, I'd knock on an abandoned door. But if I was right, I might find someone in Talbot's network... or he could be there himself.

I glanced south, but there was no telling where Ben and the others were, and I didn't even know if following the ichthys symbol would lead to anything.

I shrugged at Charcoal. "No harm in knocking on a door, eh, chap?"

He huffed in agreement and trotted beside me. When we reached the twelfth intersection, I peered west, then east. Both blocks appeared vacant, and Talbot hadn't explained the nuances of the ichthys symbol. The buildings east of the route were closer, so I turned toward them. But the first door was on the other side of the street, confounding me again. Was I supposed to count all the doors or the doors on one side of the street?

Charcoal huffed, and I turned in time to catch Neblina's tail as she slunk behind a building.

"If we're knocking, I suppose there's no harm in knocking on several doors." My stomach tightened with anticipation as I approached the fifth door on my side of the street, but when I knocked, the door swung open, its hinges complaining.

"Hullo?"

No answer.

The fifth door, counting both sides of the street, was two buildings west across the street. It also appeared empty, but I crossed the street and rapped on the door, anyway. Faint vibrations, like footsteps, echoed through the building.

My mouth dried, and I took a step backward as the footsteps approached. The words I'd rehearsed jumbled across my mind's canvas, and I took two, quick, deep breaths to center myself before pasting a smile on my face. My expression froze in a vacant smile several sizes too wide, like a grinning skull.

*Tom Staker.*

# CHAPTER THIRTY-THREE

Tom Staker and I stared at each other like mirror reflections. Meeting each other here, thousands of kilometers from where we'd last spoken, ripped every scrap of sense from me. The artist in me detached and stepped back to study the scene; two men of similar age and background, standing in a doorway with identical postures of surprise.

*How is this possible?*

"Matthew?"

Tom's voice was exactly as I'd remembered it. Memories swamped me, and my words came out in a rush. "I thought you died."

"I didn't. How—" His mouth tightened. "How do we even begin?"

"You could invite me in." My voice was impossibly calm, conveying none of my confusion, or the questions burning like prairie grass in my mind. "Around these parts, I believe the highest honor is to offer a guest a glass of water."

"Beg your pardon. Please come in." He stepped back, gesturing us into the building. Before shutting the door, he peered out into the darkening street, then led us down a long corridor into a brightly lit kitchen. On one side of the room, several glass doors stood open. The air coming through them was cooler and scented with desert jasmine.

Tom filled a glass from a tap at the base of a large crock. "I never imagined I'd see you again."

"Likewise." The last time I'd seen him had been during our sparring session on Niagara Abbey's grass lawn. Before they had abandoned the abbey. Before I learned the artists at the abbey worked for Reverend Carter.

I leaned against the counter, sipping water while Tom filled a bowl for Charcoal. My intuition gnawed on the edges of my mind's canvas. "Do I have reason to fear you?"

He wouldn't meet my eyes.

My gut tightened. If Tom was a danger to me, he might be a threat to Talbot, Akiko, and Erena, too. I straightened, but my body remained tense in case I needed to run. "Tom?"

He set the bowl down for Charcoal saying nothing, but his breath exploded from him. He sank onto a stool, cradling his face in his hands. "I'm desperately ashamed, but no, you have nothing to fear from me." He looked up, his eyes tortured. "I've dreamed of you so many times. You've haunted my nightmares, so when I opened the door, I wasn't sure if I was awake or not." A miserable, brown-green color outlined him, bringing the smell of damp granite to my memory.

"You walled me in." Betrayal stole my breath. "You *entombed* me in Carter's tower."

Tom flinched as if I'd struck him, and his shoulders slumped. "Yes. Can you forgive me?"

"Forgive you?" Every memory from my incarceration, every moment of fear and pain and rage whipped into a funnel and threatened to suck me in, collapsing me into a speck of... of *nothing*.

My heart galloped. This man had tried to kill me. Why wasn't I running away?

*Talbot.*

If I dismissed my hurt and wounded pride, could I turn this situation to my advantage? I kept my face neutral and handed Tom my empty glass. His brow smoothed, and he leaped to refill it. When he returned it to me, his face was hopeful, and his eyes pled for mercy. I drank the second glass without releasing him from my gaze. "I'll try, but no promises."

He shimmered, the murky light around him vanishing. If he heard the lie in my voice, he gave no sign. "It's more than I hoped for. Why did you come?"

Talbot's face settled onto my mind's canvas. "My cousin has disappeared."

"Your cousin?"

"Talbot Sato." I searched his face for recognition but saw none. "He's a preacher and works—*worked* with Reverend Carter."

Tom's face darkened. "Carter is a monster."

"Talbot isn't." I raised my chin and narrowed my eyes. "His injuries have left him blind, and he's disappeared from our rooms. I'm worried your colleagues grabbed him."

"They're not my colleagues. I don't follow Carter anymore." Tom gestured at the wooden table. He dropped into a chair and waited for me to join him before continuing. "After what I did, after what he did to the children—" He stopped and stared. "Did they find them?"

"Scared but unharmed. The depot re-homed the fosterlings."

Tom closed his eyes. "Thanks be to God."

I tensed again. "You *are* religious."

"I'm... faithful." Tom's eyes turned wary. "Most of us at

Niagara Abbey were. Carter twisted our beliefs by using our fears of exposure."

Charcoal's head swiveled and the front door opened.

Tom brightened. "Back here, honey."

Charcoal's growl rumbled, and I backed toward the open doors. Coming face to face with Tom had scrambled my thoughts, but Cara stepping into the kitchen shattered my mind.

*And then the world died.*

"Matthew." Horror flashed across her face, and her voice went tight and thin. "What are you doing here?"

My throat convulsed, and I couldn't squeeze enough breath out to say anything.

"Have you come to help us?" She crossed the kitchen, laying her hand on Tom's chest. "Didn't I tell you God would provide?"

He nodded, smiling at her with so much love my stomach lurched. It was too much.

"Must go," I said, bolting toward the front door. I wrenched it open and hurtled down the stairs without slowing. My breaths came in gasps, and I raced down the road toward the tower. I thought Tom called after me, but I didn't slow until I reached the Copperfield.

Bursting into the dining room, I spun, desperate to find Sally. Not only was she still in the room, so was everyone else. My chest heaved, and I made a wheezing noise.

Genevie swung around, her smile fading as she scanned me. "What the blast is wrong with you?"

A tall, dark-haired woman maneuvered past Genevie, a puzzled expression on her face. "Talbot?" She took a tentative step toward me. Before I reacted, she stiffened, her gaze and voice hardening like fire-baked porcelain. "What are *you* doing here?"

# CHAPTER THIRTY-FOUR

The room swam as I struggled with this newest shock. First Talbot, then Tom Staker and Cara, and now *her*, the reason behind our mad march across these baked, unforgiving lands.

My sister looked as I'd imagined—a strong jaw and straight, thin nose. Her mouth was generous, but her brows were like two angry slashes drawn over glaring eyes. "Erena?"

Genevie's expression turned incredulous. "No. This is River—" she stopped when Erena shook her head.

"Erena means *water route* in Japanese." My sister turned back toward me. "Where's Talbot?"

Genevie bumped her. "That's who we're looking for."

It was Erena's turn to look stunned. "*Talbot* was blinded?" When Genevie bit her lip and nodded, Erena swung toward me with clenched fists. "How *dare* you!"

The rage on her face made me step back and raise my palms. What was going on? "*I didn't hurt him.*"

Erena glared as Genevie pulled her back, looking as shocked as me.

"Should we sit and work this out?" Ben unfolded his arms and gestured at the table.

Work *what* out? Ben's question made no sense to me, and I stared at him as though I'd been struck dumb. After traveling thousands of kilometers to find my sister, all I wanted was to ask why she was furious with me. But Talbot was still missing, and I needed to tell the others about Tom and Cara.

But Sally frowned and glanced around the dining hall. "Outside."

Our group clustered outside, and I skirted my sister with the same wariness I'd give a rattlesnake. Earl touched my hand, and I clutched at it, grateful. I pulled Akiko close to us.

"Hullo, Erena," said Josephine. "We came here to find you, so at least half of our mission is complete."

"Mission?" My sister stiffened and swung toward me. "Why are you here?"

A roaring filled my ears. "Talbot said you were in danger."

When her glare didn't ease, I tried again. "Erena—" But her name stuck in my throat, unfamiliar and difficult.

"River," she said without softening. "I *prefer* River."

"Noted," said Ben. "A man named Reverend Carter threatened Matthew's parents, *your* parents, so we traveled here to warn them."

"They're not here," said River, glowering.

"I didn't know." Somehow, I kept my voice steady. "We guessed they were here based on a painting I've been working on. But Talbot asked us to travel here to ensure your safety."

River drummed her fingers on her arm. "Aren't you supposed to be in New England?"

I blinked. "I graduated more than a year ago."

Akiko leaned forward. "River, if you're Erena, are you my aunt?"

"My name is *River*." She glared at us before continuing. "Who are you?"

"Akiko Sugiyama." Akiko skipped toward my sister and thrust her small hand out, a pleased expression on her face. "Hi, Aunt River."

River hesitated, and I tensed, ready to bolt toward them. But her face relaxed, and she extended her hand. This time, her voice was kind. "Hullo, Akiko."

The greeting was all the permission Akiko needed. She leaned against Genevie and peppered River with questions, chattering about the trip and sharing gossip about us, while we stared at Erena.

Dante broke our stasis when he rounded the corner of the Copperfield. "No one invited *me* to the party. Who's this?"

"River," said Earl. "Matthew's sister."

His brow furrowed. "I thought your sister's name was Erena."

"So did I."

River scowled at us, interrupting Akiko. "I suppose I'll need to hear the entire tale." She held her finger up to prevent Akiko from launching into another story. "But first, I need to know what you know. How will you find Talbot?"

Genevie entwined her fingers with River's. "Can you ask at the Excalibur?"

Josephine stiffened. "You're Avalon Society?"

River nodded, her posture equally rigid. "Yes, I'm a weaver."

Akiko and I stared at each other before I blurted, "Are the blankets sold at the market yours?"

River nodded, her chin raising. "Why?"

"They're so neat!" Akiko lowered her voice, "We found them because—"

River cut her off. "Sorry, kid. Now is not the time. I don't know any of you, and until we find my cousin, I don't care to."

However I'd imagined the first meeting with my sister, this wasn't it. Earl squeezed my hand, and I swallowed, trying to ease the tightness in my throat. "You're right... we'll talk later." I steeled myself to deliver the next chunk of bad news. "While searching for Talbot, I found two ghosts from our past."

Ben frowned and leaned forward. "Who?"

"Tom Staker and" –I tried to swallow, but my mouth was too dry– "Cara."

"No," said Sally and Josephine in unison.

Akiko burst into tears again. "Did Cara take Uncle Talbot? Will she hurt his nose?" She buried her face in Genevie's hip, sobbing. Charcoal pawed at her leg, whining.

"Do you think they have Talbot?" Ben encircled Josephine with his arms as if to protect her from my answer.

"No, but they may know something." In hindsight, it had been foolish to flee.

Josephine's eyes flashed, and she gripped my wrist. "You can't go back there."

I patted her hand until she relaxed her hold. "I know, but if Carter's men have him, Tom and Cara could provide us with information."

Ben cleared his throat. "It's too late now, so let's table this until tomorrow." He turned to Sally. "Depending on what we decide to do, we may need you to run interference for us."

Sally grimaced like she wanted to argue, but her gaze slid toward River, and she jerked her chin in agreement.

When I peeled Akiko away from Genevie, her face was splotchy and swollen. Worse, the watery smile she gave River tore my heart more than my sister's hostility. "It's late, so I'm going to switch rooms and get Mouse to bed."

AKIKO FELL INTO A RESTLESS SLEEP ON MY BED SOON after entering our new suite, but despite the day's toll, rest eluded me. When I was sure she wouldn't wake, I slipped back to our old rooms, retrieved Talbot's hidden parcels, and packed our things.

Charcoal stirred when I let myself back into our rooms. His tail stub wiggled as I scratched his head. He'd taken my place on the bed, and I still wasn't sleepy, so I settled myself at the desk by the window.

Our new rooms were on the west side of the Tropic, across the street from the Excalibur. Under the light from the half moon, its pale walls shone like bleached bone. The longer I stared at it, the more grotesque it grew until the image on my mind's canvas was of a monstrous hulking beast-dwelling, capable of moving, like the tale of Baba Yaga's hut Talbot had told us. Talbot had regaled us with many of the fairy tales from *Before*.

My eyes stung as I pictured Talbot's calm smile, his bandaged face fire-lit as he spun story magic around us. Those happy nights had reminded me of my boyhood at the abbey back when I'd been sure the world was a good and just place. I'd been a naive child, like one of Talbot's fairy tale characters when I'd set off on an adventure to find my parents.

And now everything had gone wrong.

Talbot was injured *and* missing. My parents weren't here, but Tom and Cara were... and both had tried to kill me. Erena —*River* was a nightmare. Earl had met a handsome rancher. And until we found Talbot, we were stuck in this dreadful place.

My imagination spiraled as I pictured how much worse things could get for us. What if we couldn't find Talbot? What if Carter came for us? What if *anyone* learned Akiko's secret? A whirling fear filled my stomach with dread. It wrapped bands of anxiety and overwhelm around my heart until they crushed me, making it hard to breathe. I couldn't shoulder these problems... but if not me, then who?

Akiko moaned in her sleep, her arms and legs jerking. I smoothed her hair until she quieted. To excise my dark thoughts, I pulled out my charcoal and sketched until the mantle of sleep covered me like a blanket.

# CHAPTER THIRTY-FIVE

A furtive rustling woke me, flooding me with alarm. I bolted upright, sweaty and disoriented.

Akiko froze, then pulled the stack of drawings the rest of the way. "Sorry, but your face was on them. Why did you sleep at the desk?" She studied the top page and frowned. "It's like a castle from a nightmare."

I scowled at the Excalibur, but the morning's light had transformed it, making the compound more goofy than malignant. The bright day did little to alter my dark thoughts, but it would do little good to share them with Akiko. Forcing a smile, I took a deep, bracing breath and stretched. As I twisted, the vertebrates along my spine popped, making us both groan.

"Gross." She shook the sheet. "You used a lot of value ten."

"Mm." The sense of lurking danger remained, even though the Excalibur sparkled, benign, in the morning sun. "I hope they turn on the water early today, or my hand will carry a value of seven all day."

"Your face too." Akiko narrowed her eyes as though trying

to decide if I teased her. "But they have washrooms in the Copperfield."

Although it hadn't occurred to me, I cracked a grin like she'd caught me in a silly lie. Her answering smile of relief was an uncomfortable reminder she wasn't convinced I was on top of our current situation.

When we ran into Dante in the lobby, he looked startled. "I knocked and popped my head in, but your rooms were empty."

"We moved, remember?" Akiko skipped in a circle around us.

Dante wrinkled his nose at my appearance but held the door for us. As we walked to breakfast, he chattered about his admiration for Vegas Depot—a magical place full of opportunities. It took all my resolve to remain upbeat and not list everything I disliked about the place. I plastered a determined smile on my face, sure everyone would see through it. But it cheered Earl, Sally, Josephine, and Ben, who greeted us with matching enthusiasm.

A girl brought over three more bowls on a lacquered wooden tray as soon as we sat. "Tea?" She set two empty mugs on the table, winked, and disappeared into the kitchen.

I poked at the Nickel Yellow mush in my bowl. It had the consistency of porridge, but it was thicker and grainier.

"Corn," said Josephine, answering my unasked question.

To sell my feigned positivity, I dug in. It had little flavor, but Ben passed me pale, agave syrup and a small pitcher of cream. I added some to my bowl and tasted it again, aware of being watched. The hot mush remained flavorless, albeit sweeter. I passed the syrup to Akiko. "I didn't know I'd miss maple syrup."

She dumped the rest of the syrup on her breakfast and beamed. I opened my mouth to scold her but shoved a spoonful of corn mush in instead. What was the use of starting another argument? I ate half my meal before Genevie strolled in, holding hands with River.

"Morning, all," said Genevie, dropping into a chair. They both accepted their bowls with smiles of thanks. Genevie dug in with apparent enjoyment; if she was faking a cheerful mood, she was a better actor than I.

I hoped a good night of rest would relax my sister, but she glared at me, and the cereal turned leaden in my stomach. Every scrap of positivity I'd gathered fled. Stomach churning, I passed my bowl to Akiko in case she was still hungry. She promptly set it on the floor for Charcoal, winning even more points from him.

Dante chattered about the people he'd met, and I pretended to listen. As determined as I'd been to keep my spirits high and focus on finding Talbot, it was difficult around River's continued hostility. She focused her ire on me, but I didn't know why. And until her fury with me cooled, there was no chance of pumping her for information. Perhaps once we'd found Talbot, we could work through whatever bothered her.

Under the table, Akiko squeezed my hand, drawing my attention to my left wrist. The skin was raw and angry from rubbing it, an unhappy childhood habit I'd developed to soothe myself as a boy.

Sally tapped her sheaf of papers on the table. "I caught Francis Lee this morning and got everyone dismissed from their assigned labor hours today. Francis is eager for us to find Talbot since the depot is expecting a minstrel show tonight." She peered around the table, and we nodded. "Good. Josephine and I will speak with the librarians this morning. Erena—*River*—you'll speak to your colleagues in the Avalon Society?" River nodded with stiff, jerky motions, and Sally returned to her list. "Ben, reach out to the head of infrastructure. I believe her name is..."

"Isabella." He pushed his bowl away, his spoon clattering. "I met her the day before yesterday. You think she'll know something?"

"Even if she doesn't" –Sally pursed her lips– "knowing which buildings in the depot are occupied would be helpful."

Ben's expression turned thoughtful. "Right."

"What about me?" I asked, trying to ignore the angry colors shimmering around River.

Sally hesitated. "I hoped you and Dante would speak with Tom and Cara."

The knot in my stomach threatened to push the corn mush back up my throat. Although I'd expected this, somehow, I'd still hoped to avoid the couple entirely.

"It's the least you can do."

River's words hit me like a bucket of cold water. What did she mean? What had *I* done to her?

Dante's eyes widened, and he tossed a doubtful glance my way before turning to Sally. "You're sending me?"

"Tom Staker is an artist, too." The way Ben and Josephine nodded told me they'd already discussed it. Sally folded her arms. "Matthew and Cara have... history, so for safety, go together."

Earl stiffened, but her voice sounded normal when she leaned toward Akiko. "We get another day together."

Akiko scowled at Earl before frowning at me. "Maybe you shouldn't go."

"Oh?" I asked, through gritted teeth. If Akiko refused to spend time with Earl, there was little reason to hope for a future with the three of us together.

Akiko's eyes crossed as she pressed her finger to the tip of her nose. "Last time, Cara broke your nose."

I forced a chuckle to cover my relief. "Sally is sending

Dante with me because he can charm anyone into a better mood."

"Good point." Akiko sat back, sighing. "But watch your nose, anyway."

It was my turn to cross my eyes. Even River's lip twitched as my face sent Akiko into peals of laughter.

---

As much as I believed what I'd told Akiko, I hesitated when Dante and I reached Tom and Cara's dwelling.

"Lost?"

I shook my head. "Trying to settle my nerves."

"The dread is probably worse than the experience." He shrugged. "Besides, putting it off won't make it any easier."

"You're right."

The door flung open on my second knock. Tom's voice was breathless. "I was afraid you wouldn't return."

I swallowed. "This is Dante, from Leavenworth Abbey."

Tom smiled and nodded at Dante, but his expression was strained. "Please, come inside."

Dante stepped inside immediately, but I hesitated. Tom could barely meet my eyes, justifying my concern. "What?"

He heaved a sigh and admitted, "Cara is waiting inside."

The urge to bolt welled inside me, but the memory of River's disapproving stare made me pause. Until I found Talbot, there was no way forward for me and my sister. And while I hadn't known she existed until recently, her rejection of me was shockingly painful.

*I have to do this.*

As we followed Tom to the kitchen, the hallway stretched and compressed. The corn mush in my gut roiled, and I swallowed several times before stepping into the room.

Cara perched on the edge of a cushioned chair, her face tight. As if she'd expected him, she nodded at Dante before turning her dark eyes toward me. She was exactly as I remembered; the same mass of black, ringlet curls, the same flawless, light-brown skin, and the same heart-shaped mouth. But despite her beauty, the memory of her face twisted into a hateful snarl, her eyes wild and bulging with rage, filled my mind's canvas.

Nausea shuddered through me, and I bolted to the sink. The corn porridge came out in wet clumps, like sand on the beach following a retreating tide. I continued to retch until pain tore at my gut and nothing remained. A wave of dizziness swept over me, and I gripped the sink. When it passed, I turned on the tap, but no water came out.

"Our allotments are at eight and five." Tom's voice sounded thin.

My face burned. Not only had I humiliated myself, but I also couldn't clean up the mess. My heart slammed in my chest as I turned, but the sight of Cara weeping brought a different jolt. Shame burned my raw throat. "I'm sorry... I can't clean it up."

Tom shook his head as he wrapped his arms around Cara. He murmured to her until she shuddered and wiped her eyes. When she spoke, her eyes were red-rimmed. "The last time I saw you, I..." She stopped and hiccuped. "What I said—what I *did*. Unforgivable."

I swallowed, but my mouth was dry and bitter with bile. My word came out as a croak. "What?"

"She's told me what happened—about Wakefield." Tom's arms tightened around her. "But she was a different person. We all were."

Did people ever really change? My hands tightened on the

edge of the sink behind me. "I haven't come to discuss Wakefield *or* Welland Island."

Tom raised his chin. "Why have you come?"

His defiance unsettled me. Could asking for their help put Talbot in even more danger? If they wouldn't help, we'd have to find someone else with ties to the religious community in the depot. The secret religious community. It would take time—time I wasn't sure Talbot had. "To ask for your help." When they exchanged glances, my eyes narrowed. "I told you last night my cousin is missing."

"Yes?"

"I need to you ask your network about him."

Cara bit her lip, but Tom's chest swelled. "We aren't part of Carter's group anymore."

"But you're still Christians." My brow furrowed as I glanced from Dante to them. "And you're here in the depot's Christian safe house."

Tom's mouth opened and closed several times, but Cara licked her lips. "We're Christians, yes, but we don't interact with them at all. In fact, we're here to find help so we can separate from *them* permanently." She looked at Dante. "You're an artist, too?"

"I am." He cocked his hip and folded his arms as if waiting for another question, but she turned back toward me.

"We need your help," she said.

"You must be joking." My laugh rang, hollow and insincere.

She raised her chin. "We're looking for artists to help us build a haven for people like us."

"Like Welland Island?" I couldn't keep the bitterness from my voice.

"No." Tom rubbed his palms over his face. "But I understand why you'd think it."

The rage simmering in my gut rekindled, its bitter flames

licking at my core. "Let me see if I understand. I came for help to find my missing cousin. You won't help but you're asking for my forgiveness *and* want my help to build your dream home?" My voice had risen to nearly a shriek.

No one said anything.

Time stretched.

With each thud of my heart, I imagined Talbot in peril, in as much terror and pain as they'd caused me.

Charcoal pressed himself against my leg as if to comfort me. It broke my stasis, and I turned without another word. The hallway flashed past in a blur, and I stormed out before they recovered. Dante caught up and matched my speed but said nothing.

We neared the tower when the sharp, staccato sounds of running footsteps pounded behind us.

*What now?*

I swung around and tensed.

Tom stopped several meters away, his face pale and breathing ragged. His fists clenched.

# CHAPTER THIRTY-SIX

Tom sucked in several great lungfuls of air as we eyed him. When he caught his breath, he straightened. "We had no right to ask for your forgiveness, let alone a favor."

My jaw flexed and I gritted my teeth, but said nothing. My second interaction with him and Cara was as useless as the first, and I was no closer to finding Talbot.

"I'll help you." He glanced over his shoulder as if afraid Cara would race after us to argue his decision. "I'll find Carter's people and see what I can learn about your cousin."

"Talbot," I said. "His name is Talbot."

Tom opened his mouth as if to say something but closed it again and shuffled his feet. I braced myself for another attempt to coerce me into helping him and Cara, but it was Dante who spoke, not Tom.

"If you bring us news, we will *listen* to your proposal." My breath caught, and I glowered at Dante, but he waved away my silent protest. "Deal?"

"You're staying at the Tropic?" Hope flooded Tom's voice.

Dante didn't bother to glance at me. "Yes."

My heart thundered. "How dare you make a promise on my behalf!" I said, once Tom was out of sight.

Dante raised his eyebrow. "What matters more? Wounded pride or your cousin?"

Fury clogged my throat, and I spluttered.

"What's the harm in listening?" Dante waggled his fingers. "It's not like I promised we'd help."

I fumed as we walked south, but my anger didn't bother him. He nodded to everyone we passed and even chattered about the unseasonably warm weather.

I said nothing as I slapped my feet against the hot pavement. Dante knew nothing. Talbot meant a great deal to me. We had found Erena, so this was all about Talbot.

But what if it wasn't?

I stopped at the market's turnoff. Because the men had shouted Talbot's name, I'd assumed he was their target. But what if they'd taken him... as bait? If Talbot was bait, who were they trying to trap? Me? Akiko or Erena? All of us? And if Tom brought information, could I trust it?

"I need to check something."

Dante shrugged, waved, and continued south. Charcoal and I bounded up the stairs two at a time to burn off the wild, fiery energy boiling inside me. Winded and probably red-faced, I marched to Ruben's stall. He lifted his eyebrows and pulled back the curtain into his makeshift kitchen without saying a word.

He ignored the crate of water and reached for an amber-colored jug nestled between several heads of cabbage. I picked one up. "Imperial Purple. How odd. I haven't seen cabbage like this before."

Ruben grinned as he pulled the stopper from the jug with a *pop*. "Today, my spike is perfection."

The liquor burned, and I spluttered, but Ruben laughed.

Mindful of how the alcohol had taken Ben's legs out from under him, I allowed myself two swallows before handing it back.

Ruben reclined on his crate and took a long drink. "Bad news?"

"Infuriating." I paced around the tiny area but stopped when I nearly trod upon Charcoal. "Where do you go at night?"

"Home." Ruben shrugged. "I live west of the depot."

I pushed my toe against the crate of cabbages. "Is that where you garden?"

"So many questions." Ruben held the jug out for me, but I shook my head. Stoppering the jug, he waited, his eyes curious.

*Could Ruben ask about Talbot?*

While it was possible Tom would deliver, it wouldn't hurt to hedge my bets. The spike warmed my stomach, the sensation not unpleasant. I had no reason to distrust Ruben; he'd been nothing but helpful to me. I sighed, deflating, and sank onto another crate. "My cousin has disappeared."

Ruben tilted his head. "I thought your sister was lost."

I chuckled without mirth. "She was, but we found her."

Ruben waited.

"My cousin is a minstrel and is supposed to put on a show tonight, but we can't find him."

"Is it usual for him to leave?"

"He was injured in an accident and can't see, so it's unlikely he left voluntarily. We're afraid someone took him."

Ruben shifted, as if waiting for something.

"Can you ask around?" I swallowed. "Any information would help."

"I'll make inquiries." He heaved himself onto his feet. "Check back around four and take a torta."

"Torta?"

The last thing I wanted was another delay, but I watched him saw a golden bun in half. He loaded it with shredded cabbage, carrots, and chicken, and topped it with several sprigs of cilantro. He handed it to me. "Torta."

I took a bite and moaned. The acid from the pickled cabbage hit my tongue in a nearly painful sensation. Painful but welcome, especially when it replaced the taste of vomit.

Ruben nodded and clapped my back. "See you at four."

Returning here before dinner with Earl would be tight, but I could make it work. "Four it is."

# CHAPTER THIRTY-SEVEN

I entered the Copperfield, intending to report my progress to Sally, but no one was in the dining room when I arrived. It took several minutes to track down the porter, but he refused to tell me where Sally and Earl's rooms were. "It's not done," he said, his voice strained. "It's not proper."

"But we're part of a party."

He eyed me. "Then why don't you know their room numbers?"

My bark of incredulous laughter didn't help. He folded his arms and glared.

"Can I leave a message?"

"You can *try*."

Waves of animosity rolled off him, and I suspected any note I wrote would quickly find its way into the trash. I spun but nearly tripped over Charcoal. He tucked his tail stub and scooted out of my way, casting me a look of reproach. The porter's derisive snort reignited my ire, but I stalked out with as much dignity as I could muster.

My mood was already dark when I found Tom Staker waiting for me outside my rooms. Clearly, the Tropic's porters had less concern for security and privacy than the awful man in the Copperfield. "Why are you here?"

Tom leaned backward, his shoulders hunching into a mute apology. "You were right. I found him."

Already? It couldn't have been more than an hour since we'd left him. My key slid into the lock with a *snick*, but I hesitated. "You're sure?"

His throat convulsed, and he nodded. "They're holding him in the Mandal, south of the Excalibur."

I pictured the buildings I'd passed on the way to the warehouse. "The gold one?"

"Yes."

"What else did you learn?"

Tom hesitated. "Your artist friend..."

"Dante?"

"Yes. He said you'd listen to us. To Cara's plan."

My mouth tightened, but he raised his chin, clearly prepared to wait until I agreed. Maybe Dante had been right. Hearing them out harmed no one. "Fine. I'll listen."

Instead of looking pleased, Tom folded his arms. "It's not enough."

My hands itched to grab him and throw him against the wall, and my voice was nearly a growl. "Get inside. This isn't a hallway conversation."

I shoved the door open so hard it hit the wall and bounced back, locking with a *click*. He said nothing while I unlocked it a second time. He followed me into the room but stayed near the door as though prepared to flee.

I sank onto the corner of my bed. "Go on." Tom pressed his lips together, his gaze flicking from Charcoal to me. Charcoal's posture was rigid, and I put a restraining hand on his collar. "Speak."

Tom's eyes tightened. "I want your word you'll come to the valley."

"Why? You've already told me where Talbot is."

"I can help you get him back."

My eyebrows shot up. "You're holding him hostage... and you want a favor for your trouble?"

Tom shook his head. "I'm not holding him, but I'll risk my neck to help you get him back."

"So? It still wouldn't make us even."

"No, it wouldn't." He met my eyes without flinching. "We're desperate. We need a safe place to live and have nothing left to lose. I'll help you because I need your help *and* because I disagree with what Carter is doing."

His answer was evasive, but now wasn't the time to grill him about it. "You have a plan?"

"Cara does. I think it will work, but it's time-sensitive, and we have one shot to make it work." Having made his case, he settled into the same relaxed but wary posture I remembered. Could I trust him? Our long-ago, sparring session next to the Ontario Sea was from another lifetime. This could be a trap, but I didn't detect any artifice in his manner. If he was sincere, was his help worth the price he demanded?

"Tick-tock, brother."

I glared at him, but my gaze flicked to the door behind him, the door leading into Talbot's quarters. "If we get Talbot back safely, I'll come to your valley."

Tom studied me. "We'll need to leave the depot immediately or they could come for him again."

Vise-like pressure clamped my head and settled behind my eyes. To leave immediately meant mustering everyone for a hasty departure or leaving them behind and traveling alone with an injured man. "Our party is large; I may need time."

"We have what we have. Unless you want to risk them coming after us, we must go as soon as we've rescued him."

I hesitated, then nodded. Sally could get it done.

Tom's energy changed. He shifted his weight onto the balls of his feet, as though preparing for a fight. "You promise you'll come?"

There was no helping it. "Yes, *if* we get Talbot back safely."

Tom exhaled as though a weight had lifted from his chest. "Good. Meet me at four, at the tiny chapel. Take one of the secondary roads south, so no one sees you pass the Mandal."

My heart jolted. I was supposed to meet Ruben at four.

"Problem?"

It was my turn to hunch my shoulders. I swallowed and shook my head. "I'll make it work."

THE DINING HALL WAS EMPTY WHEN I CHECKED BACK AT the Copperfield. I ignored the surly porter and returned to the Tropic, intending to give my update to Dante, but he wasn't in his room either.

When I entered the Copperfield a third time, the porter scowled. "If you're Matthew, you have a reprieve."

"Oh?"

"Park said the administrators have canceled the minstrel show because of the incoming storm." His scowl deepened, as if I was responsible.

As a child, the only storms with enough power to cancel a minstrel show were the nor'easters on the mighty Atlantic. Compared to them, what kind of storm could a dusty place like this depot conjure? My skepticism must have shown because the porter drew himself up in a huff and turned to leave.

"Can you tell me where their rooms are now?"

He smirked. "It wouldn't be proper."

What wouldn't be proper was to punch the smug expression off his face.

*Now what?*

I'd agreed to attend two meetings, scheduled at the same time. Both were vital, but they were in opposite directions. If I showed up at the market too early, Ruben might not have information for me yet, plus I risked being delayed and ruining Cara's time-sensitive plan. "Can I leave a message... *please?*"

The porter's eyes narrowed, but he didn't leave, so I sat at the nearest table and ripped a sheet from my sketchbook. I pulled the charcoal I'd been using from my trouser pocket and scrawled, "E, I have a conflict, and Ruben is expecting me at the market at four. Can you meet him? M." I stared at the message, underlined 'conflict,' and folded the sheet. I handed the note to the porter, then pulled the buffalo figurine from my pocket. "This is for Earl. She has red hair." I dragged my open fists along both sides of my head like pulling on a pair of braids.

The porter said nothing but snatched the note and figurine from me and left. When he returned empty-handed, it peeved him I hadn't departed. His sneer back in place, he gestured toward the door.

After the day I'd had, I couldn't help myself. "You know, you don't need to work so hard to get people to dislike you."

His face turned an interesting shade of Naphthamide Maroon, giving me a malicious, little boost. On my way out, I ran into Genevie and Erena. My gut twisted, and I froze, blocking their way.

If Erena noticed, she said nothing. She bent to pet Charcoal. "You're a handsome thing."

He smiled at her and leaned into her touch.

*Traitor.*

"He's the brains behind this duo. You make a better wall than door, Artist." Genevie's eyes crinkled at the corners. "Any news?"

"Maybe," I said.

River crossed her arms. "You either have information, or you don't. Playing coy is not cute for a man your age."

Her words stung, and I recoiled, stepping backward. Genevie's brow furrowed. "River—"

She held up her hand to stop Genevie from speaking, then swung toward me. "Do you know where he is yet?"

I didn't want to give them false hope, but if I asked, Genevie would organize our departure. "Maybe. We think so. I'll find out shortly."

The humor dropped from Genevie's face. "Need help?"

"If our plan works, we'll need to leave the depot." Saying it out loud made everything more real. My stomach sank; I'd have to cancel the dinner I'd promised Earl. Why hadn't I asked to reschedule in the note I'd left her? There was no way I could ask the porter for another favor now.

Genevie's eyes sharpened. "I'll make sure everyone knows and prepare things at the livery."

River spun toward her. "You're leaving too?"

"Yes, but come with us." Genevie cupped River's cheek.

River's face softened, but she said, "I don't want to leave Vegas Depot."

Why would anyone stay here voluntarily? I knew better than to ask. "It won't be safe for Talbot to stay."

River wilted but nodded at my statement.

Charcoal circled us as I turned toward Genevie. "I'll get the things in our rooms ready and leave them on the bed. Tell the others to pack? The porter wouldn't take me to Sally or Earl."

Genevie's voice tightened. "I will. Be careful, and good luck."

Instead of echoing Genevie, River's eyes flashed. "Bring Talbot back."

# CHAPTER THIRTY-EIGHT

Even though I arrived early, Tom was already waiting for me. He fidgeted in the shade of two, gigantic pines towering over an ancient wooden building. I scrutinized the area but saw nothing out of place. This *could* be a trap... but what choice did I have?

Dirty clouds scudded across a sullen, silver-gray sky. From the outside, the building resembled a pioneer-era, frontier church complete with a steep, peaked roof and a steeple, like structures I'd seen in the western-motif paintings from *Before*.

I took a deep breath, stepped out of the shadows, and crossed the open expanse. I waited for Tom's expression to change, sure I'd see triumph when I presented myself. But his wistful expression didn't change, and he continued to study the building. "It would have been marvelous to tour the churches *Before*."

I gestured at the building. "Isn't this a church?"

"At one time. Come on."

Inside, Cara and two men I didn't recognize rose from wooden chairs. My pulse jumped, but neither man displayed more than passing curiosity toward me. Charcoal pressed against my leg as I folded my arms. "What's the plan?"

Cara held out garish, orange sashes. "You're going into the Mandal as water workers."

A shiver raced down my spine. Tom passed me a sash, but I refused to take it. "You know Talbot and I look alike. They'll recognize me."

"No one looks at maintenance workers," said the taller man. The shorter man chuckled, nodding in agreement.

Unconvinced, I narrowed my eyes. "What are we supposed to do once we're inside?"

Cara unrolled a schematic drawing across the unoccupied chairs. "Ben and the others will turn the water on soon, and workers will enter occupied buildings to open the second-story valves."

"My friend, Ben?"

"Unless there are two engineers named Ben working on the depot's water system." Cara narrowed her eyes. "Shall I continue?"

I nodded, swallowing. I'd forgotten Cara knew Ben. Knew everyone.

"The Mandal has six standpipes," said the taller man. "We'll enter here. You three will enter the service corridor, then the two of you will head upstairs. We'll mess around like the valves are stuck until you find your man."

My stomach clenched. Not only would I have to trust Tom and Cara, but I'd also have to rely on strangers. Since I hadn't told Genevie where Talbot was or where I'd gone, if things went wrong, they'd have no way to find me.

"Wait..." Tom frowned at the drawings. "How will you know when we've found him?"

The short, round man waved a heavy-looking, metal

wrench. It clattered as he tilted it back and forth. "Hit the pipes."

"When we get your signal, we're going to release water and pretend a valve busted."

A broad smile broke across Tom's face. "And during the resulting commotion, we sneak away?"

They nodded in unison.

I glanced from face to face, waiting for the punchline. When none came, I groaned. "That's it? You're going to distract them with leaking pipes?"

The shorter man narrowed his eyes. "You understand how precious water is here?" He turned to his companion and hooked his thumb in my direction. "Another guzzler."

My face burned. "Assuming the leak *is* a sufficient distraction, how do you propose we sneak Talbot away?"

Cara sighed, as if I should already know the answer. "The knacker will wait with his wagon."

The building groaned as wind gusts hit it, its timbers giving a tortured creak.

Tom turned to me. "No one will notice the wagon, either. Your horses are at the livery nearest the Wyndham complex?"

"Yes." I glanced between the sash in my hand and the Mandal's schematic. "How did you put this together so quickly?"

When Cara pressed her lips together and looked away, my heart squeezed, but she finally sighed. "We were planning to go in for our own reasons. But when Tom told me you'd agreed to come see our valley, we decided helping you get your cousin back was more important."

The plan could go wrong in a few ways... but it might also work. If the clock wasn't already ticking, I would have weighed the merits with Ben and others, but doing so now risked everything.

"Let's do it." I glanced at Charcoal, my stomach clenching. "What about him?"

"Charcoal can stay with me." She addressed him directly. "I'll be in the wagon, so you must promise to keep silent."

He licked his muzzle, his gaze flicking from me to her.

I swallowed. Cara's plan was sound but surrounded by these people, I'd never felt more alone.

# CHAPTER THIRTY-NINE

The people lounging in the lobby recognized the taller man and spent several moments joking and laughing with him when we entered the Mandal. As predicted, no one showed any interest in the rest of us. While the tall man distracted the others, Tom and I followed the shorter man through the lobby and into an opulent hallway. Spots danced before my eyes. I struggled to keep my pace measured, since the adrenaline coursing through me made me twitchy and hyper-alert to each tiny sound. More than once, I jumped when the winds gusted and a window flexed, the glass whining in protest.

Once we'd walked out of eyesight, our guide directed us toward a hidden door. We followed him through it into a second hallway. Unlike the first, this hallway was dim and unadorned, filled with pipes and cabling.

"This way." He led us deftly through the twisting passage-ways to a beige-painted concrete stairwell. "When you reach the second floor, exit and turn right. Your man should be in the third room."

He handed me a heavy wrench. It rattled when I shook it back and forth. "What pipes should we hit?"

"Any pipes connected to the toilet or sink should work. Bang three times, wait for a count of five, and repeat the strikes. Hurry—we think they check on him every ten minutes."

Tom bounced on the balls of his feet. "Should we return this way?"

The short man shook his head. "They built the building like an upside-down 'Y,' so head north. Take the exit stair at the end of the hallway. The knacker's wagon will wait on the roadside."

I took a deep breath. "Turn right, third door, strike three times, wait for a count of five, and bang the pipes three more times."

"God be with you," he said, nodding.

"And also with you," replied Tom. Their words filled me with queasy dread, but I kept silent and nodded at the man.

Tom and I bounded up the stairs. The exit from the stairwell took us through a hidden door into another ornate hallway. My heart hammering, I turned right and stopped at the third door. I hesitated, but Tom gestured for me to hurry. I tapped lightly and cocked my head at the muffled movement inside. When no one approached, I tried the knob. It turned, and I cracked the door open.

The floor-to-ceiling curtains were drawn, so the room was dim, but I spotted a figure in the corner. He was on the floor in the corner, his hands and feet bound. They had secured him to the base of a metal bed frame and stuck a canvas sack over his head.

"Talbot?"

"Matthew!"

I crossed the room in two, gigantic strides and kneeled by him, pulling the sack off his head. Why had they covered his head when he was still wearing bandages over his eyes? "I'm here." I squeezed his shoulder and examined the bindings. I didn't have time to untie every knot, but if I could release him from the frame and free his feet, we could worry about his wrists later, after we were clear. I glanced over my shoulder. "Did you bring a knife?"

Tom shook his head and peered down the hallway. "Let's go. We don't know when the guards were last here."

"How?" I struggled to untie the thick knots, then pulled the curtains back for more light.

Outside, blowing dust made the air hazy. Talbot shrank from the light but couldn't get far. My fingers shook as I fumbled with the knots. "Who is holding you?"

"Shh," said Tom from the door. "Time for that, later."

I concentrated on my task, trying to distract myself from the Rose Madder-colored bruises on Talbot's wrists and ankles, and my growing rage. At last, they released, freeing his ankles. I helped him to his feet, steadying him when he staggered. "I'll cut the wrist bindings later."

Tom checked the hallway and darted out.

"Tom," I hissed, but he didn't return. My heart thumped, and I squeezed Talbot's arm. "Wait here." I slipped into the bathroom and clanged my wrench against the pipe under the sink three times. I counted to five as slowly as I could before clanging the pipe three more times. "Okay, let's go." I led Talbot down the hallway, the heavy wrench clanking in my left hand as we walked.

We hadn't made it even halfway down the hallway before the click of a door opening froze my blood. I turned Talbot around just in time.

A man stepped into the hallway and stared at us. "What are you doing?"

"I found him wandering down the hallway." I adopted a

casual posture and kept my tone bored. "Help me get him tied up again?"

Talbot said nothing as I shoved him back into the room, but as soon as the man bent to retrieve the ropes, I hit him with the heavy wrench. He collapsed and lay without moving.

"Matthew?"

"Give me a minute." I tore a strip of dusty cloth from the coverlet on the bed and used it to gag the unconscious man, then another to tie him to the bed's frame. After inspecting my work, I pulled the canvas sack over his head. "Okay, let's go."

From the doorway, Talbot swayed. "What have you done?"

I didn't answer and maneuvered him into the stairwell.

Tom waited in the stairwell with incredulity written across his face. "What took you?"

I lifted the wrench. "Three clangs, wait for a count of five, three clangs." He didn't need to know what else I'd been up to.

Tom closed his eyes. "Right. Come on."

Talbot's legs shook as we descended, and we'd reached the final landing when Tom opened the exterior door. A moment later, the door leading to the first floor opened.

I shoved Talbot behind me as a blonde lady stepped into the stairwell. "What's going on?"

I raised my wrench. "Maintenance."

She narrowed her eyes but whirled when shouts and commotion rang out behind her. "Come with me!" She trotted down the hallway. Contrary to her order, Talbot and I rushed down the last half-flight of stairs and out the exterior door.

"Where's the wagon?" I asked, my voice thin. The brightness made my eyes tear, and I squinted, trying to find the promised vehicle.

"There!" Tom pointed through a thicket of trees and shrubs. "Come on, let's go while they're distracted."

When we reached the wagon, Cara's breath hissed. "What took you?"

She passed me a knife and banged on the front wall, then held a finger to her lips. The wagon lurched forward as I sawed through the bindings around Talbot's wrists. Charcoal squeezed himself between my legs. He panted, his eyes cloudy with anxiety. Several times the wagon shuddered when a gust hit us, but the driver neither slowed nor sped up. None of us said anything until the wagon rumbled to a stop, and the driver's muffled voice called, "Clear."

Cara's shoulders slumped as she leaned back, closing her eyes. Tom intertwined his fingers with hers and pinned me with an intense gaze. "It won't be long before they find out he's gone. When can you leave?"

Talbot raised his chin as I stood. "Leave?"

"Come on," I said, helping him climb down. "We have to get you away from the depot."

He clutched my arm. "We have to find Erena first."

"We have."

"She's here?" He reached up as if to tear the bandage off his eyes until I stilled him.

I glanced around the yard. "Not yet, but she'll be here soon." His throat convulsed several times, but he let me help him climb down from the knacker's wagon. Akiko squealed and bolted toward us. She flung herself into my arms before squirming away to hug Talbot.

"Ben will be right back," said Josephine. "He and Sally are collecting their congratulations. Genevie and River will return soon, too. We didn't have room for her loom, but River had other things she didn't want to leave behind."

I glanced around the saddled horses. "Where's Earl?"

Akiko cocked her head. "She got a piece of paper, mentioned tacos, and left. Are we having tacos for dinner?"

"Dinner?" I swallowed as a leaden weight settled in my gut. *My note.*

I grabbed Josephine's upper arm. "Does Earl know we're leaving the depot?"

"She left before Genevie delivered the news." Josephine gave me a pained look. "How long do tacos take?"

"Hullo, Talbot, welcome back." Dante popped his head out and rapped his knuckles on the wagon's rear panel. "Come, I've made a cozy nest for you." He grimaced at me. "If I hadn't made the promise to Tom, I'd stay in the depot."

I narrowed my eyes. "I wish you hadn't made the promise either."

"Too late now." Dante pointed behind me.

Cara stood in the doorway with her arms wrapped around herself.

Josephine spotted Cara. She took two, stiff-legged strides toward the doorway, then reversed direction and disappeared down the barn's aisle. Akiko watched her go. She turned toward me, her eyes anxious.

"Can you check if Uncle Talbot needs anything?" I asked, to distract her.

Akiko bit her lip but scrambled into the wagon.

I joined Cara at the door to keep her away from Akiko.

"Tom has gone for our things," Cara said. "He'll be back soon."

"You both have horses?"

She nodded. "How much longer do you need?"

"Here comes Ben and Sally," said Dante.

Cara stiffened and swung around, her expression of distaste a mirror of Sally's.

Ben's voice was full of gravel when he spoke, "Cara." He looked at me. "Is Talbot okay?"

"He'll be fine." I didn't want to say anything else in front of Cara. "We're waiting on Gen, River, and Earl."

"And Tom," said Cara, her voice tight.

Sally glowered at Cara before focusing on me. "The administrators canceled the show because of the storm. Are we sure we should leave now?"

"When the people at the Mandal find Talbot missing, they'll come after us. We can't stay here." Cara's tone turned shrill. "You *promised.*"

"And the storm?" Sally snapped. She gestured at the sky, which had turned an ugly, mottled gray-brown. "If the administrators are concerned, shouldn't we be?"

Debris swirled around us, and I squinted. "If we leave now, are we leaving in debt?"

My worry subsided when she shook her head and patted Ben's arm. "Ben's work on their water system more than covered our stay. We're set." She looked around. "Where's Earl?"

When I shook my head, she patted my hand. "She'll be along soon. I left her a note in our room."

Tom approached the livery, riding a bay horse and leading another. He handed Cara the bay's lead and leaned down to kiss her. My gut twisted, and I looked away, spotting Genevie and River. Laden with bags, they rushed toward us from the south.

For once, my sister looked relieved to see me. "Talbot?"

"In the wagon." She dropped her bags and sprinted into the barn. I helped Genevie carry them in, scanning for Earl each time I returned to the doorway.

When I'd finished helping Genevie, I hauled Bruno's saddle out and got him ready too. The big horse fidgeted as I worked, so I swatted his belly to make him settle. He did, but his eyes were reproachful. Guilt burned in my gut, and a single question blared in my mind.

What if Earl chose not to come?

Behind me, Ben finished buckling his mules into their harnesses and climbed onto the wagon's driver's seat beside Dante. Josephine and Akiko had already mounted, and Fox shied as Sally's coat flapped while settling on My Darling.

"Ready?" Ben asked.

The wind picked up, flinging grit into my eyes. My chest tightened as I struggled to breathe without coughing. "I'm not leaving, but you should go."

# CHAPTER FORTY

Everyone stilled, staring into the livery where Bruno, Oxide, and Magnesium waited.

"What do you mean, you're not leaving?" Genevie asked, boosting River onto a rangy, chestnut gelding.

"Earl went to the market on an errand for me." I swallowed, peering into the blowing dust. No one could compel me to leave Earl behind. "I'll wait for her, but you should head north."

"Are you sure Earl is coming?" The kindness in Josephine's voice stung my eyes worse than the blowing dust. Even though her question set my heart thumping with doubt, I nodded.

Akiko's face pinched with anxiety. If the men came looking for Talbot, I didn't want her here either. "Stay with the others, Mouse. We'll catch up."

She shook her head, her mouth flat and hard, but panic flared in her eyes when Ben flapped the mules' driving reins. The wagon groaned and rolled forward. Cara moved to the front to lead the group. Tom's horse danced from side to side, unhappy about being left behind, but he ignored it. "We'll

275

follow the main road north past the Strat. When you reach route ninety-five, turn west and follow it north."

"I'll be there."

He nodded. As soon as he leaned back, his horse spun and sprinted to the front of the line.

"Akiko, Sally, follow Ben." Josephine pointed at the wagon. "I'll bring Donkey."

Akiko hesitated.

"Please go," I said. "We need to get Talbot out of here."

She sighed and followed Sally but twisted in her saddle to glance back several times.

River passed by without acknowledgment, but Genevie slowed. "Don't be long, Artist."

After they turned the corner, I checked Oxide and Bruno's saddles, tightening both cinches. Magnesium whinnied, and I looked up, but the stable yard was empty, save Charcoal and Neblina. I tried tying Bruno to a pick string on Magnesium's packsaddle, but the enormous horse jerked his head back and snapped the string. In response, my packhorse pinned his ears, raising a hind leg in warning.

"Easy, fellows." There wasn't time to let the three horses sort out a pecking order, so I mounted Oxide and left the livery with both horses in hand. Bruno fussed, dancing from side to side, but I shook his rope to get his attention. "Easy, easy. Let's go find your rider, big man."

By the time I'd gotten the hang of maneuvering all three horses, the others were out of sight but not out of hearing. Oxide's sides shook as he whinnied to his herd mates. The shrill sound ricocheted off the surrounding buildings, transmuting into a series of eerie screams.

The road next to the market was choked with wagons. Harried shouts rang out as the vendors raced to pack up their stalls. The horses picked up on the restless energy and fretted—

pawing and swinging from side to side, bumping into each other, their tails swishing.

"Easy," I muttered, dismounting. There was no hitching rail or anything sturdy to tie the horses to. People hurried up and down the stairs laden with goods, but neither Earl nor Ruben appeared among the throng.

The third time a young woman with ruddy skin and close-cropped, white-blonde hair passed me, I flagged her down. Her voice was hesitant. "Yes?"

"Have you seen Ruben?"

She paused before answering. "No, but he usually uses the porters on the northwest stair."

I thanked her and led the horses to the north side of the market. Here again, the staircase rang with churning footsteps. My palms grew slick, and my stomach twisted. What if Earl and Ruben had already left? What would she do if she'd returned and found us all gone? The idea left my knees spongy, making it harder to climb back onto Oxide. I wheeled him east, and we trotted toward the livery.

*She'll be there.*

I repeated the statement like a mantra, my pulse pounding when we turned toward the livery. But finding the dusty barn empty, my hopes withered.

I turned the horses south toward the Copperfield. They jostled back and forth as I tied them to the hitching rail, making the task harder than needed. The porter's desk was unmanned, but the wooden buffalo figurine stood on the edge of the desk. I snatched it and rode back to the livery, my stomach churning. I chewed on my lip as we reached the dusty yard, unsure what to do next.

"Artist."

The flood of relief washing over me sent my heart soaring. I couldn't keep the grin off my face as I swung Oxide around.

"Butcher. The others have gone ahead, but I know what routes they're taking."

When she took Bruno from me, Earl's eyes were red-rimmed.

"Are you okay?"

She took a shuddering breath before mounting. "When I found the livery empty, I thought..."

A pang tore through me. "When you didn't come, I thought you'd still be at the market, so I took the horses to find you. I checked the Copperfield next."

She climbed onto Bruno and offered a small smile. "A misunderstanding then. Talbot?"

"Safe in Ben's wagon, sitting in a nest Dante made for him."

A ghost of a smile crossed her face. "Good."

Oxide leaped forward when I squeezed him. Magnesium's lead slid through my hand, scorching my skin before I had the wit to tighten my grip. My palm stung, but I ignored it as we turned north. Earl brought Bruno abreast on the wide road. She pointed northeast, frowning.

A dusty, orange-brown hue, like Verona Gold Ochre, obscured the eastern horizon, obliterating the barren, wrinkled mountains. Eager to catch up with the rest of our traveling herd, Oxide needed no encouragement to quicken his pace. The buffeting winds grew stronger, and I kept my head down to protect my eyes from the gusting grit.

During a moment of calm, I said, "Thank you for seeing Ruben."

Earl glanced sideway, her expression troubled. "He had a message for you and was reluctant to give it to me, so it took longer than I expected."

"What message?"

"I didn't understand it. He said, 'There are three, but

together, they don't make a whole.' But when I asked for clarification, he wouldn't elaborate."

Oxide snorted, shaking his head as a hot gust brought a new swirl of sand and grit. "That's all?"

She stiffened, nodded, and shielded her eyes.

I grimaced, intending to apologize for my tone, but another cloud of dust enveloped us.

By the time we reached the Strat, the streets were empty. The air was thick with dust, and we pulled our tunics up to cover our noses. The bulb near the top of the tower was hazy and indistinct as we passed beneath it. It was the second tower to lead us astray, and once again, my efforts to find my parents had fallen short. This trip had cost us months of travel, but I'd gained a sister. Not that I wanted one anymore. If *Home* wasn't leading me to my parents, why had I painted a tower?

The surrounding buildings moaned, their intact windows rippling and shuddering under the wind. The sky east of us had darkened further, the Sepia and Bloodstone hues pulsing as lightning flashed.

Charcoal barked and sprinted ahead of us. Sally and Akiko hunched low over their horses' necks, covering their mouths and noses with their tunics. I waved at them, urging Oxide forward to catch the wagon.

Ben squinted at me. "We need shelter!"

I didn't enjoy traveling through the storm any more than the others, but at least it provided cover. If we took shelter and our pursuers didn't, they would soon catch up. But what if the storm worsened after we'd left all shelter behind? Breathing was already difficult, and we had no way to cover the horses' noses.

*Can you drown in dry air?*

Ahead, Cara and Tom's horses were barely visible through the dusty gloom. I braced as a gust buffeted us, then urged

Oxide forward. "We need to find shelter!" Acrid dust coated my mouth.

Tom's mouth compressed, but he pointed forward. "We're heading to Mountain View, a safe house on the north side of the depot."

The buildings weren't visible, but I nodded and dropped back to relay the news. Genevie had wrapped a strip of linen around her face, leaving only her eyes exposed. River wore a matching face covering, but where Genevie's eyes showed friendly concern, River glared.

"We're riding for shelter now!"

We staggered on after Tom and Cara through swirling clouds of dust and grit. Though lightning flashed, the howling winds drowned out any accompanying thunder. By the time we turned off the principal route, my throat was on fire. Pulling under an overhang, we coughed and spluttered. Beneath me, Oxide quivered, his sides heaving.

Tom banged his fist on the glass doors until someone answered. After a hurried conversation, he waved us over. "They have room for us."

"Can we bring the horses inside?" Josephine sneezed several times, her hair gray with dust.

"No, they don't have anywhere to stable them."

Ben's voice was hoarse. "Where's the nearest livery?"

Tom trotted back to the men waiting inside the lobby. His face was pinched when he returned. "A quarter kilometer southwest."

I shook my head as Sally convulsed in a coughing fit. "Get everyone settled. I'll run the horse to the livery."

Ben coughed. "I'll help."

As each rider dismounted, Genevie pulled their bags down and tied the horse onto the end of the pack string. Even Akiko didn't protest and helped River escort Talbot inside. While the others ferried our bags inside, Oxide and I led a string of ten equines out from under the awning. Away from the building's shelter, the storm's power hit us again, and a racking cough shook me. I struggled to breathe through the swirling dust. Behind me, Ben followed in the wagon, its rumble nearly inaudible over the storm's roar.

The livery was less than a quarter kilometer away, but after the hostler rolled the barn's massive steel doors closed, I collapsed onto a bale of straw and waited for Ben to negotiate the board.

"He's agreed, but we have to stack his hay."

I groaned, looking at the mountain of dusty bales. "Let me guess, into the loft?"

"Yes. After we untack, brush, feed, and water all the animals."

When we finished the work, the hostler brought out a jug of water and a basket of stale biscuits. My legs and arms like rubber, I stretched out on the wagon's bench. I didn't have the energy to attempt a second biscuit when Ben tried to pass me the basket again. Between the storm, hay, and horses, my sweat-soaked tunic was a dismal, brown-gray, and I'd developed three, sizable blisters along my fingers. They squished when I poked them.

Ben rubbed his beard, its normal Russet color nearly a Burnt Umber. "Should we wait out the storm here?"

"We can't. We've already been gone too long." I groaned. "There may be no one left standing if we leave Josephine and Cara together much longer."

"You're right." Ben's frown deepened, and he reached over to haul me to my feet. "Let's go."

Shoulder to shoulder, we trudged back to the Mountain View with rough, cotton feed sacks pressed to our faces. When we reached the building, two men helped us shove the doors shut behind us. Charcoal shook before I could stop him, his coat releasing a cloud of dust. Ben shook too, then brushed my back for me. While returning the favor, I squinted through the clouded glass. I didn't see Neblina.

A slight man with slicked-back hair waved. "I'll take you to the others."

He led us down a wide corridor and through a large, open expanse. While the space was technically large enough to have housed our equines, we couldn't have secured them without resorting to art. There was no bedding or forage to cover the polished stone floor. A rooster crowed from a crate, and in the far corner, a trio of pigs snuffled in a temporary pen made from upended tables.

When the man led us up to the fifth story, Ben and I exchanged glances. I dropped back and lowered my voice. "I thought your engineering job only added enough water pressure to get to the second story."

"So did I."

Our guide opened the door for us, then led us south down another long hallway. This one ended at a locked set of doors with inset windows, and he pulled a key from a chain around his neck. After unlocking the first, he stepped aside to let us through. I hesitated until Genevie stepped into the hallway.

When she sprinted toward us, we spread our arms to prevent her from running headlong into the doors behind us.

"Easy, Gen." Ben's expression mirrored my confusion.

Behind us, the lock engaged with a *click*.

Genevie shoved me so hard my back slammed against the door. I gaped at her until she shoved me a second time. My knees buckled, and I landed on my tailbone. Sparks exploded along the periphery of my vision.

Charcoal put himself between us, barking ferociously, and

Ben leaped forward to wrap his arms around her. She struggled as he bellowed, "Josephine!"

When the others crowded into the hallway, my breath caught at Akiko's tear-stained face. Between her expression and the strain on Earl's face, alarm spread through me strong enough to clear my head. "What's happened?"

Genevie stopped struggling when River reached for her. In the resulting quiet, Dante helped me stand. "We're in a pickle."

Behind him, Cara snorted, but when she spoke, her words and tone were bitter. "This place is run by Carter's people. You *were* our last hope for escape."

# CHAPTER FORTY-ONE

T he hallway wobbled as I stared at Cara. She had tended toward melodramatics... but based on everyone else's expressions, she wasn't exaggerating.

*I'm trapped.*

*Again.*

My knees gave out, and I slid down the wall to the floor a second time, my mind racing. I couldn't be trapped again. All I'd wanted was to find, meet, and warn my parents. Build Akiko a safe home. Keep Talbot and River out of harm's way. And, maybe, explore the intense energy between me and Earl.

Together, Ben and Genevie attacked the doors, yanking on the handles and pounding their fists against the unyielding steel surfaces. The cacophony of their struggle added to the din of the storm and the shrieking, flexing windows wrapped around me like a steel band, stealing the air from my lungs. Panicked memories from Welland Island flashed across my mind's canvas.

Dante slid down the wall next to me and sat with his legs splayed and his expression despondent. "Feel your feels, man.

We went through it too." He waved his hands at the others. "We're a few hours ahead of you."

My mind roared as my eyes locked onto Tom and Cara. Why had I trusted them again? Carter had ordered his people to do reprehensible things... but these two had directly caused harm to me and the people I cared about. The deaths of Whistler and Bowman, my incarceration on Welland Island, and now, our present predicament. "Why are *you* here? You are Christians, aren't you?"

"Yes." Tom recoiled, his jaw tightening. "But we told you, we're not with Carter or any of the other Christian factions."

Ruben's message of three not making a whole now made sense. There were at least three sets of religious folks in the depot; the people working with Tom and Cara, the people in the Mandal, and Carter's crew here in the Mountain View.

Cara nodded in agreement as Tom continued, "Besides, isn't your cousin one of Carter's lieutenants? If there's anyone we shouldn't trust, it's *him*."

River pushed away from Genevie and placed herself between Talbot and Tom. "Talbot isn't religious. They sent him to infiltrate Carter's organization for information."

The Bible I'd found hidden in Talbot's room flashed across my mind's canvas. "But that's not entirely true, is it, Talbot?"

"How *dare* you?" River rounded on me, making me regret saying anything. Pink spots burned high on her cheeks as she took Talbot's hand. "You have no idea what he's given up on your behalf. What they forced both of us to do for *you*."

Talbot patted her hand but turned his face in my direction. "Did you bring my things?"

"Yes." I grimaced as the others stared at me.

Talbot's jaw relaxed. "Thank you. They're precious to me and not easily replaced." He pulled River closer, unaware of the uncertainty flickering across her face. "Not that I can read right now."

Josephine's eyes sharpened. "Read?" She leaned forward, narrowing her eyes. "You found a Bible and said nothing?"

"A Bible?" Cara straightened. "Talbot, you brought one with you?"

River scowled. "Of *course* not." But Talbot murmured something near her ear, and River's outrage melted into an expression of betrayal. The hurt on her face raised a lump in my throat. She pulled away from him, stooped to grab a bag, and strode down the hallway to the last room on the left.

Genevie let out a whistling sigh and rolled her eyes. "Anything else you haven't disclosed, Artist?" Her words stung, and before I could defend myself, she followed River down the hall and disappeared, too.

"Well?" Sally glared at me with her hands on her hips. "I'd like an answer too."

"Why?" Josephine's question was full of exasperation. "Are any of us sure he'll tell us the whole truth, anyway?"

My toes curled in my boots, and I glanced at Earl for support. Her gaze flicked away. A deep chill spread through me. I'd taken her continued support for granted, just like I'd assumed there would be time for us... later. After Talbot was safe. After I had the answers I wanted. Perhaps even after I'd built a home for Akiko.

*Even trapped together, I could lose her.*

I squirmed, the silent reproach seeping from everyone more uncomfortable than the storm. "It wasn't my intention to..." I swallowed. "I didn't mean to deceive anyone."

"What does the intention matter when the results are the same?" Ben sighed. "But done is done, so let's start with what you know."

I clenched my jaw, sorting my thoughts. "There are at least

three Christian groups in the depot. Ruben—a contact I made at the market—confirmed it, though I didn't know what he meant when Earl relayed his message."

"Three?" Josephine frowned and turned to Talbot. "Who were the people who took you from the Tropic?"

"Carter's competition. Deacons in his ministry, so I didn't realize—" Talbot's jaw clenched several times before he answered. "It was stupid to go with them, but I thought them friends. No one told me they'd left his organization."

My gaze dropped to the bruises around Talbot's wrists. "If you knew them, why did they tie you up?"

"They thought I was here to track them down and grabbed me to prevent me from sending word to Carter."

Dante squinted at Talbot. "But if you're *with* Carter, can't you get us out of here?"

"No." Talbot's throat convulsed. "I *was* part of his organization, but like Erena—"

"River," interrupted Akiko.

Talbot sighed before continuing. "Like *River* said, my original mission was to infiltrate Carter's organization for information."

"Infiltrate." Ben rubbed his jaw. "And now he's found you out?"

"It would appear so."

Charcoal leaned against me, and I stroked his coarse fur, grateful he was still on my side. "We are trapped, but Carter could be after me *or* you." My mouth tightened at the glance Tom and Cara exchanged. "What?"

"Or us." Tom's frown deepened, but he lifted his chin. "I raided their art supplies before we left."

Dante perked up. "You have supplies here?"

"I did, but they confiscated what I had on me. I hid the rest near our valley."

"So, you think Carter is after you for taking art supplies?" Josephine asked. She turned to Talbot. "And you think he's after you for spying on him?" She gazed at me, her expression pained. "Were we just caught in the middle?"

In truth, I didn't know. "When Tom trapped me in the cell on Welland Island, Carter threatened my parents—*our parents* —but he assumed I'd die there. Since we trailed his group, he may not know I survived."

My chest tightened as fresh tears rolled down Akiko's face, but a new thought struck me, and I turned toward Talbot. "Did you tell the minstrels you sent out who your message was for?"

"No." Talbot rubbed his jaw. "But I gave the same message to five minstrels. Perhaps one of them relayed it to Carter, and he sent someone to find out who I wanted to meet."

The image of the dead man in Angel Falls splayed across my mind's canvas. "So, he may not know who I am, but he's now certain he can't trust you." There *was* something else I hadn't told the others. "When the man attacked us at Angel Falls, I fought with him. He fell backward into the water and broke his neck. Talbot was hurt and needed urgent medical care..." –I shrugged– "so I left him there."

At this new admission, Ben groaned, and Cara and Tom exchanged glances. Josephine's frown deepened, but her expression was sympathetic rather than judgmental.

"You left a *body* behind us?" Dante looked at Earl. "Did you *know*?"

She shook her head. "You and I organized the wagon to transport Talbot to the depot." She avoided my eyes again, so I buried my flaming face in Charcoal's dusty fur.

"Right." Sally drew in a deep breath. "Anything else?"

I tensed. There *was* another secret, perhaps the biggest of them all. One that could forever change everything. But even if Dante, Tom, and Cara hadn't been present, I wouldn't have divulged it. The knowledge of Akiko's gift would threaten everyone here.

Without a qualm, I raised my head and stared at Akiko. And lied. "No, there's nothing else."

Uncertainty flickered across her face. My heart pounded as I willed her to remain silent. At last, she leaned against Sally and sniffled. "If we're done yelling at Matthew, can we pick our rooms?"

Josephine gave her a watery smile. "What was it you said earlier?"

A smile glimmered on Akiko's face. "This place is better than a poke in the eye."

I'd said the same to her when someone had stolen our bags in Toronto Depot. The bewildered, lost feeling from then perfectly captured what coursed through me now. "We need a yellow boat."

Akiko's chin raised. "And manners, *please*."

We grinned at each other; our private joke made even funnier by the mystified expressions on everyone's faces. It lifted my mood, and I clambered back to my feet. I couldn't do anything about Talbot, my parents, or finding a permanent home for Akiko now, but maybe I could use the time here to make amends to everyone... and explore the feelings I had for Earl. I hauled Dante up, then reached down to pull Sally, Ben, and Josephine to their feet. "We've been in worse situations than this before. How many rooms do we have?"

"Six." Sally ticked her fingers. "Three will go to the couples, and the six of us will double up."

"I'll share with Uncle Talbot." Akiko flashed me an apologetic look. "He tells stories at bedtime."

"Good. Makes this easy." Sally surveyed the pile of dusty bags in the hall and tugged hers from the pile. "Earl, do you care which side of the bed you sleep on?"

My heart dropped, but what had I expected? After months of traveling together, I'd only just invited her to a private dinner. We were nowhere near a couple, and if I couldn't find the courage to address the situation, we might never be. But should I talk to her now or wait until things were more settled?

Earl bent to retrieve her saddle bags and an urgency seized me, the sensation of time slipping past too fast. "Earl, a moment?"

She nodded but looked uncomfortable and shifted her feet as the others disappeared into the rooms. "What is it?"

I swallowed. "I want to apologize to you. Our dinner—"

"It's nothing now," she interrupted. "Forget it." Without another word or a backward glance, she left me standing in the hallway with nothing but Charcoal, dusty bags, and regrets.

# CHAPTER FORTY-TWO

**B**y our second day of captivity, even Akiko drooped from our communal case of lethargy. I spent the time watching the guards through the small glass panels, but they rotated often enough there was no way I could use art to remove the doors. Not that I had any art supplies to work with, anyway.

There was no other exit from our bank of rooms. None of the windows opened far enough for even Akiko to squeeze through. But even if they had, we were on the fifth floor, facing the front entrance. The exterior walls were clad with stucco-covered concrete and glass. Even Ben couldn't climb walls without finger or toe holds. Plus, even if we broke a window *and* figured out how to cling to the smooth surfaces, we'd be in full view of our captors.

We spent endless hours discussing, then dismissing escape options, until we'd exhausted our imaginations and run out of things to say. Earl avoided me, leaving me even less inclined to play Josephine's endless 'what if' games. Whenever I joined the group, River withdrew, splitting Genevie's attention.

While the rest of them contemplated escape options, I tried

to catch the attention of passersby. One woman in a swirling, red dress stopped and stared up at us. I waved frantically, but the way she turned and continued told me she hadn't seen me. Still, I watched for her and other sharp-eyed pedestrians while thinking about how to repair my floundering friendship with Earl.

None of our rooms were large enough to seat and house everyone comfortably, leaving the hallway as our only communal space. Our captors had left no chairs, so our options were to sit or lie on the beds, stand, or sit or lie on the floor. No one came to speak with us, so we didn't know if our captors wanted anything. The uncertainty we faced wore on us all.

Even more troubling were the two, meager pails of water our jailers delivered each day. As we were on the fifth floor, we had no access to water, other than what they delivered. The water sufficed to sustain fourteen people and one dog, but not enough to flush every toilet or wash. I'd trained Charcoal to do his business on a towel at the end of the hallway, but he looked mortified each time he had to do so. To his credit, Dante didn't complain when I added Charcoal's movement to our toilet for our daily flush.

Akiko wandered into our room and glanced around with little interest. She flopped across the corner of the bed, saying nothing. Charcoal trailed her in, but he at least seemed interested in my company and crossed the room to where I sat at the window.

I rubbed his ears and mustered the energy to tease her. "Talbot out of stories?"

She shrugged. "His headache got worse. He fell asleep, and he's too hot to sit next to."

"Everyone is too hot," I muttered. As soon as the sun went down, we cracked every movable window to pull in fresh air, but it did little to reduce the temperature in our living space.

Akiko eyed Dante. "What are you doing?"

He opened one eye. "Sculpting."

She sat up. "You can art without materials?"

Dante sighed and opened both eyes. He sat up, scooting back against the wall. "When I was a boy in the abbey, I had a terrible time falling asleep. I envied the other boys who fell asleep as easily as stones dropping down a well."

I leaned my head against the broad window frame, trying to remember even a single night where I'd lain awake in the dark while the other boys had slept.

Akiko propped her hands on her head. "So, what did you do?"

"Some people like to count backward from one hundred by threes or sevens, and some people focus on their breaths, but neither worked for me. Instead, I pictured a giant block of marble in an enormous, dark room. I'd circle the marble, trying to imagine what was inside."

"Did you ever find out?"

He shook his head. "Some nights, I chip away the corners before I fall asleep, but on others, I don't even pick up my chisel before I'm out."

Akiko rolled onto her back. "Are you trying to sleep now?"

"For two days, I've had nothing to do but sleep." Dante poked her with his toe. "So no, now I'm working on the sculpture I never finished."

Her eyes brightened, and she sat up. "What will it be?"

"A very beautiful man. Someone I can love." He shrugged. "Maybe it's the man I came to the depot to find."

Akiko sighed. "I hope he comes for you and lets us out."

Dante leaned forward, his face serious. "Perhaps I should keep working on my sculpture."

"Good idea." She slid off the bed and turned to me. "Want to come visiting?"

I didn't, but I let her pull me to my feet, anyway. We stopped at Ben and Josephine's room first. Like Dante, Ben sat on his bed, leaning on the wall.

Josephine lay diagonally across the mattress with her head in Ben's lap. "Hullo, you three."

I leaned against the door frame. "We're visiting."

"Good timing," said Ben. "We've devolved into spiral logic once again."

"At least *you're* not trying to convince everyone the solution is prayer." Though Ben snorted in agreement, it wasn't a joking matter.

Tom and Cara's convictions caused friction for us. We no longer gathered in larger groups for fear of encouraging them to join us. Their effect on Earl aggravated me. Faced with their unyielding certainty, Earl had withdrawn more than usual, making it even harder to find excuses to talk to her.

Josephine sighed and sat up, patting the bed next to her. "There must be a way out of here."

Akiko climbed onto the bed and scooted next to Josephine. "Matthew will figure something out."

The simple confidence in her voice made me squirm. Like Dante sculpting his dream man, I'd been daydreaming about Earl, not pondering ways to escape. As though he could read my mind, Ben raised his eyebrow. I flushed and shrugged, trying for humor. "The last time I accepted Carter's hospitality, they at least left me a *chair*."

Akiko giggled and pantomimed throwing a chair off a tall height. She pretended to watch it fall for several heartbeats, then made an explosion noise, mimicking a chair smashing against imaginary rocks far below.

"Rude," said Ben. "Think of what we could have done with one chair."

"So rude." Akiko slid off the bed and waved. "We're visiting Genevie and River next, so bye."

My stomach tightened, but Akiko grabbed my hand and pulled me toward their door. When I hesitated at their threshold, she dragged me in while making obnoxious groans, turning us into a spectacle. "Sorry," I mouthed when she released my hand.

Genevie and my sister sat on the floor near the window. Cross-legged, they held hands, facing each other.

Akiko joined them and beckoned me over. "Dante is sculpting a perfect man while Ben and Josephine plot. What are you doing?"

The corners of Genevie's eyes crinkled. "Discussing our future."

Akiko scooted over to make room for Charcoal. "What about it?"

"Where we should go."

"*If* we should go," River corrected. Her eyes narrowed as she studied me. "Talbot asked me to respect my oaths and not to answer your questions. I don't know why, but I trust *him*, so don't even try."

My sister was like a cactus—pretty, but prickly. If she hadn't been so hostile toward me from the start, I absolutely would have tried pumping her for information. But even after rescuing Talbot, she hadn't let go of her grudge. Disappointment pooled in my gut, but I pretended I didn't care and focused on Genevie. "You're not staying with us?"

She sighed. "I want to, but River isn't sure she wants to leave the depot."

Sally knocked on the door frame. "Matthew, a word?"

I pushed to my feet and joined her in the hallway. Her gaze flicked to the room as she pulled me farther into the corridor.

Once we were out of earshot, she lowered her voice. "Talbot is unwell. Come see."

My mouth tightened, and I followed her to Talbot's room. He lay on his bed, his breathing shallow and sleep restless. Sweat darkened the sheets, souring the room.

*Fever.*

He'd pushed his pillow to the floor, and I stooped to retrieve it. "Akiko said he was hot, but I didn't realize..." My throat tightened, and I lifted him without finishing. Sally slid the pillow under his head and straightened his sheet. His morning ration of water was still on the nightstand, so I brought the cup to his lips. "Talbot, drink." I dribbled water onto his lips but couldn't tell if he swallowed any. My eyes blurred, but I stared at him until Sally patted my shoulder and beckoned me back into the hallway.

She peered at me as she polished her spectacles. "He needs a healer."

"I know." I pulled his door closed and gestured toward Genevie's room. "Should we tell them?"

When Sally squinted at me, I winced. "I know—and I promise I'll work on my candor. But I also don't want to worry Akiko needlessly."

She searched my face. "We'll wait until she goes to bed." She flashed me an uncertain smile and squeezed my hand before returning to Genevie's room.

I crossed the hallway to Earl's room. For once, she was alone. She sat on the edge of her bed, facing the window. I raised my hand to knock but hesitated. What if she didn't want company, or didn't welcome my intrusion? I almost left, but I stopped myself. Pining for the easy friendship we'd lost wasn't working either. I cleared my throat, and she glanced over her shoulder, then turned to face me.

I tried a smile, but based on her reaction, my expression wasn't friendly. "Unvarnished truth?"

Her eyes softened. "Always."

*Courage, Artist.*

"I've let you down and feel terrible." I fingered the buffalo figurine in my pocket. "All I want is to know you better, but it's like we're caught on opposite sides of an ever-widening chasm."

Her lips tightened, but she shook her head. "With everything happening..."

When her voice trailed off, I put the buffalo figurine on the bed between us. "The unvarnished truth, remember?"

Her breath caught and an expression of longing crossed her face, but she didn't touch it. "I regretted leaving it behind as soon as I left the Copperfield."

"Why did you?"

When she finally met my eyes, electricity sparked through me, and my heart leaped. But her gaze slipped beyond me as someone knocked on the open door. In an instant, she stiffened, her eyes went blank, and her neutral expression settled back in place like a mask.

# CHAPTER FORTY-THREE

The hairs on the back of my neck rose, and my gut twisted as Cara said, "Sorry to disturb you."

I swallowed, turned, and somehow kept my voice even, "What is it?"

"We need a word." Cara glanced over her shoulder to where Tom waited in the hall.

I yearned to refuse, but I knew Cara. She wouldn't leave until I agreed, and any ensuing argument would further alienate Earl. "Excuse me," I said.

Earl shrugged and returned her attention to the window without touching the figurine.

I glowered at Tom while following Cara into the hallway.

He fidgeted as we approached, then launched into his pitch without so much as a greeting. "We wanted to explain our vision once we reached our valley, but since we're stuck here for some unknown time, we thought we'd explain it now—what we plan to build, and how fulfilling our vision will help you, too."

"Help me?" I blinked. "How?"

The look they exchanged told me they'd argued about this. Neither of them said anything, but they continued their staring contest, as if telepathically communicating.

I'd had enough. "If you won't tell me anything, we're done here. I was in the middle of something, so—"

Tom's words came out in a rush. "We're planning to build a cooperative Christian community. Assuming we get out of here and can talk the artists at Churchill Abbey into joining us."

"Terrific. How does it help me?"

Cara sighed. "We believe our sanctuary community will prevent Carter's followers from expanding westward."

"How? By stretching the mountains?" I asked, remembering the gigantic ranges we'd traced on the map.

"Mountains?" Cara frowned. "No, by robbing him of supporters."

The lines around Tom's mouth deepened. "Carter's following grows because people are desperate to practice their faith. But if we establish our haven—"

"When we build our paradise on Earth," Cara said. "Few will stay with Carter."

My stomach flipped. "But you're trying to do the same thing he is, so how are you any better?"

Tom leaned forward, but Cara stilled him. "It's a fair question." She smoothed her palms against her sides. "First, know I'm ashamed of my actions. I thought myself a warrior, battling for religious freedom. But I fought for my freedom at the expense of others." She leaned forward and grasped my hand. "I fought by *taking* from others. God has shown me how wrong we were."

Tom smiled encouragement, and she continued, "We want to create a community where the faithful can come to us to worship, rather than spreading our message through established communities."

Tom met my eyes. "Anyone can join us, and we wouldn't force anyone to stay. Our aim is to create a refuge. We have no plans to proselytize, and no wish to convert."

It still sounded exactly like what Carter had tried to build on Welland Island. "I understand," I lied, turning to go.

Cara blocked my escape. "We have a favor to ask."

*Big surprise.*

Tom nodded, his eyes shining. "We want to borrow Talbot's Bible."

My hands curled into fists. "He's unwell."

"We could read it to him," Cara offered, raising her chin. "It would comfort him and give us the chance to study it, too."

*They won't let this go.*

The pounding in my head resumed. "I'll consider it." Before they could continue their plea, I returned to Earl's room and shut the door behind me.

She stood, folding her arms across her chest. "What is it?"

I leaned my head against the door and closed my eyes. "They want to study Talbot's Bible."

"I suppose we should have expected it. Are you alright?"

The buffalo figurine sat on the window ledge. It was a slight gesture, but it encouraged me enough to confide in her. "Enabling religion makes me uncomfortable."

She glanced from me to the figurine, and a ghost of a smile curved her lips. "Same. What does Talbot think?"

"He's unwell." My mouth tightened, my head throbbing in time with my pulse. "Fever."

Earl's eyes softened, and she searched my face. "Can we do anything?"

I shrugged and cracked the door to peek into the hall. Cara and Tom were gone, so I pulled the door open. "Sally says he needs a healer."

Earl brushed past me and stood in the hallway, studying

the locked metal doors. Her eyes hardened. "It's time to make friends."

The speculative expression on her face made me uneasy. I shuffled my feet. "Make friends?"

"With our guards." She rolled her eyes. "They're men."

"Can I help?" If Earl had a plan, I needed to be part of it. Besides, she didn't believe men and women could be friends.

Her lips curved. "You're pretty, but not *that* pretty," she said, before disappearing into Genevie's room.

DANTE WAS STILL LYING ON THE BED WHEN I RETURNED TO our room. "Asleep or sculpting?" I asked, digging through my bags.

"I can't see his face yet, but I'm getting closer." He squinted, shading his eyes. "What are you after?"

I stared at Talbot's linen-wrapped Bible. "Reconciliation?"

His eyes closed. "Good luck."

The hallway was still empty, so I ducked into Talbot's room. His sleep was quieter, but his skin was flushed and damp.

"You probably can't hear me, but if you could, would you agree to Cara's request?" I studied his furrowed brow before unwrapping the book. It lay heavy in my hands. I flipped through the pages, catching my name printed in the upper corner.

I read the ornate language out loud, "*Ask, and it shall be given you; seek, and ye shall find; knock, and it shall be opened unto you: For every one that asketh receiveth; and he that seeketh findeth; and to him that knocketh it shall be opened.*"

My gut twisted, and I stared at the passage. "A little on the nose."

Talbot's brow had smoothed, as though the words had soothed him. Maybe he would appreciate someone reading to him. I flipped through the pages again, stopping here and there to focus on the notes Talbot had added to the margins. None were personal, and all appeared to pertain to the text. After smoothing his bedding, I slipped from his room and crossed the hallway to Ben and Josephine's room.

"I find this deeply unsettling," I said, tossing Talbot's Bible onto the bed next to Josephine.

She scrambled up with an eager look on her face, but Ben ignored it. "Stay in here with us."

"What? Why?" The way they exchanged glances made gooseflesh rise along my arm. "What don't I know?"

Josephine cradled the Bible against her chest and bit her lip. "Earl is putting her plan in motion. You shouldn't watch."

"In motion?" I rocked my weight backward onto my heels. "But that's great news. Anything to get out of here, right?" The passage I'd read earlier sprang to mind. "He that seeketh findeth..."

Sally popped her head into the room. "Matthew, a moment?"

Ben slid off the bed as I followed Sally into the hallway.

Dante, Genevie, River, and Akiko stood to one side, and Sally joined them. Their shared air of anticipation sent shivers up my spine, but nothing appeared amiss. "What's going on?"

When Earl stepped into the hallway from Genevie's room, my breath caught. It was Earl, but not the Earl I knew. Gone were the baggy overalls and blowsy tunic. In their place, she wore a fitted, Emerald tunic and Slate Gray leggings. The clothing clung to every curve. Her hair was loose and flowed across her shoulders and down her back like a wind-driven flame. The clothing and colors accentuated every physical gift she possessed, but the look on her face and her smoldering energy made my knees weak.

When I struggled to swallow, Genevie clapped. "Girl, you've got it."

Dante nodded. "Perfect."

Earl's lopsided grin slid across her face. "Let's do this."

Earl glided toward the locked doors. I took a step toward them too, but Ben gripped my shoulder and tugged me back into his room. Sally and Josephine crowded in after me. I stepped backward through the doorway, craning my neck to see into the hallway.

"Come," said Ben, pulling me into the room.

I sank onto the bed as Akiko, Dante, River, and Genevie pushed into the room too. Earl's low, musical laugh floated down the hallway before Genevie closed the door.

Sally broke through the uneasy, awkward silence by patting my leg and perching on the bed beside me. "We know this will be difficult, but we have to try."

Dante flashed me a look of sympathy. "If I could share my mind's block of marble with you, I would."

Their sympathetic expressions meshed with what Earl had said earlier. My gut tightened. "She's made herself *bait*."

"Yes," said River. "For Talbot." For once, her hostility was absent, but the softness in her voice made me even more uncomfortable.

There had to be a better way, and I longed to charge into the hallway and demand Earl *stop*. But as much as I hated what she was doing, she'd only taken action after I told her Talbot needed help. This was my fault. Earl had put herself in harm's way for Talbot. For *me*.

I swallowed and attempted to meet River's eyes. "For Talbot."

Josephine waved the book. "Speaking of Talbot, why are

you reading his Bible?"

Josephine used the book as a distraction, but I welcomed it. "I wasn't. I mean, I did, but not on purpose—" I stopped and collected myself. "Cara asked if she and Tom could study it while we're stuck here. They offered to read to Talbot."

Genevie frowned and crossed her arms. "I don't trust them."

Sally nodded, but Josephine opened the book. "Reading would help pass the time."

Akiko pushed forward and leaned against the bed. "Does it have stories?"

"Yes. Stories, parables, sayings, history." Josephine closed it and hugged it to her chest again. "Is there any harm in reading it? For research?"

I shrugged and stared at the floor. If the guards had turned Earl away, she would have returned and reported it.

But she hadn't.

Ben's rumbling voice pulled my focus back into the room. "Is there anything dangerous in the book?"

"Not in what's written. Objectively, it's a collection of stories, poems, and letters." Josephine tugged on her lip. "But for the faithful, it was everything. A rubric for life, a measure with which to judge others. Some believed every word in it was divine truth, and it gave others an excuse to persecute or ostracize swaths of the population."

"Then we would be safe to read it," said Dante, "but not the others?"

I hugged myself. "It's a *book*."

"A book with the power to send people into war, condone slavery, and justify murder." Josephine shivered as she covered the Bible with her palms. "It can harness ideals and galvanize action."

"Toss it out the window," said Sally.

"No," River and I said in unison. My gaze flicked to her, before I added, "It's Talbot's, and it's precious to him."

River nodded in agreement. "How about this? We agree but stipulate the book must remain in Talbot's presence—and one of us, too."

*One of us.*

Warmth bloomed in my chest, and I smiled at my sister. "Feels right to me."

"Yes," said Josephine. "Shall we tell them now?" She led us into the hallway. I'd expected to catch Earl batting her lashes at the guards through the window glass, but the hallway beyond the locked doors was empty. My fists tightened, and I stared at them while Ben knocked on Tom and Cara's door.

They were guarded when they joined us in the hallway, but they relaxed as Josephine explained the conditions under which they could read Talbot's Bible.

Cara beamed and hugged Tom's arm. "Done. Is one of you available now?"

Sally raised her chin. "I am."

"Us too," said Akiko, tapping Charcoal's head. "Besides, it's *my* room," she added, when I opened my mouth to object.

"Let's keep it to a half hour," said Ben. "Talbot is ill, and we don't want to disturb his rest needlessly."

I nodded, staring at the hallway doors.

The others wandered away, leaving me alone with Genevie. "She'll be all right."

It took effort to pull the corners of my mouth up. "How would *you* feel if River joined her?"

Genevie shrugged. "She plans to... if this goes well."

My chest deflated. "I hate doing nothing."

"It's difficult for me too." She leaned against the wall and crossed her arms. "Did you speak? Do you have an understanding?"

Earl's decision to flirt her way out of here bothered me. Assuming all she was prepared to trade were her smiles. Everything I'd been certain of was now murky. I scowled. "I understand nothing."

Genevie snorted, the corners of her eyes crinkling. She sat at the base of the wall and leaned back. "Shocker."

"Change the topic or I'll go mad." I pressed the heels of my palms into my eyes. "Tell me about you and my sister. How did your relationship progress so quickly?"

Genevie glanced over her shoulder, then patted the ground beside her. "It doesn't matter now, but I didn't know she was your sister."

"She's nothing like Whistler." I slid down the wall, drew my knees to my chest, and leaned my head back. "He was kind. And friendly."

"So is River." A faraway look crossed Genevie's face. "I loved Whistler, but he wasn't perfect either. No one is."

"What drew you to River?"

"Something in my soul recognized a part of hers. I'd been traveling on a lonely, dark road. But with her, I glimpsed a chance for something more, and I followed my intuition." Genevie shrugged, but her eyes were warm and soft. "Life is too short not to grab hold of love at every chance."

I blinked. "You *love* her?"

"Passionately."

She chuckled as heat flooded my cheeks. I scrambled for an appropriate response, but her eyes widened, and she rose in a single, fluid motion.

By the time I'd scrambled to my feet, the guards had secured the doors again. But in the center of the hallway, Earl stood triumphant with her arms full of clean bedding and a woven basket and six pails of water at her feet.

## CHAPTER FORTY-FOUR

Earl was magnificent in her victory, like one of the marble-sculpted goddesses from the early Greeks. She exuded confidence, her chest and chin up as the others crowded into the hallway. The flush of triumph stained her cheekbones and reddened her lips. I yearned to rush to her too, but when she caught and held my gaze over the exclamations of our jubilant friends, something dark and ugly inside me reared its head. Saying nothing, I retreated into my room.

I wanted to congratulate her, but her success sparked an ugliness festering deep in my core. Suspicion and humiliation swirled inside me, leaving my breaths coming in gasps. I stared unseeing out the window, my hands flexing into fists with strange urgency. The sounds of merriment from the hallway tightened bands around my chest, and I fought simultaneous urges to lie on the floor, wailing like a lost babe, and punch my fists through the window glass.

Someone entered the room, but the measured footsteps gave Dante away. I didn't bother to turn.

"Why are you alone in here?" He grunted, setting something heavy on the ground before crossing the room to stand beside me. "Oh, I see. What a wonder."

My eyes refocused, widening at the glorious sunset sprawling across the sky. The jagged mountains framing the western horizon were a mix of deep Perylene Violet and Ultramarine Blue. The setting sun splashed textured clouds with fire, so they glowed a deep Quinacridone Gold with iridescent streaks of Russet. The sky between the silhouetted mountains and the blazing clouds was brilliant with bands of Sapphire, Cadmium Yellow, Violet, and Carmine.

Dante leaned against the window frame and folded his arms, his posture languid and relaxed. We silently watched the show, and it wasn't until Tom spoke that I realized he had joined us.

"Miraculous," he said.

Together, we watched the colors deepen into a Burgundy Red Ochre as the sun sank beyond the horizon. The deepening twilight broke our trance, and the three of us exchanged smiles. While we had come from different places and held differing opinions on how our lives should be lived, we shared a history too. We were brothers; raised in the abbey system and forged by a common past. And now by a single, perfect sunset.

"Thank you for the water," said Tom.

I pressed my lips together and waited for my earlier rage to reignite. But when it didn't, my shoulders slumped. "Thank Earl."

Tom tilted his head. "I know we don't deserve your forgiveness, and you've shamed us with your grace."

River's hostility, Talbot's feverish sleep, and Earl's self-debasement to the contrary. My responding laugh was full of bitterness. "I've shown grace?"

The expression of sincerity on Tom's face was nearly more than I could bear. My throat tightened, but he took my hands in his, his fingertips scratchy and nails ragged.

"If you were a smaller, petty man, we may have already perished from hunger or thirst. Your party is large, and we wouldn't have stood a chance if—" he stopped speaking, his throat convulsing.

Dante and I exchanged glances, but I couldn't read his thoughts.

Tom composed himself, released my hands, and drew in a shaky breath. "If we escape this place, I will be a different man. A better person because of you."

My eyes stung, and it was my turn to swallow. "*When* we escape."

"When we escape, indeed." Dante's chin came up. "Let's see if Earl learned anything of value."

Tom's apology dampened my earlier envy, and I stayed calm when we rejoined the others. Earl's gaze flicked to the three of us when we stepped into the hallway, but her neutral mask didn't shift.

Akiko scrambled to her feet and brought a drawstring sack to me. "Look what Earl brought!"

I glanced inside, my brows furrowing at the unfamiliar, domed shapes. Akiko jammed her hand inside and retrieved two of the shapes. She popped one in her mouth and tossed the other at Charcoal. He caught it in midair and smacked as he chewed. She giggled and reached for two more. I took one from her and held the bag up, out of her reach. She grinned and shrugged, skipping back to where Josephine and Sally sat on the floor.

The domed object had a translucent, ruby color. I bit into it, squinting at its gummy, fleshy texture. The flavor was vaguely fruity, somewhere between strawberry and watermelon. It was sweet but lacked the sour tang of fresh fruit. I passed the sack to Genevie and craned my neck to see what else Earl had brought.

Besides the gummy sweets, there was a basket of biscuits, a jar of brown paste, and a small wheel of crumbly, white cheese. After three days of eating the dried fruit and meat we'd brought with us, my mouth watered. Ben spread each biscuit with paste and cut a wedge off the small wheel.

When I received my portion, I stuffed half of it in my mouth at once. The biscuit had a crumbly texture, and the stewed-onion jam made my tongue convulse with delight. The cheese was mild, but its salty tang was a perfect foil to the sweet-savory onion. I slid down the wall and sat, hugging my knees, watching the others while finishing my food.

Considering the uncertainty we'd been living under, we'd held up okay. Josephine and Akiko had even maintained their clear-eyed hope. But with everyone's faces wreathed with smiles, it was clear surviving and living were two different things.

Josephine gave Akiko the rest of her biscuit and leaned forward, her eyes gleaming. "Were you able to learn anything? Did they tell you why we're here?"

"They have a standing order to catch and detain artists." Earl looked troubled. "They have sent a messenger to Carter to inform them about the three of you."

My stomach dropped. How long would it take to get a rider to Carter and return with orders?

Sally squinted. "About them specifically? Nothing about Talbot?"

Earl hesitated. "I don't think so. All artists are supposed to be held. No one questioned me about any of us, not even our professions. We are all being held because of you three, but they never asked where you studied, your names, or where you've traveled from."

If Carter didn't know who his people were holding, we had some time. But we needed to leave before his orders arrived... or he did.

Akiko finished her biscuit and examined the hamper. A puzzled expression crossed her face as she fingered one flip-up lid after the other. She picked up the hamper and shook it hard; a brown parcel fell to the floor with a *thud*. She discarded the hamper over her shoulder and dropped to her knees next to the package, beaming. "The left lid was thicker than the right."

Josephine slid over and picked up the package. She turned it over and found a corner to pull, unwrapping layer after layer of thick paper. The texture of the discarded wrapping reminded me of the wall coverings we'd drawn on in Oklahoma Depot.

At last, Josephine reached the center of the parcel, finding a black, hardcover book and charcoal pencil. The spine crackled when she opened it, and her face fell. "It's empty." She passed it and the pencil to me.

My heart hummed as I stroked my finger down the smooth page. "It's an ancient sketchbook. Maybe from *Before*."

Akiko's eyes widened as she glanced from the pencil to the book to me. When I shook my head in the faintest of warnings, she sat back on her heels, her lips pressed into a flat line.

When I turned it to examine the spine, I noticed the word 'perfection' scrawled across the cut edges of the pages. "Ruben." My chest warmed as I ran my palm across the cover. He knew we were stuck here and had cared enough to smuggle in art supplies.

Having a sketchbook and pencil changed everything... and

nothing. While a part of me wanted to draw us out of our predicament, I still didn't know how. Rather than raise their hopes without cause, I kept my expression noncommittal. If nothing else, we could take notes or draw a schematic or—

*A map.*

Genevie reached down to collect the discarded wrapping, but I caught her arm. "Wait—we can use it."

She frowned. "For?"

I steeled myself to make eye contact with Earl. "If you'll share what you've observed, we can draw a map."

---

OVER THE NEXT TWO DAYS, TALBOT HOVERED NEAR THE edge of consciousness. His fever remained as steady as his heart, but he didn't appear to worsen.

Earl scouted the compound for us and recruited River to help her. After flirting their way out, they made themselves indispensable by taking over the compound's kitchen and laundry duties. It provided them with greater freedom to explore the building, and they smuggled in bone tea for Talbot, several books, and a skein of yarn for Akiko. By pestering everyone, she learned to play several string games and weave bracelets we all pretended to wear with pleasure.

Cara and Tom spent their time studying Talbot's bible. They took turns reading, their eyes gleaming as they argued over the meaning of the words and the application of the truths they found in the book. Ben and I spent our time working on the map, endlessly discussing the building and probing it for weaknesses. When Dante joined us, he'd relay the gossip he'd gleaned from Earl and River. He had an uncanny knack for spotting social patterns, which River tested and exploited.

Only Genevie chafed at our continued captivity and wandered in and out of rooms in a listless, discontented manner. Her flask reappeared, but she'd soon exhausted its contents, and either River couldn't, or wouldn't, procure more. Genevie started fights with nearly everyone, so we'd all grown tight-mouthed whenever she appeared.

When she returned a third time to pick a fight with me, Dante finally put a stop to it. "*Listen*, you." He folded his arms and pursed his mouth. "You're being a right pain. If you want to help, stay, but otherwise, you need to move along and keep this" –he waved his hand up and down her face– "mopey, dark cloud to yourself."

Genevie's jaw jutted. "Why aren't any of you *doing* something?"

Ben pushed himself up and stared at her. "We are."

"Planning and plotting, planning, and plotting. But what are you *doing*?"

The belligerence in her voice made me rise and cross the room. Before she could protest, I wrapped my arms around her and held her as tightly as I could. She stiffened and pulled away, but I held on, laying my cheek against her head. Her chest spasmed once, and as she drew in a shuddering breath, I swayed, rocking us both from side to side.

In movements so tiny Ben and Dante probably couldn't see, she relaxed into me, eventually nestling her head against my neck. "I hate being useless," she murmured.

"I know."

"I'm the one who fixes things." She clutched my tunic. "I'm the one with the plans."

I nodded, saying nothing.

"They're out there risking everything, and we're... stuck."

"You and me." I sighed. "We have survived by being people

of action, not thought. This is a growth opportunity for us both."

She pulled away from me. "But you're doing something. You're planning."

"And plotting."

She barely returned my smile. She'd been so unpleasant to be around, we'd purposefully excluded her.

"I'm drafting, Ben is planning, and Dante is telling us which strings we should pull to unravel our captors." I shrugged. "Why don't you join us?"

Doubt clouded her face. "To do what?"

"Nope, Ben already claimed the 'what'." I grinned at her bewilderment and pulled her toward our map. "Dante is working on the 'who'. Ben is working on the 'what' and I'm trying to figure out the 'how'. Why don't you work on the 'where'?"

Dante stared at Genevie. After a long pause, he said, "And the 'when'."

Ben explained the overall layout of the building. "We've considered making a break for it when they return, but even if we overwhelm the guards in the hallway, they have people stationed in every stairwell."

"What are these?" She pointed at two banks of square boxes.

"Elevator shafts." He tapped his fingers on them. "The elevators are inoperable, and we discussed altering them, but even with three artists, we don't think we could make the improvements fast enough."

Genevie leaned against the wall and frowned at us. "We can't climb down the outside of the building, either. It's too exposed, and they'd be waiting for us when we reached the bottom."

Dante shrugged. "Now you can see why we're stuck."

We continued working together for another hour, revisiting each plausible scenario before discarding it yet again.

"It's impossible," Dante announced. He pressed the heels of his palms into his eyes. "Utterly impossible."

Ben rose from the floor and groaned as he stretched. "Nothing is impossible. We just haven't found the right solution yet."

"What solution?" Dante made a face. "We have an old lady, a child, and a man who can barely sit up during the few minutes he is conscious each day." He paced the length of the room. "We are under twenty-four-hour guard in a locked corridor on the fifth floor of a populated building. And there are *fourteen* of us." He stopped and waved his hands at the map. "We'd need to manufacture a distraction long enough and large enough to allow fourteen of us to climb down five flights of stairs with no one seeing a thing. Forget it."

Genevie's back hit the wall with a *thud*. She grinned at us. "I've got it. I know where to get us out of here."

"How?" I waited, rolling the pencil back and forth.

She winked. "How is your department, remember? I'm the where."

Dante groaned at Genevie's joke, but Ben sat up. "Where?"

"Here." Genevie tapped the map in our present location and beamed. "Or over there." Dante looked as mystified as me, but Genevie chuckled. "They made this building from what, steel, concrete, and glass?"

Ben nodded.

She snapped her fingers, turning toward me. "You can manipulate anything present, as long as you're not breaking any natural law."

I tapped the charcoal pencil on our map as my understanding dawned. "Yes." We'd been looking at our predicament as a two-dimensional problem, but Genevie had discovered a three-dimensional solution. My head snapped up. "Yes!"

Dante raised his hands. "Hold up, you've lost me. What are we doing?"

Genevie snapped her fingers, suddenly sounding like her old self. "Keep up, Artist-the-sequel. We're going to need you to figure out the when, after all."

# CHAPTER FORTY-FIVE

As evening fell, we gathered everyone into River and Genevie's room to discuss our escape. The plan wouldn't be easy to pull off, and a hundred small things could go wrong, but we convinced everyone it was our best option forward. It was also exactly the type of project I'd been looking for to impress Earl... assuming we pulled it off.

Sally took the longest to convince, but when we'd answered all her questions, a smile flitted across her face. "Bloody flipping *frogs*. I knew you'd figure it out."

Ben raised his eyebrow. "Which one of us?"

She smirked and waved her hand in our general direction. "Sort the praise amongst yourselves *after* we get away."

Once we had a solid plan, captivity was even harder to endure. Ben passed the time by working through a multitude of possibilities, while everyone else pretended to languish, as they had all week.

Upon their return, Earl and River could barely contain their triumph. They'd spent the day scouting our potential targets and brought back enough solid information Ben and I pinpointed our exit. Even better, Dante coached them on the information he needed from our captors, and they delivered it, too.

"We're a go," he said, his smile gleaming in the dark. "As long as we're exiting around three in the morning, we'll have enough time to trot ourselves over to the livery. We'll get clean away."

Sally and Josephine offered to stay up so the rest of us could sleep. I protested, sure there was no way I'd find sleep, but Dante and I both woke, bleary-eyed, when Sally shook us. I slipped into the hall and made my way to Tom and Cara's corner room while Dante worked on the other side of the hallway.

Tom had already created a door between his room and Ben and Josephine's room, so Ben waited for me. "Tom's working on the last door now."

"Good." I pulled my sketchbook from my pocket and drew a deep breath. "Ready?"

Ben nodded and flipped the mattress up, setting it against a wall to give me more space. I'd drawn the room earlier, before dark, so I had nothing left to do but the artwork.

I closed my eyes, pulling the shadows away from my mind's canvas until it glowed as if illuminated by a single, bright, downward light. Even before I set the charcoal on the page, my fingers tingled.

I sketched with quick, sure strokes, opening the stairwell before drawing the stairs. They were very like the ones I'd climbed at Sayzar's Market, made from metal and concrete and folding back across themselves at the halfway mark. As soon as I finished the stairs, I descended to the empty room below and flipped the page.

River had confirmed the rooms beneath Tom and Cara's were nearly identical, so I'd drawn five identical rooms on my pages. In case I needed to change them, I'd sketched each room using a value of three to make them easier to correct. Upon reaching each room, I adjusted my sketch and continued the staircase down. While I worked on the stairs, I tasked Tom and Dante with creating openings between our rooms so everyone could transport their luggage to the end of the hall without the guards seeing them move. The trickiest part of their job was to alter the hallway, adding a false wall at the end. It needed to fool a casual glance, but it had to be far enough away from the true wall so the others could carry our luggage—and Talbot—to the stairwell I'd sketched.

By the time I reached the bottom floor, my tunic was drenched with sweat. My hands shook as I adjusted the sketch of the last room. Muffled footfalls rang along the stairs, and I winced at the noise the others made descending. Charcoal panted next to me, stopping occasionally with his ears cocked as if listening for discovery.

Somehow, everyone made it down without mishap. They crowded around me, and I caught Josephine's eye. "Did we get everything?"

She nodded, slipping under Talbot's right arm. His head wobbled, but he stayed on his feet by leaning on Cara and Josephine.

I took a deep breath and prepared to open a door in the wall.

"Wait," Cara said, her voice a hiss. "Where are we going after we leave the livery?"

My stomach plummeted. Had we forgotten to plan a destination?

"Tager's ranch," said Earl and Josephine in unison.

"I sent him a note via Ruben," Earl added.

Cara relaxed, but my gut tightened. At our moment of need, Earl had reached out for help from *another* man.

Akiko bumped me. "We leaving?"

I swallowed and continued sketching. The meager moonlight coming through the single window barely provided enough illumination to work with, but after I'd finished the door, the moonlight streamed in, painting the smiling faces around me with silver.

As planned, everyone slipped into the night and scattered, heading toward the deep shadows on the other side of the cracked pavement. Ben took Talbot from Cara and swept him across the open pavement with Josephine on Talbot's other side. I watched until they reached the shadows before repairing the opening.

I followed the others into the dark with Charcoal beside me. Once we reached the far side of the paved area, I looked back at the compound, savoring our triumph. Above us, the sky was a deep, purple-black, like Amethyst mixed with Moonglow. The spray of stars across the sky glittered in approval as we sprinted away from the Mountain View.

WHEN WE REACHED THE LIVERY, GENEVIE AND I ROLLED the giant doors open. The barn was dimly lit with lanterns trimmed low, throwing Bronzite Yellow pools of light. Fox nickered from the first stall, but I froze; two men sat near the door on a bale of straw.

"My man," said Ruben, holding his hand out.

"*You're* the man." A grin split my face as I pulled him into an enthusiastic hug. "Thank you."

He patted my back and chuckled. "If memory serves, your chit number is '333', correct?"

Ruben and the hostler had already tacked up our animals, so it took little time to stow our things before we were ready to leave. To be safe, I rechecked Sally and Akiko's tack before giving them each a leg up. Earl was already astride Bruno, waiting to lead us west.

"Hurry, Artist," Ben called to me. "You're the last one ready, but this time, I'm driving sweep."

Dante helped Ruben climb into the wagon, and Ruben chuckled at my expression. "Thought I'd ride with you all. My place is near the Buchner ranch."

Genevie was still working on her panniers, so I checked River's saddle. My sister gave me a brief smile and even let me give her a leg up before riding out. Magnesium bumped me with his head as I returned to my horses, reminding me to untie the donkey.

"Just in case," I muttered, unclipping his lead. He wiggled his lips, his long ears swiveling when I scratched his chest.

I'd just put my left foot in the stirrup when Oxide shifted to the side, and I hopped awkwardly next to him, determined not to fall. The snort from the hostler made my cheeks flush, but the jolt gave me the burst I needed to spring up and get my leg over. Without taking a moment to settle myself, I wheeled Oxide toward the door, nearly unseating myself when Magnesium's lead slipped through my hands.

The hostler sighed and picked it up, handing it to me once I'd settled myself. "You familiar with horses, Artist?" he asked, handing it to me.

From the wagon, Ben, Dante, and Ruben hooted and jeered. My face burned as I followed the women into the dark, but even this couldn't dampen my spirits for long. Every group needed someone to provide comic relief, and I may as well shoulder the role since I was forever bumbling through my life. My grin broadened as I rode down the moonlit track, imagining the faces of our captors when they found us gone. The wagon rumbled behind me, and Charcoal trotted alongside, occasionally stepping aside to ensure the donkey kept up.

Pale blue streaks rent the eastern sky by the time we passed under the large timber gate onto the Buchner ranch. In the side pasture, a trio of gigantic birds bolted. Taller than a man, they ran on long, spindly legs like mutant chickens. Their feet hit the dusty ground with booming *thuds*, and they hissed and trilled as they ran. Oxide went up and to the side, and I lost both stirrups and flew through the air, landing hard on my shoulder. Stunned, I lay on the ground. Somehow, I'd kept my grip on his reins, but in the distance, I heard Akiko scream. Moments later, My Darling bolted past us, riderless and bucking to dislodge his saddle.

Before I'd regained my feet, Fox streaked past us in the dark with Josephine low over his neck. She ignored Ben's shout and continued after the wayward pony.

The wagon rumbled alongside and stopped. Ben's face looked grim in the predawn light. "You okay?"

When I nodded and waved, he clucked to the mules and rolled past. I picked myself up, groaning. This wasn't how I'd planned to meet Tager, my rival. I considered brushing off the worst of the dust and remounting, but I was too tired and sore for another fall, so I walked my horses toward the ranch house, following the wagon.

A man I assumed was Tager was on the porch with Earl, but by the time I reached it, he'd disappeared. Either he'd already made his mind up about me, or he saw me as little competition for Earl's attention.

"Come on," said Earl, "the barn is this way."

To call it a barn was a stretch; it was a series of plank corrals under a single roof, but I kept my thoughts to myself. We unsaddled and turned the horses loose in the pasture.

Earl watched them go before turning to us. "Tager said to

catch some sleep. He'll send someone when breakfast is ready. This way."

Tager's bunkhouse reminded me of the dormitory at Popham Abbey, except instead of cold stone, the ceiling, walls, and floor were made of dusty wood. Sally groaned as she crawled into a lower bunk, and Akiko made me switch with her three times until she finally decided she wanted to sleep on the top bunk. As picky as she'd been about finding the perfect bunk, she was asleep before I'd even finished tucking the rough cotton quilt around her.

Sleep dragged at my eyes and made my bones ache, but I staggered to the end of the bunkhouse to help settle Talbot into a bunk.

"We have him." River waved me away, giving me a gentle smile. "Get some rest. You've earned it."

# CHAPTER FORTY-SIX

The air in the bunkhouse was hot and stuffy when I awoke, and the only other occupied bunk was Talbot's. Somehow, everyone else had left without waking me.

After checking on Talbot, I stepped outside. The air was even hotter, but it had a fresh, crisp feel to it despite the heat. I paused on the shaded porch, unsure of what to do next. It was time to tell Earl what she meant to me. Assuming I could find a moment alone with her... and it wasn't already too late.

The bunkhouse nestled on a gently sloping hill, midway between Tager's barn and the sprawling ranch house at the top of the hill. I couldn't see anyone in the barn, so I trudged up the hill, mentally rehearsing what I wanted to say to Earl. Other than the buzzing rattle of insects, the day was quiet. The wooden stairs creaked when I climbed onto the wrap-around porch.

Josephine looked up from her book and smiled.

I glanced around. "Did I miss breakfast?"

"Breakfast *and* lunch." She closed the book and stretched. "You must have been exhausted."

"Where are the others?"

She hooked her thumb toward the rolling pastures. "Tager took them on a tour of his exotics."

The memory of the enormous birds thundering away in the thin moonlight reappeared, and I frowned. "I would have liked to see them too."

"How are you feeling?"

I patted my chest and stomach as I assessed my state. "Tired. Hungry." I stared down the long, dusty drive. "Anyone come after us?"

She shook her head and marked her book with what looked like a strip of cloth. Catching my curiosity, she shrugged. "Akiko has moved onto weaving bookmarks. Blame River."

When I snorted, she smiled. "Come on, let's get you something to eat."

I followed her into the kitchen, which was cooler than I expected. In the center of the space was a long island with stools lined up along one side. Josephine gestured at the stool closest to a large cabinet. I slid onto it as she pulled the cabinet open. A rush of cool air fell out, mist furling toward the floor. My eyes widened, and I sprang closer to examine it.

The interior of the cabinet held fresh produce and glass jars with bright chunks floating in jewel-colored liquids. Josephine pulled a plate of corncakes and a small, brown jug from the top shelf and set them down on the counter. "What is this?"

She shrugged as she pulled a second plate from a drawer. "Tager called it a 'frij'. Isn't it a marvel? Everyone wanted to open and close it, to feel the rush of cool air." Doubt crossed her face, her scars puckering and rippling as the muscles underneath her damaged skin moved. "Do you want me to warm these? I'm sure I could contrive a way..."

"No. I mean, no, thank you." I grinned at her as I reached for a flat cake. "It's a novelty to eat something cold here."

She slid a jug toward me. "Syrup, if you want it."

I poured a generous puddle onto my plate and dipped the corn cake into it. The cake was buttery, and the syrup ratcheted up the intense corn flavor. The texture was dense and grainy, but not unpleasant. I wandered around the room as I ate my cake, looking at Tager's things. "Doeshelivehe—"

"What?"

I swallowed twice and cleared my throat. "Sorry. I asked if Tager lived here alone."

"Oh." She nodded and gestured toward the platter. "Do you want another?"

I plucked two more of the cakes from it. When she picked up the platter to return it to the frij, I took it from her and pulled the door open myself. It resisted, like it was under vacuum, and when it released, a wave of cold air rolled over me. "Miraculous."

She nodded as she pushed it shut, and I wanted to protest, but the amusement on her face stopped me. "Why didn't you go with the others?"

The amusement dropped, and her eyes slid sideways. "Someone needed to stay, in case someone came, or you got up, or..."

I studied her as I started on my second cake. "What aren't you telling me?"

She sighed and crossed her arms. "Ben and I got into a fight. I didn't feel like being around him."

My eyebrows shot up. "You and Ben?"

Her lip poked out. "It happens." She pushed open one of the glass doors and stepped onto the porch at the back of the house. I filled a glass from the faucet, marveled at the chill, and followed her back into the heat.

"Tell me," I said as I settled onto a wicker chair next to her.

A muscle in her jaw worked for a moment, but when her

shoulders slumped, she sighed. "Don't take this the wrong way."

I paused with the corn cake halfway to my mouth. "Okay."

"Ben has been pushing for us to settle somewhere."

A pang rushed through me, turning the cake metallic and bitter in my mouth. First Genevie and now Ben.

"I told him I'm not willing to consider it until you—" She stopped and bit her lip.

I swallowed and set my plate on my lap. "I'm not your responsibility."

She made a scoffing noise and waved her hand. "It's not that."

As much as she might protest, I knew she wasn't being entirely truthful with me... or herself. The guilt she'd carried since childhood—since the accident that had torn her face and killed her brother—drove her. I'd suspected her fierce loyalty toward me was, in part, atonement. The selfish part of me had used it to my advantage. My throat thickened, and I swallowed. Life without Ben and Josephine...

I studied the dusty fields as I considered what my life would have been like if I hadn't met Josephine. Ben and Josephine were now as much my family as Akiko, Talbot, and River.

*River.*

My birth sister resented me now, but over time, I'd wear her down. Like Dante chipping away at the marble concealing his dream man, I'd whittle through her defenses until we synced. And then there was Earl...

Josephine looked at me, her eyes sad and fierce at the same time. "Why does life get harder and more complicated?"

I had no answers for her, so I handed her a piece of my corn cake. She chewed slowly and leaned against me when I put my arm around her shoulder. The sage-scented wind brushed around us, its hot, gentle fingers lifting our hair and tugging at our clothing.

A cloud of dust marred the horizon. Josephine straightened, shielding her eyes. "That's them." She turned to me. "What are you going to do?"

"About Earl?"

"No." She raised her eyebrows. "I meant Cara and Tom, but since you've brought it up..." Her eyes danced. "I've been dying to ask."

I groaned. "I do not know what I'm doing."

She snorted. "And?"

The same feeling of helplessness swamped me as I pictured Earl's unfathomable, green eyes, and the pleasant, neutral face she pulled down like a mask. "I can't reach her."

"She's right *there*. Waiting for you to reach out."

The dust cloud moved closer.

"I've tried. But something gets in the way. Each time, something—or *someone*—interrupts or changes our plans."

I squirmed as she studied me, her scrutiny merciless. "Do things truly get in the way, or are they excuses to keep you from acting?"

When I swallowed, she leaned into me, the weight of her head against my chest comforting. "It's okay to be scared."

I caught my breath. "Shouldn't it be easier? I mean, if it's right between us, shouldn't there be some sign?"

Josephine pushed herself up. "Why?" she asked, her voice thick with amusement. "Why is easy better?"

I gaped at her. "Huh?"

"If it came easy, you wouldn't trust it, and neither would Earl."

"But..." I shrugged, my half-smile a grimace. "What if we're not supposed to be together?"

Josephine grabbed my tunic and shook it. "Was I supposed

to meet you? Were you supposed to rescue Akiko?" Color flooded her face. "We all make choices and live with the consequences of those choices. There is no grand plan, no fate, no destiny. If you want something, make it happen."

*Make it happen.*

Josephine was right. Why had I wasted so much time? "You're very wise, my friend." I clasped her hands and smiled at her. "How did you learn this?"

Her chest heaved and reddened. "From *you*, you oblivious toe mushroom!"

I shouted with laughter. "Young lady, I'm setting a daily, Sally-exposure limit for you!" The peevish expression on her face sent me into hysterics.

***

By the time the others pulled up and disembarked from the long, flat wagon, we were senseless with laughter, and no amount of prodding, questions, or scolding from them could return our composure. We laughed until tears streamed down our faces. Charcoal wiggled with delight, lapping at our tears and capering in circles on the shaded porch, his ears flat against his head and eyes wild.

River headed toward the bunkhouse to check on Talbot, and Genevie followed, shaking her head but smiling. Tager clucked to his oxen and drove Cara and Tom to the barn, leaving the others with us. Earl took Akiko inside, and when they returned, they brought a pitcher of cool water and several more glasses.

I smiled when Earl refilled my glass. Our fingers brushed when she handed it back, and she lingered a heartbeat longer than I'd expected. Was Josephine right? Was Earl waiting for me to reach out? Before I could say anything, Cara and Tom returned.

"We'd like to leave tomorrow," said Cara. Waiting for our response, they radiated tension.

"Tomorrow?" I hadn't wanted to come here, but I wasn't ready to leave yet. Staying another day or two would allow me time alone with Earl, while finding any sort of privacy on the trail would be near impossible. But what if a delay gave Ben time to talk Josephine into staying? And if he was successful, were Genevie and River far behind? If the four of them stayed, Sally might too, making it near impossible to get Akiko to continue our journey.

Our trip here had been grueling. But while determined to find her a permanent home, I didn't want to settle *here*, so I nodded. "Let's leave in the morning."

"I'm hot." Akiko climbed onto the chair with me, pushed her hair back from her neck, and handed me a leather lace. "How long to get to the valley?"

Tom squinted at the sky. "Two days if we leave at dawn."

I pulled Akiko's hair into a ponytail, but strands stuck against her neck, so I shook it out and braided it like I'd seen Earl do for Josephine. I focused on my work as the others discussed the exotic animals they'd seen during Tager's tour.

When I finished, Akiko rewarded me with a garish head-band and probed her braid. "French hair!"

Earl pushed away from the railing she'd been leaning against. "Me next."

Akiko scrambled up, and Earl settled onto the porch between my knees. She flopped her long braids into my lap and leaned back to flash me an upside-down smile before straightening. My fingers trembled as I unfastened the laces at the ends and tucked them into my pocket. Earl's hair spooled out in strands of Pyrrole Red, Red Gold, and Burnt Yellow Ochre as I loosened the twin braids. Her hair had a silky, fine texture and smelled of sun and dust and lavender when I bent forward to gather it.

A smile played on Dante's lips, but his eyes widened when Tager climbed onto the porch.

My gut twisted.

Tager *was* the sharp-jawed man from the market. He was a fraction shorter than Ben, though his frame was rangy and loose-limbed. He wore his hair and beard close-cropped, high-lighting his chiseled jaw and symmetrical features. His eyes were a deep, piercing blue with lines radiating from the corners, hinting at long hours spent under the sun. He strode toward me with a graceful, rolling stride, holding my gaze as he bent to shake my hand.

*I'm glad we're leaving tomorrow.*

His grip was firm, and his palm was rough. He exuded a polite, friendly air, but his presence made me feel young, naive, and oddly effeminate.

"Tager Buchner."

Between my knees, Earl tensed.

Everyone stared at me, and I flinched. "Of course, you are."

# CHAPTER FORTY-SEVEN

The afternoon's heat sapped our strength. We lounged on Tager's porch, discussing the logistics of traveling, our supplies, the condition of our horses, and the best route to take to Cara's valley.

Earl hadn't moved from her spot in front of me, so I toyed with the end of her braid. What excuse would get her away from the others? Nothing came to mind, so I didn't move, determined to enjoy the moment.

By late afternoon, the heat sapped even Akiko's energy. Every so often, someone murmured, rousing me from the drowsy torpor I'd fallen into.

Wheels crunched on Tager's gravel drive. I bolted upright and my legs tensed, ready to sprint away. Everyone but Tager appeared alarmed, but he remained relaxed, his expression shifting into a lazy smile. "Ruben."

A moment later, the porch creaked as the big man rounded the corner. He beamed at us and rubbed his belly. "Hot today."

Akiko popped up, inquisitive and curious, a prairie dog come to observe us. "Why are you here?"

Ruben's gaze slid to Tager. When the rancher nodded, Ruben said, "I'm here to fill my bottles."

River's voice had a hard, brittle quality. "In exchange for?"

Ruben's smile didn't waver.

"Supper," Tager said.

Akiko beamed. "Tacos?" She glanced around as if desperate to convince us. "They're great!"

"Sorry, no." Ruben's eyes gleamed. "Tonight, we're having fajitas, though I don't know what Tager has hanging."

"Dealer's choice." Tager rubbed his jaw. "I have an ostrich and a longhorn in the cave."

Earl straightened. "Can I help?"

My heart fell, but Ruben looked pleased when Tager nodded.

"What's a cave?" Akiko hugged her knees into her chest. "Is it far?"

Ben nodded, his eyes bright. "I'd love to see it too. It's how you're cooling the water and the house?"

Surprise crossed Tager's face.

"He's an engineer," said Earl.

The look he sent her made me sit forward. My hands curled possessively over Earl's shoulders. "Since I missed the first excursion today, I'd like to see it, too."

Tager's expression didn't change, but his fingers tightened on the arm of his wicker chair. "Fine. Who else?"

When everyone but Sally stood, she glared as though we'd betrayed her. "It's too hot to go anywhere."

Genevie chuckled and reached her hand down to the smaller woman. "The cave should be cool, right?"

"Yes." Josephine clapped her hands, pleased to share her knowledge. "It stays around ten degrees because the earth provides a type of thermal insulation."

Ben ruffled Akiko's hair before turning toward Sally. "Come with us."

Sally looked unconvinced

"It will be like standing in the frij," he said.

Ruben drove his wagon down the hill and waited for us at a wooden door. "Our secret," he said, waiting for us to nod.

When we did, Tager unlocked the door and pulled it open, gesturing for us to enter. The first room was cooler than outside, though not as cool as I'd expected, and nowhere near ten degrees. It was dim, but our eyes adjusted as we waited for Ben, Dante, and Ruben to drag the crates of canteens inside. Wood darkened by damp and age paneled the room. Shelves filled with dusty jars occupied one wall.

Once they'd pulled the outer door shut, Tager crossed to a section of wooden paneling disguising a door. He opened it and a wave of cooler air smelling of old copper washed across us. Akiko followed Earl inside but waved her arms as though trying to scare off the dark. Tager lit several lanterns and handed them around. We traversed a short corridor carved out of rough-hewn rock and waited as he fumbled with the third door. Icy air blasted us, and the room we stepped into wasn't dark. We gazed around the massive space as Tager and Ruben collected and extinguished our lanterns, setting them onto a shelf carved high into the stone.

Akiko spun a slow circle, her eyes as round as saucers. Unlike the rest of us, Earl kept her lantern lit, pulled aside a hanging canvas tarpaulin, and disappeared into another chamber. Charcoal followed her to the tarpaulin but hesitated and sat, looking disconcerted.

"Our hanging room is through there." Tager gestured in the direction Earl had disappeared. "Look around, anywhere."

Cara shivered and Tom put his arm around his shoulder,

but I delighted in the chilly air and laughed as gooseflesh rose along my arm. "How marvelous."

Ruben nodded and pointed to a spigot near the wall. "The well is there. Give me a hand?"

Ben followed us, rubbing his head as he tracked the network of pipes. "You're bringing water from here up to the house?"

Tager nodded. "My great-grandfather was an engineer too. He built a cistern in the house's cellar. The windmill pumps the water from here to there, and a smaller pump pulls it from the cistern into the house."

"Why is the house so cool?" Josephine asked, her eyes bright.

Tager's shoulders relaxed. "They built the house like a giant zeer pot. The walls and frij are filled with tiny pipes. They act like capillary straws. As the water inside them warms, it rises and spills into a sand-filled cavity between the inner and outer walls. The evaporation through the porous outer wall cools the interior. Earl's cottage has the same technology."

*Earl's cottage?*

If Earl had agreed to stay, I was too late and had only myself to blame. I'd had months to make my move. Tager had known her for a week, but unlike me, he hadn't hesitated.

Akiko stared at a shaft of sunlight illuminating the far corner of the cavern. "Is that a mirror?"

"Yes." Tager bent to point at another. "We use a network of them to bounce the light around."

"Ingenious," said Sally. "Your great-grandfather again?"

Tager shook his head and Josephine chimed in. "The Egyptians did something similar, thousands of years *Before* the world died."

"Why are there three doors?" Akiko asked, stroking her palm down the door we'd entered. "Why is this place a secret?"

Tager cleared his throat, but it was Ruben who answered. "If everyone knew Tager had a shady, cool place with plenty of water, it would be hard to keep them out."

And Ruben would lose a major advantage in the marketplace. But I said nothing and heaved the heavy crate toward the door.

Tager pulled Akiko away from the door for me. "No one bothers with us here, since we look like a dry, dusty ranch in the middle of nowhere."

It *was* a dry, dusty ranch in the middle of nowhere. So maybe if I asked, Earl would still come away with us. With me. The possibility cheered me so much, I lifted the second crate of water with ease. Ben noticed and lifted his eyebrow. I grinned in response.

"Where is your garden?" I asked Ruben.

"In a chamber similar to this." He winked and gestured toward the next door. "But my cave's ceiling fell long ago. I get plenty of sunlight, and the garden stays cooler than the surface does. Over the years, my family built a series of raised beds and an irrigation system, but nothing as sophisticated as this."

I grunted and heaved the crate through the last door, squinting at the dazzling light. Reentering the main chamber, I clapped his shoulder. "You don't bring this much water to your shop."

When he shook his head, River made a noise of disgust. "Guzzlers."

The smile didn't leave Ruben's face, but his eyes hardened. "I deliver water to the Excalibur in exchange for access. It's why I can get hold of near about anything."

"You're a bootlegger," Sally said. She smiled at Ruben. "Every community needs a person who can procure things."

Something like uncertainty flashed across River's face until

I picked up the last crate. Under her disapproving glare, I lugged it to the wagon.

Outside, I leaned against the wagon while Ruben pulled his faded tarpaulin over the crates. When he'd finished, he dusted his palms together. "When do you leave?"

"Tomorrow morning." The words felt as final as they sounded. I clapped his shoulder with affection. "Thank you for your help. It meant the world, knowing we had an ally on the outside."

"I like you. Plus, none of us like what they've done with Vegas Depot. If getting you gone means they leave too, I'll have done two good deeds." He shook off dark thoughts like a dog shedding water and clapped his hands as we reentered the main chamber. "Who wants to help me prep dinner?"

STARS GLIMMERED IN THE DARKENING SKY AS WE SET UP A long table on Tager's lawn. At Ruben's request, Earl cut wafer-thin slices from the ostrich's round and tip. I watched for a while, then busied myself so I'd be done with my tasks by the time Earl finished. Ben and Ruben would take over cooking the meat, giving me the best chance for a word alone with her.

"It looks like red meat," said Ben, his eyebrows raising in surprise as he watched her finish.

"It is," she said, handing him the platter of raw ostrich.

I craned my neck. "Ostrich isn't like chicken or turkey?"

"Ostrich is perfection." Ruben clapped my shoulder. "Come, you can prep the vegetables."

My stomach sank. Genevie snorted when Ruben handed me a knife, but he soon had Sally, Josephine, Cara, Akiko, and me slicing bell peppers and zucchini into thin strips. Ruben tasked Ben with slicing four onions, and we snickered as tears rolled down his cheeks. Ben glared at us with his red-rimmed eyes, but the corners of his mouth twitched.

Even though our vegetable slices were far from uniform, Ruben looked pleased with our work and showed us how to mince cilantro and slice radishes.

While we were busy, Ruben carried several spiky paddles over and showed Ben how to pop the spikes off with heat. Ruben even put Dante to work, handing him a large bowl and a pestle. "Grind these herbs into a fine powder."

The griddle heated over Genevie's mesquite fire until it hissed when Ruben flicked water onto it. "It's ready." He upended a pot of rendered bacon fat across the griddle, nodding as it melted into a bubbling sheen. The hot iron sizzled as he lay the thin-sliced, marinated ostrich along one side. "Ladies, please put the vegetables in this bowl."

Akiko grinned as they scooped the vegetables we had chopped and the sliced onion and cactus into the huge metal bowl.

"Dante, the herbs go on top of the vegetables."

Dante shimmied in a circle, poured his ground powder, and finished with a flourish. Akiko squealed and copied him, the two of them dancing like lunatics around us.

"Exactly right." Ruben nodded his approval and turned toward me. "Toss them together!"

I hesitated, poking the mass with my wooden spoon.

"Like this." Ruben pantomimed digging into soil with his bare hands, so I set the spoon aside and plunged my hands into the mix. The spices tickled my nose as I mixed the vegetables together, and I laughed when Ruben shouted, "Perfection!"

My chest swelled, and I flashed Sally a cheeky grin. "Better add me to the kitchen roster from now on, Administrator."

I glanced around, hoping I'd impressed Earl, too. But instead of admiring my newfound kitchen skills, she was deep in conversation with Tager. When he patted her shoulder, my heart plummeted, then sunk even lower when she followed him into his brightly lit kitchen.

Time was running out; if Tager convinced her to stay before I told her how I felt, it would be too late. But if I abandoned my tasks and raced after her now, I wouldn't live down the ridicule from the others. And what if she heard me out, but stayed anyway?

As soon as Ruben released me, I used Akiko as an excuse to rush to the kitchen. Feigning nonchalance, I ushered her in under the guise of washing her hands. Inside, we found Earl and Ben chopping tomatoes and peppers. My kitchen cockiness returned, and I reached around Ben to snag a piece. When I popped the chunk of green pepper into my mouth, he waved his knife at me. But his expression changed from warning to mirth at my first splutter.

Something was wrong.

Heat clawed at my mouth, and I ran to the sink to spit out the vegetable.

"Here," said Akiko, shoving a glass at me, her eyes wide with alarm.

I drank glass after glass, but nothing eased the fire crawling down my throat. Ben drove his knife into the cutting board and bent over, his shoulders heaving with laughter as he struggled to catch his breath.

Tager entered the kitchen and knew what was happening without explanation. His lips twitched, but he grabbed a glass and filled it from a pitcher of milk in the frij. "This will help."

The milk was cool and creamy but had an unfamiliar flavor. It tempered the fire consuming me, dulling it from a burn to a smolder. I wiped my eyes and nodded. "Thanks. Goat?" I asked after finishing the glass.

"Camel," he said, glancing at Ben. "Jalapeño?"

Ben's shoulders shook as he chuckled again. "It happened too fast to warn him."

Earl flashed her lopsided grin at Tager, her eyes warm. "You're a hero."

My stomach burned, but this time, the heat had nothing to do with the wretched vegetable.

Tager grinned at her until she pinked and returned to her task. When he turned toward me, his smile didn't falter despite my withering glare. "Your cousin is awake and joining us for dinner."

# CHAPTER FORTY-EIGHT

The night cooled to an almost-pleasant temperature by the time dinner was ready. We sat around the long plank table under an inky sky glittering with stars. I marveled again at the unseasonable weather. At Popham, they'd already be wearing thick sweaters and serving soups and stews for supper. But even though it didn't feel like October in this strange place, winter would come. If we wanted to choose where we overwintered, we needed to fulfill the promise Dante had made to Tom and Cara with haste.

*But not tonight.*

We'd earned a moment of respite. Of celebration. A reprieve from the forces which had put us here, together. Everyone who mattered to me was here, and it was enough.

While we passed around the bowls and platters, Ruben had Genevie and River pressing and grilling a supple, flat bread he called a tortilla. They were like the corn wrappings he'd used for tacos, but larger and more robust. We piled the grilled meat and vegetables on top and sprinkled them with the minced cilantro and crumbled white cheese.

The ostrich reminded me of tender beef. My senses swooned at the combination of herbs, softened vegetables, and seasoned meat. We ate with our hands, and I didn't even mind the juices dripping down my wrists.

When Sally passed me a bowl of brightly colored vegetables, I eyed it warily. It had bright yellow grilled corn, red onion, radish, and tomato... plus the green pepper Ben had chopped.

River raised her eyebrow. "What?"

I poked at the dish with the heavy silver spoon. "Jalapeño?"

Ruben chuckled. "Yes, but the vinegar tempers the heat. Try it. I make the best pico de gallo in the valley."

With everyone watching me, I couldn't refuse, so I put a small scoop on my plate and Talbot's before passing the bowl to Sally. I'd intended to push it around my plate, but Ruben stopped eating to watch me. Steeling myself, I picked up my fork and tried it. I chewed slowly, my eyes widening with pleasure. As Ruben promised, the vinegar tempered the heat, the jalapeño providing a bright, clean, crisp tingle. There was a sweet note in the dish, too, beyond the fresh corn and tomato.

Ruben looked amused as I dug into the crispy vegetables for a second bite. "Watermelon," he said when I couldn't place the unfamiliar flavor. "It's my secret. That, and my agave vinegar."

Unlike the rest of us, Tager ate sparingly. He pushed his unfinished plate away as we reached for seconds and thirds. "Have you decided when you're leaving?"

Cara stiffened, setting her fork down with a *clink*. She relaxed when Sally and Josephine nodded in unison.

"Dawn," said Sally, sighing. "Although you're making it very hard to leave."

"You're welcome to stay," said Tager. His voice was soft and cordial, but he stared at Earl.

"Winter is coming. We should go while it's still warm

enough to travel." My words came out louder than I'd intended, but my effort to draw Tager's focus from Earl worked.

"Let's not be hasty." River frowned. "I like it here."

"Me too," said Ruben, beaming. He pulled another tortilla from the basket and heaped it with pico de gallo.

"It's pretty, but too hot," said Akiko. "I'm ready for rain and snow."

When I nodded, River's frown turned bitter. "I've had enough rain to last a lifetime." She twisted toward Genevie. "You said you liked it here."

Genevie set her fork down and took River's hand. "I enjoyed meeting *you* here."

Alarms rang in my head. Until we left, the others could change their minds about coming. But how long could we stay hidden at Tager's before our enemies found us? "It's safer if we stay together."

"You have no right to direct my life." River's anger flashed toward me, seething and tangible. "Besides, Talbot needs more rest before he can move."

Cara shifted in her seat and clutched Tom's hand. Her knuckles paled. "We can't wait for Talbot to fully recover."

"You *promised*." Tom's eyes hardened as he stared at me. I didn't trust them any more than the other religious folks I'd encountered, but I'd given my word. I nodded, saying nothing.

Josephine glanced from me to Cara and Tom. "If you're going, I am too."

"And me," said Akiko.

Sally refilled her glass before sending the pitcher around the table. "Me as well. I've had my fill of being on my own."

Earl said nothing but wouldn't meet my eyes as she pushed food around her plate.

When Ben sighed but nodded, Genevie winced.

Dante leaned back to look at the stars. "I promised to help, too, but I'd like to return here when we're done."

River straightened, flashing Dante a brilliant smile. "Then with Tager's permission, we'll stay until Talbot is better. When Dante returns, he can tell us how to find the valley, and we'll make our decision." Triumph rang in her voice.

I wanted to argue, but Genevie's shoulders sagged in acquiescence. There was no point.

"We'll see you off in the morning," she said.

My answering smile was tight and didn't reach my eyes, but if anyone noticed, they said nothing.

***

A FAINT MIST CLUNG TO THE MOONLIT GROUND WHEN I stumbled from the bunkhouse toward the barn. Sending Charcoal off to round up the animals, I pulled out my tack and checked it over.

Ben hefted one of the wagon harnesses over this shoulder, then hesitated. "Since you're not coming, can Dante borrow Bertha?"

Genevie shrugged. "Why not?"

"Great. We can leave the wagon here." Ben hung the harness back on the wall and turned, beaming. "I'll let the mules know."

Dante didn't look thrilled with the idea, but he didn't complain as Genevie fitted her stirrups for him.

Until Josephine saddled Bruno, I wasn't sure Earl would come. I still hadn't spoken to her about my feelings, but I would once we were away from Tager and his luxurious ranch. Ben whistled a merry tune as he readied his mules, his song lightening my mood even more.

With luck, our detour to Cara's valley wouldn't take long.

Once there, we would listen as promised. Afterward, Sally, Josephine, Ben, Earl, and I could spend our time making plans for *our* future while waiting for Genevie and Talbot to arrive. And if River stayed... I couldn't keep the smile from my face. Things could go back to normal.

Akiko skipped into the barn. "Breakfast is ready!"

Even Talbot made it to the table. Tager and Earl had scrambled a mass of eggs with the remaining pico de gallo. They'd also rewarmed the tortillas, and we tucked in, our meal nearly silent, save the scraping of forks against crockery. Again, Earl avoided my eyes, but since Bruno was saddled and ready to go, I didn't let it bother me.

The sun had turned the tips of the eastern mountain gold by the time we were ready to leave. The mists had already burned away, promising another hot, dry day. Murmuring our goodbyes, we rode away, leaving Tager, River, Genevie, and Talbot waving from the porch.

Tom and Cara took the lead.

"Ben, you ride in front of Dante, and I'll ride behind to monitor him." Josephine turned toward me. "Ready?"

Akiko and I exchanged glances and nodded. Clutching Bertha's mane, Dante looked terrified but followed Ben per Josephine's instructions.

Akiko and I brought up the rear. Her spirits were high, and she bombarded me with questions and observations, but after an hour, her chatter stopped. "Look!"

I checked the horizon, afraid an approaching dust cloud would signal pursuers, but nothing looked amiss. "Where?"

Akiko giggled, pointing at the slope above us. Halfway up, Charcoal and Neblina sniffed noses, dancing around each other.

My eyes widened. "How the blast did she find us?"

Akiko made a kissing noise to her mare. "Maybe she never

left!" She squeezed Lady and trotted toward Sally to report the news.

We ate while we rode, stopping only for brief breaks when Akiko pleaded. By the time we stopped to set up camp, Ben and Dante could barely walk. Josephine smirked at Ben until he growled something about not cooking supper. Earl took over without comment and concocted a savory bean dish with chopped onion and peppers. Sally passed around bricks of the cornbread Ruben had packed for us, and we fell asleep listening to the *crackle-pop* of the fire and the hooting of distant owls.

THE NEXT DAY WAS A REPEAT OF THE FIRST, BUT OUR endurance paid off, and we reached the bluff overlooking Cara's valley by late afternoon. A large lake sparkled in the valley, and the trees lined the low hills on the northern side. Cara's joy was contagious, and we were all smiling by the time we reached the valley's floor. The air was cooler here, and the faint scent of resin from the pine trees was a welcome change from the dusty sage I'd become accustomed to.

Again, Earl was remote, her eyes focused on some distant point. While we set up camp, I waited for an opportunity to speak with her, but taking over Ben's cooking duties kept her busy, leaving no opportunity for a quiet word. I smiled at her many times during dinner, but either she didn't notice or ignored me. Each time eroded my confidence further. By the time we'd finished dinner, I was less certain than ever she'd welcome my declaration.

"Can I help with the dishes?" Perhaps it would be easier to speak while focused on a task.

Tom stretched. "Anyone care for a walk?"

"Me!" Akiko scrambled to her feet.

Ben groaned as he stood. "Me too."

Earl sprang up with the others, leaving me alone with the dishes. I watched them wander down the shoreline, my frustration growing as I scoured the pot with sand. By the time Sally took it from me, it sparkled inside and out. She said nothing, but her eyebrows raised as she dried it.

When the others returned, they dropped arm loads of firewood and Dante rebuilt the fire.

Ben sighed, staring at the glimmering sky. "I see why you call this Paradise Valley."

Cara settled herself next to Tom. "If Tom can convince the other artists to come, I think we can build a haven here." She swallowed, the corners of her mouth pulling back. "For people like us. People who want to live and worship without fear."

Josephine frowned and shifted, but it was Ben who asked the question. "Why stir up the old? They had religion *Before*, but it led them to their doom. These things caused the world to die."

Cara bowed her head. But when she spoke, her voice was clear and strong. "Because as much as you may want to believe it, people haven't changed. We nurture our faith in secrecy and fear. You may not need religion or love God, but many of us do."

The truth in Cara's words twisted my heart. Akiko's shoulders sagged, and I imagined she grieved her birth parents. They had defended their faith, given up their child, and paid for their beliefs with their lives.

The sincerity of Cara's words was also written across Josephine's face. Now it was she who wouldn't meet my eyes.

*This isn't news to her.*

If people hadn't lost their faith or their desire to commune and worship, then the rest of us had forced them to do so in a secretive, furtive, and shameful manner. No wonder scholars had confiscated the religious texts and hidden them away.

Tom cleared his throat. "Dante, Matthew, and I will travel to Churchill Abbey tomorrow to plead our case." Before we could raise objections, he said, "Along the way, we'll retrieve the art supplies I've hidden."

My jaw ached from clenching my teeth. This wasn't what we'd agreed to. He was changing our bargain yet again. I wanted to argue, but Dante and I both needed art supplies which were also not part of the original bargain.

"I suppose we should stay here." Sally sighed. "There are too many of us to ask the abbey to accommodate everyone."

Again, I waited for Earl to look at me or speak. After our trip to Leavenworth Abbey, she knew they'd welcome a few visitors. But she said nothing.

The bitterness I'd carried over the last several days caught fire. "You should stay here," I said, agreeing with Sally. I shook Akiko's hand. "Even you."

For once, she didn't argue. "How long?"

"As long as it takes." My reply was vague on purpose, and Earl's mouth tightened. The reaction pleased me. Her indifference hurt. If she couldn't be bothered with me, why should I waste my time and effort and *heart* on her? Besides, my family's safety was my priority, and if Tom thought building his paradise would keep Carter's people from advancing west, I was prepared to use all my skills to make it happen.

My focus had been and must be, my family. Earl and I... My hands clenched. If it was supposed to happen, it would have by now. I raised my chin and drew a metaphorical line with my words. "In this beautiful place, none of you will miss us." My statement was a challenge, a question to probe what I meant to Earl. This was her chance. She could protest, ask a question, or even express worry. Any response would mean she still cared. That the bond between us was worth fighting for.

But it wasn't Earl who responded.

Instead, Josephine's eyes saddened. "I hope it doesn't take long." Ben and Sally murmured their agreement, and no dissent came from Earl or anyone else.

Bitter regret washed over me. Perhaps it hadn't been fair to challenge her in front of everyone. Should I apologize? Or ask for a private word and explain?

*No.*

She had made her choice. I tightened my jaw and pasted a smile on my face. "Come. Let's wash for bed."

Josephine scrambled to her feet. "What about a swim? I've longed for one for months."

"In the lake?" Akiko's eyes widened. "I don't know how to swim."

She wasn't the only one. I tickled her, ignoring Earl. "I'll keep you safe," I said, pretending a joviality I didn't feel.

Earl faded into the dark as the rest of us ran whooping toward the lake. The water was pleasantly cool. After realizing I wouldn't let her wade in deeper than her waist, Akiko relaxed. Even Sally splashed around in the water, crowing as Charcoal leaped in. He swam around us, snorting.

The water soothed our hot, dry skin, and eventually, we quieted, floating in the shimmering dark. The moon painted silver trails across the rippling surface, and Akiko clung to my back like a burning ember as I swam out into the deeper water.

Afterward, her voice was sleepy as I tucked her into her bedroll. "Will you learn me how to swim?"

"Promise," I said. My eyes flicked to Earl's bedroll, but she wasn't there. I brushed back Akiko's damp hair and kissed her forehead. "Sleep safe and be well."

# CHAPTER FORTY-NINE

A ghostly mist floated over the lake's surface when I awoke. I lay still for a moment, dreading our inevitable parting. Akiko wouldn't make it easy, and Earl...

As much as I'd pretended bravado last night, I regretted the ultimatum I'd laid down. The public challenge hadn't been fair and had accomplished nothing. But perhaps I could make amends this morning. Assuming Earl wanted to speak with me... and I could set aside my pride.

Charcoal lifted his head from my chest and licked my cheek once before standing. He stretched, his chest down and tail up, paws out in front, before switching and shrugging his shoulders up, his hind legs behind him. He blinked and shook, jumping lightly across Ben's body.

Earl's bedroll was empty again. She slept even less than me. No one else stirred yet, so I picked up my boots and tiptoed out from under the canvas shelter we'd set up.

The damp grass soaked through my socks, but I relished the chill. The day would heat soon enough, and the memory of the cooler air would help me escape the heat, if only in my mind.

As usual, the donkey was loose. His ears twitched as Charcoal trotted toward him, and he stamped his front foot in warning.

I smiled and rubbed his shoulder. "Have you seen Earl?"

The donkey leaned into me but didn't answer. I scoured the shore and tree line for a flash of red but found nothing. In the meadow, Bruno grazed with the other horses. I watched him, remembering Earl's sunlit smile as we'd ridden to Leavenworth Abbey.

Bitterness filled my mouth. My dreadful behavior last night had been pretense, a protest of her aloofness. Had she known?

*Yes.*

Shame heated my cheeks. Earl had always seen through my words, seen through my actions to my core. And despite my many failings, she'd remained a steadfast, supportive friend.

It was time I did better.

I pulled on my boots, rehearsing my apology. When Earl returned, I'd tell her exactly what was in my heart and beg for her forgiveness.

But Earl did not reappear. She remained absent even after Ben rekindled the fire and fried bacon, its scent floating through the morning air. There was no trace of her when I sent Charcoal to fetch the horses, or while Tom, Dante, and I prepared to leave.

I dallied, finding excuse after excuse to delay our departure. I imagined her arriving breathless, laughing about losing track of time while exploring a creek or watching a juvenile bird take its first flight.

Indecision racked me. Should I stay? I could catch up to the others easily enough, especially with Dante's nascent equestrian skills. But how would I explain it? Nothing came to mind, so I continued my preparations.

If anyone else noticed her absence, they said nothing, either out of tact or for fear of upsetting my feigned indifference. At last, there was no more pretense, no more excuses for delay, and they waved a cheerful goodbye as we rode away.

THE TRAIL WEAVED UP A ROCKY RIDGE INTO THE TREES. I searched through them and on each rocky outcropping but saw nothing. The hopeful part of me waited for Bruno to come thundering after us. I imagined her tear-stained face as she leaped from her dark horse into my waiting and outstretched arms. But no one followed us except Neblina, who slipped between the trees and rocks like a shadow.

I deluded myself for nearly an hour before my hopes died.

Earl's absence had been no accident.

The admission brought an inferno of pain. I longed to sob and rage and turn around... but I did nothing but replay the scene from last night. There was a strange comfort in reliving the moment I'd wrecked everything between us. Like prodding an injury or poking a sore tooth with my tongue. And so, I continued to berate myself silently until the fires died, leaving my heart a smoldering husk of charcoal.

Near noon, Tom called for a halt. Dante half-slid, half-fell from Genevie's mare and hobbled toward the trees. His theatrical shouts of relief made Genevie's mare snort and dance sideways. Tom flashed me a smile as I settled the mare, and for a moment, the brotherhood we'd shared after our sparring session darted across my mind's canvas.

Tom must have shared my thoughts. When Dante returned, he asked, "Do you both have your swords?"

Dante compressed his lips and squared his shoulders. "Yes."

I eyed him. When he'd left the abbey, he'd carried a large bag, but it wasn't long enough to hold a sword. "You do?"

Dante fumbled with the leather strings on the back of his saddle and pulled down his bag. From inside, he pulled two curved cylinders. He handed one to me, and the other to Tom. "Take care."

The handle was round, ornate, and thicker than I was accustomed to but lay comfortably in my grip. When I slid the metal from the sheath, it sparkled in the midday sun, one edge honed like a razor. The blade was approximately forty centimeters long, and when I flicked it, it flowed with me, like an extension of my arm.

"Beautiful," I said, sliding it back into the sheath.

"It's a wakizashi blade." Dante took it back and waited. When I said nothing, he added, "Tanaka-*san* introduced them. Many of us at the abbey preferred working with them, especially for close-quarter fighting."

Tom quirked his eyebrow. "Tanaka-*san*?"

"Andrew Tanaka, the headmaster at Leavenworth Abbey." Dante smiled and jerked his thumb at me. "Another artist of Japanese heritage." Tom handed the other sword back. Dante stowed it and retied his bag onto the back of the saddle. "Will we need them?"

Tom said nothing and shrugged, passing around the sandwiches Ben had prepared for us. He had used tortillas to wrap the leftover fajita filling from the night before, like little bedrolls.

Dante studied Tom between bites. "Explain your vision to us."

"I'd like to establish an abbey and a cooperative community. The residents in both would be free to worship if they wish to."

"And you want to invite the brothers from Churchill?" I frowned. "Why would they want to leave their abbey?"

Tom compressed his lips. "I've heard they're believers."

"Was Niagara full of believers?" I lowered my meal.

Tom blinked, as though confused. "Always." His brow furrowed. "You didn't learn the connection?"

The food sat heavy in my gut as I shook my head.

"Carter is Headmaster McCully's son." Tom took another bite. "As far as I know, believers populated Erie and Niagara from the start."

"But his name is Carter." I stared at Tom. "Reverend Carter."

"Carter is his first name." Tom finished his sandwich and dug into his saddlebags for his canteen. "Carter McCully. You really didn't know about the abbeys?"

"I hadn't heard of either, but they were on a map." Appetite gone, I tossed the rest of my meal to Charcoal. "If his father is an artist, why does Carter hate us?"

It was Tom's turn to look surprised. "I suspect envy. They sent him to study at another abbey, but he failed."

*Headmaster McCully's son... a failed artist.*

My thoughts reeled, but even as I digested Tom's revelations, questions sparked, like wind-driven embers of a wildfire. "Why are some artists religious?"

Tom sighed as he stood. "Can we talk as we ride? I'd like to reach the abbey before dark." Once we were underway, Tom picked up where he'd left off. "First, you should know you're very talented."

His praise warmed me, but I wanted answers, not flattery. "That's well and good, but it doesn't explain it."

"It's not flattery, it's context." Tom rolled his neck. "Imagine if you had a moderate talent. Perhaps enough to change the color of a piece of fruit, but not enough to produce a change that mattered."

I shrugged. "At Popham, boys often failed for insufficient talent."

"Yes. Those boys left, dissatisfied. Bereft even." Tom

paused, squinting at the sun. "They witnessed greatness but could never be artists."

Dante clucked his tongue, then grabbed at his reins when the mare sped up as she'd been trained to do. "Settle, girl!"

I hid my smirk. Dante wouldn't thank me for an impromptu equitation lesson.

"Leavenworth Abbey had masters like that." Dante frowned. "Skilled at the technical aspects of art but unable to manifest physical changes. They usually instructed the younger boys, teaching perspective and abstraction."

"Exactly." Tom glanced at me. "Technicians who could teach basic skills but who couldn't alter or improve anything."

"But..." –I frowned, leaning forward– "it's what makes us artists. We transform matter." The memory of a dragon hidden in a vined mural flashed onto my mind's canvas. "Many learn to draw or paint, but they're not artists."

"True," said Tom. "Imagine an entire abbey of failed artists. Men who knew what was *possible* but for whom the ability —*the magic*—of art remained out of reach."

"Men condemned to a lifetime of teaching boys with potential, hoping some of them would have the extra spark." Dante's jaw tightened.

His words sent ice down my spine. "What a desolate future."

"Exactly."

The trail narrowed, so I dropped back and contemplated what my life would have been like if I'd studied at a place like Niagara Abbey. Every master I'd studied with at Popham could demonstrate the concepts they taught. Witnessing the astonishing possibilities of art fueled my desire to learn as well as my drive for mastery. But if I hadn't believed large improvements were possible, would I have studied with the same vigor?

At the top of a steep slope, Tom stopped his horse and

swung it around to face us. "In truth, it took every ounce of my skill to open the doorways in the walls at the Mountain View. And we only managed to manufacture the false wall you asked for by working together. Artists like us can accomplish more when working in concert with others."

Tom's admission made me uneasy, but when Dante nodded, understanding crashed through me. This was why the artists at Welland Island worked on murals cooperatively. As a group working together, they were capable of more than any of them could accomplish on their own.

"But what about Welland? You walled me in."

Tom sagged at my reminder and Dante's choked gasp. "Seven of us worked together. I followed you so you'd see a friendly face if you turned around. But you didn't. We pooled our skill to fill the hallway and stairwells with stone."

"I'm unable to do what you do," said Dante. "And I was one of the best at Leavenworth, one of the best they'd ever had." His shoulders sagged, but his tone conveyed relief, not despair. "For men like us, highly skilled and prized, the future is wide open. But you—" he stopped and exchanged a look with Tom.

The artwork I'd used to change the Mountain View required precision and meticulous attention to detail. Extending the overpass required little more than the belief I could do it. Neither had taxed me or approached the level of effort it took me to move objects with my art. If they knew what I could do, would it open their eyes to the possibilities and allow them to grow and develop their talent? Or would it cause trouble for them... and me?

"Your talent is astonishing," said Tom. "But your accomplishments diminish my small talent. If I didn't have my faith..." He pursed his lips, his eyes sad. "I don't think I could bear it."

A whistling filled my ears, and though they continued to

speak, I heard nothing more. I had allowed the trouble with Earl to distract me and pull my attention from what was truly important. For I too had witnessed a power far greater than mine, a staggering talent with unknowable potential.

*Akiko.*

But where her gift had awed and inspired me, it could drive the men Tom and Dante described to despair... and rage.

# CHAPTER FIFTY

During our next break, Tom disappeared into the woods while Dante finished his toilet. When Tom returned, he carried four, canvas-wrapped parcels and dropped them next to Dante. Dante waited for Tom to disappear before unwrapping one. "Oil pigments!"

On Tom's next trip, he brought four more parcels and turned to go again. I followed him.

We scrambled up the toe of a shale-covered slope, the stones slipping and clattering underfoot. Tom stopped and lifted a shale-colored canvas tarpaulin. "They're here."

He had cached his purloined art supplies in a shallow void, left after shale had broken away from the main rock face. I raised my eyebrows at the quantity but said nothing.

It took three more trips to retrieve the parcels. Once we had everything back, I laid them out to determine how to pack them into Magnesium's panniers.

"I think I can fit these in the left side, and those in the right, but these smaller parcels will need to go in our saddlebags."

Tom nodded, but Dante shook his head. "Sorry, my bags are full. I had to *roll* my clothes to get them to fit."

"Why? We're not staying long," I said, dividing his share of the smaller parcels into a pile for me and for Tom.

"Excuse me? We're traveling to an *abbey*. I needed outfits."

"Outfits? But we'll borrow robes while we're there."

"Doesn't mean we have to keep them on." Dante tossed his head and arched his eyebrow.

I grinned and opened the first pannier. "Hand me those." What impact had Tom's theft had on Carter's artists? They had raided the libraries at two depots, but I couldn't estimate how far their supplies would stretch. Not without a clear estimate of how many artists traveled with, or on behalf of, Carter. Leavenworth Abbey, alone on the prairie and packed full of art supplies popped onto my mind's canvas. Dante must have had a similar thought, and we locked eyes.

"They'll be alright," he said, handing me the last parcel.

There was little I could do to help the abbey now but hope they stayed off Carter's radar. When I established a home for Akiko, I'd take care to keep our capabilities and supplies from general knowledge. Better the world believed we were ordinary folk than artists. I buckled the last pannier closed, my gut twisting with unease. Ben would keep Akiko safe until I returned, but the sooner I could return to her, the better. If Tom's vision caught, it would take little effort to convince the artists at Churchill Abbey to join him.

We descended the narrow, rocky trail in near silence, save the strike of a hoof on a rocky outcropping or the clatter of shale as it slid down the rocky slopes. The exposed rock on the surrounding slopes ranged from hues of Burnt Bronzite to nearly a Venetian Red. We passed ugly outcroppings in shades of Alvaro's Caliente Gray, where the rock bulged like it was covered with pustules.

When we reached the valley floor, the vegetation was sparse and dusty. Everything had a bleached, desiccated appearance, as if an artist had attempted to capture it with the pigments left on his poorly cleaned paintbrush.

"This is where color goes to die," I muttered. The occasional flash of red-hued rock helped to keep the muted blues, grays, and tans from driving me mad.

I was *not* a child of the desert.

Tom led us east through a narrow gap in the barren hills, the rock folded like a discarded towel. Charcoal occasionally flushed grouse from the sage, but they, and giant jumping grasshoppers, were the only creatures I spotted. We followed an ancient, graveled grade, and based on the evenly spaced trees in the gully below, a river had once flowed through the dry channel. The skeletal trees were devoid of foliage, their trunks silvered from sun and death.

Tom's horse snorted and picked up the pace, telegraphing we were near the abbey. Unlike the stately, imposing facility I'd been expecting, we arrived at a dusty, two-story structure. From my angle, the building appeared nearly a quarter kilometer long on a north–south axis. It looked wrong, a trick of the dying sun and trail dust. But when we reached the corner, the building continued east toward the horizon. Tom's shoulders sagged, but he kicked his horse forward.

The structure was not in good shape, the outer cladding pitted and worn. Why wouldn't the abbey have sent boys out to repair the structure? As we rode, I examined the damaged areas and noticed they had constructed the building with some sort of Bronzite-hued brick, smoothed with a thick plaster of nearly the same color. Large, rectangular windows set at regular intervals reflected our images as we rode past. Dante preened, but I avoided my disheveled appearance.

In the middle of the building, we arrived at a set of large, wooden doors. Tom stopped and smoothed his hair, then motioned us to dismount. The doors swung open, and several brothers squinted into the sun. They wore lightweight robes of bleached linen which nearly matched the buff-colored sand underfoot, not the black robes I'd expected.

"*Ego autem—*" we chorused, stopping to smile at each other.

"Niagara," said Tom.

Dante tossed his head. "Leavenworth."

"And Popham," I concluded.

They hesitated before one stepped forward. "Are you with the others?"

We exchanged glances and shook our heads.

"Have we come at a bad time?" Tom asked.

"No, but we have little water," said the man, his look apologetic. "We make do since we get so few visitors, but you make ten this week alone. Our resources are... strained."

"If there's water for our livestock, we'll be fine," said Dante.

The first man heaved a sigh, which may have been of relief. "Then you're very welcome. I'm Lee Bendall, and this is Vail Linford. We're currently hosting artists who have traveled from the east, but I don't remember offhand if any are from Niagara, Leavenworth, or Popham."

Although Tom's posture stiffened, his voice was cordial as he introduced us, "I'm Tom Staker, and this is Dante Ruiz and Andrew Tanaka."

My gut clenched when Tom smiled with hard eyes. The deception troubled me, but I raised my hand in as genial a manner as I could muster and followed the others inside.

The doors opened into a central courtyard, which appeared as vast and as dusty as the outside. They had built the abbey as four linear buildings connected at the corners. Each stretched approximately a quarter kilometer, creating an inner courtyard of approximately three-quarters of a hectare. The courtyard contained livestock paddocks, gardens, and assembly spaces.

There were as many window openings on the inside of the courtyard as we'd seen on the exterior, and through the nearest, I viewed active classrooms. They had doors opening into the central courtyard. When the bell rang, students spilled into the vast courtyard from three sides of the compound. They threaded across the space, their shouts and jeers bringing back memories of my boyhood.

After they passed, Bendall led us to a low-roofed structure nearer the northern side of the courtyard. Like Tager's barn, it had open walls divided into a series of covered paddocks. I counted roughly a dozen horses stabled in the structure, many of whom whinnied greetings to our mounts.

The man in charge of the barn had a pinched look and sighed as he directed us to four of the open stalls. "The boys take the horses to the creek in the evenings and morning, so we stall them under cover during the day. They sweat less and demand less water."

Once we'd settled our horses, Bendall and Linford escorted us toward the oak growing in the courtyard. Its leaves had a withered, furled look, but the shade it provided was a welcome respite from the merciless sun. Polished benches made from bleached wood sat in the oak's shade, over which nearly two dozen men had gathered. Tom and Dante scanned the assembled men. When both relaxed, I assumed neither of them had spotted anyone they recognized.

"Masters Tom Staker, Dante Ruiz, and Andrew Tanaka," announced Linford. "I thought they could join you while we prepare rooms for them."

An older man with an ample belly and pleasant smile stood. He raised his hand. "Welcome, Travelers. We arrived the day before yesterday." He dragged his toe through the dusty soil in a shallow arc. The motion could have been accidental, an old man's weak leg dragging behind him as he turned to sit, but Tom made a similar motion while sitting. A partial ichthys... and a signal.

*Carter's men.*

It was pleasant enough in the shade, but my skin crawled. Tom and Dante made small talk while we waited for Linford to return. The Churchill masters wore the same tan-colored robes as Bendall and Linford. The five men wearing traditional black robes, including our greeter, were the visitors. In our traveling clothes, we stuck out, wearing neither sand nor black.

When Linford returned for us, he escorted us to the northern building and led us up a dim staircase to a second-floor hallway. Linford opened three adjoining doors. Each room boasted a sweeping view of the courtyard and the mountains beyond. A dusting of snow decorated the peaks—a jolting reminder that, despite the heat, winter was fast approaching.

"There's a communal seating area down the hall. Join me there once you've stowed your things," Linford said, handing each of us a sand-colored robe.

LINFORD GRINNED WHEN WE SANK INTO THE OVERSTUFFED armchairs with sighs of appreciation. The scarred, plank floors were scuffed, and the sun-faded, leather upholstery was worn, but the room had a cheerful, relaxed atmosphere, enhanced by a bookcase of well-thumbed books and spiky, potted plants. The communal room boasted the same sweeping, south-facing views, and a welcome breeze floated through the open windows.

Once we'd each taken a seat, Linford perched on a short wooden stool, his gaze intent. "None of you are with the

Reverend Carter?" When we shook our heads, he leaned forward. "On your honor?"

"None of us," I said, trying not to think about Tom's former association. "He is no friend of mine."

At the vehemence in my voice, his posture relaxed, and his smile warmed. "I am very glad to meet you."

Dante glanced over his shoulder toward the hallway. "Should we guard our words?"

Linford shook his head and crossed the room. "Their rooms are in the western building. Our quarters are in the east, and the students live in the south, so you have this wing to yourselves." He hesitated before pulling a pitcher from the cabinet. He set three glasses on the table and filled them each to the three-quarter mark. When we protested the water, he shook his head. "It's the least we can do for the favor we need to ask."

Dante straightened. "Favor?"

"Carter's artists have shown up to demand our allegiance... or our art supplies. Like we didn't already have enough to worry about."

After what I'd learned in Vegas Depot, I knew not to gulp my water regardless of my thirst. I sipped it, and when I set down my half-full glass, Linford relaxed. I took a chance. "Water trouble?" When Linford chewed his lip without answering, I elaborated. "We traveled from the west, along what I assumed was once a river channel."

His chest deflated in a whistling sigh. "The Carson River. Our headmaster says it was once mighty, though it was little more than a creek when I arrived as a small child."

Tom tilted his head and set his unfinished glass down. "What happened?"

Linford's chuckle turned bitter. "Silver Springs is an Avalon Society community. They closed the dam, and we could do nothing to convince them otherwise."

"But you are *artists*," I protested. The way Tom and Dante's eyes slid sideways reminded me that the Avalon Society did not welcome *all* artists.

Tom scowled and leaned forward. "If there was no Reverend Carter and no water issues, what would your abbey brothers want?"

Linford studied Tom's face for a long time before closing his eyes. "To be left alone," he said in a small voice. "To worship and live lives of faith."

"Then we've come at exactly the right time." Tom beamed at Linford. "I have the answer to your problems."

Linford leaned forward, focused on Tom. "Go on."

"I'm here to invite you to move west into a valley so beautiful, you'll see God's hand in it. We plan to establish an abbey there too."

I relaxed. Dante and I had fulfilled our side of the agreement, and we could now return to the valley with clear hearts. With Carter's men here, it was prudent to leave as soon as we could—the longer we stayed, the greater the risk they'd learn my true identity.

But Linford's demeanor dimmed. "I can relay your offer, but don't hold much hope."

Tom blinked, as though confused. "But you have nothing here. No support. No water. The nearest community is unfriendly toward you. Why would you stay?"

"This is my home." Linford's face was sad as he lifted his gaze to meet Tom's eyes. "I don't want to start over. I'm not sure any of us will."

My heart sank at the sincerity behind his words and an awkward silence filled the room until Dante cleared his throat. "Earlier, you mentioned a favor?"

Linford raised his hands and sank backward. "To lend your support should our headmaster decide to send Carter's artists away."

"I will."

I'd uttered the words without thinking, but based on the expression on Linford's face, I couldn't back out now. If Linford and his brothers wanted to fight for this sad, shabby excuse for an abbey, how could I leave without trying to help?

When I faced my companions, my gut twisted at the expression of horror on Dante's face... and the sly satisfaction on Tom's.

# CHAPTER FIFTY-ONE

I woke before dawn with my mind chewing on my decision to stay. Had it been rash? The abbey was silent, but I had little chance of returning to slumber. Charcoal crept closer and nudged me.

"All right, chap. Let's go out."

His nails clicked on the creaky, wooden stairs as he followed me downstairs. After a stop at the composting toilet, I took him outside to conduct his business in the courtyard. Puffs of dust rose behind him as he nosed the strangled weeds and stunted shrubs.

The predawn stillness held a faint chill, and I gazed up at the deep, Lunar Blue sky, wondering if Earl was awake too. Why had I agreed to help Churchill? If I hadn't, I could have ridden to the valley this morning. But now I was stuck here until Carter's men forced the issue... or left.

When Charcoal finished, we returned to the common room. I lit a candle and sat at a desk under the windows, opening my sketchbook. Last night, I'd stayed up late, sketching. The act of drawing usually soothed me, but the shame of how I'd left things with Earl, plus the pressure of waiting for Carter's men to do *something*, had filled me with restless energy. I'd filled nearly half my book with illustrations of Cara's valley and Churchill Abbey. I'd also drawn vignettes of Genevie and River, sketches of buffalo, and the ostriches racing across Tager's dusty pastures. There were doodles of Akiko grinning at Sally, and Josephine folding into Ben's embrace.

But what I'd drawn most was Earl.

Memories of her riding Bruno across the prairie, wearing her floppy straw hat. Her face half-hidden in shadow as she laughed at one of Talbot's poems beside the flickering fire. Modeling at Leavenworth Abbey in a flowing, green dress. Her eyes sparkling with wonder as she stared at the Kaskaskia dragon or filled with worry when Oxide dragged me, water-logged and half-drowned, from the river. Standing over six pails of water, a blazing monument of victory.

My head may have decided she and I were done, but my heart clearly hadn't listened. The memory I yearned to draw was her face filled with understanding and forgiveness in the pearlescent, predawn light, next to a mist-covered lake. If I'd been able to find her before leaving for the abbey, would she have accepted my apology?

*Maybe.*

My heart tore, but rather than shove the pain away, I gathered it to me. Even my painful memories of Earl were precious. If I made my feelings clear and she rejected me a second time, would my heart survive it? I tapped my pencil and stared unseeing through the window. Another refusal from Earl would hurt, but surely my heart couldn't shatter more than it already had. And if she said yes...

When I heaved a heavy sigh, Charcoal mimicked me. I closed my sketchbook with a *snap*. "We'll fix things with her when we return, eh, chap?"

He wiggled in agreement and swung his head toward the hallway.

"Why are we up so *early*?" Dante staggered into the sitting area. "It's positively indecent."

I folded my arms and shrugged. "Did I wake you?"

He flopped onto the couch and made a face at the *twang* of protest from its springs. "No. The bed was too comfortable, and I've become accustomed to the grizzled life of an outdoorsman."

I studied his smooth skin and oiled hair. "Yes, you're quite hardy."

Tom shuffled in, yawning. "What did I miss?"

"Dante's rugged masculinity."

Tom snorted and ignored the glare Dante shot him. "So... what now?"

"Wait?" I shrugged. Perhaps I could use the time to investigate the abbey's water problem. "But when we resolve the situation with Carter's men, I'm returning to the valley."

"Same." Dante stretched, catlike. "I've seen what Churchill has to offer, and it's not for me."

Tom's shoulders sagged. "I can't return empty-handed."

"Have faith." The irony of my statement made my lips twitch, and I scratched at my jaw, wishing we could bathe. "Linford said he'd relay your request, so perhaps someone will join you."

AN UNSETTLED MOOD PERMEATED THE DINING HALL WHEN we arrived for breakfast. Even the boys were subdued. Few lifted their eyes from their meals when we entered. I kept my expression neutral, but my gaze darted around. Where was the fractious energy coming from?

We joined the serving line. No one spoke. While waiting for our meals, Linford caught Tom's eye, so we carried our steaming bowls of corn mush to open seats next to him.

"Good morning," he said, sliding a piece of paper toward Tom. Tom glanced at it. His expression didn't change as he passed it to Dante. Dante scanned it and passed it to me under the table.

My pulse jumped as I smoothed the note against my thigh. It read, "We're turning them down today. Are you ready?"

So much for my plans to work on the water issues.

"When?" Tom asked.

Linford scraped his bowl loudly, muttering, "Second bell."

My appetite fled. I toyed with the frayed sleeve of my borrowed robe, my stomach flipping.

Students finished with their meals carried their dirty crockery to large tubs near the doors but poured their remaining water into a barrel strapped to a wheeled dolly.

I pointed at it. "What's the barrel for?"

Linford twisted to look. "The oak in the courtyard. We save water at every meal for Bodmer."

Dante pushed his uneaten breakfast away. "Named after Monet's painting?"

Linford nodded, the smile dropping from his face when the headmaster stood and clapped. The first bell tolled, and the remaining boys scattered, their bowls clattering into the tubs as they dashed through the doors. Although several of the masters also left, presumably to teach, the remaining men gathered near the head table. When we'd arrived, I'd found Churchill's sand-colored robes odd, but now they made it easy to distinguish between the two groups of artists. In our borrowed robes, we blended into Churchill's ranks.

Bendall stood near the headmaster's table with a benign expression as he glanced around the group. After the second bell rang, his shoulders squared and he focused on a black-robed, barrel-chested man. "Thank you for joining us." When the man nodded, Bendall continued, "We've discussed your requests but cannot assist with either."

Sweat prickled along my spine but the barrel-chested man seemed neither surprised nor disappointed by Bendall's statement.

"We are a small abbey with few resources and can spare neither supplies nor men, but we thank you for your offer." Bendall spread his hands. "Please remember us in your travels."

The man shifted and cleared his throat. "You're sending us away with neither artists nor supplies?"

Bendall shook his head, his face regretful.

"We will not return empty-handed."

The man's expression remained unchanged, but the tone of his voice sent shivers up my spine. My mouth went dry.

Headmaster Wilcox sighed. "We are sorry."

The barrel-chested man murmured to the man on his right before turning toward the headmaster. "We'll prepare to leave."

Bendall smiled as though relieved, but Dante stiffened. Of the three of us, he was the best at reading body language.

This wasn't good.

When the group dispersed, Dante strode through the door into the courtyard, and headed north, toward our quarters. Tom and I scrambled to keep up, tossing uneasy glances at each other.

Once we were out of earshot, Dante confirmed my fears. "We need our swords."

Tom stopped. "But they said they're leaving, didn't they?"

Dante's mouth compressed into a flat, thin line. Without answering, he continued north.

Our march back did little to settle my nerves. Reaching my room, I strapped my sword to my leg under the robe.

Charcoal followed me toward the door and gave me an inquisitive look when I inched out the door, holding him back with my foot. He whined, trying to push past me.

"Stay here, chap." Once I closed the door, he barked without stopping. My heart thrummed as I walked toward the common area. I hadn't fought in a skirmish since Wakefield.

Was this happening? I'd avoided the notice of Carter's men so far, but surely, they would remember the strangers who had joined the abbey's fight against them. But if I didn't help and Carter's men won, I'd risk exposing our involvement. Plus, if they searched our things, they could find my sketches, putting Akiko and the others at risk, too.

Tearing cloth jolted me back into the moment.

*Pocket.*

Following Dante's lead, Tom and I slit our left pockets open so we could draw our swords through our robes.

Dante practiced his double draw while we finished. "Ready?"

I patted my hip.

"Let's go," Tom said, in a terse voice.

We retraced our steps across the courtyard, but when we reached the dining hall, we found it empty. Dante crossed the room and stood in the hallway, his eyes watchful. A muffled *thud* followed by a *clang* reached us.

"They're after the vault," said Tom. "This way."

Down a set of stone steps, a dozen men fought in murky torchlight. Along the hallway, sparks flared as steel met stone. Wearing black, Carter's men were simple to spot. Though outnumbered, they fought with ferocity, their mouths hard and eyes grim.

My breakfast roiled in my gut. *Too late now to turn back, now.*

Dante's wakizashi blades sang as he stripped their sheaths.

He tossed the protective coverings behind him. Like mirror images, Tom and I drew our swords and waded into the fray.

The barrel-chested leader attacked me.

My mind cleared as the shock of his blows resounded up my blade and into my shoulders. I waited for a break in his attack, then went on the offensive. Because of the tight quarters, I could neither raise my sword nor swing it from the shoulder without scraping it against stone. Neither was effective, so I changed my stance, using the flat of my blade as a shield as I pushed him backward. I whirled, thrusting and parrying as best I could in the narrow hallway.

My shoulders ached, and the side of my hand stung from the kiss of his steel, but I was at least twenty years younger than him and had the advantage of momentum. My boots scraped for purchase along the stone corridor as we grappled, my calves shrieking as I drove him down the hallway. But when his expression changed, I knew another black-robed man advanced from behind me. I released my pressure on the leader and ducked, pressing my sweaty back against the cool, stone wall. Instead of continuing his attack, the leader let the other man take over while he slipped up a narrow staircase.

I ignored the leader's departure and studied my new opponent's tactics. While his swordplay was competent, his footwork was a mess. Each time he went on the offensive and swung, he allowed his weight to come onto his toes, leaving his center of gravity too far forward. On defense, his weight shifted too far back, so I went on the offensive, blitzing him with quick thrusts and parries. He stumbled backward, trying to regain his balance, but I didn't let up, my frenzy driving him into a darkened room. When he stumbled over something, I leaped backward and pulled the door shut. Having no way to secure it, I clung to the handle as he shouted, yanked, and banged on his side of the door.

I examined the hallway for some way to secure the door. There was little here, so I hung on, evaluating the ongoing fight. Not that it was much of a contest. It reminded me more of the monthly sparring drills held at Popham Abbey than a true battle. Few of the blows had lethal force. Everyone was still standing, and though crimson smeared several sand-colored robes, none of the wounds appeared severe.

This was a skirmish, not a battle.

As though my conclusions were contagious, the fighting slowed, then ceased. Churchill's brothers and Carter's men retreated to opposite walls, gasping and glaring at each other.

The man I'd captured continued to scream and yell. One of his black-robed companions advanced toward me, so I released the handle and backed away. My former opponent wrenched the door open and rushed into the hall with his sword high, but he deflated when he saw the fighting had stopped.

"Blast you!" He joined the other black-robed men inching along the far wall. When they reached the narrow stairwell, they rushed up it.

"Come." Bendall led us toward another staircase. Dante and Tom were in the dining hall when we arrived. Tom had a swollen lip, but it looked the worst of our injuries. My shoulder ached, but I suspected the pain was due more to the abbreviated motion forced by the hallway than any injury.

Relief crossed Linford's face. "You're okay?"

I nodded. "Was anyone hurt?"

"Cuts and scrapes." He shrugged. "It could have been much worse."

Dante sighed as he slid his sheaths back over his short blades. "No one wanted to harm a brother artist."

Boys tumbled into the dining hall, white-faced. Several of the smaller boys crouched along the wall, sobbing. "They took our paints!"

The masters crowded forward toward the boys, checking them for injury.

"There they go!" someone shouted. The black-robed men raced eastward, flashing past the large windows. The hollow *thud* of the exterior doors banging shut was followed by relieved shouts.

My stomach churned as the others cheered. We'd defended Churchill Abbey, but Carter's men had escaped. How much worse had we made things for myself and the others? And what about the real Andrew Tanaka?

# CHAPTER FIFTY-TWO

The three of us waited in line with Tom to see the abbey's healer. Despite the lack of serious injuries, the wait was long. Dante didn't help when he paced up and down the hall.

"We should go," he finally said. "We could make it to the valley before dark. How soon can you be ready?"

Linford's eyes clouded. "What if they come back?"

Without checking with us, Tom clapped Linford's shoulder. "We'll stay another day."

"No." Dante bristled. "We've fulfilled our obligations twice over. Shall we, *Andrew*?"

I wanted to leave with Dante, but the attack by Carter's men may have improved Tom's chances of convincing Churchill's artists to abandon this place and establish a new abbey. Long term, ensuring Tom's vision came true was still our safest course, so I shook my head. "I'm going to stay to help. Can you find your way back?"

Dante's jaw tightened, but he nodded. "Yes." He turned toward Tom. "Is there anything I should take back, *just in case?*"

Tom nodded, his eyes widening. It wasn't only the abbey's art supplies in jeopardy if Carter's artists returned. Without a packhorse, Dante couldn't carry it all, but if we emptied his bags, he could carry some of it back to the valley.

I clapped Dante's shoulder. "I'll help you pack."

"Thanks." Tom's eyes brightened. "I'll meet you in the barn after the healer releases me."

I waited until Dante and I were out of earshot. "Will you deliver something to Akiko for me?"

He shrugged and glanced at me without breaking his stride. "I don't know why you're staying. Will Carter's men return?"

"Unlikely. There's little forage or water here, and if Silver Springs is hostile, they can't regroup for a while. Plus, after raiding the classroom, they're not entirely empty-handed." I took the stairs to our quarters two at a time. "Plus, they've lost the element of surprise and know Churchill will fight, so why return?"

Charcoal glared at me when I released him from my room. As mad as he was, he refused to let me out of his sight while Dante and I packed as many of the art supplies as we could fit into Dante's saddlebags.

No one was around when we reached the barn, so I pulled Bertha from her stall and saddled her. She pawed, as eager to depart as Dante, so after I'd boosted him into the saddle, I kept hold of her reins. "This is for Akiko," I said, passing him my spare charcoal pencil and a quarter of my sketchbook. His brow wrinkled as he stared at it, but I shrugged. "Tom needs his supplies, so I ripped pages from mine. She's struggled with her letters, but Josephine will work with her while they wait for me."

Though flimsy, he accepted my explanation and tucked the pages into his outer thigh pocket. He pulled the lightweight robe over his head, ignoring Bertha as she snorted and danced sideways and tossed it to me. His energy changed, like he was about to say something important. But the moment passed.

"Hurry back," he said.

THE DEPARTURE OF CARTER'S MEN IMPROVED THE MOOD in the abbey. Chatter and laughter filled the dining hall during lunch. Tom waited until the students left for their designated rest period, then made his pitch to the assembled masters. Several men nodded at Tom's reasoning, but none agreed to leave.

"But you have no *water*." Tom's shoulders sagged. "How do you expect to survive here?"

They had no answer, and my heart ached for them. I glanced out at the dusty courtyard and the parched oak tree. "Have you tried negotiating with the Avalon Society?"

Linford shook his head. "They wouldn't even meet with us when we tried."

I tugged on my beard. It still needed a wash and a trim, and I hated the idea of approaching the Avalon Society in my present, grimy state. Even so, I said, "I could try."

When Tom frowned, I shrugged. If I could improve the abbey's circumstances, perhaps he could persuade Cara to set up a cooperative community here instead of in her valley.

"I've had some luck working with them. I'll see if they'll speak with me."

THE COMMUNITY OF SILVER SPRINGS WAS APPROXIMATELY fifteen kilometers from the abbey, and the journey took nearly two hours. As in Newfane, an ornate gate blocked the road leading into the community. Unlike Newfane, no one was tending it, so I dismounted and tugged on it. It didn't move, and when I reached through it, my fingers fumbled over a thick chain leading into the stonework.

High stone walls flanked both sides of the gate. I could draw an opening, but it wasn't in my best interest to annoy or irritate the community. Sighing, I tethered Oxide to a low branch under a flimsy cottonwood. I sat on a rock to wait, flipping through my sketchbook and staring at Earl.

Charcoal settled next to my leg, and each time he raised his head, I craned my neck to see if the gatekeeper had arrived.

No luck.

"How are we going to get their attention?"

In response, Oxide nickered.

I studied the sparkling blue water. "Thirsty?"

He pawed, raising a puff of dust with each hoof strike. I patted him and walked to the edge. The lake's surface was approximately twenty meters down, but the slope was too steep to hike. I scanned the shoreline, but this appeared as good a location as any.

"Be right back," I called. Charcoal, Neblina, and I skirted the shore until I had a clearer view of the hillside below the gate. Once satisfied, I kneeled and sketched the hillside.

The rock rumbled as I began the artwork, cutting a broad trail into the side hill. Neblina bolted away, but Charcoal huffed at the noise.

"They know I'm here, now." A cloud of dust obscured my work, but it dissipated by the time I untied Oxide.

Charcoal was already at the bottom, lapping at the water. He scowled at the horse when I nudged him sideways to make room but moved over anyway. Oxide bobbed his head and drank without stopping for several minutes. There was so much water here. Could I convince Silver Springs to share it with the abbey?

When we reached the top of the trail, a man stood by the open gate. He appeared bewildered by what I'd done. "You're an artist."

"I am."

"But not from Churchill Abbey, and we haven't seen any other artists in years."

I inclined my head.

"You best come in." He waited for us to pass before closing the gate behind us. He gestured at the track and said nothing until we reached a large, handsome building near the top of the hill. "This is our meeting hall." He pointed at a stone patio. "Please wait here."

Silver Springs was a terraced community built on the tip of a natural peninsula. It jutted into the sparkling water, surrounded on three sides by the man-made lake. A wide street followed the incline from the meeting hall to the shore. Streets cut into the rocky hillside radiated from the main street. The terracing allowed each set of structures to look over the roofs of the downhill buildings, giving every building a sweeping view of the lake.

A cooling breeze rose from the water, but the sun beat down mercilessly, bouncing light off the water and making my head ache.

"Sir?" A boy near twelve or thirteen popped out from the meeting hall. "Take your horse?"

I handed him Oxide's reins and watched them walk up and over the crest of the hill. Even if their livery didn't boast as nice a view as the rest of the community, I wouldn't blame Oxide if he balked at returning to the dusty shade of Churchill Abbey's barn.

It wasn't long before the gatekeeper returned with two

other people and introduced them. "I'm Gabe Osborn, administrator, and this is Ian Kinsey and Laila Gomez, our scholar and engineer, respectively."

I'd assumed Osborn was merely the gatekeeper. Had I known, I would have asked him for water on behalf of the abbey straight away.

When I didn't respond, his frown deepened. "You are?"

My cheeks burned at my breach of etiquette. Since Carter's men weren't here, I used my real name. "Beg pardon, Administrator. I'm Matthew Sugiyama."

"Ah," Osborn's posture changed.

The scholar looked furious. "You didn't ask first?"

Osborn shook his head and folded his arms. "His work spoke for him."

Gomez sighed. "Let's go inside."

The smoked glass covering the meeting hall's eastern wall cut the sun's glare and eased my head. Osborn and Kinsey remained outside, arguing. Gomez filled several tall glasses from a fruit-filled water pitcher.

Despite my burning thirst, I sipped mine. "Delicious."

She nodded as she filled the last glass. "We have watermelon, cucumber, and mint to spare this time of year." Glancing at the men, she sighed. "They won't stop without intervention. Please excuse me." Whatever she said halted the discourse. They glanced my way before moving off the patio, out of sight.

I wandered around the room, examining the handsome furniture. The style was plain, but the dark stain highlighted the natural grains, and each piece was polished and waxed to a high gloss. The same stone as the patio outside covered the floor, though the interior stones had a shine from being smoothed and polished. Tall tables set with stools lined the back wall, and a piano sat on the north side of the room. The cover was up, so I set my water on a coaster and sat.

We'd had a piano at Popham, but I hadn't liked the abbey's music master. All my musical knowledge was gained second-hand from the boys who had suffered through his lessons. None of the beautiful pieces I'd learned came to mind, so I played a rollicking tune—a type of sea shanty with ribald lyrics. My singing voice was worse than my playing, and it was a good thing I hadn't attempted to belt out the lyrics because someone cleared their throat as the final chords melted away.

"You must be the reason behind the fracas outside." Her voice was strong and clear, but she was the oldest person I'd ever seen. She rolled her chair forward and stopped next to me. "You're no minstrel."

I chuckled and twisted to face her. "Correct. I'm an artist."

Her mouth pursed.

"Not from Churchill Abbey," I added.

A spark of humor crossed her face. "But you have come from there, so are you here to convert us?"

My eyebrows shot up. "You know?"

"That they're religious? Why do you think we refused their entreaties?"

I hid my dismay. If Silver Springs was set against Churchill because of religion, could I blame them? Even if Silver Springs had been willing to bargain, Churchill had little to offer in trade, leaving my chances of negotiating on their behalf bleak.

Why had I offered to intercede? I'd already been away from Akiko, Earl, and the others for too long. But I was already here. What harm could come from asking for aid? "You truly won't share?" I gestured at the lake. "They barely scratch by when you have all this."

"Politics, Money, Power, Religion, and Greed." She shrugged. "Shouldn't their god provide for them?"

I winced. To be fair, until recently I'd shared her opinion. A bone-deep weariness settled over me, leaving my arms and legs heavy. "I'm wasting my time here, aren't I?" When she grinned her gap-toothed smile, I sighed and stood. "Thank you..."

"Marta."

"Well met, Marta."

"Remember us in your travels, Artist."

The others broke off their argument when Charcoal and I stepped outside. "If you can point me toward the livery, I'll be going."

Osborn frowned. "We haven't reached our decision."

"On?"

Gomez looked amused. "Whether we should invite you as a member."

*This again.* "I'm leaving."

"Good." The scholar reddened and folded his arms. "Marcus sent a warning about you and your attitude."

"Marcus." I raked through my memories, arriving at the picture of a man with hooded, piercing, blue eyes. "From Vegas Depot?"

When they nodded, I shrugged. That he'd bothered to send a messenger based on two interactions lowered my opinion of him even more. I gestured at the hill. "The livery?"

Osborn hesitated. "But you didn't make your case."

Marta rolled herself near the windows and waved. Despite myself, the corners of my mouth quirked. "If I agreed to settle with you, would you consider releasing water back into the river channel?"

The late-afternoon sunshine sparkled across the water as they squirmed.

"Then I'll go." I snapped my fingers for Charcoal, waved at Marta again, and trudged up the hill.

Before I reached the crest, Osborn called my name and trotted after me.

Had they reconsidered?

"Listen, tell Churchill they can come for water if they need it. We won't block the road you cut into the hillside."

I stared at him, my spirits sinking. "It's a two-hour trip, each way."

"If they need it, they can come." He shrugged. "I'll meet you at the gate."

# CHAPTER FIFTY-THREE

I rode away from Silver Springs empty-handed yet undaunted. I'd suspected they wouldn't help based on my previous encounters with the Avalon Society, but I'd still hoped they would prove me wrong. Churchill Abbey needed water, and while it would have been better to have the community's blessing, I wasn't yet prepared to admit defeat.

I traveled toward Churchill until I was sure I was out of sight, then swung east toward the dam. Per Linford's report, only a tiny trickle escaped from the reservoir.

The dam was a marvel, but so large it had to be built *Before*. It spanned a narrow gap between rocky outcroppings, and based on the pattern of lichen and weathering on one section of the natural rock, excess water spilled down the rock face rather than through the dam's inner workings. Without understanding the dam's inner workings, I couldn't chance damaging or destroying the structure, but I could weaken the rock face.

Charcoal and Neblina snuffled through the sparse brush while I studied the shoreline, looking for another weakness.

I dismounted, tied Oxide to a low shrub, and pulled out my

sketchbook. A dusty, blue-gray bird landed on a squat juniper tree and watched me sit on a rough boulder. Charcoal settled next to me, eyeing the bird.

Without the back cover, the sketchbook was floppy, so I turned it sideways on my knee after checking to make sure Akiko hadn't sent me a message. On the back side of a sheet, I worked on capturing the scene. The beating sun reignited my headache, but I set my jaw and continued until the blue-gray bird flew to the ground near my feet, breaking my concentration. It hopped near my boot, investigating the parched soil.

Charcoal tensed.

"Leave it," I murmured

Once my sketch satisfied me, I traced the ghostly waterway with my finger, smudging the charcoal. The water level of the reservoir was very near the top, so it wouldn't take much to release water into the dry river channel. If I made the breach between the dam and rock face appear natural, no one would question it. Besides, unless someone came to maintain the dam today, the water would wear away all traces of interference by the time they found the breach.

A flock of blue-gray birds settled onto the trees above me, their chortles annoying Charcoal. He circled the junipers, leaping and snapping at them. The birds hopped from branch to branch, their piping commentary comical. The way they worked together to pester Charcoal reminded me of the gulls I'd watched as a boy. A sharp longing to rejoin everyone in the valley hit me.

I shifted my attention to my sketch and pictured the change I intended to make. If this worked, I could feel good about leaving to return to the valley. The time away from Earl had given me enough distance and objectivity and, as Genevie had said, something in my soul yearned for her. As often as I'd rehearsed my apology, the words burned to be released.

When I returned, I would repair things with Earl. Together, we'd decide what to do next, since neither Talbot nor River would tell me where my parents were. Even if River convinced Genevie to stay in Vegas Depot, we could retrieve Talbot and find a place to overwinter. Assuming winter even came to a place like this.

Oxide's low nicker refocused my attention. I sprang to my feet and scanned the area but saw no one. The birds scattered, scolding me, then settled again when I resumed my seat.

"Enough. Get it done, Artist."

The sketch floating over my mind's canvas settled, the planes and angles sharpening under my critical inner eye. I set my intentions and went to work changing the rock face. The flock above me erupted from the tree chittering. As one, they flew to investigate the cascading water. It tumbled down the slope's stony face, splashing and deepening the hue of the rock into Rose Madder.

But when the water reached the ground, it sank into the soil and disappeared. I held my breath and waited for the channel to dampen, but nothing happened.

Was more water required?

I returned to my sketch and deepened the breach, allowing more water to escape. The velocity of water pouring from the reservoir changed in sound from a burbling to a low rumble. But although the footprint of dampened soil in the channel grew, the water still sank out of sight. I gaped at the water pouring to no effect onto the parched desert sands. All I'd accomplished was wasting a lot of precious water. It was a punch to the gut. If this much water wasn't enough to restart the river, the volume required was something Silver Springs would notice.

The birds fluttered and bathed in the edges of the small waterfall I'd created, their gleeful cries amplifying my defeat.

Their shrieks of delight followed me as I rode toward Churchill Abbey.

BEFORE I REACHED THE MAIN ENTRANCE, THE ABBEY'S bell clanged. I sighed and attempted to straighten my shoulders. But based on the way their expressions changed from hope to resignation, I knew mine conveyed disaster.

A group gathered to greet me, and I'd barely dismounted when the bell clanged a second time. Tom craned his neck to see who else had arrived, then sprinted toward the doors. Cara slid off her horse and into his arms, laughing. Their reunion made my heart ache, so I turned and led Oxide to the barn alone.

I returned to my room to wash the dust from my face. The view from my room usually cheered me, but a thick, warm gray-brown haze hung over the mountains to the south, sending my spirits even lower.

Someone knocked on my door. I grimaced, but squared my shoulders, expecting Linford. "Come in."

Cara and Tom entered the room, hand in hand. "They're allowing Cara to stay." Tom's grin nearly split his face. "Did you have any luck at Silver Springs?"

The small waterfall I'd created splashed across my mind's canvas. I shook my head. "None."

Cara smoothed her hand across Tom's chest. "What now?"

He caught it and smiled at her. "We wait. They're not opposed to our ideas, but they need time. Many have lived here their entire lives and don't want to leave."

"Then we wait." Her words were patient, her tone resigned. They stood together, their heads bowed and foreheads touching, unified.

This was love. Two people coping with an uncertain future and facing it together. Sharing a purpose, a common goal. Even here, even now, with defeat more probable than not, their joy at being together overshadowed everything else.

I ached for Earl—her smile, her scent, the light in her eyes. We should be together. Life was short and everyone deserved a chance at happiness.

*Even me.*

The animosity and bitterness I'd held for Tom and Cara dropped away. They had each done the unforgivable, yet my resentment disappeared, like water pouring onto desert sands. It left me buoyant and unburdened. My words tumbled forth in a rush. "I'm leaving tomorrow, but I wish you luck." I threw my head back and laughed, my belly shaking with relief.

After a moment, their stunned expressions turned sunny. They beamed at me, then at each other. Saying nothing, they left me to resume my packing.

When the supper bell clanged, Charcoal jumped off the bed, landing with a *thud*. He waited, staring at the doorknob then sighed when I flipped open my sketchbook. I'd intended to tear out the page showing the water access I'd created, but I found a message from Akiko next to my waterfall sketch.

"Very prity."

Her spelling made me chuckle, and Charcoal groaned when I sank onto the bed to answer her. Ignoring him, I sketched the flock of blue-gray corvids sitting on a juniper. Should I ask Akiko to convey a message to Earl? But how could she, without admitting we communicated via our sketches? Plus, my words to Earl needed to come from me, not get filtered through Akiko.

Charcoal huffed again, but I drew a thought bubble next to the nearest bird and lettered, "See you tomorrow!" Afterward, I tore out my illustration of the new water access to show Linford and the others.

Charcoal shoved his way through the door and led the way to the dining room. Tom and Cara were already seated with Linford when I slid onto the bench and handed him my sketch.

"Next to Silver Spring's main gates, there's an access road leading to the water. Their administrator has granted access to the abbey, should you need water."

Linford nodded, but his rueful smile told me the abbey was unlikely to take advantage of the offer. He tucked my sketch into his pocket, asking, "Did you see the smoke?"

The haze I'd noticed popped onto my mind's canvas. "On the southern mountains?"

"Yes. There isn't enough vegetation left for a fire to threaten the abbey, but I pity anyone traveling to or from Vegas Depot."

I sighed. We'd have to wait for the fire to burn out before we could collect Talbot. The arrival of our meal distracted me until I returned to my room and found Akiko's latest message.

"Yay! It is to empty hir." Next to her statement, she'd drawn vignettes of Cara riding east, and Earl and Dante packing their horses next to the southern route.

The route leading to Vegas Depot.

# CHAPTER FIFTY-FOUR

I stared at the page, trying to decipher Akiko's message. Had Earl and Dante already left? If they had, they wouldn't know they rode toward an inferno until it was too late.

But maybe they hadn't. The illustration of Cara revealed her riding away while Earl and Dante were preparing to leave. I studied the shadows and shading, trying to discern the time of day. The shadows beneath Cara were pointed westward, which made sense if she'd left this morning. The shadows around Earl and Dante were murky. It could have been noon when the sun was high overhead and shadows were nearly non-existent... or after sunset, when shadows blended with the falling dusk. But why would they leave after sunset? The drawing must show them preparing for an early morning departure.

*Please.*

I drew an arrow pointing at Earl and Dante and wrote, "When?" I stared at the page for a long time, even though I knew Akiko had been asleep for hours.

Night's hold deepened, and the abbey fell silent. With the doors barred, there was little chance of leaving before daybreak unless I roused the abbey. And even if I did, it was too dark to navigate a narrow, rocky trail I'd only ridden once. Under the weak light of the sickle moon, anything could lurk in the dark. I stared south, trying to decide if the dim glow was from moonlight painting the high ridges with silver... or from fire.

I could do nothing until morning.

The delay tore at me, but I lay down, stroking Charcoal's fur as he stretched alongside me. My dreams were full of disturbing images—sword fights in narrow corridors where we slashed through air as thick as gelatin, unseen desert creatures who snapped at our heels with grinning faces made of flame. An hourglass through which water poured fast. Too fast.

THE CLANG OF THE BREAKFAST BELL WAS LIKE A BUCKET of water dashed in my face. I jolted upward, spluttering and tingling with alarm. I threw on my clothes and grabbed my saddlebags, struggling to pull my borrowed robes over my head as I trotted toward the barn. I tossed my saddlebags over the seat of my saddle and looked around, but the lads charged with hostelry duties must have gone to breakfast, too.

Before I'd crossed half the distance to the dining hall, I remembered the note I'd left a note for Akiko and walked back to get it from my saddlebags. My fingers shook as I pulled the mangled sketchbook from my bags and flipped to my question. My timing was eerie—as I watched, lines appeared, darkening until I could read her words.

"An our?"

Did she mean an hour previously or an hour from now? I dug through my things for a charcoal pencil, but before I found it, an image of Ben appeared. He smiled, flipping a pancake high in the air and Sally wept as she waved south with one hand, an empty plate in the other.

My shoulders sagged. An hour hence.

In response, I sketched a picture of me sadly holding a bowl of the inevitable corn mush and wrote, "Enjoy!" before hurrying to the dining hall.

On the threshold, I scanned for Linford. He sat with several older boys. I hesitated to interrupt, but the dirty plates in front of them were empty. "Pardon me, lads. Brother Linford, a word?"

The boys slid away with shy smiles. Linford gestured at their vacated seats, but I shook my head. "Who here knows the routes to Vegas Depot?"

His brow furrowed. "If the flames have reached the routes, there's no way through."

My hands clenched, but I kept my voice even. "I'm aware. Still, is there someone here who knows the routes?"

My heart plummeted when he shook his head, then soared when he said, "But we have a map."

"I need to see it. Now, if possible."

Linford led me across the courtyard to the eastern wing and into the headmaster's office. It was empty save for a bookshelf, several ledgers, a large desk, and a padded bench. "Through here," he said, opening another door.

What I'd assumed was a closet was a short corridor leading into a smaller room. It was comfortable with an easel set up near the windows, and brightly colored, woven blankets flung over padded armchairs.

"This is where Headmaster Wilcox spends his time. The outer office is used to intimidate our truants and troublemakers."

Linford opened an armoire and rummaged through it, pulling out a half-dozen rolled documents. We unrolled several papers until we found the map. Unlike most, Silver Springs, not the abbey, was the center, denoted by a blue star. I followed the route I'd ridden from there to the abbey, which wasn't much more than a faint notation. From the abbey, there appeared to be a more direct route leading southeast toward Vegas Depot. Lines climbed from the valley floor into the mountains to meet the hilly route between the depot and the valley, the path Earl and Dante would likely travel.

I'd never catch them if I rode to the valley first, but perhaps I could stop them in time if I traveled south on a parallel route. I traced the options, committing road names to memory.

I clasped Linford on the shoulder. "Thank you. I must leave now."

Linford neither argued nor questioned my urgency. He walked me to the barn and ordered the lads to ready my horses before shaking my hand. "I'll get the doors opened for you."

In my haste to depart, I raced from the abbey and turned south without speaking to Tom or Cara. I also forgot to warn Linford about the Mountain View. I couldn't escape the twinge of guilt tugging on me—a nagging reminder of my failures. Even though I'd fulfilled my obligations, I didn't like leaving with warnings and farewells unsaid.

The wind whistled in my ears as we clattered down the dusty road. Time had turned its surface into well-graded gravel, and the engineers from *Before* had ensured they were not steep. Beneath me, Oxide flowed, his muscles rippling with every stride. Charcoal matched our speed, his body bunching and lengthening in a simple rhythm. On the hillside above us, Neblina slipped through the sage, keeping pace.

South of us, the thickening smoke obscured the mountains, but the cool morning air carried no hint of it as we galloped along the dry riverbed. We continued our pace until Oxide's footfalls lost their rhythm. By my estimate, we'd covered nearly twenty kilometers. The horses dripped with sweat, so I slowed so they could catch their breaths.

At the first pond we encountered, I stopped to let the horses drink. My plan was mad. So many things could go wrong. If Earl and Dante had left Paradise Valley before I'd departed the abbey, they could have traveled at least fifteen kilometers. We'd made up ground during the hour we'd run, but depending on their pace, they could be anywhere from twenty to thirty kilometers south of the valley by now.

Magnesium snatched a mouthful of grass, the ripping sound jarring in the strange quiet.

"Time to go." I unclipped Magnesium so he could follow at his own speed. Without complaint, Oxide settled into his ground-eating, running walk, leaving me ample time to brood and we continued southwest.

The map showed Smith Valley as a farming community. I'd hoped to find people here who could tell me about the terrain, but they had abandoned it long ago. Sagebrush and desert marigold choked the fields, and the few structures remaining leaned or sagged toward the ground. Oxide swerved toward a field of alfalfa. I dismounted and loosened his girth but held onto his rein while trying to decide on my next move.

We'd traveled nearly seventy kilometers in five hours. The horses were fatigued, but not spent. If we turned west, we should reach Topaz Lake in two hours. But during the same two hours Earl and Dante would travel farther south. From here, I couldn't see much smoke, and if I hadn't viewed the southern mountains from the abbey, I wouldn't have known about the danger.

My second option was to travel south to Bridgeport. It was another seventy kilometers, but almost due south, and I would beat Earl and Dante to it. But I didn't know if the fire had reached Bridgeport.

Topaz Lake was closer, but if they passed it before I reached it, they'd continue south toward the danger. Bridgeport was the safer bet to intercept them... but what if I couldn't reach it? If the fires spread north, the flames could cut off the route. My thoughts raced, but I breathed deep and slow, like Ben often counseled.

"What would Ben do?"

Oxide's ear flicked in my direction, but I ignored it, feeling the drag of minutes ticking by. Was there a third option? I tugged the map onto my mind's canvas and focused on this area, but they were the only two roads I'd noted.

"Let's go west."

Charcoal leaned against my leg and sighed, searching my face.

"If we reach Topaz Lake late, we can ride south and catch up. And if we beat them there, we can ride south ahead of them. When we near the fires, we'll turn back to warn them."

Charcoal huffed in agreement. He stretched and shook, clearly ready to go. Oxide quickened his eating, ripping at the alfalfa with gusto.

I checked his girth and tightened his cinch. I patted him, grateful for his strength, speed, and courage—hoping, as I swung onto his back, that we wouldn't need them to face what lay ahead.

# CHAPTER FIFTY-FIVE

True to its name, Topaz Lake sat like a glittering jewel in the desert. It nestled in a shallow basin, covering over four-square kilometers. Towering cottonwood trees shaded the shoreline, their autumnal, French Ochre and Serpentine Green foliage painting the scene with their warm green-golds.

Charcoal brushed past the thirsty horses and waded into the water. Belly-deep, he snorted and snuffled as he drank. Despite my worry, his antics made me chuckle while I searched for signs of Earl and Dante.

*Nothing*.

After the horses had drunk their fill, we stood at the crossroads, waiting in the wild-rose scented air.

Had Dante and Earl already passed by the lake?

Turning right would take me north toward Paradise Valley. Vegas Depot lay to the left. If I stared at the cracked pavement hard enough, I could discern a few scuffs which could have come from hooves, but I couldn't tell how old they were. I shaded my eyes and stared north, willing Earl and Dante to appear on the northern horizon, until Oxide moved restlessly under me.

"Good lad, let's go." I patted his neck and turned left.

My thoughts drifted like ash on the wind. Had Talbot regained his strength? Would Genevie talk River into coming with us?

Could I convince Earl to stay?

WE TRAVELED SOUTH FOR SEVERAL HOURS UNTIL OXIDE faltered, his head bobbing deep with each step. I dismounted to check his hooves for stones. The smoke in the air was stronger now. It had a resinous quality and coated my mouth, thick and astringent.

While I was bent over, something startled Magnesium. He snorted, whirled, and bolted, heading south. Oxide staggered sideways, and if I hadn't been inspecting his foot, he may have followed Magnesium.

Charcoal tensed, waiting for me to release him. When I didn't, he whined, his eyes tracking the fleeing horse.

A part of me hoped Magnesium raced to join Bruno or Bertha, but he hadn't developed a strong bond with either. I settled Oxide and pried the rock from his hoof. Setting it down, I scanned the ground for rattlesnakes or other flight-inducing dangers but saw nothing.

"Let's go."

Oxide rushed forward, his worry fueling mine. I expected to catch Magnesium around the bend in the road, but I found no trace of him.

The road climbed, the smoke thickening. Flakes of ash hovered on the wind, soft petals which disintegrated under my touch. Around the next bend, flames leaped and roared on the ridge above us. Dread punched my gut. I stopped Oxide and whistled. When Magnesium didn't appear, I released Charcoal. "Go get Magnesium!"

Charcoal streaked south, and Oxide shook his head, dancing sideways with anxiety. I glanced over my shoulder, but the road behind us remained empty, so we continued toward Bridgeport.

The fire intensified as the road bent south. A gray-blue river tumbled alongside the east side of the road, but its sound was muted by the fire's roar. Oxide marched on undaunted, but I couldn't stop gaping at the flames. Towering pines along the ridge shimmered before their foliage burst into flame. They burned like huge, thundering candles. Spots swam across my eyes whenever I let myself watch one burn. The flames pulled cooler air across the road and past us, sliding past my face like feathers.

I'd expected Charcoal to return quickly, but when he didn't, I quickened Oxide into a running walk. Ash rained thicker, and I watched for drifting embers, but the fire stayed on the ridge. The grade steepened, and the stream narrowed, rushing with silent ferocity. Pines and wild blueberries joined the desert foliage as we climbed, thickening the brush.

Around the next bend, I stopped Oxide, my heart hammering.

Because Talbot had stayed behind at Tager's ranch, the route north to Paradise Valley had appeared relatively benign. Without the wagon, the many stream crossings had been a mere inconvenience. Now, the sight of our wagon tilted precariously in the rushing water was so unexpected I couldn't make sense of it.

From the water, Genevie shouted orders I couldn't hear at someone I couldn't see. Downstream, Talbot clung to a rock. Even from here, I could see the cords in his forearms strain against the pull of the swift-moving water. I vaulted off Oxide into the river, gasping at the icy shock. My feet went numb as the rushing water swirled past my calves, then my knees. I gritted my teeth and worked my way across the slippery rocks toward him. When the water reached mid-thigh, I stopped, afraid to take the next step. Between his bandaged eyes and the roar of the water, there was no way Talbot knew I was here. I took a deep breath and continued.

The cold reached my groin like a kick, but Talbot didn't move at my miserable yelp. I closed the last two meters.

"Talbot!" I shouted, "come on!"

He didn't release the rock.

*Can he hear me?*

I lunged forward and lost my footing, grasping his arm to steady myself. He whipped his pale face toward me, fright pulling his mouth down.

"I'm here. Let's go!"

"Matthew?"

"Give me your hand."

Talbot's throat convulsed, but he waved his left hand until I caught it. With two of us walking together, we were steadier, and I got him across the roiling water without either of us falling. I led him to Oxide and left him with his hand on Oxide's saddle before working my way up the bank.

River was waist-deep in the swirling water, pulling on Magnesium's halter. He had parked himself behind the wagon, making it impossible to back it up. My sister's face registered shock when I appeared, but before she could say anything, Genevie popped around the edge of the wagon, submerged nearly to her chest. "The axle caught on a boulder!"

"Do we need it?" I gestured to the blazing, eastern hill.

Her eyes widened. "The fire moved closer!"

River grabbed my attention by slapping her hand on the

water's surface. "Your horse won't leave and he's blocking Gertie."

"Let me try." I waded in again, the cold no easier to bear a second time.

The two pack horses cowered together. Magnesium's flanks shook when I touched his hip, and he'd thrust his head so far in the wagon, his chest pressed against the rear wall. I tried pulling him backward, but he ignored me, pressing forward even harder. The wagon tilted, its wood groaning. The sound frightened the horses harnessed to the front. They whinnied and thrashed, lunging forward.

Overwhelmed, I closed my eyes to picture the scene on my mind's canvas. Three people and four horses, chest deep in rushing water. A foundered wagon. A wall of flame advancing down the slope. Somehow, using my artist's detachment dulled the intensity of the situation. My mental picture receded into shadows and planes, lines and hues, and my mind cleared. Calmer, I stroked Magnesium's neck.

"Go release the horses from their harnesses. I'll work on these two."

Genevie and River disappeared as I pulled my tunic over my head. Squeezing past my shaking horse, I climbed into the wagon and tied my tunic over his eyes. I stroked his forehead before clipping a rope onto his halter. "You're all right, lad." I put pressure on him and clucked my tongue. "Back. Back."

Water swirled between him and the wagon as he retreated. I untied Gertie's lead and jumped down, backing both horses away from the wagon. Once we were far enough, the three of us waited in the icy water until Genevie and River emerged from the water with both harness horses in hand.

The wagon shuddered. Wood cracked in a series of staccato pops.

"Watch out!" Genevie bellowed as it rolled onto its side.

The current caught the wagon's broadside, sending it careening downstream. It crashed into boulders with terrific force. The noise made Magnesium jump forward while Gertie simultaneously locked her feet, wrenching my arms in opposite directions. My shoulders screamed, but I held fast until Genevie reached me to take her mare. I steadied Magnesium's head covering, but he remained docile and followed me onto the bank. When we emerged, Oxide nickered. Charcoal whined, his brow furrowed with anxiety.

Still holding onto my saddle, Talbot shivered and hugged himself with one arm. "What should we do?"

My shoulders ached, but I ignored the pain and studied the team of horses. "Are they broke to ride?"

"Unknown—they're Tager's." Genevie shrugged. "But Gertie is saddle broke. What about Magnesium?"

I patted my horse, but he leaped skyward, his sides heaving. "He is, but I wouldn't trust him right now. Genevie, why don't you ride Gertie and lead Oxide? Talbot can ride him, and I'll walk Magnesium."

Genevie shook her head. "River sprained her ankle."

Nearby, my sister balanced on her left leg, her right toe hovering above the cracked pavement. In the river, the water had obscured her injury, and she hadn't complained when I'd directed her and Genevie to unharness the horses. She waited with numb exhaustion on her face, her body language uncertain. For the first time, I could picture her as a child. My heart ached to know this version of her.

Genevie boosted River onto Gertie, so I held Oxide for Talbot. My cousin's legs shook, but he settled himself into his saddle and clung to Oxide's mane.

The trees lower on the hillside lit with a series of snapping booms. Even in my soaked clothes, the heat rolling off the fire was like a weight.

The delay had cost us. "Let's move."

Genevie took both of Tager's horses and we trotted after the others. But we made it around two bends of the road, before River yelled, "Heads up!"

Eyes wild with fear, Bruno and Gertie galloped toward us with Earl and Dante clinging to their backs. When they saw us, their horses slowed and stopped, their sides heaving.

If finding us on the road surprised him, Dante didn't show it. "The fire has jumped the road." Dante's sides heaved, and he gasped for breath. "Turn around!"

Genevie shook her head. "We can't. There's a wall of flame behind us too!"

Earl swayed in her saddle, and I jumped forward to steady her. She gave me a tight smile but sat up straighter and pulled into herself. The rejection stung. Despite the urgency of our situation, my help was neither appreciated nor wanted.

"What now?" Genevie twisted toward me. "Dam the river? Make a fire break?"

The water disappearing into the desert floor splashed across my mind's canvas. "No. Water will do what it will do—I can't control it."

My nerves zinged as I waited for their next suggestion. But no one said anything, deepening the hollow weight in my gut. Even Genevie, my stalwart friend who had been through everything, sighed as though conceding defeat.

A bone-deep anger welled up inside me. I'd waited my whole life to meet my family. I deserved more time. Time to get to know my sister and to deepen the bonds with my cousin. To guide and shepherd Akiko as she developed her gift. And even if she'd given up on me, I hadn't given up on a future with Earl.

*This is not the end.*

The fire had grown, but the brush east of us hadn't caught yet, leaving us a potential escape. But here, the hillside across the river was too rocky and steep for the horses to climb. With Talbot and River's injuries, we couldn't leave the horses behind.

Earl's voice was strained, "Can you do anything?"

I swallowed. "This slope is too steep, but let's go back and look for a place to climb out of this canyon."

# CHAPTER FIFTY-SIX

River galloped Bertha up the road, back the way we'd come. I followed the others on foot, leading Oxide and Magnesium. My shoulders ached, and holding both horses didn't help. Despite the pain, I continued to scan and assess the canyon wall across the river, looking for a pass out of the canyon. The fire's heat scorched my exposed skin and, having no free hands, I wiped my right cheek across my shoulder multiple times.

When River returned, her eyes were wild. "There's nowhere! We have no way out!"

"We're trapped." Dante's voice was thick with despair. "What do we do? Stand in the creek until the fire consumes us?"

Genevie's jaw hardened as she scanned the steep slope. "It's not over until it's over." She grinned. "Besides, we've been in worse places, backed against a wall."

Despite the dread twisting in my gut, a broad smile split my face. "Can you take over for me?"

She nodded, the corners of her eyes crinkling as I handed her my horses and patted Talbot's leg.

Charcoal refused to wait behind and jumped into the river when I waded in. Though he paddled as fast as I'd ever seen him swim, the current swept him more than fifty meters downstream before he reached the far bank. After making sure he'd emerged safely, I continued across, bracing as my boots skidded across unseen and slippery stones. I nearly made it across before I lost my footing. The icy water closing over the crown of my head left me gasping as I scrambled onto the bank. I glanced back, my heart sinking. Compared to the wall of flame behind them, our group was impossibly tiny and vulnerable.

I scrambled up the loose, steep slope. While the first ten meters were passable, higher on the slope, thick stands of trees blocked my view of the terrain.

Neblina yipped. Charcoal scrambled past me up the slope, but I whistled him back. Unwilling to waste time on a fruitless search, I scanned the slope north of me. Maybe we could work our way north on this side of the river. I slid partway down the slope and scrambled along the bank. "Come on, chap."

Charcoal obeyed until Neblina made a yowling noise. Charcoal turned back toward her, but she disappeared into the trees. He swung his head toward me, then to where she'd been. When she reappeared, he followed her, disappearing into the brush.

I whistled, but he didn't return.

On the far bank, everyone moved closer to the river. Genevie had her forehead pressed into River's, Earl appeared to be holding Talbot's hand, and Dante stood in knee-deep water, his face a mask of strain.

*We're out of time.*

It took me a half-dozen lunging strides to make it up to where Charcoal and Neblina had disappeared. My heart pounded as I leaned my right hand on the first tree, struggling to catch my breath in the smoky air. The trees were spaced farther apart than I'd assumed, and I followed a faint track at a sideways angle to the slope. When I reached the last clump of trees, Charcoal appeared above me in a narrow gap. I followed him through a shallow gully leading to an open ridge at the edge of a forested basin. From my vantage, the basin appeared flame free, and a small lake nestled at the bottom.

Neblina's smile was wolfish when I whooped. "Yes!"

I retraced my steps, my arms windmilling as I half-slid, half-ran down the slope. I shouted, waving the others over. Dante shouted back, but I couldn't hear him over the rush of water or the hiss and roar of the fire.

Dante turned to the others and Genevie's head came up. When I gestured for them to cross to my side, she raised her fist in a victory salute before gesturing for River to ride into the rushing water. Gertie made it to the center of the water before halting. Rather than kick the mare forward, River patted her neck, then twisted to beckon Dante in. Dante nodded, keeping Bertha upriver of Gertie. As soon as he'd passed River's position, Genevie gestured again. Earl kicked Bruno toward the water, leading Oxide. My heart hammered as they progressed across the swift water. Her lips moved constantly, as though to reassure the horses. Her face and posture remained calm, but her hand shook when she handed me Oxide's rein.

His legs trembled, but his eyes were soft and alert. Never fond of water, the horse's quiet crossing was an enormous achievement. Even though he couldn't see me, I beamed at Talbot and patted his leg.

On the far bank, Magnesium balked at the river's edge. Genevie held Tager's team in one hand and my horse in the other, but he danced and reared, jerking her toward the flaming hillside. River turned Gertie back, but Genevie said something to stop her. River glanced from us to Genevie, and when I stepped toward the water, she shook her head. Genevie blindfolded Magnesium and let him back away from the river, toward the fire.

Brush fifteen meters from the road caught.

Magnesium bunched like he would spring forward over her, but Genevie drove him in a circle until he slid backward into the water. She continued to back him across the rushing water, pausing when she passed River to hand her one of Tager's horses. When they reached us, my horse emerged from the river, rump first. Like Oxide, his legs trembled, but his snorts were victorious.

Genevie was wet nearly to her neck, but her smile lifted my heart. "We do enjoy our adventures eh, Artist?"

I grinned at her as River and Gertie climbed from the water. "This way. If you're on a horse, stay low."

Despite my warning, Dante remained upright. As he battled with the face-level, pine branches, his curses and yowls of frustration struck me funny, making me laugh hard enough that it was a struggle to climb the slope.

Once we'd made it to the ridge, we scanned the basin. The smoke in the basin had thickened, but the fire hadn't made it over the ridge. "Let's go."

At the lake's shore, River scanned the trees above us. "If the fire breaches the ridge, we'll need to get into the water."

Dante pointed. "You mean *when* the fire breaches the ridge?"

Tree after tree burst into flame. No one spoke as we watched the mesmerizing wave of orange sweep down the slope toward us.

"If you have a plan, Artist, now's the time," said Earl. "I can't—"

"Swim, I know." I pulled out my sketchbook. My heart

twisted at the malicious joy with which I'd excluded her from our moonlit swim. "I remember."

*What now?*

I turned toward Dante, but he shrugged. "Even if I had your talent, you know I can't make art under pressure."

My gut twisted as more trees caught. If Akiko were here, she could create a boat, but this wasn't the time to practice creating. I could attempt to summon an existing boat, but the only boats I knew well enough to draw from memory were the sailboat I'd given Bryer to deliver mail around the Ontario Sea and Gunther's *Marybelle*. And even if I could transport a boat across the continent, I couldn't pull either man into the path of the hungry flames.

I couldn't do nothing—without some sort of intervention, we wouldn't survive. It took all my concentration to close my eyes and imagine the scene like it was a painting. In it, the edges of the lake steamed as the fire lapped at the shore, and we...

*We huddle on an island in the lake's center.*

My movements were feverish as I sharpened my charcoal, my gaze darting around the lake's shores to assess the shape and size of the exposed boulders and submerged logs. The island needed to be large enough to provide refuge for seven horses, two canines, and six people... but far enough from the shore to keep us safe from the flames.

When I was ready, I sketched the lake from this perspective, pausing occasionally to check my ridge-top memories. I folded these into my sketch to ensure my drawing was as accurate as possible. Still, I asked Dante to review it before I proceeded.

He pointed out several of the near-shore trees I could include to anchor the perspective.

After I changed my drawing, I said, "Keep tight holds on the horses."

They nodded. Drawing in a deep breath, I began. As the tingle spread through my fingers, the water shuddered. In an instant, a roiling so fierce it looked as if the lake boiled replaced its calm. The horses snorted, plunging at the ends of their leads, their eyes rolling in terror. Trusting my friends to deal with them, I drew the soil and rocks up from the lake's bottom, creating a mound in the center of the water. I drew the island in layers, each course spreading the land mass wider and higher. Once the shape was correct, I softened the edges with reeds and boulders, giving it a natural look.

"Time to swim," said Genevie.

Earl held her rein out. "Take Bruno for me?"

Genevie barely hesitated, climbing onto the large, dark horse. Once up, I handed her Tager's horses. Her mouth quirked. "Here goes nothing."

Considering his earlier reaction to my art, Bruno entered the water willingly enough, but snorted and backed when the water reached his shoulders. Anticipating it, Genevie pulled Tager's horses tight to his hindquarters, giving him nowhere to go. The big horse leaped forward and hit the water, discharging a tremendous splash and dragging Genevie under the water.

I held my breath.

Popping up, Bruno snorted and paddled toward the island, Genevie and Tager's horses trailing behind him.

"You're next," I said to Dante. "When the water rises, float beside the mare, and hold on to her mane so you don't get left behind."

He paled but nodded and kicked Bertha forward. When the water rose to his seat, he shrieked, but followed my directions and let Bertha tow him to the island.

"We're up," said River. She took Oxide's rein from me. "Ready, Tal?"

My cousin buried his fingers in Oxide's mane. "Ready."

Near the island, Dante released Bertha and paddled toward the shore. Genevie waded in and helped him to his feet before catching her mare. River and Talbot were more than halfway across, so I turned toward Earl. I gave her a quick smile, but it slid off my face when she took a step backward. "Don't worry. I'll take you across."

She glanced from me to Magnesium. "What about him?"

I pulled his blindfold off and stuffed my tunic into the nearest pannier. The swim wasn't far, and I wasn't going to destroy any more art supplies. "He will pull us to the island. We stay calm and float."

Doubt crossed her face, so I stepped closer and took her hand, turning her toward the burning ridge. The fire had spread in both directions, and trees halfway between the lake and the ridge were already smoking. "We can't stay here."

She squeezed my hand. "I'm scared."

"Me too." I pulled her hands to my mouth and kissed her knuckles. "Trust me?"

"You've got me?"

I leaned so close her face blurred. "Always. Ready?"

She bit her lip and then nodded. "Stay calm and float."

"That's it."

I waded into the water, holding Earl with my right hand and Magnesium with my left. "Time to go, chap."

Charcoal swung his head from me to Neblina and barked once. She lowered her head but followed him to the edge of the water.

"What if she doesn't come?"

"It's her choice to make." I took a deep breath and smiled when Earl copied me. "Ready?"

When she nodded, we waded in until we were chest deep. Earl clutched my arm, her breath coming in gasps.

Before Magnesium could change his mind and back out, Oxide nickered. Magnesium whinnied and lunged forward, jerking me off my feet. My shoulder screamed at this fresh assault, but I tightened my hold on Earl as Magnesium swam toward the island.

"I've got you," I murmured, until she stopped struggling. I relished the moment of quiet, the sensation of her gathered in my arms. I pressed my warm lips to her cool temple. "Float with me."

When we reached the island, Dante and Genevie waded in to help Earl out of the water. Charcoal and Neblina waited their turn, then shook their coats, spraying me with the musty lake water.

River laughed, her mirth setting Genevie off. Earl soon joined, their peals of laughter floating above the fire's roar.

# CHAPTER FIFTY-SEVEN

Dante joined me as the fire raced toward the shore.

"Was this enough?" I'd done my best, but doubt squeezed my heart. Perhaps I'd bought us merely a few precious moments of hope. "I couldn't think of anything else to do."

Onward the fire came, lighting everything in its path. The scorched skulls from Brookfield grinned and gaped at me from the leaping flames. There was no smoke, the air as clear as any I'd experienced, even though searing winds buffeted us from all directions.

Neblina paced back and forth in the shallows, her whines agitating Charcoal. He pressed his muzzle into my knee and pawed at my calf. I kneeled to hug him, comforting us both while steeling myself for what I needed to do next. I had things to say, and it didn't look like I could put them off any longer.

But before I started, Genevie cleared her throat. "If this is it, I want you all to know it was my honor to know and love you." She sat on the muddy bank with her arms wrapped around River, her eyes warm and bright.

I blinked back the sting in my eyes. Dante joined Genevie and my sister, wrapping his arms around the women. Talbot leaned against Oxide, his face turned to the sky, his lips moving without sound.

Earl stood alone near the water's edge, hugging herself when I joined her. "Cold?"

She shook her head. "Is this it?"

"I hope not. I have something I need to say." I swallowed and took her hands. "Even though Genevie said it first, don't think this doesn't come from me."

She waited, her green eyes locked on me.

"First, I'm sorry. I'm sorry for how I acted at Mountain View, and for calling you out in Paradise Valley. I've regretted it every moment since."

She flinched when the trees near the farthest shore burst into flame with a splintering *crack*. "And second?"

"Everyone deserves to be happy. Life is too short—" I stopped, a wry grin twisting my face as I gestured at the flames surrounding us. "And we all deserve a chance at happiness. Even me. Even now."

I took a step closer, my breath ragged. "I love you, Earl. You're the most amazing woman I've ever met. Since the day I met you in Star Creek's filling station, you've rarely left my thoughts."

The fire had nearly reached the shore.

I fought my panic down. Earl's eyes had darkened, but she hadn't said anything, so I squeezed her hand one last time. "Thank you for listening. Excuse me, I need to send a message."

I left her and crossed the small island to where Magnesium waited in the huddle of horses. He was calm and nosed me when I approached. "Hey there, lad. You've been a good boy."

He made a bobbing motion with his head, his mouth licking and chewing.

I unlatched the pannier and pulled out my tunic and sketchbook. The cloth was completely dry and rasped over my tender, heat-scalded skin. I flipped open my sketchbook past my sketch of Churchill Abbey, to the last message Akiko sent. It was time to say goodbye, but no words came. Her birth parents had died saying nothing, and I couldn't do that to her again. I needed to tell her how much love I held for her. How dear she was to me.

I searched my memories for words or images to convey the depth of my feelings. The images rolling across my mind's canvas stopped at the memory of her kneeling in the grass, wonder on her face while she watched Beck's dragons soar and wheel above us. I sketched as fast as I could to capture the scene and printed below it.

"Every time I think of you, this is how I feel. Thank you for letting me be your dad."

This time, the tears came, spilling out of my eyes and tracking down my cheeks. They tasted of salt and ash, and my heart wrenched as I set the charcoal against the paper.

*Is it enough?*

The lump in my throat thickened, and I tapped the pencil against my sketch of Churchill. Flakes of ash settled on the page, and I blew them off. We had failed to convince them to move. If we had, and Cara had built the haven she'd promised, Akiko and I would have been safer.

I turned to the sketch I'd made of Paradise Valley. Broad and deep, the ground was likely fertile. There was easily enough land there for two communities. Or for one community and an abbey.

Genevie splashed into the shallows. "We should wait in the water."

As if to prove her point, a glowing ember landed on my knee. I slapped it away, my mouth bitter and dry. The fire neared the lake on all sides. Its searing heat made me long for the relative cool of Vegas Depot under the midday sun. I nodded as River hobbled toward Genevie, clutching Talbot for support.

Dante and Earl waded in, holding hands. They didn't get farther than knee-deep before Earl stiffened and turned to escape the water. Dante wrapped his arms around her, and though she struggled, he didn't let go. When he sank to his knees, she followed suit, so they kneeled nearly chest deep in the shallows.

Her voice quavered when she called to me, "Come on, Artist."

I glanced from Earl to Genevie to my sketchbook. If we weren't going to survive this fire anyway, what was the harm in one more improvement? Especially one that could ensure Akiko's future safety or happiness?

"I've one more thing to do," I called as the horses slid into the water, their tails flicking water as they stood side by side, belly-deep.

When I settled cross-legged onto the ground, Charcoal crawled toward me. He lay alongside my thigh, panting, his gaze locked on my face. I bent forward, burying my face in his thick fur. "Love you too, little chap." He sighed, and I straightened to focus on my sketches.

This would never work.

*But if it did...*

I flipped back and forth between the two drawings, trying to decide which to alter. The abbey was the more complicated sketch, but the drawing of Paradise Valley was better anchored. What I needed was sheets of translucent vellum so I could layer both together, but I had neither the supplies nor the time.

*Out of time.*

Hesitation gone, I ripped the sketch of Paradise Valley out and lay it on my left thigh. I closed my eyes and calmed my breathing, picturing the finished product. Even if it took everything I had, I could leave the world safer. The fire's roar dimmed as I opened my eyes and began.

As before, waves of energy pulsed through my arms as I drew the lake and horizon, shudders racking my body. I imagined a great wrenching sound in the air as I sketched faster, blending and shading the lines in a variety of values. My vision blurred as I drew the trees alongside the lake, and someone called my name as if from a great distance. The fire consumed all the air, and my chest heaved as I gasped, my tunic dripping with sweat. A crackling near the edges of my vision darkened my eyes, narrowing my focus until I could only see the portion of the sketch nearest the tip of my charcoal. The roaring increased, and even that speck of vision, a pinprick of light, faded until there was nothing left.

# CHAPTER FIFTY-EIGHT

Cocooned in delicious warmth, I floated, luxuriating. It had been so long since I'd wallowed in a deep tub. This had to be the afterlife Cara believed in. But Cara's dream had been wrong. Heaven wasn't a castle in the clouds. Rather, a peaceful eternity floating in a bathtub.

A ghostly presence neared me. "Stay with us."

"Always and forever, for death was only a doorway," I murmured, sliding back under the water.

A force cradled my head, the sensation like what I assumed a babe felt when his mother bathed him. "I love you, too."

This was what Talbot hadn't wanted to tell me. My mother was dead, and he hadn't known how to break the news.

No matter. We were together now, and if Cara's stories were to be believed, we had an eternity to catch up.

"Of course, you do," I said, in what I intended to be a soothing tone. Being dead, it was no longer necessary to hold on to the anger and betrayal her abandonment had caused. Why hamper our future relationship with hurts from the past? "What's not to love?"

The mother-spirit left, and another took her place. This one was familiar, her scent like a summer's morning.

"With an eternity together, I will make you love me, Earl."

"Too late, Artist." The Earl-spirit bent forward and pressed her ghost lips against mine. A million lightning strikes fired at once, the jolts leaving me breathless and senseless. Why hadn't I kissed her while we were still alive?

"Better late than never."

"What did he say?"

I tried to frown, but it took too much effort. The voice was familiar and unwelcome. Moreover, the owner of the voice was not a fan of mine either. Who knew a sister could be such a pain? I sank back into the bath, but rough hands grabbed my shoulders and wrenched me from the tub.

"Ow, what the blast?" My eyes popped open, and Genevie gaped at me, her face covered by soot and surprise.

"You're alive," she said, poking her finger into my chest.

It hurt, and I squirmed. "This is *not* the afterlife they promised me."

"Afterlife?" Genevie blinked three times in rapid succession before throwing her head back and bellowing at the smoke-obscured sky. When she did, she lost her grip on me and my face went back under the warm water.

Earl grabbed my right shoulder and Dante my left, and together they dragged me onto the island. Earl collapsed next to me, grinning the lopsided smile I loved so much.

The fire had largely burned itself out, but smoldering remains glowed, bathing the area with an eerie, Burnt Sienna glow.

Charcoal stepped onto my stomach, and I groaned. When I tried to push him off, he stretched out on top of me. Without warning, he attacked my face with his tongue.

I squealed under the onslaught of canine kisses. "Quit!

Help, help!"

Talbot's chuckle floated through the night air. "You deserve everything you're getting right now."

"Exactly," said Dante. "Like, thank you for saving our lives?"

I lunged upward, but Charcoal refused to move, so I gave up, wincing as my head landed on a stone.

"None of us thought we'd make it, especially after you passed out," said River. For once, I couldn't detect any hostility in her voice, and when I tilted my head to look at her, she smiled, her warmth entirely unfamiliar to me.

"I thought I was dead, and my mother was too."

River sighed, the smile fading from her face. "No such luck. She's still in Seattle Depot, like a spider secure in her web."

Talbot groaned, and Charcoal scrambled off me as I bolted upright. "My mother is in Seattle Depot? Where's that?"

"Northwest," said River. She shrugged at Talbot. "What's the point anymore? All her plans have gone awry. You're not in Carter's retinue, I'm not in the Avalon Society, and he's not secure in some tiny hamlet in New England."

Talbot's mouth twisted. "We promised."

"I absolve you of your oath." My heart soared. "Seattle Depot? Is it far?"

Talbot's frown deepened. "From here? It's over a thousand kilometers across multiple mountain passes. We wouldn't make it before winter hit."

"Unless we travel by ship." River shrugged, laying her head in Genevie's lap. "But as the headmaster of Alcatraz Abbey, Papa is closer."

*Headmaster.*

A light, airy sensation filled my chest. "Alcatraz Abbey." The name was unfamiliar. A thrill shivered through me. "Is it far?"

When River grinned, her energy was completely open to me. It surrounded us, bringing our hearts closer together. "About four hundred kilometers west," she said.

My throat thickened.

*Four hundred kilometers.*

I'd never considered the possibility my parents lived apart. Should we hurry north and risk getting stuck along the way to Seattle Depot, or postpone the trip north until spring and visit my father first?

This late in the year, the risk of getting stuck in the northern mountain passes was too high, but if we went west, there was a good chance the others would settle there, leaving me and Akiko to continue north in the spring by ourselves.

My father was a five-day ride away. He was a headmaster, and if we traveled by ship, his abbey was on the way to Seattle Depot and my mother.

I scrambled to my feet. A wave of fatigue and dizziness left me swaying. I bent forward to catch my breath, then collapsed onto my knees. "I vote we ride to Alcatraz Abbey after retrieving the others from the valley."

"I wish you luck, but I'm heading back to Vegas Depot." Dante's eyes sparkled. "I finished my sculpture."

Earl's chin came up. "Tager?"

Dante blushed and looked down, nodding. "If you think the way is clear, I'll take his horses back to him so you can leave as soon as possible."

It hadn't occurred to me to consider who Tager was interested in. I grimaced. I'd wasted so much time worrying about Earl falling for Tager.

"He's very pretty," I offered.

When everyone but Talbot nodded, Dante's blush deepened.

Earl turned toward me, taking my hand. "So, Alcatraz

Abbey first, and then on to Seattle Depot."

I hesitated. "Are you sure?"

Her green eyes glinted. "Did you, or did you *not* profess your love for me?"

"Finally," said Genevie. She snorted and wrapped her arms around River. "You even sealed it with a kiss, so there's no backing out now."

My spine stiffened. "We kissed? I missed it?"

Earl's lips curved up as she leaned forward. "Maybe your third kiss will take."

When her lips brushed mine, I forgot to breathe. My heart stilled, and in that moment, there was only her. I leaned forward to increase the pressure, craving her touch. There was no future, no past, and even though I didn't know what to do next, this was enough.

This pressure, this heat, this moment.

But when her tongue brushed my lips, a thousand sunsets burst behind my closed eyelids. I startled. My eyes flew open as my lips parted. The tips of our tongues brushed like the shy nod of the first snowdrops in spring. My heart and soul ignited. The world fell away as our kiss deepened until Charcoal squeezed between us and swiped at our faces with his obnoxiously wet tongue.

Earl squealed, and I pulled back. Starved for breath, my chest heaved.

"If you were his second and third kisses," Genevie asked, "who was his first?"

⟍▬▬▭

THANK YOU FOR READING CHARCOAL AND SMOKE. I HOPE you enjoyed the journey. Please leave a review to help other readers find the book. Your reviews really help me out!

# AUTHOR'S NOTE

One of the things I love most about writing is the opportunity to immerse myself in someone else's experience. To sink into their heads, viewing the world through their eyes. It may sound strange since characters are born in the writer's imagination, but our characters are often so different from ourselves that they feel like completely separate people. For example, Matthew is open and guileless. He saunters through his world with a confidence born of his privileged upbringing and skill as an artist. His effortless ability to connect with others is something I admire, and a talent I wish I shared!

Writing gives us authors an opportunity to explore. We have a wonderful freedom to delve into themes, ideas, and worlds very different from where we live. We get to dream about what might have been, and sometimes, what could be. Since I set the Elemental Artist books several hundred years in the future, they've given me a vehicle to weave together a different kind of world. In them, I've gotten to merge the landscape of the present with the practices of the past. But although I'm writing about places that exist in the present, it wasn't until last fall, while writing Charcoal and Smoke, that I got to visit several of the locations from Graphite and Turbulence. It was almost surreal to stand on the shore of Lake Ontario (the Ontario Sea), to visit Pultneyville (aka Pultney), and to walk along the beach of Oneida Lake where Matthew and Akiko landed their flier after nearly crashing.

In November, I visited Las Vegas for the first time. As I walked along the Vegas Strip, my imagination scrubbed out the cars and electric lights until I was left with the post-apocalyptic version that Matthew visited. It was so much fun to take pictures of the Mandalay Bay hotel (the Mandal), the MGM Grand (the Copperfield), Excalibur, and the STRAT Hotel and SkyPod (the Strat). Furthermore, I was likely the only tourist in Vegas to take photos of the ornate, multilevel self-parking garage behind the Caesar's Palace and Forum (Sayzar's Market), but it's fitting that something so beautiful, albeit mundane, get a mention in a story somewhere!

This book was such a pleasure to write. And why not? At its heart, Charcoal and Smoke is a story about love. Who doesn't yearn to wallow in love? Familiar love, romantic love, playful love, affectionate love, and, not in the least, self-love. From family, to pets, to friends, to community... love makes each of these relationships more dear.

Thank you so much for reading Charcoal and Smoke. I hope you enjoyed reading it as much as I enjoyed writing it. Please consider reviewing it on Amazon, Goodreads, or any other book site. Reviews help immeasurably to bring reader attention to a book. Matthew's story will conclude in Ink and Waves, Book 4 of the Elemental Artist series.

# THE ELEMENTAL ARTIST

Matthew's origin story is available for free when you sign up for my email newsletter and updates on my books and other fiction at:

***What would you paint if you could change
the physical world with your art?***

Seventeen-year-old art student Matthew Sugiyama has his heart set on winning the coveted position of Head Boy, but so have the other thirteenth-grade boys in the abbey.

Winning the spot will secure his future after graduation, but is his art magic strong enough to win?

## THE ELEMENTAL ARTIST SERIES
## READING ORDER

A Garland of Cedar and Snow
Oil and Dust
Graphite and Turbulence
Charcoal and Smoke
Ink and Waves (forthcoming)

Matthew's story will conclude in Book 4 of the Elemental Artist fantasy series, Ink and Waves. Be sure to join my newsletter for updates!

# ACKNOWLEDGMENTS

Once again, I have oodles of people to thank for the feedback, guidance, refinement, and encouragement that was necessary to bring Charcoal and Smoke to the page.

Thank you to the presenters, organizers, and other attendees of the 2022 Rainforest Writing Retreat. The creative space, motivation, and inspiration provided by the retreat were invaluable to my process. I wrote nearly a quarter of this hot, dusty story while watching a misty rain patter down on Lake Quinault.

I also want to thank the Jamigos; Jami Sheets for those many 5 AM Writer's Club sessions, and Jamie Sogn for her constant support and encouragement. Thank you, ladies!

Next, I'd like to thank the 20Books community on Facebook. Your personal stories and unending encouragement are hugely motivating. Likewise, I'm grateful for the ongoing support from fellow authors Erin Staves, AJ Calvin, and Kat Kinney. Thank you for reading, reviewing, and recommending my books to your audiences.

This book was made better by my fabulous team of beta readers. Erik Shimizu's notes on continuity, Doug Fairleigh's feedback on relationships, Richard Odey's thoughts on pacing, and Susan Keillor's guidance on romance beats all improved this story.

Thank you also to Deb Correia. Not only did she take the manuscript on vacation with her to give it an emergency read, her feedback helped me move forward with bringing the story to print.

Next, I'd like to thank my editors. Charlie Knight (CKnightWrites) thank you for ensuring the tone and style of Charcoal and Smoke mesh with the world created in Oil and Dust and Graphite and Turbulence. Your notes about the emotional impacts of scenes helped so, so much. To Warren Layberry (Dark Water Editing), thank you for your sharp-eyed read! Your work has been invaluable in tightening my prose, catching factual errors, and filling plot holes. Last, thank you Hyper-Speller (https://www.wordrefiner.com) for your lightning-fast capture of typos, homonyms, and homophones... and for your notes on what pieces of the story resonated with you and made you laugh.

Thank you also to Andrew and Rebecca Brown (Design for Writers) for a third, beautiful cover.

For inspiration, I follow several amazing charcoal artists on Instagram. Thank Celia de Serra @celiadeserrastudio, Henrietta Abel Smith @henriettaabelsmith.art, Petra Domčíková @dpetra_art, and Barbara , @barbara_skrzyniarz_ for sharing your work.

Again, I'm grateful for the tool makers behind Scrivener, ProWritingAid, BookFunnel, reMarkable, Publisher Rocket, Reedsy, BookSirens, and Vellum. Your products and platforms make it much, much easier to be an independent author.

A special thanks to P. Welte, who was the first person to preorder Charcoal and Smoke directly through my website.

Last, to every reader who has left (or will leave) a review, thank you, thank you, thank you. Your kind, thoughtful words will fuel me through the writing of Ink and Waves, the last book in this series.

www.ingramcontent.com/pod-product-compliance
Lightning Source LLC
Chambersburg PA
CBHW011217190726
48287CB00008B/2648